Kris Webb and Kathy  in Brisbane.

Kris worked as a l Kong until having he Hong Kong with her ~~~~~~~~~~ daughters.

Kathy worked as a marketing executive in Sydney and now has her own consultancy in Brisbane, where she lives with her husband and son.

Sacking the Stork is their first book, and is the result of lots of emails, phone calls, coffee and wine.

KRIS WEBB & KATHY WILSON

PAN

Pan Macmillan Australia

First published 2003 in Macmillan
by Pan Macmillan Australia Pty Limited
This Pan edition published 2004 by Pan Macmillan Australia Pty Limited
St Martins Tower, 31 Market Street, Sydney

National Library of Australia
cataloguing-in-publication data:

Webb, Kris.
Sacking the stork.

ISBN 0 330 36453 7.

1. Motherhood – Fiction. 2. Friendship – Fiction.
I. Wilson, Kathy. II. Title.

A823.4

The characters and events in this book are fictitious and any resemblance
to real persons, living or dead, is purely coincidental.

Typeset in 11.5/13 pt Bembo by Post Pre-press Group
Printed in Australia by McPherson's Printing Group

Papers used by Pan Macmillan Australia Pty Ltd are natural recyclable
products made from wood grown in sustainable forests.
The manufacturing processes conform to the environmental regulations
of the country of origin.

To Mum and Dad

ONE

In retrospect, I should have realised there was something odd about my hormonal levels when I found myself making a banana cake one Sunday afternoon.

Despite this glaring inconsistency in my behaviour, I still hadn't seriously considered that I might be pregnant, not even when I skulked into the chemist's shop. After all, I'd heard that extreme amounts of exercise could affect some women's cycles and I had been making it to the gym at least twice a week over the previous couple of months.

I am convinced that chemists put pregnancy tests in the hardest possible place to find, in a deliberate attempt to toy with the already volatile emotions of the women who come looking for them. My furtive casting around for the pregnancy test section must have immediately alerted the staff, but I was given ten minutes to uselessly circumnavigate the store before the signal was given and an assistant swooped on me.

'What are you after, love?' she asked.

A very cleverly worded question and one obviously settled on after lengthy research. You see, it requires a definite answer, and the standard 'I'm fine, thanks' doesn't work unless you're prepared to be really rude. What it does do is force you either to confess what you are after, or (and the only option as far as I was concerned) to lie and ask for something else.

'Ah . . . I need some sunscreen,' I stuttered.

'Certainly,' the assistant answered, guiding me to the sunscreen section (which I'd passed six times), waiting as I chose a tube to add to the collection in my bathroom cupboard.

'Was there anything else?' she asked loudly as I hesitated.

I glanced around guiltily. Although I didn't recognise anyone, I had long ago learnt that despite the fact Sydney has over four million inhabitants, everyone always knows a lot about everyone else's business. If someone here recognised me and told a mutual friend what I'd asked for, the power of email could have the information spread to the four corners of the world by lunchtime.

'No. Just the sunscreen,' I answered, deciding to try somewhere else on the way home.

The staff in this shop had obviously been off form when picking the location of the pregnancy tests, because as I walked towards the cash register I spotted the telltale packages out of the corner of my eye on a bottom shelf behind a poster for painkillers.

The woman who had been serving me looked

crestfallen as I presented both the first pregnancy test my hand fell on (no comparison shopping here) and my sunscreen. However, she rang both items up without comment, both of us pretending that my first priority had been to ensure I didn't get skin cancer when I was sixty-five and that as an afterthought I'd decided to see if I was going to bring another human being into the world in seven months time.

The next morning I dutifully followed the instructions in the pack then put the little tray with its vertical stick on the bathroom sink as I jumped into the shower.

Five minutes later I stuck my shampoo-lathered head out of the shower to check that all was well and had already let the shower curtain fall back when my mind registered that there were not just one but two little blue lines on the stick. Pulling the shower curtain back slowly, I tried to convince myself that I was mistaken. But no, those two lines were still there and would not become one, no matter how I squinted at them. I lurched out of the shower and grabbed the instructions, hoping that I'd somehow got confused and two lines actually meant a negative result. Nope.

Emotions hit me one after the other.

The first was, of course, denial – an old favourite of mine. The chemicals in the kit were obviously hopelessly out of date and they would have responded in the same way if Alfred, my sixty-year-old boss, had peed on them. After checking the expiry date on the packet, I reluctantly discarded that theory.

After that came terror. In the past I'd had a few tense moments flicking through my diary counting

3

days, but on each of those occasions my technique of wearing a pair of white trousers had brought on my missing period. Somehow I'd assumed that if I were to get pregnant accidentally, it would have happened years ago, not at the age of twenty-nine after ten years of successful contraception.

The realisation that I was actually pregnant made the blood drain suddenly from my head and I sat down heavily on the edge of the bath as my mind whirled in panic.

Every good friendship has some rules and one of our household's, which was unstated, but well-understood, was that we never, ever, disturbed each other in our bedrooms. However, for the first time I ignored that rule and, pausing only to wrap a towel around myself, ran into my flatmate and best friend's room.

Fortunately Debbie was alone as I leant dripping over her bed waving my stick in her face.

'I'm pregnant!' I screamed.

She opened one hungover eye and looked at her red-faced and terrified flatmate.

'I can't even begin to respond to that without caffeine in my system,' she said calmly. 'Make me the strongest coffee you can, bring me the leftover pizza in the bottom of the fridge, put some clothes on and then let's talk.'

I'd met Max, the other half of the pregnancy, during one of my fits of lunacy some people call an exercise phase.

Every now and then I decide that I'm going to change my life and become a runner. What I seem to forget between each of these little episodes is that one cannot 'become' a runner. One is either born a runner or a non-runner and I fall squarely into the second category.

During one such phase I decided I would enter the Sydney City to Surf. I struggled determinedly over the course and managed to finish, although the crowds of supporters had long since departed by the time I lurched over the finish line.

No one was waiting to cheer me as I staggered to a halt beside Bondi Beach. I had thought my best chance of having a receiving committee was if Debbie and co were on their way home from the International, their nightspot of choice at the time, but they'd obviously had a relatively early night and made it in before sunrise.

Despite my exhaustion, I noticed a group of men standing about ten metres away. They were a particularly good-looking group (I have always thought there should be a name for a group of good-looking males – maybe a testogaggle) but my eyes were drawn to the one who was talking. He was quite tall with dark curly hair, and as he delivered the punch-line to the story he threw his head back and laughed loudly. I would like to say that it was Max's joie de vivre that first attracted me to him, but I have to admit that it was actually his gorgeously straight shoulders complete with appropriate muscles, and his lovely legs clad in little running shorts.

The testogaggle moved off and on impulse I

grabbed my bag from the runners' station and followed them onto a bus heading for Glebe. The bus wasn't going totally the wrong way for me to get home to Coogee, three suburbs away from Bondi; nothing an extra hour or so's travelling wouldn't fix, anyway.

The bus was packed. I just managed to get a hold on the bar above my head as it took off, but I still swung in a precarious, but cunningly directed, arc before I regained my balance. As I straightened, I found myself looking right into the face of the object of my attention, who smiled at me.

I had a sudden vision of how terrible I must look. At better times my short blonde hair and brown eyes could be considered reasonably attractive. However, just walking up a decent flight of stairs was enough to make my face go red, so I could only imagine how it looked after almost two hours of running (well, mostly running). The only good news was that my grimy running cap covered my limp and sweaty hair, which was plastered to my skull.

What the hell was I doing following a guy onto a bus after running for fourteen kilometres? I had a worrying thought – maybe I had heatstroke and it had addled my brain.

Oh well, at least I would die happy, I thought. Struggling to stay upright, I smiled back, hoping desperately that my active-person deodorant was living up to its claims.

'So, how did you go?' he asked.

'Great, thanks,' I replied honestly. After all, finishing was a major accomplishment as far as I was concerned.

'What time did you do?' he enquired with a raised eyebrow.

'Personal best,' I hedged, not wanting to tell him that the timers had all quit by the time I made it to the finishing line. 'And you?'

'Sixty-five minutes,' he smiled. 'I'm pretty happy with it.'

Pretty happy with it! I'd have been putting my name down for the Olympic trials if I'd done that kind of time. I tried not to show my dismay. This guy wasn't just a runner, he was a good runner. There went any ideas of suggesting a jog around the Botanic Gardens after work. He'd be done before I even made it down the steps of the Opera House.

'So do you run a lot?' he asked.

I considered lying and telling him running was my life, but decided a statement like that could well bring a bolt of lightning from above. Besides, I was too tired to do anything but be honest.

'Not really,' I replied. 'I'm actually considering a ceremonial burning of my runners when I get home.'

He did the throwing-back-his-head-and-laughing thing again (which convinced me that at some stage someone must have told him how sexy it looked) and then stuck his hand out.

'Max Radley,' he said. 'Nice to meet you.'

'Sophie Anderson,' I replied.

We smiled at each other just as one of the testogaggle grabbed Max's shoulder.

'Our stop, mate. Your fry-up awaits. Let's go.'

'Bye,' Max said with what I optimistically

interpreted as a touch of disappointment. 'Best of luck with your running career.'

'Thanks,' I said dismally as I watched him bound down the steps.

Cursing my idiocy, I tried to spot something out of the bus window that would help me figure out where I was and how I could get back to Coogee before sunset on the sporadic Sunday public transport.

When I was glancing through the run times published in the paper the next morning I found myself looking for Max's name. Radley was a pretty unusual surname, I figured, and flipped open the telephone directory. Sure enough there was only one M Radley.

Before I could change my mind, I pulled out a 'With Compliments' slip that had my name and contact details. After scrawling, *Congratulations, Max, great time. Regards, Sophie Anderson (ex-runner)*, I stuck it in an envelope and put it in the office out-tray.

Over the following twenty-four hours I see-sawed between thinking that the note had been a gutsy modern-woman kind of thing to do and thinking it was the most pathetic and embarrassing act of my life (despite there being some serious competition on that front). However, I consoled myself with the fact that none of my friends would know what I'd done.

The next afternoon I was head down in a huge pile of paperwork when the phone rang. I reached over and picked it up, eyes still on the document I was reading.

'Sophie Anderson speaking,' I said automatically.

'Is that Sophie Anderson, the ex-runner?' asked the voice on the other end of the phone.

I jerked the phone away from my ear, and stared incredulously at it.

'Yesss . . .' I replied cautiously, holding the phone back to my ear. Could any of my friends possibly have got wind of what I'd done?

'It's Max Radley, Sophie. I just received your note. Fancy a drink after work?'

By a stroke of remarkable good fortune, I was wearing my best suit that day and for once actually looked like I arranged major events for a living. Debbie had insisted that I wear the suit (which she'd bullied me into buying for an astronomical price) for a 'salary review' meeting earlier that morning. She'd rejected my argument that my oldest, most tattered suit would provide me with grounds for my assertion that I was underpaid and convinced me the extra confidence the outfit would give me was tactically vital. She had even insisted on lending me a matching handbag and shoes to complete the effect.

Unfortunately the image of the sharp, efficient businesswoman I'd seen reflected in Debbie's full-length mirror had only lasted until I spilt my morning coffee down the front of my crisp white shirt. As a result I hadn't been able to remove, or even unbutton, my jacket all day, although my boss hadn't seemed to notice and had even agreed to a pay rise.

We arranged to meet at a bar halfway between his office and mine. When I arrived, the place was absolutely heaving. I didn't know what was going on, but it looked like everyone who worked within a five-kilometre radius had decided to meet there. Suited men and women hung out of the windows and spilt out of the doorway, while frantic doormen tried to keep control.

Suddenly the whole thing seemed like a bad idea. I couldn't even really remember what Max looked like. How on earth was I going to find him in this place?

I was hesitating in front of the entrance when I heard a voice behind me. 'Not exactly the right place for a quiet drink.'

I turned around to find Max standing behind me. I needn't have worried about not recognising him. Despite the fact that he was now wearing a suit, he had the same casual grin and rumpled hair.

'Well, no,' I replied, feeling awkward suddenly.

'Do you come here often?' I flushed as I heard the bad pick-up line emerge from my lips. My capacity for inane comments still managed to surprise even me.

Max didn't seem to notice.

'I've been here a couple of times,' he answered.

We turned to head inside but were almost knocked out of the way by an exiting group of men who looked like they'd been there for a while. I thought about sharing my testogaggle theory with Max, but decided against it.

'Don't suppose you fancy going somewhere else?' Max asked.

'That sounds like a great idea,' I replied as yet more people forced their way inside.

'Have you ever been to the Centennial Club?' he

asked, naming one of the oldest private clubs in Sydney.

'Um, no, can't say that I have. I didn't actually think they allowed women.'

'New rules as of the start of this year – apparently the old boys have been forced to move with the times and allow in the weaker sex. So do you want to risk it?'

Several years previously I'd had a particularly humiliating experience at a similar club. I'd been curtly refused entry to its bar, where I'd arranged to meet a colleague who was new to the club and as unaware of the rules as I. As a result, I'd vowed to boycott all such places forever more.

I struggled with my conscience for at least a second. 'Sure, that sounds great.'

Some female rights activist I would have been, I thought guiltily. I probably would have unchained myself from the gates of parliament if a good-looking man had asked me to join him for a coffee.

'Have you been a member for long?' I asked as we walked, surprised and a little put off that Max belonged to that type of club.

'Well, you can have the truth or an elaborate lie, which would you prefer?' Max replied, producing that grin again.

'Definitely the lie,' I smiled.

'They approached me several years ago, begging me to be their only honorary member for my good deeds to humanity.'

'Okay,' I nodded with mock seriousness. 'And the truth?'

'It isn't my membership. My boss has a corporate membership and in a fit of generosity last week suggested that I borrow it sometime. I figured I'd do well to take him up on it and see how the other half lives before my popularity diminishes.'

As we entered the oak-panelled foyer a stern-looking man with a ramrod-stiff back held out his hands to take my jacket.

'Ah, no thanks, I'm fine,' I stuttered.

The man raised his eyebrows, my uncivilised behaviour obviously only confirming his opinion of the new rules.

'Planning to make a quick exit?' Max asked out of the corner of his mouth as we walked into a high-ceilinged room filled with overstuffed leather chairs grouped in small circles.

'I can't take my jacket off,' I whispered.

'Why?' he whispered back.

Reluctantly I opened my jacket to reveal the tan stain stretching from my collar to my waist.

Max threw back his head and laughed. A few heads turned. Obviously, unrestrained laughter wasn't heard around here terribly often.

'How about we sit under the airconditioning vents?' he suggested.

It may have been a meeting of the minds, or it may have been the numerous gin and tonics we each drank, but from the second we sat down, Max and I seemed to have a lot to say to each other and it was late before we finally left.

When I was recounting the evening to Debbie the next day, I was mortified to realise that despite telling Max all about my job and the golf event I'd just organised, I had no idea what he did.

Debbie instantly decided that Max was hiding something.

'He must have a dodgy job – he's probably a drug courier or maybe a parking inspector.'

'How many parking inspectors do you know who wear a suit and work in the city?'

'All right, so maybe he isn't a parking inspector,' Debbie conceded. 'I'm going with the drug courier theory then. What do you know about him?'

'Well, he's thirty-one and he grew up in a little town in western New South Wales and he still visits his parents a lot.'

Debbie dismissed this. 'Could just be part of the front – anyone can fabricate a solid family background. What else?'

I hesitated, and she looked at me shrewdly.

'What else?'

'Promise you won't laugh?' I knew even as I said the words that I was wasting my breath.

'Sure.'

'When he was fourteen he used to play the guitar in a Kenny Rogers tribute band.'

To her credit, Debbie tried hard to suffocate her laughter behind a cushion. Hearing her muffled choking I couldn't help but join her.

'I didn't believe him either until he recited all the words to "The Gambler". Do you need any more proof than that?'

That fact alone convinced Debbie that Max wasn't hiding anything. Despite my worry he'd be too embarrassed by his confession to see me again, he called the next morning and I was able to report to Debbie that he held a perfectly respectable job at a large advertising agency.

Max and I were soon seeing each other regularly and discovered we both enjoyed heading out of the city at weekends. We rarely knew exactly where we were going when we left and would stop wherever we felt like it.

One Friday night before my twenty-eighth birthday, Max pulled up outside my flat driving a rented 1950s MG convertible. I had thought we were heading out for dinner but he told me he was kidnapping me for the entire weekend.

'You have five minutes to pack your bags. You need to take something to wear out to dinner, something to wear during the day and something to swim in.'

I opened my mouth to ask a question, but he held up his hand imperiously.

'No, that's all the information I'm authorised to disclose. Oh, and everything needs to fit in a very small bag because the boot in this car is about the size of Debbie's makeup case.'

Half an hour later, feeling rather like I was 99 to Max's Maxwell Smart, we were on the road and heading west. As we left the city Max slipped a CD into the portable player he had set up on the back seat and Vivaldi's 'Four Seasons' filled the car.

Catching my look of disbelief, he laughed. 'Yeah, all right I borrowed the CD from a woman at work. I thought you might like it better than Dolly Parton.'

Three hours later, we turned onto a rough dirt track.

'Are you sure this is the right place?' I asked. After I'd directed him into three wrong turns, Max had relieved me of my navigational duties and for the last half hour had been both driving and reading the map.

He held the map up and twisted it around to try to catch some light, doing the same with a brochure he'd been keeping in his top pocket. Being a city car and not exactly built to go off the road, the MG had no internal light and its head-lights were almost useless.

'I think this has to be right. If it's not I have no idea where we are.'

After several hundred bone-jarring metres, we reached a rusty gate. I could just make out a sign for Oboloo Springs Cottage.

'Bingo!'

Max looked like he'd just won a Boy Scouts' prize for orienteering.

As I left the car and opened the gate, I was struck by how much darker it was here than in the city.

'I told the woman who runs this place that we'd be in late,' Max said as I rejoined him. Glancing at his watch he added, 'Although not quite this late. She said she'd leave the cottage door unlocked and we could check in properly in the morning. I hope it's as good as it looks in the brochure.'

Rounding another corner we saw a small stone cottage set back from the road. The lights were on inside and cast a welcoming glow.

'This is it,' Max announced, pulling up to one side of the cottage. 'Let's leave the bags until later,' he said as he turned off the ignition. 'They're wedged in so tightly, I don't actually know if I'll ever be able to get them out again anyway.'

He bounded up the stairs and opened the door, ushering me in before him.

Although the cottage was lovely, with a vaulted timber ceiling and a stone fireplace, the most striking design feature was the amazing collection of lace doilies. I had never seen so many crocheted doilies in one place. There was one under every item on every shelf, on the back of each chair, and even an enormous one covering the round table.

'Well, at least this answers one of life's universal questions,' Max said, trying to keep a straight face. 'Doilies do in fact breed if left together for too long.'

Further exploration revealed that the door off to one side of the living room opened onto a bedroom containing a huge wooden bed covered by a patchwork quilt – and mercifully fewer doilies.

Max's head was buried in the fridge when I returned to the lounge and he directed me sternly to sit down on the deck, which stretched in front of both of the cottage's rooms. Settling into a canvas easy chair, I tipped my head back and gazed at the stars, finding it hard to believe it was the same sky I could see at home.

Eventually Max emerged bearing a wicker tray on which balanced a bottle of champagne, two glasses, a baguette and a plate filled with an enormous wedge of cheese and an equally large slab of pâté. We managed to finish all of the food and the best part of two bottles of champagne before falling into bed.

We woke the next morning to the sound of kookaburras and, after an enormous country breakfast at the main house, spent the day exploring. We had a fantastic evening at one of the well-known restaurants in the area, despite the fact I had forgotten to pack any evening shoes to wear with my silk slip dress. Faced with the choice between ankle-high leather boots or sandshoes, I'd opted (against Max's advice) for the boots, which looked distinctly odd.

We spent Sunday morning lounging around the cottage drinking coffee, reluctantly wedging our bags back into the car around midday. Neither of us felt like heading home straightaway and I happily agreed to Max's suggestion that we try to find the farm we'd been told made the fabulous goat's cheese we'd eaten on our first evening.

The road to the farm looked like it had never seen a grader and we parked the MG off to one side of the unmarked gate and let ourselves through, heading towards the farmhouse we could see on a rise.

'What the hell are you doing in here?'

I turned guiltily towards the sound of the voice to see an old man striding towards us. Although he wasn't carrying anything, he looked as though he wished he had a shotgun in his hands.

'Just what do you think you're doing?' he bellowed again, despite the fact that he was now only a couple of paces away.

Max answered – rather bravely, I thought.

'We've been staying at the Oboloo Cottage and tasted some of your cheese. We really enjoyed it and thought we'd drop in and see if we could buy some more to take home.'

If anything the compliment seemed to make him even more aggressive. 'Does this look like a supermarket to you?' he demanded.

'Well, no,' Max admitted.

'Exactly, so kindly go back the way you've come and stop scaring my goats.'

Chastened we retraced our steps, half expecting to hear shots whistle over our heads. 'Bloody hell,' Max muttered as we climbed back into the car. 'That guy isn't exactly into customer relations. What's his mission statement? Keeping city folk in the city?'

Despite this experience, we often speculated about what it would be like to own one of the guesthouses or wineries we came across on weekends away. The idea of taking a few years out to run a small business in one of the beautiful spots we discovered appealed to both of us.

However, blissful thoughts of making my own jam, while gazing at Max tilling the fertile soil of our farm, were a long way from my mind the day I discovered I was going to have a baby.

TWO

There is only one thing worse than being pregnant to a boyfriend who breaks out in a sweat if there is a baby in the same room as him. And that is being pregnant to someone like that who is no longer your boyfriend.

Max and I had broken up four weeks before I ran into Debbie's room brandishing the pregnancy test.

It had been coming for a while. After two years together, I was sick to death of carting my clothes between flats and worrying about whether leaving a change of underwear and a toothbrush at Max's place would be overstepping the mark.

I'd decided that Max was the person I wanted to spend the rest of my life with and had been hoping that he would come to the same realisation. While I didn't want a wedding ring, or even vows of eternal love, I did want him to be able to tell me that I was the one he wanted to be with and that he was willing to make plans past the next Friday night. Max, however, still very pointedly avoided any discussion of the future, and we both looked uncomfortably at our feet whenever someone tactlessly asked when they could expect an announcement.

A couple of months before we broke up, Max and I had been on a boat on Sydney Harbour celebrating a friend's thirtieth birthday. A girl I didn't know had reached a messy stage of drunkenness and had collapsed into tears right next to the group of people we were talking to. Although we all pretended not to listen, it was impossible not to hear what she was saying.

'He . . . he said that he thought he loved me,' she sobbed. 'But he said he couldn't get over the feeling his Elle Macpherson was going to walk around the corner one day.' It was several seconds before she could speak again.

'He said that he didn't want to miss out because he was with someone else,' she finished, burying her face in her hands.

I raised my glass to my mouth to try to hide my discomfort and caught sight of Max's profile. Ignoring the conversation we were part of, he was staring at the girl, a look of surprise on his face. My first thought was that he knew her, or her boyfriend, but a split second later it dawned on me that it was the boyfriend's feelings he recognised.

I lay awake beside Max that night, trying to convince myself that we had a future. Finally I had to face what I'd really known all along – I could spend the next ten years waiting for Max to decide if it was me he wanted, and even if he did, I would never be sure that I wasn't just a consolation prize.

So it seemed that I had to either accept the situation or break up with him. But each time that I resolved to finish the relationship, we would have a fantastic night out, or a great Sunday doing nothing but reading the papers and wandering along the beach, and it would seem stupid to throw away something so good.

It was Max's ability to get on well with people from all walks of life, as much as his creative talent, that had propelled him quickly through the ranks at his advertising agency, but a promotion to art director was something he still expected to be a few years away. So when he came to the flat one evening to tell me he'd just been offered the job, it seemed like a major cause for celebration.

I was halfway to the fridge to pull out the bottle of champagne that always lived in the crisper (a habit of Debbie's I wholeheartedly agreed with) when Max said, 'There's more, Sophie.'

It was his tone of voice rather than his words that made me turn around slowly.

'The position is in San Francisco.' Max was watching my face carefully.

'Oh,' I replied, leaning on the kitchen bench and looking down at my hands.

'They want me there by the end of next month,' he continued apprehensively. 'But you could come and visit me and I'll be home for Christmas.'

It was blatantly obvious that I wasn't being asked to go with him.

Taking a deep breath, I looked up. 'You're right, Max, I could,' I said. 'But you know, having a long-distance relationship with someone who doesn't know what he wants out of life, or even who he wants in it, just doesn't sound that great to me. It really doesn't seem like there's much point in us being together any more.'

Max looked as though I'd slapped him in the face.

'Sophie, it's not that I don't want you in my life. I just don't think I'm ready to have you move to another country because of me. I don't even know if you'd be able to work in the States. Why don't we just give it some time and see?'

Strangely, more than anything else I felt relief that we'd finally got to this point.

Shaking my head firmly, I replied, 'Max, it's not just this move. I don't want to get married or even move in together, but I do need to feel that we have some kind of a future, that I'm the person you want to be with.'

To my great frustration I always cry when I am in an emotional situation, but I forced back the tears which threatened, determined to say what I wanted to. 'It's just not enough any more. It's over, Max.'

I'd never seen him look so shaken.

'But Sophie, I'll be here for another six weeks or so. Why don't we talk about it some more and see what happens?'

'I'm sorry, Max, I just can't do that,' I replied.

The celebration champagne stayed where it was. Despite Max's efforts, I hadn't changed my mind by the time he left half an hour later.

Although I had been determined to make a clean break, I saw Max several times over the next few weeks. He tried to convince me not to make any big decisions until he was home at Christmas, but I figured that if after two years he still didn't know what he wanted, another couple of months wouldn't make any difference.

And nothing had changed by the time I found out I was pregnant.

My first instinct was to pick up the phone and tell Max. But even in my panic-stricken state I knew I had to think things through before having that conversation. Over the next couple of weeks I picked up the phone to call him dozens of times, but always hung up before the call connected.

My first visit to the obstetrician was scheduled for the day before Max was due to leave and Debbie had agreed to come with me.

If it is possible to have a phobia of all things medical, Debbie has one.

While my home breast-check regime has never consisted of much more than feeling guilty when I read an article about cancer or saw a mobile mammogram clinic, I do manage to get to a doctor for periodic checkups. Debbie, on the other hand, claims that going to a doctor for anything less than a life-threatening injury is a waste of time and she has never set foot in a doctor's surgery unless forced to do so.

Although I realised the significance of what I

was asking of Debbie, I was feeling in definite need of some moral support. Anyway, as I'd assured her, I'd seen enough episodes of medical soap operas to know that in order to see the baby, all they had to do was run a scanner across my stomach.

Debbie paced the waiting room nervously while I pretended to be absorbed in a two-year-old copy of *Cosmopolitan*. I have always wondered why doctors don't feel they can spare ten dollars a week to provide reading material that is in any way current. Flicking through the pages, I realised that several of the glamorous courting couples that were pictured had already been married and divorced.

Debbie's low wolf whistle broke the silence and the eyes of all the waiting patients turned to her. Oblivious to their attention, she urgently beckoned me over to where she was standing.

'All I can say is that I hope that's Dr Daniels!' she said loudly, not taking her eyes off the wall.

Where I would have liked to have seen photos of my soon-to-be obstetrician nursing cherubic babies he'd carefully brought into the world, there were different shots of a man, presumably Dr Daniels, engaged in various life-threatening activities, ranging from parachuting to bungee jumping.

Great, I thought. I was putting my unborn child in the hands of an adrenalin junkie in the middle of a midlife crisis. Well, maybe not a midlife crisis, I corrected myself, looking at the photos of the decidedly attractive man who didn't seem much older than me.

I am a strong believer that young, attractive male doctors should be sent to some remote corner of the world until they are old enough not to have an effect on their female patients' blood pressure. Years ago I made an appointment to have some ugly warts on my foot removed. However, after meeting the doctor who was six foot two and blond, I was totally incapable of unveiling my festering foot and ended up limping out of his surgery with a list of vitamins, having claimed that I'd gone to see him because I was feeling run-down.

'Debbie,' I said fiercely, 'if you attempt to pick up the man who is going to be spending the next seven months prodding intimate parts of my body, I will never forgive you. Understand?'

Taken aback by my intensity, Debbie held up her arms as if to ward off a blow.

'All right, all right,' she said. 'My hands are definitely off.'

As it turned out, I had more immediate problems. After Dr Daniels had ushered us into his room and we'd had a quick chat, he asked me to take off my clothes from the waist down and lie under a sheet.

I momentarily registered that he looked even better than his photos, before resolutely crushing the thought and focusing on the framed qualifications on the wall.

'Why don't I leave the room for this bit?' Debbie suggested, a note of panic in her voice. 'Just give me a shout when it's time to do the X-ray thing over Sophie's stomach.'

'Oh, we won't be doing an external ultrasound today,' Dr Daniels replied calmly as he pulled on a pair of latex gloves, seemingly oblivious to Debbie's distress. 'An internal camera allows us to see the baby much more accurately at this stage.'

'Don't worry,' he said to me. 'It won't feel any different from a Pap smear.'

Given that I wasn't in the habit of taking my best friend along to my Pap smear appointments, his statement didn't give me a whole lot of comfort. This added a whole new dimension to my friendship with Debbie. It even made the time she had vomited in my bed after a particularly big night seem like she had been doing me a favour.

I tensed as I felt the cold metal instrument.

Obviously in search of something other than Dr Daniels and my sheet-clad body to look at, Debbie's eyes fixed on what looked like a television screen beside the bed. 'What is that thing flashing?' she demanded.

'That,' Dr Daniels said, 'is the baby's heart beating, and if you look you can see its arms and legs too.'

'Oh my God,' Debbie breathed. 'There's a baby inside you.'

I couldn't speak as I looked at the fuzzy shape on the screen. While riding the emotional roller-coaster that had been my life for the last two weeks, I'd been focused on the changes, mainly bad, that a baby was going to make to my life. But as I stared at the tiny outline that, while admittedly blob-like, did look something like a baby, the whole thing felt real for the first time.

I had always felt vaguely envious when I saw a hurt or upset child run into its mother's arms and it was bizarre to think that I would now be that mother. I vowed to myself that I would give my child all the love I could.

Dr Daniels broke the silence. 'Within the next few weeks the baby will develop all its remaining parts, so that by the time you are twelve weeks pregnant every single organ and body part, down to finger and toenails, will be fully formed,' he said. 'All it will have to do after that is to get bigger.'

Glancing away from the screen, I was amazed to see Debbie wipe a tear off her cheek. Even more amazingly she wasn't even slightly embarrassed but instead smiled at me.

'Can you believe that, Sophie? The baby is what, the size of a prawn?' She looked at Dr Daniels for confirmation and received a somewhat uncertain nod. I doubted he'd had babies compared to crustaceans before. 'But everything is there. That is absolutely incredible.'

I smiled back at Debbie, suddenly glad, despite everything, that I'd brought her along.

When Max called later that day and invited me out to Manchetti's, obviously in a last-ditch attempt to change my mind, I knew I couldn't put off telling him any longer.

Manchetti's was a little Italian restaurant around the corner from my flat. Max and I had been in the habit of eating there a couple of times a week. Max loved to cook, while for me it was a chore best avoided. As a result, we'd developed a pattern of eating in when we were at his apartment in Manly and eating out whenever we stayed at mine.

Apart from our favourite dessert there was nothing very remarkable about Manchetti's, certainly not the service. Max and I had come to the conclusion that Sydney waiters had developed a restaurant equivalent of 'chicken', where the first waiter who actually responded to the needs of a patron was the loser.

All was forgiven, however, come dessert time. The house specialty was lime cheesecake and I was very happy to support the claim on the menu that it was the best lime cheesecake anywhere outside of the village in Italy where the recipe had originated. In happier times, Max and I had even considered a pilgrimage to Italy to make the comparison for ourselves.

But even the lime cheesecake couldn't help me this time and I had picked my way through a dinner that tasted like cardboard, hardly saying a word. Max obviously assumed that I was unhappy about him leaving and was trying desperately to keep the conversation alive.

Eventually the bill arrived and I realised I was out of time.

'I'm pregnant,' I blurted, interrupting Max's story about something that had happened at work that day.

Max sat back in his chair and looked at me with an unreadable expression on his face.

'You're sure?' he asked slowly.

I nodded.

'How did it happen?' he asked. 'I thought you were on the pill.'

I tried to ignore the accusatory tone of his voice. 'I was,' I replied. 'I always thought that the manufacturers were just covering themselves saying the pill is only 99 per cent safe, but maybe not.'

'Jesus,' Max swore, running his fingers through his hair. 'Are you going to have it?'

'Yes,' I replied, trying to stop my voice trembling. 'That's the only thing I am sure about at the moment.'

Part of me had hoped that Max would tell me that, despite the lousy timing, having a baby was something marvellous and we'd sort it out together. But any visions I'd had of us living together with a white picket fence and a dog called Fluffy were quickly crumbling into dust.

'This is an absolute disaster,' Max mumbled, eyes focused on the breadcrumbs he was grinding into the tablecloth with his thumbnail.

'Really,' I answered, but my sarcasm was wasted on him.

He looked up finally and I could now read his expression, which was unmistakably angry.

'Listen, Sophie, maybe you should think about this some more. A baby changes everything.'

My patience suddenly evaporated.

'Max, I've done little else but think about this since I found out. Of course I thought about an abortion – I just can't do it.'

I pushed back my chair and picked up my handbag.

'Just get on your plane tomorrow and don't worry yourself about it. This isn't something I did deliberately to trap you. I'm not asking you for anything. I just thought you had a right to know.'

Without waiting for a reply I headed for the door, the image of his face in front of my eyes. Within a block, tears replaced my anger and I leant against a tree until my sobs subsided.

As I entered our apartment building I caught sight of my reflection in the mirror that ran the length of one wall. My face was red from crying and my eyeliner had smudged. I wiped my eyes in an attempt to repair some of the damage, hoping that Debbie hadn't invited tonight's date home. I decided that if she had, I'd pretend I had a migraine and go to bed. I just couldn't face being sociable tonight.

To my surprise, Debbie was alone. Even more surprisingly, she was sitting on the sofa reading. The last book Debbie had finished was *The Catcher in the Rye* and that had been for our senior exams when we were seventeen. I didn't need much more evidence that she had been waiting up for me.

She took one look at me. 'Didn't go well, then?'

Not trusting myself to speak, I shook my head. I slumped into a chair and managed, 'He told me it was a disaster.'

Debbie handed me the tub of chocolate chip ice-cream she had been eating. 'Here, the doctor said you need to eat a lot of dairy products.'

The ultrasound photo of the little life inside me was still sitting on the coffee table and I picked it up.

'I don't know what I expected Max to say, but it wasn't that.'

'It certainly doesn't sound like his finest moment,' Debbie said dryly. 'What happened then?'

'Not much. I just said it was my problem and I'd deal with it by myself, and then I left.'

As if on cue, my mobile rang. Debbie reached for it and switched it off. 'I think you need to decide just how you're going to manage this before you talk to anyone – especially Max. Have you thought about how you can support a baby by yourself?'

It was a logical question, but I still couldn't help bursting into tears again. Lately it seemed to be my response to everything.

Debbie perched on the side of my chair and put her arm around my shoulder. Gradually my sobs slowed down and stopped. When that happened Debbie stood up and walked out of the room. She returned a couple of minutes later, bearing a bottle of red wine, two glasses, a pen and a block of paper.

'I'm not great at emotions, so what I think we need to do is to look at this rationally,' she said in a businesslike tone as she pulled the cork from the bottle. She poured two glasses of wine, one enormous and one tiny, and pushed the small one across the coffee table to me.

'How much does a kid cost, anyway?' she asked, pen poised over the paper.

Neither of us had the faintest clue about what having a child entailed, let alone how much it cost. However, by the time the doorbell rang an hour later, we'd managed to fill a page with figures and Debbie had practically emptied the bottle of wine.

I looked at her.

'Do you want me to answer it?' she asked.

I hesitated momentarily. 'No, I can manage.'

'Okay, well, I'll make myself scarce,' Debbie said. 'Just yell if you need any moral support.'

Max was standing on the doorstep, looking as though there were a lot of places he'd rather be.

'Come in,' I said, standing back as he walked inside.

He perched awkwardly on the sofa he had thrown himself across on hundreds of previous occasions, and I sat in the armchair opposite.

'Sophie, I'm sorry I handled things so badly in the restaurant,' he began. 'You just took me by surprise. I've been walking around for the last hour and I've had a chance to think about things. What I want you to know is that I will help you support the baby.'

Any last glimmer of hope I'd had disappeared. Financial assistance was not what I wanted from the father of my child.

'Max, I don't want your money,' I said flatly.

'Just think about it for a minute, Sophie,' he said. 'You've got a good job, but can you really afford to bring up a child by yourself?'

I just looked at him, not trusting myself to speak.

He turned his eyes away and then looked back at me. 'Sophie, I care about you a lot, but I don't want a wife or a child. Certainly not now and maybe never.'

I'd thought that I'd been hurt all I could be by Max, but I was wrong. Surprisingly I felt no urge to cry, just anger at how easy it was for him to walk away from the situation. The last thing I wanted was for Max to be sending me cheques to support a baby he didn't want anything to do with.

'Don't worry, if you don't want to be part of this baby's life then I don't expect you to foot the bill,' I said coldly. 'I can manage by myself.'

'Look, don't make a decision now,' he said. 'Let's talk about it some other time and see what we can figure out.'

'I won't change my mind,' I said evenly.

There wasn't much more to say after that and Max left.

He called me the next day on the way to the airport, wanting to talk about money again. I'd spent the night crying, but on the phone I was calm and rational, explaining again that I didn't want him to be financially committed to the baby and that I thought it would be easier for both of us if we didn't stay in contact.

He called each day from San Francisco for the next week but I didn't change my mind and eventually he stopped calling.

THREE

My obstetrician had explained that the first three months of pregnancy was the most likely time for something to go wrong and had suggested that I not broadcast it before then. That was fine by me. At this stage, the looks of pity from people when I told them that Max and I had broken up were enough to deal with.

Despite women now having the vote and careers, surprisingly little seemed to have changed since the days of Jane Austen. The unspoken conclusion everyone obviously came to was that Max had refused to marry me and so we'd broken up, leaving me firmly on the shelf at age twenty-nine. Lacking the energy to clarify the situation, I usually left people to think what they liked and was dreading having to reveal that I was 'in the family way'.

The one person I knew I had to tell was my father, who had moved to London with his English wife seven years earlier. The day after Max left the country, the telephone rang at the time my father usually called and I hovered uncertainly over the receiver until the answering machine clicked in. It wasn't uncommon for us to miss each other, I told myself guiltily, as I listened to the familiar voice leaving a message. I'd call him the following night when I felt more like talking. However, it was almost a week before I finally picked up the phone and called him.

'Sophie!' he exclaimed with pleasure on hearing my voice. 'How are you, darling?'

'Pretty good, Dad,' I lied. 'How are you and Elizabeth?'

We talked for a couple of minutes before Dad asked the question I knew he'd been waiting to tactfully ask.

'And how are you about Max?' he ventured. 'Are things getting any easier?'

Dad tried to play the role of both parents, which he generally carried off surprisingly well, but it had always been glaringly obvious that discussions about my relationships were something he felt uncomfortable with.

'Ah, no, they're not actually, Dad,' I replied. 'In fact they've just got a lot worse, because you see I'm . . .' I took a deep breath and launched into it. 'I'm pregnant.'

The pause couldn't have been more than a second but it felt like an eternity.

I managed to see past my own misery for long enough to feel bad for my father. What on earth do you say to your unmarried daughter who has just broken up with her boyfriend and now delivers news like this from the other side of the world?

'Oh, darling,' he replied. 'Does Max know?'

'I told him last week,' I answered. 'But what he says can't change anything. We'd already broken up because he didn't feel he could commit to me long-term. The fact that I'm pregnant doesn't change that, and anyway, I don't want to live the rest of my life wondering if he's with me because he truly wants to be or because he was forced into it.'

'I guess you're right,' my father said slowly. 'But bringing a child up by yourself is one of the hardest things you can do. You have no idea how many nights I lay awake wondering whether I should have just married someone who could have been a mother to you, even if she wasn't the love of my life.'

My eyes filled with tears. My father's life had changed totally the day my mother was killed in a car accident when I was two. Not only did he lose his wife, but at thirty-four he was suddenly faced with raising a young daughter alone.

Dad never talked much about the years without my mother, or about the problems he faced looking after me, and I had a sudden picture of all the deci-sions he had had to make alone as I was growing up. For the first time I glimpsed how lonely and difficult the years ahead could be. I felt sick to my stomach.

Despite a number of subtle, and not so subtle, invitations, my father had refused all offers of perma-nent female company and I had been convinced that he would never marry again. Elizabeth had changed all that when they met at a barbecue when I was eighteen. She was out from England to do a year's teaching in Australia and she fell in love not just with my father but also with his country.

Elizabeth was definitely not a wicked step-mother and I loved her from the second my father nervously introduced us. He seemed to find a new lease of life with her. Within a month they were throwing legendary dinner parties which went until four in the morning, and within six months they were married.

'But if you had married just anyone, you wouldn't have found Elizabeth, Dad,' I said.

'No, but would things have been different for you if you'd had a mother all those years?' he said in a tone that made me realise this was something he still worried about.

'Dad, as far as I'm concerned I had a great child-hood and you are a wonderful father,' I said. 'Maybe there were times when I missed having a mother, but never enough to want to see you with someone you didn't love.' My voice wavered. 'Although, come to think of it, I'm still emotionally scarred by some of the hairdos you sent me off to school with,' I added, trying to lighten the conversation and avoid breaking into tears.

My father's artistic skills, which made him a highly regarded architect, deserted him whenever a hairbrush and hairband were put in his hands and I'd had some humiliating experiences with ponytails sticking out at all angles until I learnt to do my hair myself.

He laughed briefly and then became serious

again. 'All I'm saying, Sophie, is give Max a chance to be involved if that's what he wants. A child deserves two parents, even if they don't live together.'

'Okay, Dad, I will,' I promised, doubting that it was ever going to be an issue, considering the way Max felt.

'You do know what this will do to my image, don't you?' he asked.

'What?' I asked apprehensively, worried that he would say he'd be shunned in London social circles because of his daughter having an illegitimate child.

'Well, I'll be a grandfather,' he said. 'People will stand up for me on the bus and offer to help me across the street. Elizabeth might even decide that she should dump me for a younger man.'

I laughed for the first time in days. 'Sorry, Dad, your image has not been top of my list of worries over the last couple of weeks.'

'No, I guess not,' he replied. 'Well, what we need to do is figure out how Elizabeth and I can help. We'll come across for the birth, obviously.'

'That would be great, Dad,' I said, feeling suddenly happy as I hung up. His reaction had reminded me that we weren't living in the fifties. Far from being a scandal, having a baby alone was almost a status symbol, I decided. Determined to enjoy this rare moment of optimism, I managed to ignore the fact that most single-parent celebrities earned about fifty times more than I did and seemed to spend most of their life on European beaches.

*

After I found myself in floods of tears midway through a Sunday afternoon rerun of *An Officer and a Gentleman*, I knew that my movie viewing habits had to change. Out went my all-time favourite *Breakfast at Tiffany's* and in came films like *Reservoir Dogs* and *Psycho*.

By some bizarre hormonal twist I attributed to being pregnant, I wasn't even slightly disturbed by haunted houses and mass murderers, but I had suddenly developed a tendency to cry whenever I heard a sad country and western song. It got so bad that Debbie banned me from listening to the local country music radio station (a habit I'd picked up from Max) because every time another cowboy lost his woman, his pick-up truck or his dog, I'd end up sobbing on the couch.

Debbie also disapproved of the fact that I no longer felt like going out and spent most of my evenings at home. The last thing I felt like doing was being sociable, and given that I couldn't even drown my sorrows with alcohol, a night in front of the television was infinitely preferable to being with people who regarded me with a mix of sympathy and pity now that word was out about my impending motherhood.

I'd broken the news to Karen, my only friend who had children, in the park down the road from her house. We were standing at the playground watching her eldest two, Emily and Jack, attempt to throw themselves off the highest point on the climbing frame, while Pat, her eighteen month old, sat in the sandpit shovelling handfuls of sand into his mouth.

Karen is happily married at thirty-five, which in this day and age is statistically improbable. To make her even more remarkable, she has managed to retain a sense of herself (and a high-maintenance hairstyle), and with or without the kids, she is always fun to be around. Despite the fact that she only comes up to my shoulder and wouldn't weigh more than forty-five kilos wringing wet, she also has an amazing ability to down spirits without getting drunk and can outdrink most people, including men, if the need arises.

Any looming mortal danger to her brood forgotten at the enormity of my revelation, she turned to me in astonishment and pulled her dark shoulder-length hair back from her face.

I was getting used to people's responses to news of my pregnancy and I braced myself for the standard list of questions about whether Max knew, how I was going to support myself and the baby, and how I was dealing with it all.

'That's wonderful news, Sophie!'

For that response alone, I nearly fell into her arms in gratitude. Instead, I just smiled weakly.

Karen went on seriously, 'I'm sure everyone has told you about how hard it will be and how much your life will change.'

I nodded grimly, trying to hold back the tears that had suddenly appeared – again.

'Take it from me, there is absolutely nothing better in this world than having a child,' she said. 'Mind you,' she mused, 'if you'd told me yesterday when all three of mine were competing for horror

40

child of the year, I might have had a different reaction.'

I still couldn't speak around the lump in my throat and she looked closely at me.

'This can't be easy, I know. It's a frightening enough thing to deal with when you've got a husband and actually set out to get pregnant. But, believe me, there'll be more good times than bad.'

'I've got a huge knot in my stomach all the time,' I confessed. Karen stayed silent as I groped for the words to explain how I felt. 'I don't even have one tiny memory of my mother. Not even the smallest impression. What if I get it all wrong?'

As the tears poured down my face, Karen took my hand. Dimly I noticed that Emily and Jack had indeed thrown themselves off the play equipment, but by some miracle had managed to survive.

'Sophie, all you have to do is love them,' Karen said softly. 'I promise you, everything else will work out from there.'

I tried to hide my disappointment in her answer. I had wanted her to tell me that I'd make a perfect mother, that my maternal instinct would kick in and I wouldn't put a foot wrong.

'Maybe there's some kind of hormone released during labour that compels you to grow tomatoes and always have a chocolate cake in the freezer?' I asked hopefully.

Karen laughed. 'No such luck. The last time I had chocolate cake in the freezer was when my mother came to stay. Are you going to find out if the baby is a boy or a girl?'

I shook my head. I hadn't given it a lot of thought, but I liked the idea of having a surprise to look forward to at the end of the labour.

'What about names?'

I started to shake my head. I was only just starting to come to terms with the fact that I was pregnant, and a name for the baby seemed like way too much reality.

A sudden thought struck me. 'Actually, maybe I do know what I'll call the baby if it's a girl. My mother's name was Sarah – I think I'd like to call her that.'

Karen smiled. 'That sounds perfect.'

Karen had sent me home with two pregnancy books. She said that one of them was funny and reassuring, and that the other was a Nazi-style manual but contained useful information as long as it was taken with a large grain of salt.

Even without Karen's advice I would have been prejudiced against the second book as its cover featured a photo of a glowing pregnant woman wearing denim overalls. I'd never seen anyone who wasn't pregnant in denim overalls and immediately vowed to myself that they would not make their way into my wardrobe.

Figuring that I may as well get the bad news first, I opened the Nazi manual randomly, trying to ignore the cover, and found myself looking at the 'Eating for Baby' section.

The author declared that you didn't need to totally avoid alcohol and that it was perfectly acceptable to have half a glass of champagne on special occasions. Resisting the urge to throw the book across the room, I pressed on. Pâté, sushi, prawns, soft cheese, meat rarer than shoe leather . . . The list of prohibited foods sounded like a rollcall of all things good in life and I was only surprised to see that chocolate didn't rate a mention.

The next paragraph showed the reason for that omission, as the book warned against the dire consequences of overeating and suggested restricting sweet foods to the special treat of one square of chocolate after dinner at weekends. After all, it proclaimed, low-fat yoghurt sweetened with a little organic apple juice was a perfectly good substitute.

Deciding it was time for a bit of down-to-earth reassurance, I turned to the book Karen had said was more down-to-earth. This one was part of a series which covered pregnancy and early childhood, but as I read the title I realised Karen had accidentally given me a book that came later in the series.

I opened the cover anyway. Ten minutes later I was still reading, mouth open in horror and eyes glazed with shock. The book should have been emblazoned with a warning that it was not to be opened by any woman who had not given birth, I thought with a touch of hysteria. It began with a description of the state your body would be in and how you should expect to feel post-labour. Although I slammed the book shut after reading the section comparing the bleeding to something Lady Macbeth would be proud of, it was too late and the graphic images the book conjured up stayed in my mind.

Turning back to the first book I thumbed desperately through the index for the section on elective caesareans. Despite the disapproving discussion of such an option in the text, I immediately decided that the only way this baby was coming out of me was with the help of a surgeon and under general anaesthetic.

When I had made the decision to bring the baby up alone, I pictured myself as a fearless Amazon gazing into the middle distance with my child clasped to my breast and hair billowing behind me (although when I'd heard that the Amazons cut off their right breasts to allow for better arrow shooting, my regard for them had dipped significantly). However, it didn't take long for those strong and noble feelings to fade, leaving me lonely and scared.

Max had been a big part of my life for the last two years and his sudden disappearance left a huge hole which I had no idea how to fill. I used to love waking up on weekend mornings to see him lying beside me, with the prospect of a whole day to wander through shops, spend on the beach or just sit in a cafe eating and drinking. Suddenly that feeling of weekend anticipation had been replaced by a dread of the empty hours I'd have to fill before I could get back to work and bury my head in paper to make the pain go away.

I also missed the phone calls during the day. We'd often call each other for no real reason – sometimes it was just to share a particularly good Far Side cartoon from the desk calendars we had coincidentally given each other at Christmas. It wasn't until Max had been gone for a couple of months that I finally changed the quick dial button on my work phone that was programmed to his work number.

Knowing that he was halfway around the world didn't stop me half expecting to run into him and looking for him in our favourite haunts. Even though I'd said there was no point in talking about things any further, I perversely hoped it was him every time the telephone rang, and I found myself looking in the newspaper each morning to see what the weather was like in San Francisco.

Karen had convinced me that perhaps a caesarean was not the answer and so, deciding that I should try to find out about the birth process, I enrolled in antenatal classes at the local clinic. I felt conspicuously alone amongst all the couples. There was no one for me to hold muttered discussions with, or to ask questions on my behalf, and everyone looked at me in disapproval when I snorted involuntarily at the suggestion that aromatherapy was a pain-relief option. Pain-relief drugs were something to which I was giving serious consideration, but no one was going to convince me that burning scented candles would help take my mind off the process of moving a baby from inside to outside my body.

However, in my more positive moments, I convinced myself that the drama of being pregnant helped take my mind off Max.

By the time I'd reached the stage where I could leave the house in maternity clothes without feeling that people were laughing at me, the hurt his departure had caused was reduced from a constant stabbing pain to a dull ache. The day I walked past a building site dripping with workers without one whistle or catcall coming my way, I realised that I hadn't thought of him at all for at least forty-eight hours. Once I could no longer tie my shoelaces without major contortions, life alone seemed normal and my time with Max a thing of the distant past.

FOUR

As the nurse handed me my four-day-old baby, I barely resisted the urge to handcuff myself to the hospital bed and make her promise not to make me leave until this helpless little bundle was a teenager.

But it was too late. Sarah was already dressed in her street wear (a purple and red grow suit, which had received some disapproving stares from the older members of the hospital staff) and it was time to go home.

So, putting on a face I hoped resembled that of a cool, calm and collected mother, I laid Sarah in her pram, loaded the net carrier underneath with flowers, hung some more baskets of flowers over the handles, grabbed my suitcase with the other hand and headed for the lifts. Debbie chattered away next to me, carrying only her designer handbag and a small pink teddy bear someone had given Sarah.

As we entered the car park and I spotted the familiar red car, I stopped in my tracks.

'Debbie, you said you were going to go and pick up my car. I cannot fit two thousand flowers and a newborn baby in your tiny convertible,' I exclaimed.

Debbie had the good grace to look slightly shamefaced as she tried to explain. 'I meant to pick up your car last night but everyone was going for cocktails and then we went to this great little French restaurant for dinner and I know you don't approve of drink-driving and –'

'Enough, Debbie,' I interrupted. 'Just explain to me how you were planning to take Sarah without her capsule?'

'Ah,' she brightened. 'Her capsule was still at my place from when we bought it, and Alexander discovered that there was already a hole in the back seat to hook it into. So it's all safely installed ready for Sarah's first trip.'

I stifled a smile. Alexander, Debbie's latest love, struck me as someone who had never done anything more practical than change a light bulb, and I could picture him being reluctantly pushed out of bed to install Sarah's capsule this morning.

'There's heaps of room,' Debbie continued. 'If I can fit the bags from a day's shopping in, then a baby and a few flowers will be easy.'

Debbie had a point, given that the results of her shopping trips could usually fill a small truck. However, I looked enviously at the couple on the other side of the car park who were carefully strapping their baby into its capsule in their station wagon, stopping when they'd finished to gaze in wonder and then kiss it tenderly. I'd never been accused of doing things the traditional way, and usually that was fine with me, but sometimes, just sometimes, it would be nice if things weren't always so . . . untraditional.

I sighed and gingerly picked Sarah up. Debbie leant against the car, reapplying her lipstick as I lowered Sarah into her capsule, and after a few false starts I had my tiny daughter securely strapped in.

Finally we were off, and I had to admit Sarah did seem pretty pleased about her first road trip. Warm in her capsule, a little flannel rug dotted with pink bears tucked around her, she stared wide-eyed in wonder at the blue Sydney sky.

Debbie, meanwhile, seemed to have suddenly learnt how to drive. Normally she was a menace to other drivers, cutting in and out of lanes with reckless abandon and braking without warning. Today she was driving as though I was an examiner and she was hoping to get her licence.

I hadn't made it to the age of thirty, however, without learning that sometimes it is best to say nothing, and we sat in silence.

My friendship with Debbie had been cemented forever when we were eleven years old and she took pity on me and showed me how to kiss.

It was the afternoon of our first school social and Mark Johnson had asked me if we could 'see' each other that night. Even the lapse of almost two decades hasn't allowed me to delude myself that he was the coolest guy in the school, and I recall all too clearly that he was short and spotty with greasy blond hair and carried his school books in a vinyl briefcase.

But at eleven years old, it was shaping up to be the most intimate moment I'd ever had with a man.

Somehow, even at such a tender age, Debbie knew about such things, so it was natural that I turned to her for advice. To her credit, she treated the matter with the seriousness I thought it deserved and I spent two hours alternating between slobbering over a mirror (to observe how I looked) and a sliced rockmelon (Debbie thought it best that I be prepared for the worst possible scenario).

The night itself was less than momentous as Mark lost his nerve and we didn't even speak to each other, let alone join the other kissing couples on the school football oval.

In fact, despite my preparations, I didn't actually score my first kiss until I was nearly fourteen, by which time Debbie was threatening to disown me and find a best friend who had done more than hold hands with a boy on the train on the way home from school.

Despite vowing to be friends forever, we lost track of each other after high school until I ran into her in a bar a week after I'd moved to Sydney.

I was out with people from my new job, and although they were trying hard to include me, I was feeling a bit like an interloper and was about to call it a night. I recognised Debbie immediately. She was dressed in a slinky orange dress (Debbie was never one for muted colours) and even at two a.m. looked spectacularly glamorous with her long hair falling seductively around her face and her makeup as perfect as if she had just left home. My black trousers and pin-striped shirt, which had looked all right when I left home, now felt incredibly boring and I was sure that after an evening in hot, smoky bars, my mascara had created raccoon rings around my eyes.

However, the bonds of first boyfriends and first kisses were too strong to ignore and I pushed my way across the crowded room to where Debbie was chatting to a very attractive man dressed from head to toe in black.

They were talking animatedly and I stood awkwardly behind Debbie for a few seconds before tapping her on the shoulder.

'Hi, Debbie,' I said as she turned around. 'Do you remember me, I'm –'

'Sophie!' she screamed, throwing her arms around me. 'How are you? I can't believe we've actually run into each other again after all this time. What are you doing, are you living in Sydney?'

She suddenly remembered the man she'd been talking to and turned back to him with one arm still around me.

'Peter, this is one of my oldest friends, Sophie. Sophie, meet Peter.'

Peter looked less than thrilled to have had his cosy chat with Debbie interrupted by my arrival and announced that he was heading to the bar.

'A vodka, lime and soda for me, Peter,' Debbie said.

'I'm fine, thanks,' I muttered in response to Peter's raised eyebrow, which I gathered was a half-hearted attempt to offer me a drink.

'Peter,' Debbie called after him, 'fresh lime, remember?'

Peter waved over his shoulder and headed into the throng surrounding the bar.

'I've just moved to Sydney,' I said, answering one of Debbie's questions. 'Dad married a really lovely English woman and they moved to London a couple of years ago. So there was nothing to keep me in Brisbane. I decided I wanted to live in a big city, applied for some jobs in Sydney and here I am.'

I had packed up to move into a flat with friends at the same time as Dad and Elizabeth sold the house to move to England. Even in a new job and new flat I'd felt their absence strongly and Brisbane had never really felt like home after they'd left. So after a couple of years I'd found a marketing job in Sydney, packed my worldly possessions into my little hatchback and headed south.

'Well,' Debbie told me with the kind of sincerity that comes from having consumed more than the recommended weekly alcohol intake in three hours, 'you know, sometimes you have to believe in fate. I just kicked out my obsessive compulsive flatmate yesterday. Do you need a place to live?'

And so it was decided. Drunk and without knowing what suburb she lived in, I had agreed to move in, thinking that it would have to be better than sleeping on a distant cousin's floor, which I had been doing for the past two weeks.

Despite its impromptu start, our flatting relationship turned out to be a huge success and Debbie and I lived together in various parts of Sydney until we moved to Coogee three years before Sarah was born.

Debbie is, to use a cliché, everything that I am not.

She is continually mystified by the fact that I will not spend $500 on a pair of designer shoes that were in the latest issue of *Vogue* when I can get a perfectly good copy at a chain store for $60. Having said that, I am definitely not above borrowing her Gucci loafers or Prada sandals.

Debbie always knows the cool bands and has the latest CDs as soon as they hit the market, while I still think that I am on the cutting edge of music because I own Alanis Morissette's *Jagged Little Pill*. She also knows all the musical legends of the last fifty years and can reel off the names of albums by artists I've never even heard of.

Debbie's makeup bag looks like something a professional would carry around a movie set, and she has at least fifty lipsticks from the most exclusive cosmetic companies. My makeup bag contents consist of an eyeliner, mascara and foundation (all of which have come from bargain bins at chemists), and I own two lipsticks at latest count, one of which is so worn down I have to stick my finger in to get any out. I long ago came to the conclusion that I would make fewer mistakes if I didn't use much makeup and my standard face for the day (which incidentally is the same as my special occasion one) can be applied in the time it takes me to go one stop on the bus on the way to work.

Debbie's wardrobe is neatly arranged in colour groups, with trousers on the bottom rack, suits, skirts and blouses on the top, and dresses to the right. She is the only person I've ever met who can actually do the 'From Work to Nightclub Transformation Using Only One Scarf and a Red Lipstick' that women's magazines exhort us to practise. I tried it once but decided that I looked like Dustin Hoffman in *Tootsie*.

When Debbie buys a new blouse, it will produce seven different outfits when combined with her existing clothes. I, however, am an impulse buyer and my cupboard is dotted with expensive items that look fabulous on the rack but go with absolutely nothing else I own.

Debbie has always been surrounded by men who fall over themselves to get her attention. Our flats all had a revolving parade of men who each lasted anywhere from one night to three months. Debbie looks mystified when women complain bitterly about the fact that Sydney is full of gay men. A drought for Debbie is a Monday night in with a video.

In stark contrast I had had only two serious boyfriends before I met Max (Mark Johnson was not one of them, I am glad to say) and have spent considerable periods of my adult life without a man.

Debbie is five foot nine and has long hair which is always impeccably coloured a rich auburn with just enough wave to keep it back off her face. Although she scorns all forms of exercise, she never seems to waver from a perfect size ten. While I'm the same height (and fortuitously the same shoe size) as Debbie, my short blonde hair is often overdue for both a cut and a colour and I tend to fluctuate between a size twelve and a size fourteen (although in a fruitless act of denial, I refuse to buy anything bigger than size twelve).

The glaring inconsistency in Debbie's life is her job. She should have been a senior executive at a major fashion house or a globetrotting business consultant mingling with the world's beautiful and exciting people. Instead, she is in fact the buyer for a chain of stores called 'Mr Cheapy' that sell no item for more than five dollars and are crammed with very unglamorous items like toilet doilies and cans of air freshener. Debbie goes to great lengths not to divulge the nature of her job and only rarely admits to working for a 'discount retail chain'. For the last five years she has been combing Asia for the bargains that made the company a household name and, despite her frequent tirades about the rubbish she has to buy, shows no signs of leaving for more exciting but less lucrative pastures.

Debbie pulled up outside my house and hovered while I took everything inside.

My house is a sandstone terrace with a small patch of grass behind it. In an effort to become more motherly during the later stages of my pregnancy, I'd tried to cultivate some herbs in one of the garden beds. While they had never actually died, neither did they seem to get any bigger. Given that picking enough herbs for one pasta sauce would have decimated my entire crop, I had continued buying my herbs from the local fruit shop, leaving my crop to its own devices.

I had always known that living with someone else's baby was way too much to expect of any friend, let alone someone who lived like Debbie, and that eventually I would have to move. That had become crystal clear to me one Saturday morning as I lay in bed listening to Debbie have sex with her latest conquest.

I was trying to concentrate on that week's instalment of 'What appalling things are going to happen to your body next' in the pregnancy book I had bought after my traumatic experience with the tomes Karen had lent me. Operating on a strictly need-to-know basis, I was only reading one week ahead of my rapidly expanding body. I was starting to feel like an elephant, and as my spatial awareness hadn't changed quickly enough to keep up with my shape, I was constantly knocking things off shelves and desks.

As the noises from the next room floated through the air, I happened to read that the baby's ears were open and could hear sounds from the outside world. I remembered hearing that children who had classical music played to them in the womb had grown up to be concert pianists and I didn't even want to think about what hearing Debbie's sounds of passion could do to my baby.

Piling all my pillows on my bump, I tried to go back to sleep. However, the sounds in the next room began to reach a crescendo. Five years of living with Debbie in various flats with thin walls had taught me that this could go on for quite some time, so I gave up all thoughts of sleep, dressed and headed out to find the real estate section of that morning's newspaper.

House-hunting in Sydney is not something to be undertaken lightly (or at seven months pregnant). One of Sydney's miracles is that you can live literally on the beach and only be thirty minutes from the city centre. One of its realities is that you have to be a millionaire to be able to do it.

For we mere mortals who can't afford $1000 a week in rent, understanding real estate ads is a fine art. 'A water view' means you have to lie on top of the bathroom cupboard to catch a glimpse of the horizon, and 'easy walk to cafes and beach' means take some change because you'll need to get a bus.

So by eleven that morning, when I and my bump-that-could-hear were headed for Saturday morning coffee at the King Street Cafe in Newtown, I had seen two flats which smelt so bad I couldn't get in the door and one that was so dark I couldn't even tell how many bedrooms it had.

Newtown is Sydney's answer to London's Camden. When I'd first moved to Sydney, it hadn't rated at all on the list of cool places to be, but in the last couple of years the young professionals had begun moving in and I'd recently discovered that, despite the suburb's grungy feel, even the Newtown rental market was out of my league.

As usual, finding a park near the cafe was almost impossible. I was forced to drive several blocks down King Street and was almost in the next suburb by the time I spotted a park in a side street. As I pulled up, I noticed an old ivy-covered terrace house with a

'For Rent' sign. A real estate agent was showing a couple through and, on impulse, I followed them in.

Although the house was certainly not palatial, it had a good feel (if you managed to ignore the bathroom, which looked as though it had been stuck in a seventies time warp), and it was certainly big enough for me. I had no idea how much space a baby needed, but as it wouldn't even be able to sit up for the first few months, I figured it couldn't be too demanding.

The whole of the lower floor was open-plan, with the lounge leading into the kitchen which led into the garden out the back. Upstairs were three small bedrooms and a bathroom. I had recently read with horror that babies weren't toilet-trained until they were about two, so I figured I had a fair while before I had to worry about sharing a bathroom. That was probably a good thing, I reflected as I looked around, because it would take at least that long to get rid of the mould lurking in the corners.

'How much is the rent?' I asked the agent after a quick look.

My heart sank at the answer. I had decided to use the money I'd been saving for a deposit on a house to finance some time off with the baby before I faced the reality of going back to work. The amount had seemed like a lot when it was a figure on a bank statement, but the rough (and very depressing) budget I'd drafted showed that I'd be lucky if the money lasted much more than three or four months.

I'd always thought that owning a bed, sofa, fridge and washing machine was very grown up, but now realised that I'd need to buy more furniture if any new home of mine wasn't going to look like a student's flat. After putting aside money for the least amount of furniture I figured I could get away with, I'd decided that three hundred dollars a week was the most I could spend on rent, and the landlord was asking four hundred.

Obviously, moving away from the beach and into a relatively unknown suburb didn't mean the dip in rental prices I'd optimistically expected. Nevertheless, I told the agent that I'd like to make an application for the property, figuring that the landlord could only reject my offer.

This irritated the couple on whose inspection I had gatecrashed, but they were still arguing about who cleaned the bathroom more often. That was one advantage of being single – at least I didn't have to confer with anyone on my decisions.

The real estate agent looked at me uncertainly. My pregnant belly gave me an initial aura of respectability, but that was lost as soon as he looked at my bare ring-finger. Still, I was well-dressed (although by Newtown standards that only meant I wasn't liable for arrest for indecent exposure) and he gave me an application form to return to his office on Monday.

After deciding that I could manage three hundred and twenty dollars at a push, I lodged an application for that amount, together with glowing references from our current landlord and my boss. Even in my more positive moments I didn't hold out much hope that my application would be accepted and I continued looking at dingy places that no amount of bright paint and plants could redeem.

The following Wednesday I had just hung up the phone after a very tense discussion with a printer who was trying to renegotiate the pricing for a run of posters for our next event, when it rang again.

'Yes,' I snapped into the receiver, assuming it was the printer again.

'Sophie Anderson, please?' said the voice on the other end of the phone.

'Yes, speaking,' I replied more warmly as soon as I realised the print cost war wasn't about to be immediately resumed.

'Sophie, this is Adrian Henry from Barker & Henderson Real Estate. We met last Saturday.'

I tried to recall an Adrian in the line-up of real estate agents I'd met, but failed. Eyeing the stack of agents' cards I'd collected, I replied in what I hoped was a convincing tone, 'Yes, Adrian, how are you?'

'Very well, thanks, and I'm calling with good news,' he continued. 'Your application for the house at 32 Henry Street has been accepted.'

'Are you serious?' I asked incredulously, never having heard of a landlord taking that kind of rent drop.

'Certainly am,' he replied cheerily. 'The landlord decided that you sounded like the perfect tenant and so is prepared to compromise on the rent.'

I pushed my chair back and gazed out the window, unable to stop the smile spreading across my face. Maybe we didn't have much else, but at least my baby and I now had a home.

FIVE

Having driven us home from the hospital, Debbie left and I lay Sarah on the sofa. I looked at her blankly, wondering what on earth to do next. Years of reading magazines like *Cosmopolitan* and *Cleo* hadn't prepared me for this. Somehow articles like 'An Afternoon with a Baby, a Minute-by-Minute Account' didn't seem to have made it into those publications.

A sudden attack of panic hit me. What did the hospital think they were doing letting someone as irresponsible and unreliable as me out the door with a human being as fragile and vulnerable as the one looking up at me? For God's sake, I couldn't even remember to put out the recycling bin on the right day!

The nursing staff had threatened dire consequences for anyone who should dare to take their baby home without a capsule (thankfully they hadn't made it as far as the car park and spotted Debbie's convertible). However, they seemed not to realise that the risk of a car accident was minimal compared with the danger Sarah faced by being left alone with a mother who could coordinate a sporting event for 10 000 people but had not the first clue about how to deal with a tiny baby. Somehow I'd expected that the baby would come with an instruction manual, or at least a checklist of dos and don'ts, but they had sent Sarah, Debbie and me out into the world with barely a goodbye.

At the hospital I'd watched intently as they showed me how to change Sarah's nappy and bath her. Not having had any brothers or sisters or other babies around when I was growing up, I'd managed to reach the age of thirty without ever having changed a nappy. When I was five I had a doll called Mandy who wet herself when you fed her water. However, I gathered by the nurse's expression when I explained this to her that it really wasn't the kind of thing you put on your nappy-changing résumé.

If I'd thought nappy-changing was tricky, bathing looked like one of those activities television programs urge you not to try at home. Just holding Sarah coated with slippery soap in a bath full of water seemed to me to be a big enough accomplishment, let alone actually cleaning any part of her body. As the nurse twirled Sarah in the water with one hand, while cleaning inside her ears with the other, I looked on in awe. I hoped that she was doing a good job, as I didn't think I'd be able to execute that technique for at least another six months.

Figuring that now we were home there was no

point in putting off my first unassisted nappy change, I carried Sarah into her room, which I'd painted bright yellow during the long weekend mornings of my pregnancy when no one else I knew was awake.

'What do you think of your room, darling?' I asked. She seemed rather unexcited by it, which I supposed could have had something to do with the fact that she couldn't focus on anything more than twenty centimetres from her face.

The change table was in about ten pieces on the floor.

Debbie had arrived with it one day, claiming that it had been a sample from one of Mr Cheapy's suppliers. Either Mr Cheapy was going through an identity crisis, or Debbie had bought it herself knowing that I was struggling to afford everything. The price tag I'd later spotted on the bottom of the box had confirmed my suspicions, but when I'd tried to thank her, she'd denied everything and stuck firmly to her original story.

I had been very efficient with my baby goods buying, dividing the necessary purchases into different lists headed 'five months', 'six months', etc, both for the sake of my bank balance and to help myself ease slowly into the fact that I was actually going to be a mother. Somehow, buying a pram would have been unthinkable when I was four months pregnant, but was quite manageable psychologically once I had a stomach you could balance a beer can on.

There were some items that I couldn't bring myself to buy even at eight months pregnant, and those purchases, and jobs like assembling the change table, were on my list of things to do after I'd stopped work a week before Sarah was due. However, her early arrival had ruined my grand plan.

With a surprisingly small amount of persuasion, Debbie had agreed to drive me to the hospital and to be my birth partner during the initial stages of labour. The one condition she had insisted on was that her presence wouldn't be required during the actual birth.

Debbie was so serious about her role she had decided on a self-imposed alcohol ban for the entire week before the baby was due. Unfortunately, however, no one had told Sarah that most first babies come well after their due date, and the night before the ban was to start, I found myself suddenly awake. Turning onto my other side I tried to get comfortable. Almost asleep again I felt a faint pain in my belly. Jolted back into consciousness, I sat upright and stared down at where my lap used to be, trying to figure out if this was the real thing.

Fifteen minutes later I had just decided that I must have imagined the pain when I felt it again.

After two more of what I was now pretty sure were contractions, I dialled the hospital number Dr Daniels had given me.

'Ah, hi,' I stammered. I tried again. 'I think I'm in labour,' I managed, feeling vaguely stupid. I was reminded of the uncomfortable work conferences I'd been to where people were required to introduce themselves by stating their name, job and 'something personal'. 'Hi, I'm Sophie, I'm an events coordinator and I'm in labour,' would certainly have livened things up, I reflected.

'Just one moment, I'll transfer you to the labour ward,' answered the receptionist. Of course, a switchboard. My feeling of stupidity was now not at all vague.

'Labour ward,' a brisk-sounding woman announced.

'Yes, hello. Um, could I speak to a nurse?' I wasn't taking any chances this time.

'I'm a midwife.'

'Right. Ah, my doctor told me to call when I started having contractions. And, um, well, I think I am.'

The midwife asked me various questions, sounding rather unimpressed when I told her that the contractions were about fifteen minutes apart.

'Well, I'd say you've still got a long way to go, love,' she pronounced. 'You can either stay at home for a while yet or come straight to hospital.'

Was she kidding, I wondered?

After informing her that I'd be straight in, I dialled Debbie's home number. I wasn't surprised when she didn't answer and I tried her mobile. Even before I heard her voice, the background music and laughter told me that I'd be needing an alternative form of transport.

'Hello?' she answered merrily.

Her inebriated tone changed as soon as she heard my voice.

'Ohmigod,' she gasped, 'but the baby can't come now, it's not due for another week.'

Debbie's hysteria was obviously getting the better of her blood alcohol level. 'But I can't drive you. I'm in town and I've just had the best part of a jug of margaritas. I couldn't even find the car, let alone drive it. What on earth are you going to do?'

'It's all right, don't panic,' I said, reflecting wryly that I should be the hysterical one, not the calming influence. 'I'll call a taxi and you can meet me at the hospital.'

'Yes, yes of course, a taxi,' Debbie stuttered. 'But do they take women who are about to give birth?' she asked nervously. 'Wouldn't that be an insurance risk or something?'

'Of course they do,' I reassured her, pushing away the sudden worry that she could be right. 'I just won't scream in pain as the taxi is pulling up,' I added.

'Scream in pain? It's not really that bad, is it?' Debbie seemed to have totally lost her sense of humour.

As she spoke I felt another contraction begin. I looked at my watch, suddenly unable to remember the time of the contraction before. Had it been fifteen minutes already, or only ten?

At the thought that the contractions were getting closer together, panic flared. Delivering the baby on my bathroom floor in front of a fireman (someone had once told me they had the fastest response time of all the emergency services) wasn't what I had had in mind.

'Sophie?' Debbie asked and I realised I hadn't answered her question.

Gritting my teeth, I tried to think of an appropriately calming answer, afraid that my birthing partner was about to stand me up.

'No, Debbie.' I took a deep breath. 'I'm just joking.'

Debbie obviously detected a lack of conviction in my voice. 'Are you sure?' she asked nervously.

The contraction eased.

'I'm fine,' I managed, more firmly. 'Look, I need to get going, I'll see you there, okay?'

'Okay,' she answered in an uncertain tone.

After ordering a taxi, I grabbed my toothbrush from the bathroom and stuffed it inside Debbie's Louis Vuitton overnight bag. She'd insisted that I borrow it, declaring that if I was going to do something as disgusting as give birth, I'd better do it in style.

Ready to go, I sat down at the table. After flicking aimlessly through the newspaper, I stopped and looked around the living room, trying to comprehend the fact that the next time I walked back in the door it would be with a baby.

The taxi tooted outside. Another contraction grabbed at my stomach and I leant against the wall. For a moment my composure left me and I was suddenly terrified.

A cartoon I'd seen years before leapt into my mind. It had shown a pregnant woman being wheeled into the delivery room, proclaiming that she'd suddenly changed her mind. The cartoon had seemed funny at the time.

I forced myself to remember what we'd been told

at antenatal classes. Breathing! That was supposed to help. I concentrated on deep breaths in and out, not convinced of their benefit by the time the contraction finished. Looking at my watch, I was comforted to see it was still more than ten minutes since the last contraction. That didn't seem too much of a change.

The taxi tooted again. Turning off the light, I headed out the door.

'Where to, love?' the young cab driver asked cheerfully as I lowered myself onto the back seat.

I assumed he hadn't seen my profile, as I couldn't think of too many places a pregnant woman would be going with a suitcase in the early hours of the morning.

'St Bartholomew's Hospital.'

The penny obviously dropped and his head snapped around. 'Right, right,' he muttered nervously. Throwing the car into gear, he took off so fast that the rear tyres squealed.

'Ah, could you slow down a bit, please?' I asked tentatively.

'Sorry, sorry,' he apologised, without slowing the pace at all. 'It's just that you could have the baby at any moment,' he continued nervously. 'I've read about taxi drivers delivering babies on the side of the road. A bloody nose makes me feel faint. I don't even want to think about what a baby would do to me.'

I seemed destined to spend my whole labour reassuring others. 'It really doesn't work that way,' I yelled over the roar of the motor. 'I've spoken to the hospital and they think it will take hours more but they've told me to come in just to be safe.'

'Really?' he asked disbelievingly, slowing marginally.

'Really,' I said forcefully. 'Do you think I'd want to have my baby in the back of a taxi, miles from a hospital full of people who actually know what they're doing?'

'Guess not,' he acknowledged grudgingly, slowing a little more. 'Where's your fella, then?' he asked in an obvious attempt to make conversation. 'Meeting you there?'

'Ah no, he's moved to San Francisco actually,' I answered flatly.

'Oh, right,' he replied uncomfortably.

Conversation lapsed after that, but I could see him flicking nervous looks at me in the rear-vision mirror.

I looked at my watch. Six minutes since the last contraction. I tried to calculate whether we were likely to reach the hospital before I had another one, concerned that one groan would see me deposited on the footpath.

At ten minutes we approached a red traffic light. The driver slowed reluctantly, tapping his fingers impatiently on the dashboard.

'C'mon, c'mon,' he muttered.

The lights changed and he accelerated quickly.

I spotted the hospital a few blocks away. But instead of the relief I'd expected, I felt a sinking in my stomach and a sudden sense of impending doom. I'd been able to deal with being en route to the hospital, but somehow arriving there felt very different, as if it actually committed me to this whole baby thing. I willed the taxi to slow, but it whizzed along the empty road and pulled into the hospital.

As it stopped, I felt a warm sensation on my thighs.

What on earth? I wondered, looking down.

Realisation dawned as I felt my boots filling up with liquid.

No description I'd read about waters breaking had explained just how much liquid was involved, and the puddle I was sitting in grew and continued cascading onto the floor.

The taxi pulled up at the hospital entrance.

'Well, we're here,' the driver said, in obvious relief. 'And all in one piece.'

Opening my mouth to enlighten him, I closed it again, unable to bring myself to break the news. Maybe the next passenger would just think someone had spilt a drink in the back seat. After all, drunks threw up in cabs. That was a lot worse than this, wasn't it?

I leant over and handed the driver a fifty-dollar note.

'Keep the change,' I muttered guiltily.

'Really? Thanks,' he answered.

Feeling like a coward, I slid off the back seat and out of the car.

Following the signs to the maternity ward, I squelched up to the reception desk and stood there dripping. The nurse took in the situation at a glance (to her credit, not even sniggering) and within ten minutes I was in a hospital room, having discarded my sodden trousers for a pastel-coloured floral nightgown which tied at the back.

Debbie had obviously recovered her composure on the trip to the hospital, because she laughed as soon as she saw me. 'Oh, very you, Sophie,' she said. 'I'm sure everyone will be wearing one of those this year.'

'You're a comedian,' I groaned, feeling more than usually outclassed by Debbie as she clattered into the room on her high heels, wearing a silvery grey sheath, which I knew had cost a fortune.

Once the nurse had hooked me up to a couple of monitors, she left us alone. Debbie wandered around the room, opening drawers and fiddling with various gadgets.

'So what happens now?' she asked, her earlier unease returning.

'It'll probably take hours before anything much happens,' I said. 'I'm getting contractions about every ten minutes, but they don't last too long and so far they don't hurt too much.'

'Right, right,' she muttered, obviously only half listening.

Her head jolted up. 'Where's the doctor?' she asked suddenly.

I'd been through this with Debbie a few weeks ago but, as I'd suspected at the time, not much had sunk in.

'He only gets here once I'm into the second stage of labour,' I said patiently.

'Run it by me again. You've got to be, what, fifteen centimetres expanded before that happens?' Debbie asked with a grimace.

'Ten centimetres dilated,' I corrected her. Only in

Debbie's presence did I resemble any form of expert on the birth process.

'Well, that doesn't sound too hard, does it?' she said hopefully.

Another contraction started and I suddenly tired of my role as calm, collected patient.

'Debbie, I have no idea, all right? *You're* supposed to be keeping *my* spirits up, not the other way around.'

'Okay, okay,' Debbie muttered in an offended tone.

The situation was saved by the entrance of the nurse bearing a pot of black coffee, which I'd requested as soon as I arrived, in the hope of bringing Debbie back to something approximating a sober state.

She took one sip and shuddered, replacing the cup on the saucer. 'That is absolutely disgusting. It tastes like it was brewed about the time this baby of yours was conceived.'

Alcohol always made Debbie hyperactive and she looked around the room in search of something to do. I saw her eyes light up as she focused on an object over my shoulder. Sensing danger, I turned around in time to see her pick up a plastic mask, hold it over her face and fiddle with a knob on the wall.

'Debbie, what are you doing?' I demanded.

I could see her smile even behind the mask.

'Happy gas,' was her muffled reply.

She took a deep breath and then took the mask off. 'I haven't had gas since I went to the dentist when I was a kid,' she said. 'Why do they stick a needle in your mouth rather than giving you this lovely stuff, do you think?'

'Debbie, you can't do that,' I spluttered, ignoring her question and looking nervously over my shoulder towards the door. 'What if the nurse comes back?'

'Just one more puff?' she pleaded.

'Absolutely not,' I replied firmly. 'Put it back. Now.'

Like a sulky two year old, she replaced the mask and threw herself into the chair beside the bed.

Five minutes later she was asleep. Deciding that a sleeping Debbie was better than a drunk Debbie, I left her to it. With a sigh I pulled a magazine out of my bag and flicked it open. I found, though, that I spent the time after each contraction dreading the next one, and soon gave up attempting to read.

Staring out of the hospital window into the darkness I tried to be positive, but a feeling of loneliness swamped me. Dad had been determined that he would be in Sydney when my baby was born, but a month ago, he'd had a minor heart attack. The doctors lectured him fiercely about his high blood pressure and he complained bitterly about the changes to his diet and lifestyle they had dictated, and which Elizabeth enforced with an iron hand. They'd forbidden his flying to the other side of the world.

I pulled out the walkman in my bag. My pregnancy manual had suggested having a nature CD, filled with the sounds of birds and waterfalls, to play during labour. Unable to bring myself to buy such an item, I had, however, included a selection of easy-listening CDs and I inserted one of them.

Within seconds, though, I realised that my weepy mood had abruptly changed to one of anger that I was doing this with only Debbie's snoring to keep me company, and that the syrupy music was making me feel like punching something. Pulling the CD out, I rifled through my bag, looking for something more in tune with my emotions.

Bruce Springsteen's *Born in the USA* went into the machine, and I relaxed slightly. Another contraction began and I cranked the volume up, trying to pretend I was aware of nothing but the music. To my surprise this worked, to an extent, and helped to sustain me through the next hour until a nurse arrived to check the monitors. Depressingly, she informed me that the contractions weren't strengthening and that there was still a long way to go. I'd been trying to convince myself that every contraction brought the end one step closer, but it seemed that all I was really doing was marking time.

As she left, though, the blackness outside the window began to lighten and the dawn lifted my spirits. I halfheartedly nibbled on an energy bar (one of the ten I'd included in my food pack, which looked like it would sustain me for a three-day hike) and turned on the television, cheered that other people were up and watching the early morning news shows.

At eight Dr Daniels poked his head around the corner.

'So it's all happening, hey?' he said calmly. 'I've

just done a C-section and I thought I'd pop in and see how you're doing.'

'I'm fine, I think,' I said. 'Nothing much seems to be changing, though. Is that normal?'

'Totally. This stage could go on for a while yet, or things could hot up suddenly.'

As if she sensed the male presence in the room, Debbie stirred and opened her eyes. For someone who had consumed numerous cocktails the night before and had had only a few hours sleep in a chair, she looked remarkably good, I thought with a touch of irritation.

'Hello, Doctor,' she said brightly. Suddenly she sat upright and grasped the arms of the chair. 'Does this mean the baby's coming?' she asked in panic.

'No, no,' he reassured her. 'We've still got a way to go. I just dropped in to see how it was going.'

'Thank God,' she exclaimed, flopping back into the chair.

Not for the first time, I tried to remember exactly what it was that had led me to believe Debbie would be a good person to assist me through this process.

As if reading my thoughts, she came over and perched on the edge of the bed. 'Soph. Are you okay?'

Mollified slightly, I nodded. 'Everything's still pretty much the same as when I arrived. The contractions feel sort of like a bad stitch.'

Debbie smiled up at Dr Daniels. 'Have a seat,' she invited, pulling a chair up to the bed.

'Thanks.' He was smiling at Debbie in a way that

I recognised and would rather not have seen on my obstetrician's face.

'I've decided that I'd like to try to manage without an epidural.'

My statement had been more an attempt to interrupt the moment than the result of a lot of thought, but once the words were out it sounded like a good plan.

'That's fine.' Dr Daniels tore his gaze away from Debbie and looked at me. 'You may want to change your mind later, though, just let me know.'

Debbie glanced at her watch. 'Eight o'clock! I'd better call work and tell them I won't be in today. And I don't know about you two but I'm ravenous. Do they do breakfast here?'

'What an excellent idea,' Dr Daniels agreed. 'I'm sure the nurse will be able to organise something for us.'

'If it's anything like last night's coffee, I'm not sure I'm interested,' Debbie declared. 'I've got a better idea. I think there's a coffee shop not far from here. Fancy a walk?'

At first I thought she was talking to me, but I quickly realised that her question was directed at Dr Daniels.

'Sure,' he replied, standing up.

Debbie leapt off the bed as if she'd just had eight hours sleep, and grabbed her handbag. 'Will you be okay if I head out for a couple of minutes?' she asked.

I nodded reluctantly. It was my own fault. I shouldn't have tried to sound calm for Debbie's sake. I'd obviously been too convincing.

'Back in a moment, Soph,' she flung over her shoulder as she headed out the door with my obstetrician.

Feeling distinctly left out, I viciously flicked through my magazine for the umpteenth time.

By the time they walked back in, laughing, fifteen minutes later, I had begun to feel distinctly queasy and had no interest in the bacon bagels and steaming coffees they were bearing.

They checked that things hadn't hotted up while they were out, then settled themselves in the corner and tucked into their food, appearing to have become the firmest of friends during the breakfast run.

By the time they had finished eating, the contractions were coming closer together and starting to hurt a lot more.

Involuntarily I groaned.

Debbie and Dr Daniels both looked up at me.

'Are you okay, Soph?' Debbie asked, in a tone that made me feel I was interrupting something.

'Fine,' I said through gritted teeth.

'Oh good,' she replied and they both turned back to their coffee.

They laughed at something I hadn't heard and I shot them a furious look which neither of them noticed. Something was definitely wrong here. I was in a hospital room with my obstetrician and my best friend. But instead of feeling pampered and protected, I had the distinct feeling I was behaving highly inappropriately by giving birth in the middle of a hot date.

Ten minutes later I was finding it hard to keep

calm. 'Excuse me?' I said sarcastically, but obviously not loudly enough.

'Excuse me?' I repeated much louder.

Both of them turned to me with raised eyebrows.

'I'm really sorry to interrupt, but do you think I could have a hand over here? These contractions are really starting to hurt.'

Finally I had their attention and they both came over to the bed.

'What can I do to help?' Debbie asked.

She looked so concerned, I found myself about to reassure her that everything was going to be all right, but suddenly I wasn't so sure myself.

'Can I get you some ice chips?' she asked.

If I hadn't been in so much pain, I would have laughed. They always seem to have ice chips on hand in the birth scenes in movies, but unless they were laced with vodka, I really couldn't see how they were going to help.

Dr Daniels looked up from the print-out which showed the timing and strength of my contractions.

'All right, I think we're down to the serious end of things now. You might want to leave pretty soon, Debbie.'

Despite the fact that Debbie had made him promise to warn her when the birth was close, she looked at him in horror.

'Leave? Are you serious? I'm not going anywhere.'

Another contraction started, almost on top of the last one, and I pushed my head back into the pillow and closed my eyes, unable to focus on anything but the pain. When I opened them again, Debbie was emerging from the bathroom, having abandoned her shimmering dress and stiletto heels for a loose T-shirt and a pair of elastic-waisted trousers she'd obviously found in my bag.

'Right, I've changed my mind,' I announced, figuring I didn't have long before the next contraction. 'I want drugs. Give me an epidural now.' I couldn't imagine what had possessed me to decide not to have one.

Dr Daniels was moving around the room and giving instructions to a nurse who had suddenly appeared.

'Sorry, Sophie, but it's too late,' he threw over his shoulder as, to my horror, he pulled on white gum boots and a plastic apron. His words took a moment to sink in but as they did I sat bolt upright.

'What? You told me I could let you know if I changed my mind!'

'Yes, I know,' he replied calmly. 'But you've advanced through this stage very quickly; we don't have time for an epidural now.'

'You have got to be kidding!' I exclaimed. 'Why didn't you tell me this might happen?'

Dr Daniels stopped what he was doing and walked over to the bed.

'You can still use gas, Sophie. Here, take a deep breath of this.' He pulled the mask towards me but I brushed it aside.

'Do they give you happy gas when they cut your leg off?' I yelled.

Debbie put her hand on my shoulder.

'Soph, it will be all right, just relax.'

I caught a look that passed between them and opened my mouth to comment. Before I could, though, I felt the next contraction and gripped the sides of the hospital bed.

Debbie dislodged one of my hands and put it around hers.

'Here, squeeze this. Right, I think we need to focus on the name for this baby. What about Humperdink? Now, there's a name you don't hear enough these days.'

The contractions came one after the other and I didn't have the energy to argue any more. All of my energy was focused on just getting through each one.

Debbie stayed resolutely at my head, not even glancing towards Dr Daniels and the midwife. She mopped my forehead with a cloth and kept her hand in mine throughout the next hour.

When the little wet and screaming body that was my daughter finally appeared, Debbie burst into tears.

Dr Daniels handed my baby to me and I looked down at her in awe. Every part of her was perfectly formed, from her tiny ears to the nails on her long fingers. I noticed with a pang that the large gap between her first two toes was an exact replica of Max's.

'Hello, sweetheart,' I whispered, reaching out a finger to touch her nose.

Looking up, I saw Debbie smiling through her tears at me.

'It's a little girl, Debbie. I have a little girl,' I said in a voice that I couldn't stop from trembling.

'Oh, Sophie,' she said, her eyes not leaving the baby. 'She is absolutely beautiful.'

'Hello, Sarah,' I said, any lingering doubts about naming my daughter after my mother gone.

As if she heard, Sarah opened her eyes and looked up at me. In a moment all the doubts I'd had during my pregnancy about whether I really wanted a baby were swept away. Now that she was here, I couldn't imagine not having her. I was under no illusions that bringing her up by myself would be easy, but I was certain I could handle whatever came along. From now on there would always be the two of us and suddenly that felt exactly how it was meant to be.

'Oh, Sophie,' Debbie whispered again. 'Think of the clothes we can buy her.'

SIX

My first day home was clearly not the time to attempt to decipher the instructions on erecting the change table, which seemed to have been written by someone whose knowledge of the English language rivalled my high school French. Figuring babies had probably been changed on floors before, I lay Sarah on the rug and grabbed the bag with nappies and various other bits and pieces from the living room.

What had seemed, not easy, but definitely achievable, when I had someone holding Sarah's legs for me, suddenly became impossible now that I was alone. I tried desperately to remember how the nurse had managed to hold Sarah's squirming legs and clean her simultaneously. Thankfully, Sarah seemed to sense that I had absolutely no idea what I was doing and stopped moving. After sticking down the second nappy tag, I looked at my watch – ten minutes. Doing a quick calculation in my head, I figured that if I changed Sarah twelve times a day (which I had been informed was quite a conservative estimate) then, unless I managed to streamline the operation, I was going to spend two hours a day just changing nappies.

Given that I had fed Sarah just before we left the hospital and I had now changed her nappy, I couldn't think of anything else to do with her except put her to bed in the hope she might be tired. Thankfully, the family I'd bought the cot from through the classified ads in the newspaper had taken pity on my obviously single state and had not only delivered the cot but had put it back together for me before leaving.

Wrapping Sarah in a bunny-rug was a skill I hadn't even come close to mastering in the hospital. In about three quick moves the nurses had managed to make a little bundle that resembled a straight-jacket, while my attempts produced something Sarah could dislodge with a decent-sized yawn. Nevertheless I did my best and settled her in the cot, which suddenly looked huge compared to the tiny figure that was my four-day-old daughter.

During the later stages of my pregnancy I had found the feeling of the baby moving around in my belly amazing. Without even having seen the baby, I knew that I loved it, and by the time I was eight months pregnant, I couldn't imagine the feeling becoming any stronger once it was born. As I looked at Sarah now, I realised how wrong I had been.

Every time I looked at her I fell a little bit deeper under her spell. I felt like a cartoon character who spies a love interest and whose heart starts to swell and beat faster and faster until it fills the whole room.

Although I knew that the little miracle in the cot had been inside me a week ago, I still didn't feel as though she was mine. I half expected a real mother wearing a housecoat (whatever that was) to knock on the door, thank me for looking after Sarah and say, 'I'll take it from here.'

Miraculously Sarah closed her eyes, and I backed quietly out of the room, wincing as I turned in the doorway without remembering to add the extra clearance my newfound figure now required. I hadn't always had DD-cup breasts, any cleavage I'd previously managed being solely the result of a bra with a large amount of foam in it.

The transformation had occurred on the third night after Sarah was born, while a friend was visiting me in hospital. It was actually quite appropriate that it happened in front of Andrew as, one way or another, he'd been trying to change my body shape for years.

The company I worked for when I first moved to Sydney had a tiny gym which consisted of not much more than a couple of running machines and some huge weights. It had been roundly ignored by all of the staff until the CEO had a midlife crisis and found fitness, deciding that healthy bodies equalled healthy minds. He hired Andrew's services as a personal trainer and enlisted him to design an exercise program for all employees who were interested. The project had become something of a standing joke in the office and Andrew spent more time staring at the four walls of the dingy gym than revitalising our flagging energy levels.

However, one depressing day when I discovered I couldn't do up the button on my favourite pair of black trousers, I snuck down to the gym at lunchtime in desperation. On walking into the gym, I spotted a very muscular blond man bench-pressing lumps of metal that looked like they weighed as much as a small car. Horrified, I began backing out. However, Andrew had spotted the movement in the mirrors, flicked the weights back onto the stand and bolted upright, greeting me with enthusiasm. Cornered, I was coerced into what turned out to be the first of many fitness regimes designed for me by Andrew.

Despite my initial reservations, I found myself enjoying Andrew's company, and on discovering his weakness for red wine and double espressos, I decided I could overlook the fact that his idea of a great morning was jogging ten kilometres on his toes (to strengthen his calves, he informed me enthusiastically).

Debbie recoiled in horror when, soon after I'd met Andrew, I told her that he was a personal trainer.

'Sophie!' she shrieked. 'Have I taught you nothing? If there are two rules to live your life by, one of them is never give your phone number to a man wearing sandshoes and jeans, and the other is never, ever make friends with anyone who receives an income in any way connected with fitness.' Her words would ring in my ears whenever Andrew had me sweating over some gruelling course.

Despite outward appearances, Andrew's IQ far

exceeded his bicep measurement. For his twelfth birthday, his grandfather had given him a small portfolio of shares. Until he'd turned eighteen he had had to justify each trade to the old man, thereby learning the value of research and understanding the economy. He had been buying and selling shares ever since and his gym bag was usually crammed with issues of financial magazines and business papers rather than the muscle magazines you might expect. I'd learnt never to seat him at dinner next to Karen's husband Sam, who worked for a big American bank, as they could be guaranteed to spend the evening talking endlessly about recent moves in the NASDAQ and Nikkei.

Andrew's biggest problem was his taste in women. Over the years I'd seen a succession of women, all of them fitness junkies who had six-pack stomachs and biceps that would do the average male proud. The trouble was that once we'd exhausted the topic of their latest exercise regime, conversation would come to a screaming halt. I had never been able to figure out what he saw in them. The best that I could come up with was that he'd fallen into the habit of asking women out because they looked good, never giving himself the chance to find out first if he liked them.

Andrew had become a good friend over the years and on that fateful third night he sidled uncomfortably into my hospital room bearing a huge teddy bear, obviously feeling distinctly out of place in the maternity ward. My years of private hospital insurance had finally paid off and I had a room to myself, for which I was very grateful – all other considerations aside, I didn't think I could have fitted my mini florist's shop into anything smaller.

From what I could gather, the first few days of breastfeeding were a bit of a warm-up period to get both Sarah and me ready for the main event when my milk arrived. Things had seemed to go quite well so far. We were getting very good at the 'latch' (otherwise known as opening your baby's mouth and sticking it on your breast), and Sarah spent a lot of time sleeping, which I assumed meant she wasn't starving to death. However, I struggled not to smirk every time the nurses told me in hushed tones that my 'milk would soon be coming in'. I pictured a carton of milk standing outside my door, politely knocking until I let it in.

I was sitting on the bed and Andrew was perched on a hard hospital chair beside me. He had just been quizzing me as to whether there was anywhere in the hospital grounds where I could get out for a brisk walk, when I noticed him look at my chest for about the fourth time in the last five minutes.

'Sophie . . .' Andrew said tentatively. 'No, don't worry,' he quickly added.

'What on earth is wrong, Andrew?' I asked.

'Well,' he squirmed in embarrassment. 'Have you had a look at your chest recently?'

I looked down quickly, expecting to see that Sarah had thrown up on me when I wasn't looking.

'Oh my God!' I exclaimed, sliding off the bed and rushing to look in the wall mirror on the other side of the room.

I had refused to receive visitors in my pyjamas and was wearing a linen shirt that buttoned down the front. While I had been aware of a vague ache in my breasts since Sarah's last feed, I hadn't given it a lot of thought, but now protruding out of the top of my shirt was the biggest cleavage I had ever seen on any person who didn't work in Hollywood.

Oblivious to Andrew's presence, I pulled my shirt away from my body, peered down the front and let out a gasp. It looked like someone had glued two medicine balls, which were only vaguely disguised as breasts, onto the front of my chest.

'Will you look at this?' I asked Andrew, pulling my shirt down to reveal my bra, all considerations of modesty out the window in this moment of crisis.

He looked at me with his mouth open and it took him several seconds to find his voice. 'I hope you packed your little red bikini in your hospital bag,' he said. 'So you can audition for *Baywatch*,' he continued weakly on seeing that I did not consider this a laughing matter.

As I gazed down at what used to be my breasts, I became aware that the dull ache was becoming worse. While I had often wished for slightly larger breasts, these huge bazookas that had emerged from nowhere were way beyond what I had ever contemplated and I wasn't entirely sure that they were normal.

Andrew had obviously decided that he did not want to be in a hospital room with a three-day-old baby and a woman with decidedly bizarre things happening to her body and a crazed expression in her eyes. As I looked up from another contemplation of the mounds of flesh under my shirt, he was edging out of the room and muttering his goodbyes.

As soon as he was gone, I called the nurses' station and asked one of them if they would come in and see me. I was still examining my new figure in the mirror when a brisk, no-nonsense nurse arrived.

'Yes, Sophie, how can I help you?'

'Well . . .' I began, not quite knowing what to say. 'Look, I know your breasts are supposed to get bigger when you breastfeed, but I think there's something wrong with mine.' I showed her, half expecting her to turn pale and run for a doctor.

'Ah,' said the nurse matter-of-factly, 'your breasts are engorged.'

After ten months of pregnancy (don't let anyone tell you it is nine months, unless of course forty weeks equals nine months by your calculations) and the act of childbirth, I had heard a lot of hideous terms for the things that happen to your body, but this was a new one to me.

'Engorged?' I echoed nervously. 'Is that serious?'

'No, it's perfectly normal when your milk comes in,' the nurse replied as she tidied up the various items I'd been using to bath Sarah when Andrew arrived.

'Although some women do get it worse than others. It looks like you've got a pretty good dose, but it should settle down in a couple of days.'

The pain seemed to be rapidly getting worse and a couple of days sounded like an awfully long time.

'Is there anything I can do to help it?' I asked, trying not to sound too desperate.

'The only things that really work are icepacks or frozen cabbage,' she replied.

'Please tell me you eat the cabbage,' I pleaded. That at least got a smile out of her.

'Sorry, Sophie, but no, you put it on your breasts. There's something about the chemical makeup of the cabbage that helps to reduce the swelling.'

'The icepacks will be just fine, thanks,' I replied firmly, refusing to contemplate sticking cabbage leaves down my bra.

An hour later, after a series of icepacks that had done nothing to alleviate the pain, I was back on the phone to the nurses' station requesting cabbage leaves.

Something you realise pretty quickly about hospitals is that the doctors and nurses have seen it all before and don't flicker an eyelid at personal indignities that make patients shrivel up in mortification. The nurse didn't even snigger as she delivered my frozen cabbage leaves and explained what I should do with them.

As soon as she left the room, I stuck them underneath my bra and the relief was immediate. What I wasn't prepared for, though, was the smell. The heat radiating from my burning breasts cooked the cabbage, and within a couple of minutes there was a distinct smell of steaming vegetable that brought to mind memories of my grandmother's kitchen.

As a green watery substance soaked through my only nursing bra and dripped down my stomach and into the waistband of my trousers, it struck me as highly unfair that humankind could clone Dolly the Sheep, but had been unable to come up with a better remedy for milk-filled breasts than a frozen vegetable.

SEVEN

Saturday mornings at a favourite cafe had been an institution of ours for years (long before they took it up on *Friends*) and today was Sarah's official 'coming-out'.

The weekly ritual had begun when Ben, a friend of Debbie's younger brother, quit university in the fourth year of his medicine degree and, much to the horror of his parents, bought the King Street Cafe. His claims that he could still use his first aid skills to patch up the drunks who came in for a pick-me-up coffee hadn't cheered his parents up much.

Ben threw himself into redecorating the place, removing the grease-laden brown wallpaper and replacing it with brightly coloured paint and furniture. He scrubbed the whole place from top to bottom, bought every magazine that had been published in the last two years and threw open the doors with great enthusiasm.

And not a soul turned up.

In those days Newtown was still considered a bit dangerous and people from the eastern suburbs didn't often make the journey across town (even though it was all of fifteen minutes). Debbie heard about Ben's plight and immediately insisted that a group of us meet for breakfast at the cafe every Saturday morning.

While we could all munch our way through a lot of fry-ups and drink a lot of flat whites, our efforts alone wouldn't have been enough to keep Ben afloat. Luckily, though, his business grew quickly as Newtown became a place to be seen and people discovered the King Street Cafe. By then our habit had stuck and we all still took these weekend sessions seriously. The group had changed with time – Debbie's brother had left for a job on Wall Street, and various others had drifted in and out – but five of us had been meeting almost every Saturday for the last few years.

The rule was that you must appear regardless of where and when the night before had ended, the only exception being if you had arrived home after six a.m. This rule had recently been amended to include childbirth as an acceptable excuse, although only after considerable debate, as a number of our group, with the notable exception of Ben, had believed it would be appropriate for me to give birth on the premises.

Ben's wife Anna, while insisting that she wasn't paranoid, could see no reason to tempt fate by having Ben surrounded for twelve hours every day by pretty young waitresses in midriff tops and had decreed that only men could work in the cafe. Ben's rather bizarre sense of humour led to the cafe being predominantly staffed by burly tattooed men who looked like they'd be more at home on a building site than whipping up macchiatos.

The service in the cafe was very relaxed and people were welcome to sit on one cup of coffee for a whole morning if that was what they felt like doing. People came back because of this, but they all seemed to bring friends as well, so it was very common to see whole groups downing plates of bacon and eggs and one coffee after another.

Max had never been a King Street Cafe regular, but he and Ben had become good friends when they spent three months training together for a half-marathon. When we broke up, I couldn't help but wonder how much Max had told Ben, and things had been a bit awkward between myself and Ben for a while. My suspicions were confirmed when, far from being surprised when I told him I was pregnant, Ben had smiled and produced a bottle of nonalcoholic champagne. Still, he had never tried to push Max and me back together. He had mentioned once that Max's job was going well in San Francisco, and while I had pretended to be pleased, I could tell he noticed my lack of enthusiasm.

The only other time we had discussed Max was when I asked Ben to let him know when the baby was born. Ben had promised to call him, but I hadn't been able to bring myself to ask what Max's reaction had been.

Some mornings the group would all sit reading

the inch-thick weekend papers, other mornings the papers sat unopened on the floor as we caught up on the week's activities over a breakfast dictated by the previous night's level of alcohol intake – fruit salad and toast for those who had abstained, heavy-duty fry-ups for those who hadn't.

During my pregnancy I had arrived bright-eyed and bushy-tailed on the dot of eleven, while the others had dragged themselves in some time later with bloodshot eyes and the stamps from clubs where they'd spent the early hours of the morning still on their forearms.

Most of the people I know who have had babies say that they didn't miss alcohol and they found it easy not drinking for nine months. I did and it wasn't. By the time I was six months pregnant, I was heartily sick of lime sodas and was dying to have more than one glass of wine or to slug a beer like a normal human being, not sit on it for four hours while it got hot and flat.

Being sober in bars was a totally new experience for me. While the hours between ten and two used to disappear in a blur of laughter and music, they seemed to last an eternity when I was nursing my third mineral water of the evening, well aware that being seen chatting to a pregnant and obviously sober woman was social death. Usually I gave up my pretence of having fun after the fourth or fifth round of drinks and headed home for a bowl of pasta – the lack of alcohol making me all too aware that I'd missed dinner.

However, there were benefits to not drinking. For

one thing, I knew exactly what everyone else had got up to when they were drunk. For once I could be the person who said the next day, 'I couldn't believe it when you . . .' or 'Did you actually realise that you were . . . ?', instead of lying in bed the next morning trying to piece together the night's activities and figure out whether I'd done anything truly awful. I also discovered a whole lot of extra time in the weekend, namely the hours before ten a.m., and spent some fabulous mornings wandering along the beach at Bondi. It was a joy to find a parking space right beside the beach and I was back home before the hard-core partiers had even figured out whose bed they had woken up in.

So it was that at eleven o'clock on the Saturday morning eight days after Sarah had entered the world, I strapped her into the baby sling, checked that she wasn't suffocating against my cleavage and headed out the door towards Newtown. On the phone the night before, my father had assured me that you got used to living without much sleep when you had a baby. But after only a week, I still constantly felt like death warmed up and suspected he had just been trying to make me feel better.

As I walked down the street on my way to the cafe, Sarah's presence converted passers-by into beaming friends. As with most big cities, Sydney's unspoken rule is that you don't look at strangers, and no matter what you do, never, ever smile. Suddenly all those rules were out the window and people were not only smiling at me, they were stopping to talk – to Sarah, that is.

Even though it was eleven-thirty before I made it to the cafe, having been stopped every few metres, I was disappointed to see that I was the first to arrive.

'Morning, girls.'

I spotted Ben's lanky body next to the cash register. Although he was smiling, his greeting struck me as a little reserved. I felt that a bit more excitement was in order for Sarah's first coffee group experience. However, I reminded myself that everyone else had a life and Saturday morning coffee wasn't the social highlight of their week.

'Hi, Ben,' I said, hiding my disappointment as I took Sarah out of her baby sling. 'Could I just have a coffee to start with?'

The piped music in the cafe suddenly went silent and there was a drum roll. With a loud crash, which Sarah slept through obliviously, the song 'Baby Love' started playing. At the same moment, the kitchen door opened and out came my weekly breakfast companions. Using wooden spoons as microphones, they sang and sashayed their way through the tiny cafe, throwing streamers and popping miniature champagne bottles.

The other cafe patrons seemed startled at first (more, I suspect, by the uncool music than the bizarre behaviour of the dancers) but quickly returned to their newspapers or watched, smiling, the rest of the short procession.

In a congo line, Debbie, Andrew, Karen, Ben and Anna snaked through the tiny cafe, stepping out briefly onto the street to circle the tables on the footpath, looking for all the world like a collection of drag queens rehearsing for their next show.

Debbie was the first to reach us and she kissed Sarah, murmuring, 'Welcome to the world, little one,' before standing aside.

Andrew was next in the queue. As usual he was dressed in running shorts and a singlet and, judging by the amount of sweat still on him, had just arrived from whatever gruelling course he had set himself that morning. Andrew was a very vocal advocate of exercise as the best way to cure a hangover and would drag himself out of bed for a twenty-kilometre run only hours after he'd stumbled home. Judging by his bloodshot eyes, the endorphins he swore by hadn't quite been able to overcome the excesses of last night.

'Well done, Sophie. She's beautiful.'

'Thanks, Andrew. Where's Helena?'

Helena was the current body of choice. She was the kind of woman who had shoes to coordinate with each gym outfit and always knew when to clap in aerobics classes.

'We broke up,' Andrew said morosely.

I tried hard to prevent an 'I told-you-so' look from reaching my face, but clearly had little success.

'I know, I know, but I really thought she was different – you know, that we really had something.'

He seemed genuinely upset and I was about to remind him that I wasn't terribly successful in the romance department either, when Sarah woke and let out an enormous wail. A look of terror came into Andrew's eyes and he hastily retreated to the far side of the table.

Oblivious to the noise, Debbie produced a bottle of champagne and six champagne flutes. 'We couldn't have let this moment pass by!' she exclaimed. 'I mean, how often does a child have her official coming-out?'

'And besides,' Andrew commented dryly, 'it's not every day that Debbie has an excuse to drink champagne this early on a Saturday morning.'

'Well, it's a lot more natural to be drinking champagne than running twenty-five kilometres,' Debbie retorted.

Debbie and Andrew had a tendency to go head to head if they were allowed to and bloodshed in Ben's cafe was always a distinct possibility.

'If you two don't stop, I'll have Jake and Bruce bounce you,' Anna threatened, gesturing towards the two muscle-bound staff standing behind the counter in their tight T-shirts.

Unlike Ben, Anna had made it through medical school and was currently working in the accident and emergency department of an inner-city hospital. Just under six feet tall with cropped brown hair, Anna seemed to be trailed by disasters. While she was a part-owner of the cafe, a series of mishaps, the last of which had resulted in the flooding of the entire premises, had led Ben to refuse to leave her there alone. It was a constant source of amazement to all of us that someone as vague as Anna could deal with the pressures of saving people's lives on a daily basis.

Karen (she of the three children and pregnancy manual library) offered to hold Sarah, who was still crying, as Debbie handed me a glass of champagne. We had first met Karen several years ago when she'd come into the cafe one Saturday morning. All the tables had been full and, seeing her hesitate, I'd suggested she join us. Despite the fact that her life at home with three children was radically different to ours, we'd all hit it off and she'd quickly become an integral part of the group.

Karen had reached a deal with her husband Sam that our Saturday breakfast sessions were her time off. Rain, hail or shine, she could always be counted on to turn up. While she was with us, Sam took the kids to McDonald's and then put them in front of a video before retiring to his study with the *Sydney Morning Herald*. Karen had come to the conclusion that her sanity was more important than whatever damage Big Macs and back-to-back videos were doing to her children.

As soon as Karen took her Sarah fell silent. Stunned, no doubt, to be held by someone who knew what she was doing.

'To Sarah,' Ben proclaimed, holding his glass in the air.

'To Sarah,' the others chorused.

'How are things going?' Karen asked after everyone had taken a sip.

'Fine, I think,' I answered. 'I've still got no idea what I'm doing, but Sarah seems to be pretty happy most of the time, so I figure I can't be making too many serious mistakes.'

'What do you actually do with her?' Andrew asked. 'It's not like you can kick a ball around with her in the back yard.'

Andrew had a point. I'd read an article when I was pregnant that had suggested putting flashcards in front of a baby soon after they were born. Karen had set me straight on that and suggested that the article best belonged in the bin, but I still hadn't figured out just what I should do with Sarah in the limited time she was awake.

'Shaking a couple of toys in her face and jiggling her on my knee for a while is generally the best I can come up with,' I admitted. I glanced sideways at Karen to see if she was horrified at the lack of mental stimulation in Sarah's life, but she was happily drinking her champagne.

'Talk us through an average night,' Ben said.

'Well, last night I fed Sarah at seven, nine-thirty, midnight . . .' I paused to try to pick the times out of my weary brain. 'Then I think it was about three and six,' I finished.

Debbie, Ben and Andrew all looked aghast, while Karen and Anna just nodded sympathetically.

'You're kidding, right?' Andrew asked.

'Afraid not,' I answered, glad that they were as horrified as I'd been after the first couple of nights, which had each felt like an eternity. 'Although I'm told it should get better,' I added in an attempt to be positive. I looked questioningly at Karen, who nodded, although not as emphatically as I would have liked.

'How do you know when to get up?' Andrew asked. 'Do you set an alarm?'

Everyone looked at him in amazement.

'Tell me that was a joke,' Debbie demanded.

'I'm serious,' Andrew insisted, bemused at our reaction.

'The baby cries, Andrew,' Debbie said slowly, as if speaking to a two year old.

'Yeah, but what if you don't hear it? I can sleep through a ringing telephone, so I doubt that a baby the size of Sarah could wake me.'

'Trust me, hearing her is not my problem,' I said, thinking how I often found myself in Sarah's room, picking her up before I'd even consciously registered the fact that she was crying.

The conversation moved away from my life (or lack of it) and the rest of the morning passed quickly, the usual laughter and high spirits heightened by the champagne. Before I knew it, it was one o'clock and the party was breaking up. Debbie had consumed the best part of a bottle of champagne so I convinced her to come home with me for some lunch before driving back to her place.

I'd only been home for two days but had already come to the conclusion that I couldn't last any longer without shopping for some essentials that had been too unpleasant to contemplate before Sarah's birth but had suddenly become urgent. The thought of putting Sarah in the car and taking her shopping with me was way too daunting at this early stage, so the only option was to leave her at home with someone.

I looked sideways at Debbie as we walked home. 'Deb?' I ventured.

'Hmmm,' she muttered distractedly.

'How would you feel if I left Sarah with you for an hour?'

'What?' Debbie stopped in her tracks and looked at me in horror.

'There are some things I've just got to buy but I really don't want to cart Sarah around a shopping centre. Do you think you could stay while I slip out? I'll feed her and get her to sleep before I go, so she shouldn't even wake up while I'm gone,' I finished hurriedly.

'But what if I have to pick her up or, God for-bid, change her nappy?' Debbie said, still refusing to budge, as though I were aiming to trap her in the house with Sarah and run away.

'Debbie, I've only been doing this for about a week. You know as much as I do.'

'Yes, but you're a mother,' she said, as if that made all the difference.

Admittedly, despite Karen's advice otherwise, I had subconsciously thought that having a child would transform me from a self-centred almost thirtysomething into an earth mother who would effortlessly feed great groups of children and adults around her pine kitchen table and know the words to all the nursery rhymes. However, all it seemed to have done was make me a self-centred thirtysome-thing with a baby.

The bribe of dinner at Manchetti's eventually did the trick and I left Sarah asleep with a suddenly stone-cold-sober Debbie, who had called twice to check that my mobile phone was working before I'd even left my street.

The shopping centre had a couple of baby shops and I headed there, picking up what I needed before heading for the bookshop in search of baby reference material. There were signs over the shelves indicating the types of books they contained and I spotted one headed 'Parenting' at the back of the shop. As I got closer I noticed that it was sandwiched between two signs saying 'Humour'.

'Very funny,' I muttered as I scanned the book-shelves until I found a book called *The A to Z of Babies*, which looked as though it might have enough very basic information to get me through the coming weeks.

As I emerged from the bookshop I saw Olivia, a workmate of Debbie's whom I'd met a few times.

I did not feel like chatting and for a split second I considered diving behind the nearest pole, but she'd already seen me and so I halted my sideways lunge, fixed a smile on my face and walked towards her.

Olivia's husband, Paul, looked at me in horror. 'Sophie, what on earth are you doing here?'

'Out shopping for some essentials,' I muttered, holding up the bag I was carrying, which was emblazoned with the name of the baby shop I'd been in.

'But you must only just be out of hospital. Sarah was born last Friday, wasn't she?' said Olivia.

'Well, yes, but there were some things I've just had to buy which I didn't manage to get before she was born. So I've left Sarah with Debbie for an hour.'

'Debbie!' they exclaimed in unison.

'You left a week-old baby with Debbie?' Olivia repeated incredulously.

'She'll have given Sarah French nails by the time you get back,' Paul said, swallowing his smile as Olivia shot him a look that clearly said this was not a joking matter.

'Look, it was a minor emergency,' I explained. 'Sarah's coming a week early totally messed up my shopping plans.' Somehow I didn't think it would help matters if I mentioned how much champagne Debbie had drunk that morning, so I kept that piece of information to myself.

'But surely you could have sent someone else to buy them – other than Debbie, of course,' Olivia said. 'I didn't even leave the house for two weeks after Jennifer was born.'

They were really making this difficult. I checked my watch. Despite the fact that I had lived thirty years of my life without Sarah, half an hour away from her seemed like an eternity. I felt an almost physical pain at being separated from her and had a sensation in my stomach that I usually associated with job interviews.

Deciding to be frank, I gestured at my chest. 'It's a bit hard to send someone else out to buy maternity bras for you when you have no idea what size your own breasts are going to be at any point in the day. Look, I've really got to get back, I'll see you soon.'

Having escaped Olivia and Paul, I raced down the escalator and was about to head for the doors when I heard someone calling my name. To my disbelief, I saw Alice and Steve, two of my good friends from university days, waving wildly at me. In all the time I'd lived in Sydney I'd never run into so many people I knew in one outing.

'Sophie, how are you? How is Sarah? You look marvellous,' Alice exclaimed excitedly.

I did not look marvellous. The effects of my

morning coffee and champagne were wearing off and my eyes felt as though someone had thrown a handful of sand in them. I hadn't even considered makeup and had thrown on an old pair of jeans and a pale blue T-shirt that had seen better days. However, I'd already discovered that one of the great benefits of having a baby is that everyone expects you to look like absolute death afterwards, with the result that if you look even slightly less than horrific you are treated like a supermodel.

I smiled at Alice gratefully and was about to launch into an explanation as to why I had left Sarah in order to cruise the shopping malls, when I followed Steve's gaze to the front of my shirt. As the stain spread over my left breast, I realised that a detailed description of the contents of my shopping list was not necessary. I also realised why you never see women with young babies in light-coloured tops.

'Yes, well, there were certain items I didn't get around to buying before Sarah was born . . .' I stammered, once again waving around my shopping bag by way of explanation.

They both nodded and Steve started edging away, looking as though even that brief statement contained way too much information.

'Well, I'd better be off. Sarah is with Debbie and I don't want to be away long,' I said.

That halted Steve's sideways shuffle, and both he and Alice looked at me incredulously.

'Debbie?' Steve said. 'You left Sarah with Debbie?'

The reactions I was getting couldn't have been

much worse if I'd announced that I'd left Sarah with Hannibal Lecter.

'Well, yes, but only for an hour. Look, I have to go,' I said and raced through the doors of the shopping centre and out to the car park before anyone else I knew could confront me.

Everyone's horror at my having left Sarah with Debbie had made me worried and I raced home, running a couple of lights that were more red than amber and taking the corner to my street with a squeal of tyres. My feet hit the bitumen as soon as the car stopped and I ran up the path and flung the front door open. However, instead of the team of paramedics working uselessly on Sarah's lifeless body which I'd pictured on my way home, I found both Debbie and Sarah fast asleep.

EIGHT

I had no doubt that Sarah's first doctor's appointment at six weeks was not to check her at all but to test whether I was capable of getting the pair of us out of the house and to the surgery within one hour either side of the allotted time.

To make it even more challenging, whoever it is that decides such things had decreed that it would be a good idea to schedule an obstetrician's check-up at the same time. As Sarah's paediatrician was in the same building as Dr Daniels, I had booked the appointments close together.

Determined to pass, I had started planning the outing with military precision twelve hours beforehand. I'd booked the first appointment for ten in the morning, and at ten the night before I packed my bag.

When I'd found out I was pregnant I'd made a vow that I wouldn't cart around enough baby-related paraphernalia to fill a small suitcase. I had also decided that what stuff I did have to carry (at that point, I was vaguely imagining a cute fluffy toy and maybe a sunhat) would just have to fit in a bag that wouldn't shame me in the trendier parts of town. When I was six months pregnant I'd ventured out to buy a baby bag and come home three hours later empty-handed and depressed. Every baby bag I had looked at was either lemon yellow, baby pink or light blue and had pictures of animals all over it. They were also big enough to fit a whole baby inside, and for some strange reason most of them were padded. Obviously I had missed something, as it didn't seem to me that baby stuff was terribly fragile.

Being a typical Sydney girl, about ninety per cent of my wardrobe is black, so we are talking a major (and very dubious) fashion choice to add something as eye-catching as a pastel baby bag to my attire. There should have been a 'How to Accessorise with Your Baby Bag' session at antenatal classes.

I had tried to explain my concerns to a shop assistant at one of the baby shops. 'Don't you have something a little plainer than this?' I asked, referring to the bag I was holding, which was yellow with red farm animals all over it.

The shop assistant nodded enthusiastically and produced the same bag in two shades of yellow.

'No,' I replied. 'I want something really plain. You don't have anything in black, do you?'

The shop assistant shook her head and looked at me as though she was seriously revising my IQ. 'This is a baby shop, we only sell things for babies,' she explained, as if I could have failed to notice that I was surrounded by cots, prams and clothes in tiny sizes.

I decided to try a different tack. 'Do you have anything smaller than this one, then?' I thought that perhaps if I found something which wasn't the size of an overnight bag, I could dye it black.

Now the shop assistant was starting to look worried, obviously convinced I was some kind of deviate. 'No,' she replied carefully. 'A baby bag can't be any smaller than this because you need to fit in at least four nappies, two changes of clothes for each of you, toys, baby wipes, bottles if you're not breast-feeding, a cloth to clean up vomit –'

At this point the picture she was creating started to make me feel faint. Preferring to maintain my current idea of motherhood, which consisted largely of a vision of me gazing tenderly at my cherub fast asleep in its cot, I interrupted her.

'Okay, okay. I'm sorry but I think maybe I'm not ready to deal with this just yet. Thanks anyway.'

The shop assistant looked relieved as she turned back to serve a normal pregnant woman trying to decide between a Mickey Mouse baby bag and one with felt birds sewn all over it.

In the end I just bought a black cloth shoulder bag, the same size as my largest handbag. As well as being something that wouldn't get me laughed out of town, it was also about half the price of any of the pastel numbers I'd seen. The shopping I had done to date had me convinced that Debbie's designer purchases were a bargain compared to anything intended for babies.

So, packing for our first medical visit, I turned to the checklist in my baby book. Nappies were first on the list. I have to be honest and reveal that I had absolutely no intention of changing Sarah's nappy when we were outside the four walls of the house. It was hard enough to do it at home on a specially designed table with all the necessary aids an arm's length away. I knew that my level of proficiency was not great enough to manage it in public. Despite this, I put in a couple of nappies. After all, the doctor might ask to check what I had in my bag and if he realised that I obviously intended to leave Sarah in a sodden, dirty nappy until we got home, he might call up a social worker and have them take her away.

So nappies went in, as did baby wipes and Vaseline (for the nappy change which wasn't going to happen), vomit cloth, baby rug, sunscreen (it was 10°C and cloudy but the book said to put it in, so I did), a rattle, a couple of changes of clothing for Sarah and a spare shirt for me.

My wallet and chequebook were relegated to the side pocket and I stuffed Sarah's things (just) into the main section. I'd abandoned my makeup bag and brush, figuring that I never even managed to brush my hair at home these days so the chances of attending to my appearance in public were pretty slim.

The next morning Sarah woke at five forty-five for her third feed since nine the night before. In only six weeks my definition of morning had changed from the start of the morning radio traffic report at seven-thirty, to any time on the digital clock which started with the number five. One consolation was that I'd finally found a use for the Nike sports watch

Andrew had given me last Christmas. After having gathered dust on my chest of drawers for the last six months, it was now in constant use as it had a digital face and a light, perfect for night feeds.

I tried to figure out Sarah's likely feed and sleep times over the next few hours, only just resisting the urge to do a time line for the morning's activities. Miraculously, it all seemed as though it should work — she'd have a sleep and then another feed at about nine, which would take about thirty minutes, so that would leave me thirty minutes to get her in the car, drive five kilometres to the doctor's surgery and get her out of the car.

I had known before Sarah was born that babies feed about every two or three hours in the first few months. What I hadn't known was that the two or three hours runs from the start of each feed, which means that if it takes you an hour to feed the baby, it can be only another hour before you're on the job again. I also hadn't realised that breastfeeding wasn't like filling up a car at a service station.

Everything went according to plan and at nine-thirty I was balancing Sarah against my shoulder as I tried to open the car door with my spare arm. I was about to swing her down into the capsule when I felt something dripping on my shoe. Assuming she had been sick, a not infrequent occurrence, I straightened up.

'Strange,' I thought as I noticed she didn't have anything on her face. I decided that she must have been leaning over when it happened. Peering around Sarah I looked down at my shoe and groaned. What was on my shoe was yellow, not white, and Sarah's pink grow suit was soaked with the stuff.

I raced back inside, threw Sarah on the change table and pulled her grow suit off. I started to wipe the back of her body from her neck to her knees, then decided that the only viable option was to hold her under the shower. As I dressed her in a fresh grow suit, I grappled with her arms, trying to pull them through the tight hand openings, which seemed to have suddenly shrunk.

Finally we were ready. I looked at my watch – nine-forty. I raced out the door, threw Sarah in the capsule and drove to the doctor's surgery. There was a parking lot behind the surgery and, after pulling in, I leapt out of the car to grab the pram from the boot. No pram. I'd left it behind in the rush. Refusing to be flustered, I flung the baby bag over one shoulder, hefted Sarah on the other and kicked the car door shut behind me. I looked at my watch as I walked towards the receptionist's desk: nine fifty-eight, not bad at all.

'Sarah Anderson to see the doctor for her six-week check-up,' I announced triumphantly, expecting the receptionist to leap to her feet and congratulate me for being not just on time but early. Strangely, she looked very underwhelmed and just nodded, pointing me to the waiting area.

The woman sitting next to me smiled. 'Your little boy is lovely,' she said.

'She's actually a girl,' I replied. 'Her name is Sarah.'

'Oh,' the woman said. 'I'm sorry, it's just that she

'does look so much like a boy.' She was looking at me dubiously as if I could have got it wrong.

'Well, she's definitely not,' I retorted slightly sharply, wondering how anyone could think my beautiful daughter with her big blue eyes and rose-bud lips could be anything but a girl.

At ten-fifteen I was finally ushered in to see the doctor.

He asked me to put Sarah on the examination bed, gesturing to one end where I should put her head. Having been about to put her the other way around, I lost my balance as I swivelled her body in midair and deposited her on the bed with enough force to make her blink her eyes, too surprised to scream.

I couldn't believe it. In six weeks I hadn't so much as jolted Sarah and the second I walked into the doctor's office I dropped her. Tensing, I expected the doctor to push me aside as he swooped to check Sarah for brain damage. However, when I looked up, I was surprised to see him smiling calmly.

'You're obviously a confident mother, moving her around like that,' he said.

Confident mother! Did this man know nothing, I wondered as I pasted what I hoped was a Madonna-like smile on my face.

After examining Sarah and pronouncing her per-fectly healthy (I presumed this meant no long-term injuries from the crash onto the bed), the doctor turned to me. 'So, do you have any questions?'

Everything I'd read said that the first couple of months of a baby's life were vital in their long-term development. But, as I'd said to Andrew at Sarah's coming-out party, I still wasn't sure just what I should be doing in that department. My baby book wasn't much help. It exhorted me to have fun with Sarah. Fine, but I needed specifics, and at six weeks Sarah wasn't exactly providing me with much feedback on how I was doing.

'What exactly should I do with Sarah when she's awake?' I asked.

'Not much,' the doctor answered with a smile. 'You can forget mind-expanding activities and educational experiences for a good while yet. Just talk to her and love her. The rest will look after itself.'

Comforted that I wasn't reducing Sarah's IQ by poor mothering, I smiled at him gratefully as I picked her up and headed for Dr Daniels's office.

Sarah behaved perfectly throughout the second appointment. The only time I felt uncomfortable was when Dr Daniels mentioned Debbie.

'So, how's that friend of yours? What was her name?' he asked.

His casual tone didn't deceive me. I'd had too much experience with men bedazzled by Debbie. She had promised to call him but hadn't. She'd declared that she felt like it was her baby he had delivered and that she couldn't contemplate anything vaguely sexual with him.

Life with Debbie was never boring, I reflected. Most women spent their first doctor's visit post-birth discussing pelvic floor exercises. Mine, however, was spent trying to gently tell my lovestruck obstetrician that he had been dumped by my best friend. I shook my head as I put the car into gear and headed home.

NINE

I was feeding Sarah one morning a couple of weeks
later when the phone rang. On several previous
occasions I'd tried unsuccessfully to reach the ringing phone on the other side of the room by shuffling
towards it with a still suckling Sarah clutched to my
chest. However, I had now learnt to bring the cord-
less phone with me when I sat down to feed her.

'Hello,' I said, tucking the phone between my left
ear and shoulder as I swapped Sarah, who had finished one breast and was still demanding more, to the
other side.

'Sophie, it's Max,' said the voice.

I jolted upright and dropped the phone on
Sarah's head. Nothing could distract that child when
she was really hungry, though, and she continued
determinedly with the task at hand. Grabbing the
phone with my free hand, I held it back to my ear.
Despite everything, my first reaction on hearing his
voice was pleasure. We'd had so many good times

over the years – it was impossible just to put them all aside.

'Sophie, are you there?' Max was asking.

'Yes, yes, I'm here, Max,' I said, feeling this wasn't exactly the best time to go into a detailed description of why I'd dropped the phone.

'So . . . how are you doing?' he almost stammered.

I understood his discomfort. There wasn't exactly an established protocol for what to say when you call your ex-girlfriend to whom you haven't spoken for nine months and who has just had your baby.

'I'm fine, Max,' I answered.

Unsure as to whether Max wanted to know how Sarah was, I hesitated. Deciding to take a middle line I said, 'We're both doing really well, Max. Sarah's wonderful.'

'That's great, just great,' he said.

The silence seemed to last forever.

'What are you still doing up, anyway?' I asked eventually. 'It must be the middle of the night for you in America.'

I'd never managed to get the time difference sorted out, but I knew that if it was a sociable time in Australia it was the opposite in San Francisco.

'Actually, I'm not in the States, I'm in Sydney. I'm just here for a couple of weeks for a pitch.'

Knowing that he wasn't talking to me from the other side of the world shouldn't have made a difference, but it did. As I tried to think of something to say, Max spoke again, obviously trying desperately to come up with what he thought was appropriate small talk with the mother of a young baby.

'So, do you still feel tired from the birth? I've heard some pretty awful stories.'

I didn't quite know how to respond to that. Was I still tired? I couldn't remember what it felt like not to be tired – it was just situation normal. 'Um, yes, I guess. Sarah wakes up two or three times a night but you just sort of get used to it.'

'Sophie, can you hear that noise your end too?' Max asked suddenly.

The drawback to talking on the phone while I was feeding Sarah was that she made huge gulping and slurping noises. These noises were obviously audible on the other end of the phone, as my callers frequently made tactful comments like, 'Oh, so Sarah is there too, is she?', or in the case of close friends, tactless comments like, 'God, that child is a guzzler!'

Unable to face explaining the source of the noise to Max in this already uncomfortable conversation, I replied in what I hoped was a convincing manner, 'What noise? Oh, you must be hearing the washing machine in the next room.'

'Right,' Max replied dubiously.

Trying to think of a way to change the subject, I struggled to remember what people talked about when they didn't have babies. Of course – people with lives worked, it was all coming back to me.

'How's work?'

'Work's great. Except for the fact that everyone except me talks strangely, it's all pretty much like being in the Sydney office.'

'Don't ruin it for me,' I joked. 'Tell me it's incredibly glamorous, that you have a personal stylist, lunch with Nicolas Cage every week and play squash with Sean Connery every second Tuesday.'

'No,' he replied and I could hear from his voice that he was smiling. 'Sean and I play lawn bowls on Thursdays – he's not as young as he once was, you know. And Nic likes his privacy so I'm really not at liberty to tell you about that.'

I laughed. 'And how's the Incredible Hulk enjoying the change?'

The Incredible Hulk was our nickname for Max's boss, Barry, who was one of the mousiest men I'd ever met and who had been transferred to San Francisco at the same time as Max. Being stuck next to him for an entire dinner was the ultimate torture; every conversational gambit was met with a single word or, if you were really unlucky, a nod.

Max and I had long ago decided that no one could be that boring and that this was in fact just a false persona for a superhero – kind of like Clark Kent but less interesting. Adding fuel to our theory was his claim he was highly allergic to any form of shellfish. We had become convinced that this was not an allergy at all, but the trigger to his miraculous transformation into superhero form and that one mouthful of oyster soup would result in his skin turning green, his muscles rippling and stretching, and his conservative Oxford shirts tearing down the middle.

Unfortunately, neither of us had ever been brave enough to test this theory (as to get it wrong would have meant a dead dinner guest) so we had no real proof either way.

'Barry was sacked about six months ago – no one quite knows why. I've actually been promoted to his job,' Max said.

'Wow, that's great news!' I enthused and then, not wanting to seem like a total uncaring witch, I added, 'Although I guess not for Barry.'

'No, I guess not – but maybe he's off keeping another company safe in a galaxy far, far away,' Max replied.

I couldn't help but laugh. One thing Max and I had always had in common was a sense of humour no one else appreciated.

'And how's Debbie?' Max asked, clearly unwilling to give up the topic of mutual acquaintances and friends, which was a big improvement on our earlier stilted efforts at conversation.

'Oh, you know, Debbie's Debbie. She just broke up with another guy last night – something about his choice of aftershave.'

There was another long pause and, deciding to make things easy for Max, I tried to wind the conversation up. 'Well, I guess I should go . . .'

'Sophie,' Max said abruptly. 'Could I see you?'

My heart skipped a beat. But after the initial feeling of elation that he should want to see me, I realised nothing had changed. I was now a package that included Sarah and there was no point in my seeing Max, given that there was no place for her in his life. I refused even to think about the possibility that I still wasn't over him. As my father always said, 'What's done is done' and there was no going back now.

'I don't know, Max,' I hedged. 'It's pretty hard for me to get out without Sarah.'

'I want to see both of you,' he replied firmly.

My mind whirled as I tried to figure out exactly what this meant. 'Sure,' I managed to get out, trying to play it cool. 'Why don't you drop around some time?'

'What about now?' he asked.

'Now?' I echoed, looking around at the profusion of baby rugs, vomit cloths and rattles, and down at my very unglamorous attire.

I was unable to think of an excuse quickly enough and before I knew it the words, 'Sure, come around' had somehow made their way out of my mouth.

Thankfully Sarah had dropped off to sleep while she was feeding, so after I had given Max the address and hung up, I dumped her unceremoniously into her cot, calculating that I had about twenty minutes before he arrived.

After throwing off my clothes, I jumped into the shower and, with one hand, lathered my hair, which hadn't been washed in days. With the other hand, I swiped soap across my body. The possibility of shaving my legs crossed my mind, but I quickly abandoned that as too ambitious given that I didn't even know where my razor was. In record time I leapt out of the shower and grabbed the hair dryer, more to dry my hair than to attempt any great styling. After all, I didn't want Max to know that I'd had a shower especially for his visit.

Throwing open my wardrobe doors, I wondered

desperately what to wear. Karen had sternly warned me to put my jeans at the bottom of the cupboard and not to even think about trying them on for at least six months after Sarah was born. However, this was a crisis, and after all they'd always been a bit baggy before I became pregnant. With one hand I grabbed the jeans off the hanger and stepped into them while the other hand kept flicking through the possible tops. Suddenly I stopped what I was doing and looked down. Not only would my jeans not do up, I couldn't even get them over my hips.

This was a matter of serious concern. However, I didn't have time to wallow in depression and after a quick look at my watch I grabbed my white three-quarter maternity pants and a bright pink shirt.

Somehow I had always been under the impression that the moment my baby was born I would be able to relegate my maternity clothes to the bin and start wearing normal clothes again. Wrong. I was still wearing all my elastic-topped trousers, although I was now able to wear normal shirts (with the notable exception of the figure-hugging ones), which had helped my sanity slightly.

My emergency house-cleaning technique – aka throwing everything into the cupboard and shutting the door – allowed me to get the place looking in reasonable shape in under five minutes and I had just thrown the last toy under the sofa when the doorbell rang. I pushed my hair back behind my ears, took a step towards the door and then paused, turned back and grabbed a book off the shelf, which I put half opened on the sofa. I didn't want Max to know that the most intellectual thing I'd managed to read since Sarah was born were the change table instructions.

Max stood on the doorstep looking exactly as he had when I'd last seen him.

The first thing that hit me was a feeling of familiarity – almost as though the last year hadn't happened and he was just picking me up to go to one of our old breakfast haunts. That feeling was quickly replaced by the realisation of how much my life had changed since those days and how much Max had missed.

'Hi,' I greeted him nervously. After hesitating for a second, I stood back and invited him in.

Looking as apprehensive as I felt, Max stepped inside and looked around.

'This place is great, Sophie,' he said. 'It must be nice finally living by yourself.' He realised what he'd said as soon as it was out of his mouth and smiled apologetically. 'Sorry, it's kind of hard getting used to the fact that you've got a baby.'

'Don't worry,' I answered. 'I still struggle with the concept myself.'

'You look terrific,' he said. 'I didn't really know what to expect, but being a mother obviously suits you.'

'Thanks,' I replied. 'It's not always easy, but so far the good bits far outweigh the bad.'

The stilted conversation lapsed and I tried desperately to think what to say to this man with whom I'd spent two years. As I was frantically considering and discarding topics, I noticed that Max was looking at me strangely. My first thought was that I'd forgotten to do up the zip on my trousers in my mad rush to get ready, but a quick glance established that this was not the case.

With a flash of horror I realised why Max was staring. I was so used to rocking back and forth with Sarah in my arms that I was still doing it, even though she was fast asleep in her bedroom.

Get it together, I told myself fiercely. Max was going to think that I'd lost my mind if I didn't manage to act slightly normally.

'Sarah's asleep,' I said, in case he thought I had just shut her away in a cupboard. 'Would you like to see her?' I added tentatively.

'Yes, I would, very much,' Max replied.

I led him up the stairs, opened Sarah's door and stepped back. Max stood in the doorway looking at the cot for a moment and then walked slowly across the room. He didn't say a word, just gripped the edge of the cot and stared at his daughter, who was fast asleep, both her arms flung up beside her head. Her long dark lashes rested on her cheeks, and with her loose dark ringlets she looked the spitting image of Max.

I hadn't realised before I had Sarah that everyone who sees a new baby is desperate to determine who it looks like. The fact that Sarah looked like a smaller and (I hoped) more feminine version of Max and not at all like me had caused great problems for my visitors, who had flailed around desperately looking for some feature of Sarah's which they could attribute to me.

After what seemed to be a very long time, but was probably only a couple of minutes, Max loosened his grip, turned and walked back down the stairs into the lounge room.

I followed him down, but before I could say anything Max blurted, 'Look, Sophie, I've got to go, I'll give you a call.'

Speechless, I watched him practically sprint out the door and down the path. I frowned, trying to figure out what exactly had gone wrong.

TEN

Several days later I was still shaken by Max's visit. I was angry that he had decided to intrude into my life and then disappear once again.

I decided, though, that there was no point in looking backwards. I had a beautiful daughter, a great place to live and a good job to go back to when my money ran out (which was looking like being sooner rather than later).

While there was nothing I could do about the situation with Max, something I could tackle was the jeans problem.

Even without Andrew's reminders, I realised that to ever be able to go to the beach again in anything more revealing than shorts and a T-shirt was going to take some physical effort. However, Andrew's program for me to return to the land of the taut and terrific was the stuff horror movies are made of and if he'd had his way I would have been doing sit-ups as I was wheeled out of the delivery room. So I had found it hard to contain my delight when Dr Daniels had told me sternly that I was to refrain from any sit-ups or strenuous activity for at least six weeks after Sarah's birth. He explained that this was in order to allow my stomach muscles, which had separated during my pregnancy, to heal (I hadn't had the courage to ask him to elaborate on this horrifying description).

Dr Daniels seemed to mistakenly think my relieved smile meant I thought the whole stomach muscle problem was humorous, but after I had asked him to put his instructions in writing, he looked as though he was giving some serious thought as to whether he should refer me to a psychologist for treatment for post-natal depression. Somehow I couldn't summon up the energy to explain to him that, given my history of inventing all kinds of excuses for avoiding twenty-kilometre runs, I needed documentary evidence to convince Andrew.

Andrew had grudgingly accepted the ban on sit-ups (although only after suspiciously perusing Dr Daniels's name and qualifications at the top of the page) but had still managed to produce a program that looked as though it would also be suitable if I resolved that climbing K-2 was my next goal.

I decided that right now a body inspection would be a good place to start and, despite the fact that Karen had also warned me against this, stripped down to my underwear and stood in front of the mirror. Ignoring my breasts, not an easy task, it was not a pretty sight. My pregnancy book had exhorted me not to feel embarrassed about any stretch marks but to bear them as 'a badge of motherhood'. Sometimes

I had the distinct feeling that the author of the book was having a serious laugh at her readers.

Despite all the promises I'd heard that breastfeeding would 'strip off all that extra weight', there was definitely an additional layer around my middle and over my hips. Ignoring the layer, however, I could see no way that the extra roll of skin, which didn't seem quite to have contracted to its pre-baby size, was going to disappear. My knowledge of biology was pretty elementary, but I was reasonably sure that there was no connection between stomach muscles and skin, and I failed to see how even an Andrew-driven sit-up regime could snap that skin back to where it used to be.

Before Sarah was born I had allowed myself to be reassured by the spate of articles which had appeared in magazines featuring before and after pregnancy photos of glamorous celebrities. All of them looked at least as good, if not better, than before they'd had their little bundles of joy.

I was suddenly suspicious now. There was no doubt in my mind that those paragons of womanhood would have been able to avoid any extra padding, but I was sure the skin-stretching issue was one even they must face.

Marching into the spare room in my underwear, I rifled through the stack of old magazines in the corner until I found the ones with the articles that I had remembered.

'BABIES – THE 21st CENTURY FASHION ACCESSORY', 'FROM SUPERMODEL TO SUPER MUM' the covers declared. I snorted as I reread what had sounded perfectly feasible pre-Sarah. While I loved my daughter dearly, anyone would have a very hard time convincing me that a four-kilogram package which could cry, vomit and poo within the space of ten minutes was a cooler thing to be seen with than a Gucci handbag.

But it was the pictures I was most interested in. I looked at them again and had to admit that the featured celebrities did look pretty damn good post birth. But something was odd. After looking at them closely for several minutes I realised what it was. In all the photos the mothers' midriffs were cleverly concealed. Even the bikini shots, which had particularly impressed me previously, were frauds. In all of them babies were positioned squarely in front of their mothers' stomachs. I rifled through the stack of magazines again and found some more articles complete with swimwear shots – exactly the same technique had been used.

'Ah ha!' I exclaimed triumphantly.

My discovery hadn't done anything to improve my chances of being able to walk down a beach in nothing but a bikini (actually, come to think of it, I'd never been game to do that even before I became pregnant). But at least I didn't feel like I was the only modern woman who had let the side down by not looking better after having my baby than I had before.

As I'd already tried on my jeans and done an inspection of my body in the cruel daylight, I figured that I might as well complete the trilogy of things promised to drive a new mother to deep depression and weigh myself. I strode determinedly into the bathroom, stood on the scales, took a deep breath and looked at the dial.

The needle was positioned firmly at seventy kilos.

Some of the women in my antenatal classes had put on little more than the combined weight of the baby and all the accompanying bits and pieces, and one woman had actually managed to weigh less at nine months pregnant than she had before she'd con-ceived. No one had ever referred to me as being 'all baby', as I had heard those women described, but I'd managed to avoid falling into the whole eating-for-two trap, had kept myself pretty active and had hoped that the fallout wouldn't be too disastrous. But the reality of five extra kilograms was staring me in the face and I decided now was the time to address the situation.

My last birthday present from Andrew had been a six-month membership to a gym with a crèche. No time like the present, I figured, and marched into the bedroom to get dressed.

There was no way I was going to wear my dis-gusting maternity bike pants, but I decided it was way too soon to consider something as bottom hug-ging as a pair of little gym shorts (even if I could squeeze into them, which I seriously doubted). My old running shorts with the stretched waistband seemed like the ideal compromise and I slipped them on. A top was the next dilemma. My sports bras looked ridiculously small compared with my gener-ous new shape, so I settled for an aerobics bra which didn't have any cups in it, with a big T-shirt pulled over the top.

I loaded Sarah into the car and drove to the gym. Given that the time of day didn't mean a lot to me at the moment, it hadn't occurred to me that my sudden desire to hit the fitness trail had come at five-thirty, which meant that I arrived at the gym just as hordes of office workers descended. Turning around and heading back to the safety of my home seemed a very appealing option, but I summoned up a mental picture of the number on the scales and pushed on.

My local gym was a small one, which meant that all the staff had known me there and, more importantly, known my limitations. As a result I had always been pretty much left to my own devices, unless I tragically mistimed my visit and found myself there at the same time as Andrew. Unfortunately, though, that gym didn't have anywhere I could leave Sarah. Determined that I wouldn't be able to use the baby as an excuse not to exercise, Andrew had bought me membership to the very large and very slick gym outside of which I was now standing uncertainly.

The entrance was taken up by a long reception desk at which three tracksuited staff sat. Feeling somewhat out of place, I presented my card to the nearest official-looking person. He swiped it and looked up from the computer with a big smile.

'Good evening, Sophie, how are you doing?'

'Good,' I stammered, thinking that Andrew had peppered the place with spies, until I realised my name would have come up on the computer screen.

'Could you tell me which floor the crèche is on?' I asked.

'Sure,' he replied. 'Head up to the fourth floor and follow the signs.'

There was an escalator behind the front desk and I headed towards it, stopping suddenly as I realised that I'd never taken a pram on an escalator and wasn't quite sure whether I could do it without causing serious harm to Sarah and myself.

However, I had no time to ponder the situation any further, as a tide of keen exercisers swept us onto the escalator, where I managed to balance the pram precariously until we reached the top. Not wishing to tempt fate, I decided to abandon the remaining escalators for the safety of the lift, which I spotted at the opposite end of the floor, and I manoeuvred the pram towards it, dodging sweaty bodies as I went.

Pre-Sarah I'd always been a morning exerciser and I now remembered that one of the major reasons for this was that in the evenings gyms were full of beautifully groomed people who had no intention of raising a sweat. The whole concept of a gym as a pick-up place had never really made sense to me. I never feel less alluring than when I am exercising under fluorescent lights with my hair pulled back in a rubber band and sweat running down my face. Any spare energy I have is always needed to draw oxygen into my lungs, not make small talk. But at this time of day the place was full of women in designer exercise wear with full faces of makeup and hairstyles I'd be happy with if I was heading out to a black-tie function. Judging by the chatting going on across the stepping machines, their efforts were paying off.

The crèche was a sanctuary, with soothing background music instead of the thumping techno beat which reverberated through the remainder of the building. I left Sarah smiling up from her pram at the very capable-looking supervisor and headed back into the fray.

Self-discipline had always been one of my fundamental problems when it came to exercising. The 'no pain no gain' concept had never made any sense to me. I found it very difficult not to stop, or at least slow down, when any significant discomfort was involved. However, the presence of a yelling aerobics instructor, a room full of people who were working hard, and mirrored walls which showed any low-energy performances off to all and sundry, did help somewhat, so I decided to opt for the aerobics class that was about to start.

As soon as I entered the room I realised that it was full of women who were kitted from head to foot in the latest gym wear. My pinkish-white T-shirt (a result of one of Sarah's little red socks getting stuck in the washing machine), sagging shorts, and sandshoes which bore the traces of mud from a walk I'd done a few weeks before Sarah was born, stood out like a sore thumb.

Refusing to be intimidated I marched to the back of the room, grabbed a step and some blocks and assembled them in a spare spot. Only when I'd finished did I look up and realise I was the only person in the room who had a step in front of them.

Obviously my assumption that this was a step class was wrong. Ignoring the pitying glances of my fellow aerobicees, I pulled the step apart and returned the pieces to the piles behind me, wondering what this aerobics class was if it wasn't step.

A tiny instructor, who couldn't have been any more than five feet tall, bounced into the room and up to the front. Fixing her headset and slapping a tape in the machine behind her, she started marching furiously on the spot and yelled, 'Right, everyone, let's fight!'

My vain hope that I had misheard her dissolved as I saw the words 'Fight Class' emblazoned on her gym top and shorts and realised that I'd unwittingly stumbled into one of the new wave of exercise classes that were based on boxing and martial arts.

Everyone except for me leapt into a boxer's crouch and followed the instructor in a series of moves which she said was a warm-up but looked to me to require serious flexibility and strength. I was starting to get sideways glances from my fellow exercisers, and after I saw two girls off to my left look at me and smile at each other in amusement, I figured I'd better at least make an effort.

When I tuned in to the instructor I heard her say that the aim was to fight yourself in the mirror. I concentrated on trying to do a slow neck chop and then a series of chin jabs to my reflection, but couldn't quite figure out why everyone else looked like Mike Tyson while I looked like Mr Bean trying to punch himself in the face.

Determined to persevere, I followed everyone in

a fast sideways shuffle from one side of the studio to the other. As I shuffled, I suddenly realised that my breasts were moving at a different pace to the rest of my body. Having always dismissed as grandstanding the complaints of my better-endowed friends, I was now faced with the reality that DD-cup breasts do not move as part of your body but have a life of their own. In an effort to stop the painful jiggling, I clamped an arm across my front. Unfortunately this threw my balance out and slowed down my already snail-like motion, which meant that all of the people to my left who had been shuffling towards the right-hand side of the studio were bunched up beside me. Nevertheless I shuffled gamely on and managed to resume my original position.

There was a pause as the instructor changed the music for the main part of the class. I took the opportunity to lean over, my hands on my knees, to try to get my breath back. From under my arms I could see the rest of the class throwing punches and Bruce Lee-style side kicks as they prepared themselves for what was to come.

I reached the sudden decision that no degree of fitness was worth this amount of public humiliation. There was no way of sliding out discreetly so I decided on the brazen approach, marching between the instructor and the rest of the class and out the door.

The aerobics schedule was posted outside the door and I ran my eye down it so that I could avoid Fight Class should I ever have an exercise urge again (which at this stage I felt was extremely unlikely).

The names of most of the classes were all totally foreign to me – 'Jazzercise', 'TBC', 'Kickbox', 'Latin Dance'. Didn't anyone do plain old aerobics classes any more?

I toyed briefly with the idea of using one of the battery of machines lined up against the window, on which people were jogging, sliding or stepping, but decided that I had had enough for one day and headed back up to the crèche. The woman minding Sarah smiled at me as I opened the door.

'First time back?' she asked.

'Yes,' I admitted sheepishly, given that she would hardly have had time to take Sarah out of the pram while I was away.

'Don't worry, love,' she replied. 'I see it all the time. Just take it easy, your mind and body are working overtime at the moment, anyway.'

Feeling slightly mollified, I gave her a grateful smile and wheeled Sarah away.

Having not expended any energy whatsoever, I felt restless once I arrived home. One thing that my baby book said was good for babies was a varied environment.

'Right, Sarah,' I said. 'We're going for a walk.'

One mothering skill I had picked up with ease was talking to Sarah and describing to her what was happening, although on a couple of worrying occasions I had found myself still doing it after I'd put her to bed.

I unfolded the pram and slung the baby bag in the

carrier underneath. When I was buying baby equipment I had looked longingly at the expensive jogging prams in the shop. The thought of actually jogging with one filled me with horror – after all, jogging was a hellish enough activity without pushing a baby in front of you – it was just that they looked so cool. I had briefly considered saying that a jogging pram had been stolen from my front verandah and claiming it on insurance. However, I had always been an obsessively law-abiding citizen (my heart rate doubled if I jaywalked at an intersection) and even if I had been capable of insurance fraud, I was sure that any half-competent insurance inspector would have been able to figure out that I wasn't the jogging-pram type before he stepped out of his car. So I had settled for a more traditional number which I'd managed to pick up second hand.

It was nearing seven on a Friday evening. The traffic was picking up and people were streaming along King Street, heading for happy hour at their favourite bar. As I walked past Effervescence, my old Friday evening haunt, I looked in wistfully. Not working had a lot of advantages, but I did miss that wonderful Friday evening, start-of-the-weekend feeling which I could see reflected on the faces of the people I passed.

Sarah seemed to be having a lovely time as I pushed the pram along the footpath, although she was focused more on the row of little teddy bears that hung across the pram than on the big wide world. Given the things that sometimes happened in Newtown, that probably wasn't such a bad thing.

Deciding that it would be nice to sit down for a while, I wheeled Sarah towards some tables and chairs set up outside a busy bar. There was a spare table at the back of the terrace and I headed for it. Driving a car is not one of my most highly developed skills and unfortunately I had found that there is a direct correlation between car-driving skill and pram-driving skill. The space between the two front tables looked quite big enough for the pram to fit through, until the wheels hit the chairs on either side. I smiled sweetly in apology at the chairs' occupants and pushed on through as they shuffled their chairs back. After making a sharp right turn I headed towards the empty table, only to sideswipe the one next to it with the pram, causing all of its occupants' drinks to slop onto the table. My sweet smile didn't work as well this time as they had obviously been watching my whole rally-driving progress. Ignoring their annoyed looks I dropped into the seat and took a deep breath.

Sarah took a deep breath too and released it in the form of a high-pitched scream. The few people in the cafe who hadn't already been watching me turned to look, frowning at this interruption to their Friday evening revelry.

Picking Sarah up and jiggling her didn't improve the situation and I wished vehemently that I'd kept walking. She must be hungry, I decided. Lying her on my lap, I lifted up my shirt and tried to undo the flap on my bra. Despite my increasingly vigorous efforts I couldn't undo it with one hand. Surely they had tested the damn clasp in this kind of pressure situation, I fumed to myself. Tilting my knees upward to stop Sarah rolling onto the floor, I took my other hand off her and stuck it through the neck of my T-shirt. As Sarah balanced precariously on my legs, I managed to get the clip undone, lifted up my shirt and pulled her face towards my chest. The whole cafe gave a collective sigh of relief and turned back to their conversations as Sarah stopped mid bellow.

A waiter approached (he'd obviously been hiding around the corner until I had got the situation under control) and asked me what I'd like. I was about to order a lime soda but, catching sight of some cocktail glasses on the table beside me, changed my mind and asked for a margarita instead. It was Friday, after all.

Sarah's slurping noises became louder as she settled in, and I wondered whether I should hum loudly to drown them out. Thankfully, though, the new CD which had begun playing in the background was louder than the previous one and I relaxed slightly.

My drink arrived and I closed my eyes and took a large mouthful. When I opened them I was looking straight at a couple of middle-aged women sitting at a neighbouring table. They were staring at me with disapproving faces. For a second I wondered if my whole chest was showing, but a quick look established that my T-shirt was discreetly tucked over Sarah's head and I wasn't displaying my breasts for the crowd.

Suddenly it hit me. These were the Mother

Police Karen had told me about. Her theory was that there was an underground organisation of women who patrolled the streets looking for unfit mothers. She swore she had seen members of this group make notes on their clipboards with grim faces when they spotted her children out in temperatures under 30°C without a jacket. She was also convinced she had seen them peering in her baby bag trying to count the number of spare nappies she carried with her.

Judging by the looks on the faces of the pair sitting near me, drinking a cocktail while breastfeeding was enough to earn me a significant number of demerit points. No one, however, was going to prevent me enjoying my drink and I pointedly turned my back on the disapproving duo and took another sip.

ELEVEN

By the time Sarah was nine weeks old I'd decided that having a baby wasn't all that hard. A piece of cake, really. Either that or I had an amazingly good baby. Yeah, sure, it was boring getting up to feed her every four hours through the night, but she was so cute, and when I put her back down she just went back to sleep again. No big deal.

However, on the day Sarah was nine weeks and one day old, I found out what the big deal was.

Suddenly, she seemed to realise that she liked being held – always.

The first time it happened was after one of her early morning feeds. I put her down exactly as I had every other time. But instead of drifting off to sleep, she opened her eyes, gazed at me for a long second and then let out a bloodcurdling scream.

I grabbed her, certain that something was terribly wrong.

Silence descended.

I took off her nappy and checked that it didn't need changing. She looked at me calmly as I established this wasn't the problem. Slightly worried, I rocked her back to sleep again.

Sighing with relief, I put her back in her cot, and immediately her eyes opened and she let out another bloodcurdling yell.

Confused, but less panicky this time, I picked her up. Maybe, I thought, she had wind which caused her pain when she was lying down.

For a second time she was silent as soon as I picked her up.

Bringing her back out into my bedroom, I grabbed a baby book and lay down on the bed with her on my chest.

Instantly, I heard her sigh and relax into a deep sleep.

Okay, I could sort this out. Let's see . . . Sleeping – page 162–3.

Flipping to the appropriate page I started to read.

'There are as many sleeping habits as there are babies and unfortunately a lot of them don't suit their parents. One thing that is vital though, is that she must be able to fall asleep by herself, not while being held or rocked. Often this doesn't come easily and your baby will protest when left alone in her cot. The best (but not necessarily the easiest) way to deal with this is to let her cry herself to sleep.'

Quickly I slammed the book shut, causing Sarah to jump. That just wasn't going to work. For a start, Sarah was way too little, and secondly, I could never just let her cry. There had to be another way.

Three days later I opened page 162 again, acknowledging that my sixty-centimetre-tall daughter had defeated me in our battle of wills.

The only way she would sleep was lying on my chest. The second I tried to move, either to put her beside me or back in her cot, she was instantly awake. Consequently, for the past three nights I had only slept for about fifteen minutes at a time, terrified I would roll over and suffocate her.

I was so tired I felt as though a fog had descended over my brain. When I discovered the cereal packet in the freezer, I knew something had to be done.

I tried calling Karen for advice, but for the first time she told me she couldn't help.

'Sorry, Soph, you're on your own. This is one of those decisions only you can make. All I can say is that you gotta do what you gotta do.'

Just as I hung up the telephone, it rang again. I pounced on it. Maybe Karen had decided to take pity on me and tell me what to do.

My heart sank as I heard Debbie's voice.

'Hey, Sophie. Do you fancy coming shopping with me? I've got the day off and Lisa Ho has a sale on.'

To my horror, I burst into tears. Through my sobs I tried to talk. 'I just . . . I just can't . . .' And then I had to stop for breath.

'Sophie, I'm sorry. I know you don't have heaps of money, but I thought we could have fun anyway.'

Frustrated I shook my head, although the gesture didn't help Debbie on the other end of the line.

'I just can't . . .' I tried again, 'get Sarah to sleep.'

This statement was greeted with silence and then a tentative, 'Oh.'

'I've tried everything I can think of and nothing helps. Warming the sheets with a hot-water bottle so that the cold doesn't give her a shock, singing nursery rhymes . . . hell, I've even tried tilting the cot on two legs and rocking it while I hide underneath.'

More silence from Debbie and then a hesitant, 'What does Karen say?'

If I hadn't felt so desperate, I would have laughed. This was definitely not Debbie's area of expertise.

'She says I have to decide by myself. I know you're supposed to let them cry. I just can't do it. I can't . . .' To my dismay I dissolved into tears again.

'Okay,' Debbie said, obviously trying to stay calm. 'I remember seeing this on an episode of *Oprah* once. Don't you have to leave them cry for five minutes, then ten and then twenty, until they go to sleep?'

'That's what they say,' I agreed glumly.

'And once you've done it for a couple of days, aren't they supposed to drift off to sleep by themselves?'

'But . . .' I could hardly say the words. 'What if Sarah thinks I don't love her, that she's been abandoned?'

'Well, I'll take her out drinking when she's eighteen and set her straight,' Debbie replied more firmly. 'I don't know much about babies, but I think you'd have to do more than that before you ruin her life. If you were talking about abandoning her wrapped in an old cardigan on a church step, I'd be a bit more concerned.'

I knew Debbie was right and I was overreacting, but it didn't help much.

'What about if I come around tonight and keep you company? It'll be like a pyjama party,' she continued. 'Only with alcohol.'

'And a screaming baby . . .' I muttered.

By the time the doorbell rang at seven that night, I had decided to send Debbie home. It was ridiculous to think that I couldn't deal with this on my own, and I certainly didn't need Debbie, of all people, to hold my hand.

When I opened the door, though, I knew there was no going back.

Standing on the doorstep like the three wise men were Andrew, Debbie and Ben. However, instead of bearing gold, frankincense and myrrh, they were holding beer, wine and pizzas.

'Just how long are you planning on staying?' I asked nervously as Debbie produced her entire *Twin Peaks* video collection, a family block of chocolate and a huge tub of caramel swirl ice-cream from the bag over her shoulder. 'You look like you packed for a siege.'

'Well, if we're going to do this thing we might as well have fun,' Debbie replied merrily.

The sick feeling in the pit of my stomach increased. I wished fervently that I hadn't said anything to Debbie. She, Andrew and Ben had no idea what they were in for.

During the afternoon I had been to the local library and borrowed six books on children and sleeping. The librarian had looked up at me as she scanned the titles.

'Won't sleep, hey?' she asked sympathetically.

I felt tears looming again, so I just shook my head, willing her to change the subject. The last thing I needed was advice from a perfect stranger.

'I don't know what the right thing to do is, but all I can say is, don't do what I did. My three year old still sleeps with us and I suspect she probably will until she hits high school. Plays havoc with your sex life.'

I couldn't believe a complete stranger was telling me this. Smiling in what I hoped was a consoling way, I headed for the door. At least I didn't have to worry about the effect Sarah's refusal to sleep was having on my nonexistent sex life.

By the time my support team had arrived that evening, I had read six different theories about babies and sleep, each one warning of dire consequences for choosing the wrong option. All I knew for sure was that this couldn't continue. This was my life too and I simply couldn't live on snatches of sleep and keep breaking into tears all the time.

So, control crying it was. I decided that I'd give it two nights and if things hadn't improved, I'd think of something else to do.

Glass of wine in hand, Debbie took control of the situation, gathering the four of us around the table as though she were a football coach conducting a pre-game strategy session.

'Okay,' she said, 'here's the plan. The first time Sarah starts to cry we'll leave her for five minutes and then Sophie will go in and settle her down. After that, we leave her for ten minutes, then fifteen, and so on. We just need to be tough and stick to it. Shouldn't be too hard.

'Got it?' she asked.

We all nodded and I half expected her to call us into a huddle to produce a rousing chant.

Seven hours later, at two in the morning, I found myself standing between Debbie and the door to Sarah's room.

While Sarah hadn't quite been crying the entire time, neither had she done much sleeping. I'd fed her twice, putting her straight to bed each time. After each feed it had taken at least half an hour of crying before silence had descended, the time until she started crying again was all too brief.

Andrew and Ben had headed home at eleven, having spent four hours downing the beers and pizza while desperately trying to pretend they were having a good time. Their departure had come soon after Andrew had suggested that maybe the best option was just to turn the music up as far as it would go, so that we couldn't hear Sarah crying, an option neither Debbie nor I found in any way amusing.

Despite her brave words, Debbie had quickly shown herself to be more affected by Sarah's crying than any of us, including me. Far from having her play the bad cop role as I'd expected, I'd actually spent most of the night trying to convince her that we were doing the right thing and Sarah wouldn't hate us for it for the rest of her life.

Once Andrew and Ben had left, we gave up any pretence of having fun and sat on the floor with our backs up against the wall next to Sarah's closed door, trying to will her to sleep. However, a particularly hysterical burst of crying finally broke Debbie and she sprang to her feet.

'Sophie, it's not working – there must be another way,' she pleaded. Then, abandoning her attempt at negotiation, she threw herself at the door.

Having anticipated her sudden move, I jumped up, spreading my arms protectively across the doorway as she grappled for the doorknob.

Suddenly, blissfully, there was silence. Debbie and I both stared at each other. The silence stretched for one minute, then two. Once fifteen minutes had passed and I'd tiptoed in to check that she was still breathing, we went downstairs and perched ourselves on the edge of the sofa.

After half an hour we allowed ourselves to contemplate the fact that she might finally be asleep.

'Thank God,' I breathed quietly. 'I think we need a drink to celebrate.'

'Are you mad?' Debbie asked, looking at me incredulously. 'If that child is going to sleep, then so are we. We can celebrate another time.'

She strode towards the spare room, shedding clothes as she went, and I paused only for a moment to attempt to take in this abrupt change of roles before heading for my bedroom and the blissful oblivion of sleep.

The next two nights, while not exactly wonderful, were a huge improvement, and by Friday morning I was feeling slightly closer to human and optimistic that we had almost solved the problem.

When the doorbell rang at ten-thirty I opened it to find Debbie standing on my doorstep dressed in a black trouser suit with high-heeled boots and holding a bottle of wine in each hand.

'It's okay, Deb,' I assured her. 'Sarah only cried for about half an hour last night. I think I should be able to make it to lunchtime without alcoholic assistance.'

'They wanted me to buy musical toilet brushes,' Debbie said, ignoring what I'd said.

'Sorry?' I said, thinking I must have misheard her.

'They wanted me to buy musical toilet brushes,' Debbie repeated. 'I've found tea cosies in the shape of the Sydney Opera House, coat hangers you can fold up to put in your pocket, and enough rubbish to fill ten warehouses, but I told them that a toilet brush which plays "Jingle Bells" when you stick it in the toilet bowl was just too much. I suddenly realised that I had to draw a line in the sand and say there were some things I just wouldn't do. So I resigned.'

'You resigned from Mr Cheapy?' I asked, open-mouthed.

'Yep,' she said. Far from looking devastated, she seemed to be very pleased with herself.

'But what are you going to do? You've been with Mr Cheapy forever.'

Still standing on my doorstep, she grinned and waved the wine in my face. 'Well, to start with, I'm planning to get horrendously drunk. I know you can't drink much without making Sarah drunk too, but as long as you'll have two glasses, I'll drink the rest. Deal?'

'Sure,' I nodded, still stunned.

Debbie walked past me into the kitchen, grabbed wineglasses and the bottle opener and headed for the lounge room. I followed and sat down on the sofa beside her, watching her pull the cork out of the first bottle like a woman possessed.

She poured two huge glasses of wine and took a big mouthful. When she spoke again she was no longer smiling. 'I'm over it all. I was standing in the shower this morning washing my hair and listening to the radio.' She looked sideways at me and added, 'Which I can now do as loudly as I like because my grumpy flatmate moved out to have a baby.'

I pretended I hadn't heard her. Debbie's habit of listening to the radio in the bathroom at volume ten so that she could hear it over the water hadn't bothered me so much. I had just been foolish enough to talk to her on behalf of the neighbours once, a conversation which hadn't been a success.

'Anyway, the guy who usually reads the news bulletins wasn't on air and there was an announcement that he'd had a heart attack two nights ago and died. I couldn't believe how sad I felt.'

Debbie was not the kind of person who usually felt sorry for strangers, so I knew something was really wrong.

'I realised that if it was me who'd had the heart attack, I would have been really pissed off,' she continued. 'It suddenly dawned on me that I'm thirty-one and that maybe a job with a big company isn't actually what I want. I know for a fact I don't want to be combing Asia for stuff that breaks after twenty minutes or sits unused in the back of people's kitchen cabinets for ten years. I'm even starting to think that maybe I want to have children some day.'

She smiled wanly at my raised eyebrows and shook her head.

'No, let me finish. I'm only just figuring this stuff out for myself as I say it. My mum felt like she was stuck at home raising kids when what she really wanted was an exciting job. I grew up thinking that life without a career would be a failure and that I had to make the most of the opportunities that came my way.'

I nodded, agreeing with what she said, despite my amazement at hearing the words from Debbie's lips.

She continued. 'But, you know, I'm not sure that we're actually better off than the generation before us. We feel like we need to achieve so much and own so much to be happy. I think that by trying to have it all, a lot of people actually end up with nothing.'

'I think you're right,' I said slowly. 'After two months off work, I really don't want to go back. I'm starting to think that if somehow I didn't have to work for the money, I would love to stay home with Sarah. I'd kind of feel, though, that everyone would think that I was taking the easy option.'

'Yeah, the initial excitement of wearing expensive suits to work and having power lunches in the city wears off pretty quickly,' Debbie said. 'Maybe half the problem is that we've both always worked for big companies we don't believe in – I certainly didn't dream about scouring the world for Mr Cheapy when I was a little girl.

'You know,' she sighed as she drained the remaining wine in her glass and reached over to fill it up again, 'the absolute best thing about resigning from that place is that I won't have to listen to thirty minutes of Mr Cheapy jokes every Saturday morning. My job has entertained everyone but me for years.'

'So what will you do now?' I asked. 'I presume you're not planning on asking Jeffrey for some housekeeping money each week?'

Jeffrey was Debbie's current man. They'd met the week before in the dry goods aisle at the local supermarket. She is the only woman I know who has ever managed a romantic liaison while shopping. The only people I ever seemed to run into were harassed women with three children throwing cans on the floor, or old ladies ruthlessly squeezing fruit to figure out what was ripe.

Debbie did try to educate me as to how to spot a single man from the contents of his shopping basket (dry pasta and 2 in 1 shampoo and conditioners were major clues, apparently, while a man with any form of green vegetable was definitely married or cohabiting) but it always seemed too hard.

'I think Jeffrey and I are reaching the end of the road,' she said. 'And no, I don't have a clue what I want to do. My boss came into my office to talk about the exciting new ideas he had for the Christmas range about an hour ago. First on the list was the singing toilet brush and all of a sudden I knew I'd had enough. I told him I couldn't do it any more and left him sitting on the other side of the desk with his mouth open, then headed straight for the bottle shop and came here. This has been coming for a long time, though – it was really just the toilet brush that broke this camel's back . . . There are plenty of jobs out there; I guess I'll just have to get my résumé together again and see what's around.'

A sudden thought struck me. 'What about setting up some kind of business together?' I asked impulsively. 'Both of us have got to earn money but are sick to death of big companies. We're reasonably intelligent and skilled, surely we can come up with something.'

'Mmm, I guess . . .' Debbie replied uncertainly.

I was suddenly excited about the idea of being able to earn money without leaving Sarah and so I ignored Debbie's lack of enthusiasm. 'It's something I used to think about every now and then, but it always seemed a lot easier to have a pay packet coming my way each week. Maybe we need to put our skills together and give it a go. What about something like corporate parties and client functions?' I suggested. 'Or maybe a gift service for busy executives?'

'You know, maybe it's not such a bad idea . . .' mused Debbie. 'But we've got to think about it. Providing a service means that unless you or I are working, there's no money being generated. If you want to be with Sarah and I want to have enough time to figure what else I want to do with my life, we need to do something different.

'What we need is a product,' she continued.

'That way if we get the product out it can be selling and making money for us while we're asleep or sitting on the beach.'

Debbie drained the last of the first bottle of wine into my glass and absently opened the second one. 'Mmmm,' she said as she stared off into the middle distance. 'All I know is that it's not going to be made of plastic. I've bought enough plastic in the last five years to sink a battleship. I would love to sell something I thought was a great product which would really work for the people who buy it.'

'I like the sound of that,' I agreed. 'Just once it would be great to promote a product I believe in. What are some of the good things you've seen on your travels? Maybe furniture, or clothes?'

'You know,' said Debbie, 'what we really need to do is think of something that will fill a gap in the market. We want something that buyers for big stores will go for because they don't have anything like it.'

'Special candles?' I suggested vaguely. 'Or massage oils?'

'No, all that kind of stuff has been done to death,' said Debbie. 'Even if we get products that are really good, it would be too hard to differentiate them from everything else on the market. What about baby stuff? There's a stack of money in babies and weddings. They're things people are emotional about and so are willing to spend ridiculous amounts of cash on.'

'Deb, I'm only just figuring out which way up I'm supposed to hold Sarah, I don't really think I'm up to the stage of spotting gaps in the baby products market,' I replied. 'How about your specialty – men. Maybe you could write a manual for men coping with rejection – or one for women telling them how to juggle five men at once.'

My one glass of wine had gone straight to my sleep-deprived head and I was finding it hard to be serious about what Debbie was suggesting. The remainder of the bottle, which Debbie had drunk, seemed to be having the same effect on her and she took my suggestion seriously, considering it for a moment before shaking her head.

'No, writing isn't my thing,' she said. 'You know, Sophie,' Debbie continued in a sudden change of subject, slurring her words slightly as the full force of the wine hit her. 'It still seems very weird to me to see you with a baby. Are you really happy doing all this stuff?'

'I can't even remember what life without Sarah was like,' I replied honestly. 'I find it hard to comprehend that Max and I made this little person and that she's mine. Somehow I keep expecting someone from the hospital to arrive to take her back. What it does is put everything into perspective. Being with her as she grows up and learns to do things seems much more important than sitting in tense board meetings debating how best to make a company even more money.'

'So you still haven't heard anything from Max since he did his disappearing act?' Debbie asked.

'Nope,' I replied shortly. Despite my best efforts, I couldn't help but be hurt by the fact that Max hadn't called.

Suddenly Debbie's mobile phone rang. She answered it and the normal, invincible Debbie re-emerged as she arranged to meet Jeffrey and a group of friends for lunch in the city.

'Got to go, Sophie,' she said as she hung up. 'Although I think I need some water before I do.'

I poured her a glass of water, which she gulped down before pulling a brush through her hair, putting some lipstick on without a mirror (a technique that never failed to impress me) and heading out the door.

'Thanks for the chat,' she said as she left. 'Maybe another twenty drinks at lunch will make things crystal clear.' A look of uncertainty passed briefly over her face before she pulled herself together and smiled brightly. 'Talk to you soon,' she said, kissing me on the cheek then bounding down the path in search of a taxi.

TWELVE

A lull descended over the table as those with hang-overs (which was everyone except Karen and me) tucked into their fry-ups the next morning. Even Anna, who normally worked the Friday night shift at the emergency ward, had been out the night before and was looking decidedly under the weather. Karen's seven a.m. breakfast was a thing of distant memory and her eyes lit up as Ben set her flourless chocolate cake in front of her. The King Street Cafe cakes were sensational and Karen always had one while everyone else looked on in total amazement that anyone could eat anything sweet before lunchtime on the weekend.

My multigrain toast and jam wasn't quite as compelling as either the plates of bacon and eggs or Karen's cake, and as the others attacked their plates, I looked up from the paper and gazed out the window across King Street. A short man in leather biker's gear turned to cross the street revealing that the front of his outfit was in fact all of his outfit. What actually made the whole thing stay on didn't bear thinking about and I pulled my eyes away from the bizarre sight back to the cafe, where I caught sight of a yellow packet sticking out of my bag.

As I'd headed out the door the previous day, I'd picked up a parcel that had arrived in that morning's mail and shoved it into the depths of my bag where it was still sitting unopened. Pulling it out, I turned it over to see the name of the sender.

On seeing that it was from the woman who had lived next door to my father and me' for years, my enthusiasm levels dropped. I loved Evelyn dearly but she had been charmingly dotty since I was a teenager and in thirty years of birthdays and Christmases I had never received anything vaguely useful or practical from her. I pulled out the present and unwrapped it. It was a baby record book.

Sarah's lack of a baby book was something I had felt vaguely guilty about. The only ones I could find looked like they were designed for a 1960s nuclear family – hardly the situation Sarah and I were in – and I'd given up in frustration.

Opening the front cover of the book, which featured a pastel pink stork dangling a cherubic baby from its mouth, I saw that this book was similar to the ones I'd looked at. The first page was headed 'Waiting for Baby' and had a caption requiring me to insert a photo of 'Mum and Dad just before Baby was born'. That wasn't going to work without some serious photo doctoring, so I turned to the next page, which was headed 'Baby's Birth' and had a section requiring me to complete 'The weather on the day Baby was born was . . .'

I shook my head and turned back to my companions. 'Anyone have any idea of what the weather was like the day Sarah was born?' I asked.

The initial hit of cholesterol was making its way into their bloodstreams and they were sufficiently revived to look up from their food. Everyone looked at me strangely, obviously wondering if I had finally lost my mind.

'Ah, no, Sophie,' Andrew said slowly. 'Are you trying to decipher some bizarre astrological prediction for her?'

I ignored him and tried again. 'All right, how about the news headlines that day?'

I received more blank looks and gestured to the book in my hands. 'A friend sent me this baby book and I'm yet to find one section I can actually fill in.

'Look at this,' I said, holding up a page entitled 'My Dad'. 'What exactly can I put in here?'

'How about scrawling "Gone to San Fran" across it in felt pen?' Debbie asked helpfully, briefly looking up from the newspaper.

Debbie's concentration span (never very great on a Saturday morning) was broken as she spotted one of her ex-boyfriends in the social pages with a tall brunette. 'Don't do it!' she bellowed at the page, as if saying it loudly enough would make the girl drop her handbag and run. 'He'll wine you, he'll dine you, he'll send you flowers, but get him into bed and you'll die of boredom.'

She looked at the rest of us sheepishly as if she'd forgotten we were there. 'He's just like a slice of take-away pizza. Looks good, smells good but ultimately unsatisfying.'

I couldn't resist the opportunity to get in a dig. 'If the noises coming out of your bedroom are any gauge of satisfaction, I have to agree. I had more sleep in the three weeks you were seeing him than I did in the rest of the time I was living with you.'

Everyone except Debbie roared with laughter and Ben stopped on his way to deliver four break-fasts to the next table. Ignoring the desperate sounds from table five as they spotted their hang-over cures hovering temptingly a few metres away, he asked, 'What gossip am I missing out on this morning?'

'Just talking about Debbie's sex life,' Anna said. 'She spotted George Bailey in the social pages.'

'Was he the guy Deb walked out on in Tahiti when she decided the resort he'd taken her to wasn't up to scratch?' Ben asked. 'No, no,' he corrected him-self. 'He's the guy she was seeing at the same time as she picked up that male stripper.'

'Wrong on both guesses,' Andrew said. 'He was the guy who couldn't keep up with her between the sheets.'

'Well, that doesn't exactly narrow the field,' Ben remarked. 'Half the straight men in Sydney, and for that matter some who were straight before they met her, fall into that category. Deb, you need to look closer to home, I'm sure one of the fellas here would be perfect.' He gestured towards his burly staff members. 'On second thought, stay way away from them, I wouldn't get any work out of them for a week after you'd been near them.'

Debbie couldn't maintain her angry expression and a reluctant smile spread across her face. She pushed her black sunglasses up on her head (Debbie wore sunglasses from the moment she got out of bed on weekend mornings until at least an hour after the sun had gone down). 'One of us has to maintain the strike rate for the group. Three of you are married; Andrew keeps going for fitness freaks who look great but are asleep by nine p.m. after having expended ten zillion calories during the day; and Sophie – well, she's going to be out of action for at least another six months.'

'What do you mean?' I bristled. 'I'm not exactly ready to jump back into the dating scene yet, but I haven't contracted leprosy.'

'Sophie, I'm talking about sex, not dating,' Debbie retorted.

Andrew sniggered. 'Interesting to hear that you actually distinguish between the activities, Debs. I thought the two words would have been inter-changeable for you.'

Debbie ignored Andrew's interjection and con-tinued. 'You can't tell me sex has featured in your thoughts since a certain little someone was born,' she said, gesturing towards Sarah, who was asleep in the pram beside me.

My eyes glazed over at the thought, but this was a matter of principle. 'Maybe not this weekend, but I'm definitely not giving up sex for good.'

Sarah stirred in her pram and I was relieved to see her settle back into a deeper sleep. The cafe was full of people looking rather tender from the previous night's activities and I didn't think that baby noises, regardless of whether they were happy, would be very well received.

Karen picked up the baby record book and tactfully changed the subject. 'I agree with you about the book, Sophie. It's not just that the books all expect everyone to have the standard family unit, they don't seem to accept that times have moved on and that we don't all do the things our grandmothers did when our parents were born. I'll bet you there's a page for the christening and another one for the birth announcement.'

Flicking a couple more pages, she turned the book around to show that she was right. 'See! None of our kids have been christened and I don't know anyone who's ever put a birth announcement in the newspaper. Somehow I don't think baby book authors have made it into the twenty-first century to realise that we now have email. I ended up just buying a big scrapbook for each of my kids and putting in the stuff that seemed relevant to me.'

Andrew took the book from Karen and rifled through it. 'Unbelievable,' he muttered. 'They don't even have a section for pictures of the baby's head-wetting! Where are you going to put the photos of Sarah's King Street Cafe coming-out party?'

Ever since Sarah was born, I had been paranoid that I would turn into a mother who couldn't maintain a decent conversation that didn't involve Sarah or her bodily functions, and I felt that a ten-minute discussion about baby books on Saturday morning was probably enough.

'You're both right,' I said, shoving the book back into my bag. 'I think this can go into the cupboard with all Evelyn's other presents. So tell me what you all got up to last night while I was trying to master the third verse of "Mary Had A Little Lamb"?'

'Does it have more than one verse?' asked Andrew doubtfully.

'Trust me, it does,' I said. 'Would you like a rendition?'

'No thanks,' he answered hurriedly, obviously recalling a drunken karaoke effort of mine from a couple of years before.

'Well, Jeffrey and I have split up,' Debbie announced.

'Debbie, you can't split up from a relationship that lasts less than a week,' said Andrew. 'Anything that lasts for less than seven days definitely falls into the category of casual sex and by definition can't be broken up.'

'Thank you for enlightening me on the finer points of dating, Andrew,' Debbie said sarcastically. 'And how was your reunion date with Helena? Did you manage to get her to stay up past nine p.m. or to lash out and have more than two standard drinks?'

She had obviously hit a sore point, because Andrew looked away.

'I knew it,' Debbie screeched, sensing victory. 'What time did you take her home?'

Sheepishly, Andrew just shook his head.

'All right, I'll guess. I'll bet it was before ten. Am I right?'

Andrew nodded.

'Just tell me it wasn't before nine? Nobody goes home on a Friday night before nine.'

Realising that Debbie wasn't going to let up, he finally confessed. 'All right, I dropped Helena home at eight forty-five because she needed to work on her aerobics routine for a class this morning, and it's definitely over. Happy now?'

Debbie nodded vehemently. 'I have just two words for you,' she said gleefully. 'Gym bimbos. You should know by now they're all as boring as batshit. Next time you find yourself interested in someone, take a good look at her abs. If you can see any muscle tone at all, save us all a lot of grief and give her a miss.'

'Yeah, thanks for the big tip, cupid,' Andrew said. 'Speaking of muscle tone, does anyone want to come and see the new Bruce Willis movie tonight? One of my clients is handing out free tickets like lollies. My theory is that it's a crappy movie and they need to fill the cinemas to give it any chance of survival. Still, you gotta love a freebie.'

Karen and I both passed on the invitation and I tried to convince myself that I'd rather be at home with my baby and a bad video on Saturday night. The sad thing was that an early movie session at the local cinema seemed as exciting a prospect as a cocktail party would have in my previous life.

I sighed. If a Saturday morning coffee session was as thrilling as my social life was going to get, I might as well make the most of it. Defiantly I ordered another coffee, ignoring the sneaking suspicion my morning's caffeine intake would probably keep Sarah awake for most of the weekend.

THIRTEEN

There were some advantages to being a single mother, I reflected as I put Sarah in her cot for a sleep on Sunday morning. I looked down at my once-trendy pyjamas which were now splattered with stains of different colours. When I went out, I could get it together enough so that at least people didn't stare, but at home when it was just Sarah and me, I didn't even pretend. Believing that I had to maintain some standards, however, I did have a pact with myself that I wouldn't stay in my pyjamas later than ten a.m. – even on Sundays.

I glanced at my watch and, seeing that I still had nearly an hour left, I padded into the kitchen to make myself another cup of coffee, just as the phone rang.

'Can you believe I don't have a hangover?' said a voice I immediately recognised as Debbie's.

'Morning, Deb,' I said. 'What are you doing up this side of midday on a Sunday?'

'I decided my body needed a bit of respite after my alcohol intake on Friday and went straight home after the movie. I was asleep by eleven and I feel like a normal human being this morning. This quiet life is sensational, Sophie, I don't know what you've been complaining about.'

'Trust me, the enjoyment wanes after you've done it for a year,' I said darkly. 'Surely Ben and Anna wanted to go for a drink afterwards?'

'They cancelled at the last minute – something about all the fuses in the cafe being blown.'

'Anna?' I asked with a wince.

'Afraid so. When I spoke to Ben he was threatening to ban her from the cafe altogether.

'The reason I'm ringing is because I've had an idea for our business – well, actually, you sort of had it.'

I frowned into the phone while she continued.

'Remember yesterday at the cafe when you brought out that hideous baby book?'

'Deb, hideous is a bit strong – it was a present,' I protested.

'Trust me. I bought hideous stuff for five years. I can recognise it from twenty paces, even with a hangover that would have killed a horse. Anyway, I was going through some boxes of sample stock I brought back from various business trips and I stumbled across a range of notebooks I picked up in Hong Kong. They were made in Thailand and are very cool. There are different patterns or you can get plain colours in a kind of silk finish.'

'Uh huh,' I said, not sure what this had to do

with Evelyn's baby book. 'What are you thinking of doing with the notebooks?'

'Nothing with the notebooks. But what about if we used covers just like them and designed and printed pages for our own baby book? The books could come with all the different pages loose and you could just clip in whatever pages you want for your baby.'

'Kind of like a do-it-yourself baby book?'

'Exactly. It won't be tacky because of the cover and the way we design the pages,' Debbie said. 'We could have pages like the baby's head-wetting or . . . What do I know about what mothers want in their baby book? That's your department. But what do you think of the idea?'

I hesitated. 'Deb, I think it's probably got merit. I have to tell you, though, the idea of sitting for eight hours every day in a shop talking to new mothers doesn't do it for me. I'd rather go back to my old job . . .'

'I'm not talking about a shop,' Debbie interrupted. 'I'm talking about designing the book and then wholesaling it to the big department stores. They're always looking for interesting stuff to buy.'

'Do they really buy things like that from small companies? I would have assumed they'd import it themselves.'

'They do import a lot of their own stuff, but for individual products like this they're happy to buy from anyone if they think it will sell. I have a contact who is the national buyer for Handley Smith. I'll give him a call and see what he thinks.'

Handley Smith was one of the largest department store chains in the country, and knowing Debbie, I was suspicious of the connection. 'This contact of yours . . . You haven't slept with him by any chance, have you?'

'Sophie, I'm shocked you'd think that of me. Of course not!' Debbie protested.

There was a pause as I let a disbelieving silence fall. Finally, Debbie broke.

'All right, all right. I did make some moves on him one night about a year ago, but nothing happened. It turned out he's been living with a woman for five years or something. Definitely not the kind of guy who would cheat. Shame, though – he's not ugly.'

'That sounds more like the truth. I guess if you already know him it can't hurt to run the idea by him. Do you need me to do anything?'

'Not at the moment,' she answered. 'Although you could start giving some thought to how we would make every new parent in Australia aware of the books with a marketing budget of about twenty cents. The department stores are more likely to take on a product if they know we're going to be doing our own marketing and pushing people into their stores.'

I hung up the phone and grabbed a piece of paper to scribble a couple of ideas that had hit me while we were talking. Chances were nothing would come of it and Debbie would find something more glamorous than baby books to occupy her time, but I figured it wouldn't hurt to have a bit of a think.

★

The next day I was just heading out the door with Sarah when the phone rang. I hesitated, trying to figure out whether or not to answer it. After all, the period of time in which Sarah didn't need either to sleep or feed was a very short window of opportunity and I was heading to Karen's for a much-needed chat. Talking to a baby was all very well, but it wasn't exactly mentally stimulating.

However, I've always found it hard to resist answering a ringing phone, regardless of the fact I have an answering machine, and after a moment's hesitation I picked up the handpiece.

'Hello?'

'Ms Anderson, this is David Fletcher.'

'Oh, hello,' I said vaguely, racking my brain to try to figure out who on earth David Fletcher was.

My tone had obviously given me away as he said, 'I'm a buyer for Handley Smith. Your partner Debbie Campbell spoke to me earlier today about your range of baby books, which you're interested in placing in our stores.'

Suddenly I wished I hadn't picked up the phone.

'Oh, yes of course, David. Debbie said she'd had a positive discussion with you this morning,' I replied, inwardly cursing Debbie, who had told me nothing of the sort.

'Debbie told me that your initial order of books is ready to be shipped to Australia and that you are in the process of placing them in various outlets.'

Thankfully he couldn't see the look on my face, or the fact that Sarah had chosen this moment to vomit all down my black shirt. I was still attempting to wear black, largely because I didn't own much else, but the combination of black clothes and white vomit just wasn't working for me. I tried to ignore the mess both Sarah and I were now in and concentrate on figuring out just what untruths my 'business partner' had told this man, who could buy thousands of baby books from us if he decided to.

'Yes,' I replied lamely, trying vainly to recall how people conducted business discussions. 'We're very excited about the product and have a number of outlets interested in stocking them.'

I figured that if Debbie had told this man the screaming lies it seemed she had, then a couple of small additional ones from me wouldn't hurt.

'Well, as I said to Debbie, if the books are as good as they sound, we could be interested in doing a deal with you.'

My mouth fell open as I thought about what this could mean for us. Getting a grip on myself, however, I recalled that we didn't actually have any products, or in fact any clue about what we were doing, or who would make them.

At that moment Sarah decided that standing still in the kitchen was insufficient excitement and started to cry. Figuring that David Fletcher wouldn't be too impressed if he knew just how hands-on my baby book research was, I coughed loudly into the receiver until she had stopped and was staring up at me, obviously trying to figure out whether her mother had lost her mind.

There was a silence from the other end of the

phone and I said, 'So sorry, David, I can't seem to shake this cold. What were you saying?'

'I was saying that an exclusive deal isn't out of the question.' He sounded a touch impatient now. 'But we'd have to move quickly. I have to finalise the products we're stocking for the December season by the middle of next month, so I'd like to get a look at your products, talk numbers and decide whether we want to get them into stores for Christmas.'

'The middle of next month...' I repeated inanely. 'That's what, six weeks away?' I was thinking that six months would be a more realistic deadline at this stage.

'Just under,' David answered. 'But Debbie seemed to think that the timing is achievable for you. We'd need the actual products in the store by the start of November.'

Had Debbie been taking mind-altering drugs? Our business venture to date consisted solely of a ten-minute telephone discussion, but she had been doing a deal with Handley Smith that had us on a five-week deadline.

Turning my attention back to Sarah, who was squirming in my arms, I realised that another yelling session was imminent. Figuring that David would think I had some deadly disease if I produced another coughing fit, I unceremoniously dumped her on the hallway rug and retreated to the kitchen, where I could see her but hopefully David couldn't hear her. The hideous pattern on the 1970s wallpaper seemed to appeal to her and she lay happily staring at the wall.

Now I could concentrate on the conversation, I figured that as Debbie had leapt in with both arms and legs I might as well do the same. 'Yes, that shouldn't be a problem, David,' I said. 'Tell me what you need from us between now and then.'

'First up I need to know your colour range.'

'Colour range? Yes, of course . . .' I replied. 'Well, obviously we've got the traditional pink and blue . . . but not insipid pastels. They're both really vibrant colours,' I added with sudden inspiration. Rapidly running out of ideas, I looked frantically around the kitchen. I spotted the fruit bowl on the kitchen table and said impulsively, 'And we thought we'd round the collection out with lime green, strawberry, orange and banana yellow.'

'Sounds good,' said David, obviously taking notes. 'Now when can I see them? Would Thursday work for you?'

I had been on a roll with my descriptions of the books and had almost convinced myself they were something other than a figment of Debbie's and my imaginations. However, David's question pulled me up with a jolt.

'Let me check my diary,' I said, desperately playing for time. I had absolutely no idea how long it would take for Debbie to get some samples that would roughly approximate what I'd just been describing, but as I couldn't even get a letter to the other side of the world in less than a week, I figured three days was probably a little short.

Unable to think of a good reason to put the appointment off for more than a week, I said, 'This week's really bad for me – could we make it next week, say Friday?' I looked at the calendar on the fridge as I spoke. My activities for the week consisted of one baby massage class and lunch with someone I'd met at antenatal classes who'd had a baby a week after Sarah was born. Not exactly wall to wall with appointments . . .

'I guess that will have to do,' David said reluctantly.

He was obviously used to people falling at his feet to try to get their products into his chain and seemed to be rather taken aback by my lack of enthusiasm. Had I a product to show him I'm sure I would have been at his office within the hour, but the present situation didn't give me much option. I could only hope that he thought I was planning to talk to other retailers first.

Sarah's fascination with the wallpaper seemed to be waning and I decided I should get off the phone before the conversation, which hadn't been a resounding success to date, deteriorated any further. I wrote down David's address details on the back of an unopened bill and made a time for the appointment.

'I look forward to seeing you and your baby books next Friday, Sophie,' he said by the way of goodbye.

As soon as we were disconnected, I dialled Debbie's number.

'What on earth were you thinking, telling David Fletcher we were ready to go with our baby books?' I yelled into the receiver as soon as she answered.

'Oh damn, did he call you already?' she replied calmly. 'I figured he wouldn't do that just yet and so

I've been trying to get some research done to stop you going ballistic when you heard I'd slightly exaggerated our position.'

'Debbie, we don't have a position,' I retorted. 'We have a vague idea about a concept for some books, no idea of what they'd look like, where we'd get them from, or if we even want to go ahead with it!'

'Yeah, I know,' she said sheepishly. 'But when I started talking to David, he was so interested in the idea, I figured there'd be a good chance he'd try to get someone else to do it if we didn't, so I decided to go for it.'

'Well, we have an appointment on Friday week to show him our range of books, which, by the way, come in bright pink and blue, lime green, orange and banana yellow. Oh, and strawberry.'

'Hmmm,' Debbie mused, 'you couldn't have come up with colours that were a little more standard, could you?'

'Debbie . . .' I growled.

'All right, all right, I understand you were in a difficult situation. The good news is that there's a gift expo in Hong Kong in a few weeks. There'll be suppliers there from all over Asia, including some that make silk- and paper-covered books. If we can wing our meeting with David and get him hooked, I'll be able to find something very similar, if not identical, to the notebooks and sort out our pricing and lead times.'

'Hold on, Debbie,' I said. 'We really need to figure out whether this is what we want to do before we get too carried away.'

When we'd vaguely discussed it yesterday, starting our own business had sounded like the perfect solution to my problem of having to earn money but not wanting to leave Sarah with someone else for ten hours a day. More than half of the money I'd put aside to live on until I went back to work had gone, and while I'd been trying not to think about it, I knew that at this rate I'd have to go back to my job within the next month or so. The thought of spending some of my quickly dwindling savings on a venture that might go nowhere gave me a sick feeling in the pit of my stomach.

'Sophie, I think we've got to follow this a bit further,' Debbie said seriously. 'We can see a gap in the market, there's a major department store very interested, and I've got a pretty good lead on where to get the stuff from. I could get an airfare to Hong Kong on frequent flyer points, so we'll only have to pay for my costs while I'm there. What do you say we see what I can come up with? If it doesn't go any further we haven't lost much. If it does work out and we each put, say $10 000 or $15 000 in, we'll double or triple our money and maybe be able to roll it out into a full-scale business with a whole range of products.'

I didn't have $10 000, let alone $15 000. But if I wanted to get off the corporate treadmill I was going to have to take a chance sometime, and I knew that passing up an opportunity like this was the kind of thing I might always regret.

'Okay, okay,' I said, taking a deep breath. 'Book your ticket and let's see if we can figure out how to come up with something vaguely resembling a baby book, before the meeting.'

The next couple of days passed quickly as I spent every second Sarah was sleeping trying to come up with a design for the baby book pages. Debbie had found someone who would supply a patented binding system, which made the whole book easy to personalise by inserting individual pages in any order. My challenge was to come up with some pages that looked great and would appeal to different people.

Having spent years coordinating the printing and design of event invitations, designing some pages for a baby book should have been a piece of cake. However, it was proving surprisingly difficult. What to take out of the standard baby books was easy. It was what to put back in that was slightly harder. I sat staring at a blank piece of paper for a number of hours. I decided to think about the things that I wanted to remember and I thought Sarah would one day like to know.

First Pictures: This page could be whatever the parents wanted it to be. For Sarah, I decided it would be a picture of the first ultrasound Dr Daniels did.

Birth Announcement: This would assume that the news had been spread via email, which was how Debbie had informed our network of friends of Sarah's arrival. I also wanted to figure out a way that some replies could be slotted in (some of the ones I'd received had been hilarious, one of my friends even having penned a limerick to celebrate the occasion).

First Visitors: In Sarah's case it would have to be Debbie, who unfortunately had avoided being captured on film in the very unglamorous outfit she'd worn during the delivery.

First Party: Of course this would have to be Sarah's coming-out at the King Street Cafe.

Baby's Family: This was a tricky one, but I figured if I left it at that, people could put in what worked for them. At least they wouldn't have to deal with things like glaringly blank spaces in sections dedicated to the baby's father.

Baby's Family Tree: Sarah's family tree needed a bit of work, but I thought it was important for her to know where she came from.

Vital Statistics: This wasn't just the standard baby weight, length, etc. It was also a calculation of the number of times the baby fed, woke during the night and had its nappy and clothes changed over the first ten days. I'd found myself totting these things up in sleep-deprived moments and figured it wouldn't be bad for Sarah to have some idea of what she was up to in her early days.

List of Accomplishments: I felt that just recording things like first smile and sitting up missed out a lot of milestones that were significant to me. After all, as Sarah wasn't going to read this book for quite some years, it was my book as much as it was hers. So I decided to add a checklist of things that had proved hugely daunting on our arrival home from hospital, but which were already second nature. Jotting down the first couple of things that came to mind, I listed burping the baby over your shoulder (which I only tried for the first time after I put a pillow behind me in case I dropped Sarah over my back), and my personal nemesis from the early days – fingernail cutting.

After a bit of thought, I put back some of the more traditional options I'd initially excluded. This book was supposed to be about options and a lot of people still had babies in wedlock and had them christened.

With an initial list of pages in hand, I visited an old friend of Max's who ran a design studio overlooking the water in the harbourside suburb of Balmoral and to whom I'd given a lot of work over the previous couple of years. Single and childless, Simon might not have been the best choice to design a baby book, but I wanted the book to look different from all the others on the market. One thing I was sure of was that Simon wouldn't come up with a design sprinkled with storks and chubby babies. Besides, I sometimes missed the buzz of a design studio and it was a good excuse to visit – even if it was only briefly.

'So let me get this straight, Sophie,' he said. 'You're looking for a contemporary feel for a baby book . . . Has no one ever told you that kids and cool don't work?'

'Simon, shame on you. Haven't you seen Cindy, Elle or Catherine lately? A baby is THE accessory. You're just not in the loop if you don't have a baby.' I wasn't even sure that I believed this argument, but I felt I had to at least put up a fight.

'Well, I'll settle for the latest Mooks trousers myself. When do you need these designs back?' He laughed at the look on my face. 'You'd think, after nearly fifteen years in this industry, I'd stop asking that, wouldn't you? Let me guess, you've got a meeting with the head of Harrods tomorrow morning.'

'It's not quite that bad. It's not Harrods and the meeting isn't until the end of next week.'

'Actually, you're in luck. I've just had a new designer start this week. I'll throw her this one to warm her up before I give her a real job.'

Despite Simon's professed lack of enthusiasm, I had worked with him for long enough to know that he would relish the challenge, and I left knowing there was a good chance he would spend more time than his junior designer on the project.

FOURTEEN

Debbie had taken upon herself the responsibility of ensuring that I didn't slip into social obscurity, and had been trying to convince me to go out with her since I'd arrived home from hospital. The day after my meeting with Simon, she was at my house to talk about the books and had obviously decided she was no longer taking no for an answer.

'Sophie, there's a group of us going out for some drinks tomorrow night. There's only one acceptable excuse for your not coming and that's if you're doing something more exciting. Which, I would have thought, is highly unlikely,' she added confidently.

'Deb, I'm just not sure about leaving Sarah at night,' I answered. 'And besides, I've been out of circulation so long I don't think I'd be able to hold a sensible conversation with anyone.'

'I don't think I've ever had a sensible conversation on a Friday night,' Debbie retorted. 'Trust me, as long as you don't talk about Sarah's nappies, or start flashing her photo around the bar, you'll be fine.

'I've already spoken to Karen,' she continued, 'and she would love to look after Sarah while you're out. She tells me that Sarah sleeps from about eight until three these days anyway, so she won't even know you're gone. You can feed her before you go and be back in plenty of time to feed her at three.'

Debbie saw me start to protest and cut me off. 'Sophie, you're in grave danger of thinking that a chat over a cup of tea and a Tim Tam is a social occasion. Read my lips. It is not. We need to get you back out there.'

She was right, I knew. Sarah would be fine with Karen – more than fine, in fact, as Karen knew about a hundred times more about babies than I did. For the first time I admitted to myself that the reason for my hesitation had more to do with me than with Sarah. I was the mother of a small baby and my life was filled with feeds, nappies and nursery rhymes. My last experience of bars had been as the only sober person present, and while this had not been a lot of fun, at least then I had been working and so had something in common with the people around me.

'Karen also tells me that you could express,' Debbie screwed up her nose in distaste, 'some milk and leave it just in case Sarah wakes early. Please do not tell me how you do that. I do not need to know.'

A lot of baby-related activities sound a lot worse than they actually are. However, expressing milk is not one of them. Suffice to say that all jokes about cows and pumps are horrifyingly close to the truth and that it is as undignified an activity as you would care to imagine.

Figuring that I was just prolonging the inevitable if I didn't go along on Friday, I decided I might as well surrender.

Walking out of Karen's front door without Sarah on Friday night, I felt as though I was missing one of my arms. For the last two and a half months Sarah, her pram and my bag of Sarah stuff had accompanied me everywhere, and to be heading out with only a handbag was decidedly strange.

I'd been about to throw on trousers and a shirt when it had suddenly dawned on me that as I wouldn't have to feed Sarah, I could wear a dress. My excitement was short-lived, though, as the first dress I tried was way too small in not just one but a number of places, and after one look I threw the next two on the bed without even bothering to try to squeeze into them.

The last dress in the cupboard was one I'd had for several years. It was dusky red with vague violet outlines on it and a deep V-shaped neck. Pulling it over my head and zipping up the back, I turned to look in the full-length mirror on the inside of my cupboard and laughed aloud. With my normal breasts the neckline had never been anything remarkable, but now my Sarah breasts were prominently displayed in all their glory. I'd been living with these breasts for a while, but until now they'd just made for a better shape in T-shirts and tight jumpers, and this look was a revelation.

The dress was already half unzipped when I stopped. After all, I told myself, my breasts were just on loan and the cleavage I was displaying was something that no amount of padding in a bra could produce. With a surge of bravado I rezipped the dress, pulled on a pair of strappy shoes, gathered Sarah and her luggage, and drove straight to Karen's.

After a moment's hesitation Karen promised me that my décolletage was not obscene. Thankfully, her husband Sam wasn't home, as I soon realised that in order to give Sarah her last feed I had to unzip the back of my dress and lift the whole thing up to my shoulders. When dressing I'd decided that, as no one was going to see them, pantihose were a much better option than uncomfortable stockings and suspenders, and even Karen was unable to suppress a smile at the very unglamorous picture I presented. As soon as I was finished and had reassembled my clothing, she chased me out the door, assuring me that everything would be perfectly fine.

Feeling like a country cousin who'd just come into town, I pushed my way through the crowds at Altitude, a bar that had become fashionable during my absence from the drinking scene.

'Sophie!' Debbie cried, grabbing my arm as I headed past. I hadn't seen her next to the towering blond man she was talking to.

'Here,' she said, shoving a drink in my hand. 'There was a crowd at the bar so I thought I'd get you one while I was there.

'Actually,' she corrected herself, 'I thought Jason could get you one while he was there.' She gestured at the Adonis in front of me. 'Wow,' she said admiringly as she looked at the front of my dress. 'That's got to be the first benefit of having a baby I've seen so far.'

Being in a bar with Debbie, attendant men and the various other people I knew, felt like old times. Smiling happily I took a big gulp of my drink, feeling the tingle of the tonic water and the subtle taste of gin as it slipped down my throat. No matter how much I told myself straight tonic water should taste the same as tonic water containing gin, it just didn't.

Within fifteen minutes of my arrival, I thought I was going to have to call the nearest hospital to have them send someone to deal with the cases of whiplash I was causing. Each time I spotted someone I hadn't seen for a while the reaction was the same. They smiled at me, obviously saw something in their peripheral vision, looked down, clocked my breasts and then jolted their head back up again to check that it was really me.

Never having been an exhibitionist, I felt I'd come out half dressed and wished fervently that I'd chosen a turtleneck jumper instead of my low-cut dress. I tried to hide the display by holding my drink across my chest, but Debbie spotted me from across the room and frowned her disapproval. Abandoning any attempt at modesty, I resorted to alcohol, and before I knew it, was draining the dregs of my second gin and tonic from around the ice.

Two drinks a night was my self-imposed limit while I was feeding Sarah and my spirits sank as I contemplated the rest of the evening on lime sodas.

However, at that moment another drink miracu-lously appeared in my hand, courtesy of Brian, a friend I hadn't seen since Sarah was born.

Well, it would be rude not to drink it, given that Brian had bought it for me, I thought as I sipped my first vodka and cranberry juice in a very long time.

'How are you, Sophie?' asked Brian after the now-expected double take.

'Great,' I answered truthfully as the alcohol began its job of soothing away all my concerns and making me feel that being in this bar with these people was the only thing in the world I wanted to be doing right now. This mildly drunken feeling was the thing I'd missed the most, that feeling that the whole world was my friend.

'You look fantastic,' Brian said admiringly, greatly helping my state of mind. 'You know, I've read about women with babies who look sensational but I've never met one. I can't believe I finally know a yummy mummy.'

Despite suspecting that the drink in Brian's hand was by no means his first, I was pleased by his com-ment. Yummy mummy indeed, I thought to myself.

The vodka and cranberry juice was gone by the time I left Brian and I felt a flash of resentment at the fact that I was the only person in this bar counting my drinks. Reaching the bar I ordered drinks for a number of people and, about to order a mineral water for myself, changed my mind and ordered another gin and tonic.

I looked around and caught the eye of a man standing nearby. Damn, I thought as I saw him move towards me. Being pregnant had made me careless. I was so used to men spotting my pregnant belly and making large detours around me, that I had forgotten one of the fundamental rules of drinking in bars – never make eye contact with someone you haven't made a conscious decision to talk to.

Relax, I told myself as he headed towards me. He looked okay and I had to get used to meeting new men.

'Hi there,' my new companion said. 'Having a good night?'

'Yes, I am, thanks,' I replied. 'The music's good, isn't it?'

I mentally patted myself on the back. While my conversation wasn't exactly breathtaking, it was better than asking him if he had kids.

'Yeah, it is,' he said. 'My name's Nick, by the way.'

'I'm Sophie,' I smiled.

'I'd like to dance, but all my marathon running has hurt my knees. If I danced I'd have to ice down my knees afterwards, otherwise I wouldn't be able to walk for days,' Nick volunteered. 'I've just had an arthroscopy on my left knee. When I went to the physiotherapist he tried to tell me I couldn't do anything active for months, but I said to him, "I'm an athlete, I have to exercise." I've got good genes, though – my dad died recently at eighty-nine and my grandfather was ninety-four when he died.'

'Right . . .' I ventured.

Oblivious to my lack of enthusiasm, Nick continued on with the saga of his running career. If this was the singles scene, then I'd take an evening with *Baywatch* any time.

How could I get rid of him? I discarded the idea of showing him my stretch marks, although only after having given it serious consideration. Getting another drink was the only option, I decided, looking at my full glass. Swallowing the contents in one gulp, I leapt in as soon as Nick drew breath and said, 'Lovely to talk to you, Nick, but I've got to get another drink. I'll catch you later, okay?' and dived back into the crowd.

As I shouldered my way back through the throng towards my friends, Vicky arrived with a tray of vodka jelly shots, a house specialty. She wouldn't take no for an answer as she moved around the group with the tray, dispensing the dollops of vodka-infused jelly which sat in small plastic cups, a toothpick sticking out of the top.

Just one wouldn't hurt, I told myself as I expertly cut the jelly away from the cup with the toothpick, upended it on the back of my hand and swallowed it in a single gulp. Eating jelly shots was definitely an acquired skill and could go horribly wrong. I still shudder to recall an occasion years ago when I'd been with a man I desperately wanted to impress, and had ended up with jelly half in and half out of my mouth for what seemed an eternity.

Our group grew increasingly raucous as the drinks kicked in and the music thumped in the background. There was nothing like Friday nights, I thought in a pleasant fog as I accepted another jelly shot. People were in high spirits, the reality of Monday morning seemingly an eternity away.

Altitude had a long bar running its length and various tables dotted around. A song finished and a short, dark-haired girl jumped on a nearby table with a microphone in her hand and, to the delight of everyone around her, proceeded to sing 'Stands to Reason', a song which had recently rocketed to the top of the charts.

The girl looked very familiar and I racked my mind to think where I had seen her. Suddenly I realised she was Fleur Stanhope, the pop star who had made the song a hit. I recalled now that she lived in Sydney. Open-mouthed, I watched the rest of the performance, impressed that I was in a bar so cool that singers popped in to perform impromptu renditions of their hits.

After she'd finished, I rejoined a large group of my friends who were standing off to one side. 'Can you believe we just heard Fleur Stanhope sing?' I gushed during a pause in the conversation.

'What?' asked a small man called Laurence who sported slicked-back dark hair.

'Fleur Stanhope,' I repeated. 'Wasn't she great?'

'Are you serious, Sophie?' asked Sandra, a tall, blonde girl. Seeing that I was, she and the rest of the group burst out laughing. 'Sophie, that was Joyce Johnston. She was miming the song using her hairbrush.'

'Oh,' I replied inanely, belatedly remembering that the place I'd seen Joyce Johnston was at the supermarket near home, not on television. My gin and vodka haze was not thick enough to prevent me seeing the amused glances exchanged. Muttering something about going to the bathroom, I turned to leave. Unfortunately, as I did so I tripped over nothing and lurched away.

Finding myself adrift amongst groups of loud drinkers I didn't recognise, I decided that the quiet of the toilets might not be such a bad idea. A cubicle at the end was vacant and I headed towards it. However, as I turned into it, the room seemed to tilt and I hit one side of the door and then the other as I tried to fit my body into what seemed to be an impossibly narrow space.

Finally managing the manoeuvre, I closed the door and leant against it, trying to figure out what was going wrong. Deciding that going to the toilet was way too difficult, I pulled the door open and walked back out. A woman with big breasts, hair standing in peaks in several places and eyeliner smudged around both of her eyes, looked back at me in the mirror. Thinking optimistically that I might be able to repair some of the damage with a comb and some lipstick, I opened my handbag. Wedged in on top of everything else was a breast pad in its plastic packet. For a moment the gin and tonics and vodka shots were swept away, and I remembered with a jolt what I'd managed to forget for the last few hours. I was a mother, who was due back to look after her daughter – I looked at my watch – one hour ago.

The alcohol and its effects surged back, but the memory of Sarah didn't disappear. Abandoning any attempt to restore my appearance, I stumbled back out into the bar in search of Debbie.

'There you are, Sophie,' Debbie said before I'd

gone two steps. 'I've been looking for you. Laurence said you might need a hand.'

'I've jush realised the time, Debbie,' I slurred. 'I've got to go in case Sarah wakes up an neesh feeding.'

'Okay,' Debbie answered, obviously agreeing with my decision. 'Come on, I'll take you back to Karen's.'

I allowed myself to be led out of the bar and deposited in a taxi which was mercifully cruising by, the rush on cabs not yet having started. Debbie slid in beside me and I dimly heard her telling the cab driver something, before I put my head on her shoulder and instantly fell asleep.

What seemed like two seconds later, the cab pulled up and Debbie shook me awake. 'Come on, Sophie, we're here,' she said, pulling me out of the taxi onto the footpath.

'Do you have a key or do we have to wake Karen up?' she asked.

At Karen's name my memory stirred. 'No,' I said. 'I've got a key. I'm going to sleep in the study with Sarah.'

'Thank God for that,' Debbie muttered as she felt around in my handbag for the key, which she pulled out and put in the lock.

Helped by Debbie's guiding hand, I made it down the corridor without dislodging any of the pictures on the walls, and into the study. Spotting Sarah's portacot I lunged for it and hung onto the top looking at my beautiful daughter fast asleep.

'Sophie, do not wake that child,' Debbie whispered fiercely in my ear as she prised my hands off the cot and sat me down on the mattress on the floor. After pulling off my shoes, she pushed me onto my back.

'Go to sleep, Sophie. I'll call you tomorrow.'

My eyes clanged shut and I was lost in dreamless oblivion before she'd even left the room.

The sound of a baby's crying reached me as though from a great distance. Rolling over I pulled the pillow across my head in an effort to shut out the noise. It didn't go away, however, and I was gradually pulled up through the layers of sleep to consciousness. With a start I realised that it was Sarah crying, and the realisation of where I was hit me a fraction of a second before the crushing headache.

I had no way of knowing how long it had taken for Sarah's crying to wake me. Karen's kids' rooms weren't far from the study, though, and I picked her up in a panic, desperate to quieten her before she woke the whole household. Past experience had taught me that nothing but milk could pacify Sarah at this hour and I went to pull up my shirt to feed her.

'Shit!' I realised that I was still wearing my dress. Laying Sarah, who was now hysterical, on the mattress, I struggled with the zip at the back of my dress, finally pulling it over my head.

A beautiful silence descended as I held Sarah to my breast and she started feeding. In an attempt to try to calm the vicious thumping in my left temple, I closed my eyes and leant against the wall. I must have dozed off and was woken when Sarah made a noise. She had finished feeding and was looking up at me, obviously trying to figure out was going on.

It was as I lowered her back into her cot that I suddenly realised the milk Sarah had just drunk must have had an awful lot of gin and vodka swishing around in it. Panic and guilt hit me simultaneously as I tried to think what effect my binge would have on my poor, trusting daughter.

My first thought was to wake Karen and find out how serious she thought the situation was. However, some perspective returned as I visualised myself leaning over Karen and Sam's bed and shaking her awake to tell her I'd fed Sarah after a night on jelly shots. I'd never heard of a baby having its stomach pumped because of an overindulgent mother, so I figured that there was nothing more I could do tonight.

Lying down, I tried to go back to sleep, but despite the heaviness of my eyelids and the thumping inside my head, I tossed and turned for the next couple of hours until I heard the sound of someone in the kitchen.

Sarah was still sleeping as I pulled on the clothes I'd left in the room the night before and stumbled out. Karen was standing at the coffee machine in a pair of jeans and white T-shirt, looking like someone out of a breakfast cereal commercial.

'Good morn –' Her greeting trailed off as she registered my hungover appearance.

'Hi,' I answered glumly, sitting down heavily on the bench seat running the length of the table.

'Big night?' Karen asked cautiously.

'You could say so,' I answered. 'I don't know what happened; one minute I was finishing my second drink and contemplating the rest of the evening on soft drink, and the next I'd had half a dozen jelly shots and God knows how many gin and tonics. Karen, I honestly forgot about Sarah for a couple of hours.'

Karen was about to speak but I interrupted her. 'And the worst thing is that I fed her a couple of hours ago before I even thought about what the alcohol would do. Could it hurt her?' I was almost in tears.

Karen sat down and put her arm around me. 'I don't really know, but I don't think it will do anything worse than give her some heartburn and make her feel a bit off–colour for the day.'

'Did you ever do it?' I asked, hoping to hear that my lapse was normal.

'Well, no . . .' Karen said. 'But I know a few women who did,' she continued quickly. 'And their babies are fine. When Sarah wakes up you can give her the bottle you left, and by her next feed most of the alcohol should be gone anyway. In the meantime, I think you need a very strong coffee.'

After I'd drunk my coffee and refused all offers of food, Sarah woke up. She was uncharacteristically grumpy and every time she cried I felt a stab of guilt. She wouldn't drink much of the bottle of milk, so I decided to head home, wanting to deal with my first hangover in over a year and my unhappy daughter in my own home.

Mercifully, Sarah fell asleep as soon as we arrived

home, and I wasn't far behind her. When we both awoke it was almost eleven. For ten minutes I told myself I wouldn't go to the King Street Cafe, that I'd plead illness or a death in my family, anything that would prevent me leaving the house within the next week. Eventually, though, I dragged myself into the shower, pulled some clothes on and tottered out the door with Sarah in the baby sling.

For the first time in months I was the last to arrive at the cafe. As I walked in the door Andrew leapt to his feet with a salt shaker in his hand and everyone burst into a rendition of 'Stands to Reason'.

I glowered at Debbie from behind my sunglasses for several seconds, realising that I should have expected the story of my exploits last night to have reached the cafe before I did. Despite myself I started laughing, then sat down beside Anna, trying to decide whether one fried breakfast would be enough or whether I should order two.

FIFTEEN

Debbie had insisted that I go to the meeting with David Fletcher. She had justified this at great length on the basis that (in her words) my skills of tact and persuasion would be much more use than her rather blunter approach, given that we had to convince David to make a strong commitment on the basis of a mocked-up baby book and some pretty vague prices. However, I had my suspicions that her reluctance to go had more to do with the fact that David had rejected her advances, a situation Debbie was very unaccustomed to dealing with.

If I was going to attend my first business meeting post-baby, I was determined to at least look the part. So the day before, I showed up at my hairdresser, hoping a cut would restore the damage done by motherhood. You'll notice I say 'cut' and not 'trim', having once been chastised by a hairdresser who was hurt by my having called his masterly re-creation of my existing style a trim.

Real estate agents say that the three most important factors for property investment are location, location and location. I believe that this is equally true for hairdressing salons. I am constantly amazed that hairdressers set up their flashy salons on busy streets with huge plate-glass windows which allow everyone to see exactly what is going on inside. When I am sitting in the chair, half my hair wrapped in aluminium foil and the rest of it plastered to my scalp, I do not want anyone I know to peer in the window and wave at me.

My theory is that all hairdressers are privy to a closely guarded secret imparted to them when they finish their apprenticeship, regardless of whether they work in a cut-price joint in suburbia or a swanky establishment in the middle of town. That secret is that they must make their clients look as ugly as possible before they start to cut their hair. And so they dress you in a big black waterproof poncho, wash your hair (ensuring that any makeup runs in the process), wrap your hair in a bottle-green towel and then put you in front of a huge mirror under fluorescent lights that turn any facial blemish a bright red.

By the time they ask, 'Well, what would you like us to do today?', I'm always so demoralised that I'll agree to anything they suggest. I also feel like a cat-walk model if the hairdresser manages to get the haircut even half right.

Despite years of negotiating with difficult clients, I'm still unable to tell a hairdresser that I don't like something they've done, or that I'd like them to do something they obviously don't approve of.

I'd had my hair in a bob of varying lengths for about ten years (except for the tragic perm episode, which I'm still not able to speak about). About five years ago I took the brave decision to have it cut really short. Perry, the hairdresser, looked at my obligatory photo of the actress whose hair (and face, body and life) I wanted, looked at me and decreed that he would cut my hair like that if that's what I desired, but did I really want to show off my protruding ears? Funny, isn't it, how you can get through twenty-five years of life without realising something as fundamental as the fact you have protruding ears. Luckily, Perry's skill and training allowed him to help people with deformities like mine, and he created (his words) a cropped kind of haircut that swept forward over my cheekbones (and over my ears).

Nice concept, except that I can't stand having hair on my face. But do you think I managed to tell that to Perry or any of the three hairdressers who have succeeded him but have maintained the same hairstyle? Oh, no. Instead I wait until I'm outside the hairdresser's to pull out my brush, rip out the spray and push my hair back behind my ears.

Today, however, one of the younger stylists was washing my hair, and the combination of the warm water and months of very little sleep was threatening to send me into a coma. I was concerned that if this happened no one would be able to wake me and they would have to leave me propped up at the basins for the rest of the day, so I tried to think of something to concentrate on that would keep me awake.

Naturally, my mind turned to the meeting and I wondered, not for the first time, whether David would like the design Debbie and I had agreed on. I had shown her the three different page layouts Simon's designer had presented and we had sat in silence as she examined each one in turn.

I appreciate thoroughness as much as the next person, but after five minutes her silence started to unnerve me.

Just as I had decided that enough was enough and that I'd jump across the table and hold her down until she told me what she was thinking, she looked up and smiled.

'They're all good, but I think this one is pretty close to spot on,' she said, holding up the design which was my favourite.

The designer had kept a lot of clean white space and had just added decoration with vivid splashes of colour on each page.

'Of course,' Debbie conceded, 'I'm probably the worst person to test this on. We should see what Karen thinks. Maybe even some other mothers?'

'Why don't we wait until you come back with some ideas for covers?' I suggested. 'That way we can see what kind of reaction the whole package gets.'

'Works for me,' Debbie agreed. 'I just hope I can find what we're looking for at the trade show. Trekking around deepest darkest China trying to unearth baby book covers doesn't really appeal.'

I snapped out of my musings as my hair was twisted into a towel (steel grey in this salon – obviously an acceptable variation on bottle green in the hair-dressers' manual) and I was propelled back to stare at myself in the mirror. A new addition to my customarily unattractive reflection in the huge mirror was big black shadows under my eyes. Next visit to the hairdresser I really would trowel on the makeup, I silently vowed.

When dressing I was tempted to pull one of my conservative suits (which ranged from black to navy and back to black) out of the depths of my closet where they had hung unworn from the point in my pregnancy when I could no longer do up the buttons on the jackets.

However, I decided that the high-powered corporate look might be a bit over the top for someone selling baby books. I opted instead for a pair of bone-coloured trousers and a light pink top – all made of that wonderful man-made material called microfibre which didn't need ironing and made me wonder who on earth still bought crushable clothes.

I eyed Sarah speculatively as I dressed, trying to figure out if she looked like she was in a vomiting mood. I decided that I would take my chances for the trip to Karen's place, where she was going to stay while I was out.

The phone rang. When I answered it I could hear a child screaming in the background and after a couple of seconds Karen spoke. 'Sophie, it's me. I've got a problem. Jack's just fallen out of the jacaranda tree in the back yard and broken his arm. I'm on my way to the hospital at the moment. I'm really sorry but I'm not going to be able to look after Sarah for you.'

'God, Karen, don't worry about that,' I said. 'Do you need me to do anything?'

'No, it's under control. Emily and Pat are with the next-door neighbour. Don't worry, I'm pretty good at this drill, I just about know all the emergency room doctors' names. I'll call you later.'

I hung up, hoping that I'd prove to be as unflappable as Karen when Sarah started running around and hurting herself. Dialling Debbie's number, I decided I'd give her the choice of looking after Sarah or going to the meeting herself. I suspected that any reluctance she felt about seeing David would be overcome by the prospect of being alone with Sarah for several hours.

Her home phone rang out and I dialled her mobile, which clicked straight onto her voice mail. I hung up and looked at my watch in panic. I didn't have enough time to track down someone else to look after Sarah, so there was nothing for it, I'd just have to put the meeting off.

Pulling out my diary, I called David Fletcher's number. 'David, it's Sophie Anderson,' I said when he answered.

'Hello, Sophie,' he said. 'I'm looking forward to seeing you soon – there's not a problem, is there?'

'Actually, there is,' I answered. 'Something unavoidable has just come up and I'm not going to be able to make our meeting. Would it be possible to reschedule for next week?'

'No, it wouldn't,' he replied, obviously annoyed. 'I'm off to Perth this evening and I actually booked a later flight so I could see you this morning. If we're going to do this deal then I have to see you today. Surely you can move your other commitment.'

Sarah stared up at me from where she was lying on the bed and I suddenly decided I didn't have any choice but to be honest.

'Look, David, this is the story,' I said. 'I have a baby and the person who was going to look after her while I was meeting with you has had an emergency and had to cancel. Believe me, if it was just another appointment I'd move it in a flash, but a baby's a bit trickier to cancel and I can't line someone else up in the next five minutes.'

'Well, why not just bring her along?' David said, as if that was the logical solution. It was obvious he had absolutely zero experience with children if he thought we could calmly do business while I jiggled Sarah on one knee or, God forbid, breastfed her.

About to enlighten him on the top ten flaws in his suggestion, I realised that if I didn't meet with him this morning the deal was off. Given that I couldn't meet with him without Sarah, I didn't really have a lot to lose.

'Fine,' I said briskly. 'Sarah and I will be with you at eleven.'

I dressed Sarah in what I had thought would be a fantastic ensemble of a little dress, cardigan and socks, then realised the dress was still way too big and the combined effect was to make my beautiful little girl look like a bag lady. I wasted five more minutes reversing the process, prodding Sarah's little arms back through the openings I'd just shoved them through and putting her back into the hot pink and white striped grow suit she'd been in originally. Determined not to be late on top of everything else, I grabbed Sarah under one arm, my briefcase under the other and headed out the front door.

Handley Smith's flagship store was located in the centre of town. Pushing the pram into the lift to the executive levels and punching the button for the fourth floor, I grimaced as I caught a glimpse of my very unprofessional-looking self in the mirrored walls.

When the doors opened, I wheeled Sarah into the reception area and up to the desk. 'Sophie Anderson to see David Fletcher,' I told the receptionist.

'Do you have an appointment, Ms Anderson?' she asked dubiously, obviously thinking that I was a disgruntled shopper there to complain about the state of the store's toilets.

'Yes, he's expecting me,' I replied, trying to appear businesslike. Not an easy thing to do given that I was jiggling the pram with my left foot.

The receptionist picked up the phone and informed David of my arrival. Visibly surprised to hear that I did in fact have an appointment, she gestured me to the door that led off the reception area.

'He's free now, Ms Anderson,' she said. 'Go on through.'

Despite my jiggling, Sarah had decided that this whole thing was way too much fun to sleep through.

I manhandled the pram through the door, praying that she wouldn't do anything too horrific.

Once I'd successfully negotiated the doorway I looked up. I could see why Debbie had tried to work her feminine wiles on David Fletcher. He was tall, with a strong, angular face, dark brown hair and bright blue eyes behind a pair of tortoise-shell glasses.

I held out my hand. 'I'm Sophie Anderson.'

David smiled and shook my hand. 'Pleased to meet you, Sophie. And who is this?' he asked, gesturing towards Sarah.

'This is Sarah – it's her first business meeting,' I replied, attempting to make light of the situation.

David smiled awkwardly at Sarah. 'Hello, there.' He reached out his hand but at the last minute held back from touching her.

'My sister had a little boy a year ago. I was too terrified to touch him until he was big enough to crawl. They just seem so fragile, don't they?'

I was about to reply, when Sarah suddenly let out an enormous bellow. My heart sank. Had I really expected this to go smoothly?

'Not when she yells like this,' I said. 'I'm really sorry – I know this probably isn't how you're used to holding meetings.'

I scooped Sarah out of her pram and she stopped crying. Not looking at David, I quickly spread a bunny rug on the floor and hung a rattle off a nearby chair leg. The Mother Police wouldn't approve, but I figured David knew even less about babies than I did and wouldn't report me.

'Don't worry about it,' David said. 'This shouldn't take long, anyway. Please sit down.'

I sat as instructed and watched as he settled back in his chair. Handley Smith obviously hadn't adopted the casual dress habits that had swept through the world's capital cities – David was wearing a navy suit with a white shirt and conservative tie. I looked at his desk surreptitiously. It was perfectly neat with papers stacked in labelled trays and pens lined up above the blotting pad. Interestingly, I couldn't spot the expected silver-framed picture of the beautiful girlfriend. The only picture on his desk was of a sailing boat.

'Perhaps I should start, David,' I said briskly, very conscious that the situation could go horribly wrong at any moment. 'As you can see, I have just had a baby.' I gestured at Sarah. 'But for six years I held marketing jobs in various companies and am on leave from my current job at International Events Management. As Debbie told you, she has left her position at Mr Cheapy and we've decided to pool our skills and produce a baby book to fill what we believe is a significant gap in the market.'

Sarah seemed to be getting restless on the floor, so I quickly leant down to attach a new toy to her makeshift mobile. As I did, I was dismayed by the unmistakable odour of a dirty nappy and the telltale yellow stain spreading down her leg. I also spotted a large splotch of vomit on the toe of my right shoe.

I couldn't imagine how David could miss the smell, but decided that if I ignored it maybe he would too. I just hoped that there wasn't enough overflow from the nappy to seep through the rug onto the beige carpet.

I smiled at him in what I hoped was an efficient yet calm and motherly way, and continued. 'We're waiting on our first specially designed covers in the range of colours we've already discussed,' I said, crossing my fingers in a superstitious attempt to ward off any consequences of my lie. 'However, I have a couple of mock-ups which are very close to what the final product will look like.'

I pulled my briefcase onto my lap and removed the cover and a manila folder. Turning it around, I showed it to him. 'The concept is that each baby book will consist of a cover in one of a range of vibrant colours and a set of these pages which, as you can see, slip into the fastening system inside the cover to look just like a normal book.'

I opened the manila folder and handed David a set of pages.

'Wow,' he said involuntarily as his eyes caught the bold design on the first page. As he looked through each of the pages, I kept talking to conceal my nervousness.

'The idea is that these books take into account that times have changed and so have families, and that people want to put different things in a record book for their babies' first years. We've provided a lot of different options, both traditional and untraditional, and also some plain pages with the same design for anyone who wants to come up with their own ideas.'

David looked up. 'I think it will sell. As you can tell, I don't have kids myself and wouldn't know one end of a baby from the other, but since I spoke to you last week I've talked to a number of colleagues who are very positive about the marketability of an item like this.'

'That brings me to my next point,' I continued. 'I have some ideas for marketing. It's no good putting them in stores if we don't tell people they're there. Promotion should definitely be a component of any agreement we reach.'

'What do you want to do with these books?' David asked. 'Are you wanting to sell them to as many outlets as you can, or are you interested in doing something exclusive with us?'

'It really depends on the terms you offer,' I replied frankly. 'If we'd sell more books by putting them in every department and gift store in the country, then we'll do that, but there's definitely an appeal in doing something just with you.'

'Fair enough,' David replied. 'What are your costings?'

As I slid the spreadsheet across the desk, I couldn't believe how well this was going. Despite the gurgling, smelly bundle at my feet and the vomit on my shoe, I could hear myself actually sounding very businesslike.

'These are rough figures,' I said. 'We need to firm up our cover pricing.' I grimaced inwardly at this massive understatement. 'But it will give you something to work with and I'll have final figures to you shortly.'

'Okay,' David said. 'Leave it with me and I'll get back to you in the next couple of days.'

I had run out of toys with which to entertain Sarah and when I sneaked a glance at her I saw with a jolt that she had screwed up her face and was about to let out a scream. Trying to look as though I did this all the time, I quickly slung her over my left shoulder, stood up and shook David's hand with my right.

'I look forward to hearing from you,' I said, desperate to be gone.

I decided it was too much of a risk to put Sarah back into her pram. Moving her into the crook of my right arm, I turned the pram around and headed for the door. My one-handed steering needed work and I clipped the doorframe as I went. The jolt startled Sarah, who started to cry.

I nodded quickly to the receptionist and pushed the down button for the lift, only barely resisting the urge to keep my finger there in a vain attempt to make it come more quickly. Finally it arrived and I stepped in, sighing with relief as the doors closed. I was so relieved that the meeting was over, I didn't even care when a couple already in the lift sidled away from us.

It did, however, remind me that Sarah badly needed a new nappy. Without a clue of where there might be a parents' room in the CBD (hardly a big call for it, I reflected), I headed for the ladies' toilets on the ground level of Handley Smith in the hope that the sink would be wide enough to rest Sarah on while I changed her.

No such luck. The basins were the fashionable freestanding kind, which looked good but were no use to me. With a sigh, I abandoned any pretence at being professional and lay Sarah on top of her bunny rug on the tiled floor. Ignoring the procession of people that had to step over us to reach the toilets, I quickly cleaned her and changed her into a plain white grow suit.

Feeling somewhat calmer and more presentable, I put Sarah in her pram and headed back to the foyer. My entrance through the revolving doors before the meeting had clearly entertained several onlookers. Just as I was taking a deep breath in preparation for a repeat performance, I caught sight of David walking out of the lifts, talking on a mobile phone.

My heart sank. Marvellous! While I'd avoided any major catastrophe during our meeting, he was now going to witness me trying to make my escape through the revolving doors.

He put the phone away just as he reached us, and I was surprised to see a genuine smile on his face. 'Still here? I thought you two would be long gone by now.'

'I've found that when people move away from Sarah in lifts, it probably means it's a good time for a new nappy,' I answered with a smile.

David laughed, obviously blissfully unaware of the peril his office carpet had been in fifteen minutes earlier. 'Can I give you a hand to your car?'

I shook my head. 'Thanks, but we're not far away. I've got the routine pretty sorted by now.' I was sure that the last thing he wanted was more time with Sarah and me.

To my surprise, David fell into step with me as I walked towards the exit. With relief I spotted some automatic doors off to one side and headed for them.

'I don't suppose you're free for lunch?'

I was caught off guard by his question and didn't reply immediately.

'I was supposed to be having lunch with a client but he's just cancelled,' David continued. 'If you've got time we could head there now.'

I did a quick mental calculation. Sarah would need feeding in the next hour or so, which meant doing it at lunch. Having lunch with a breastfeeding mother was certainly more than David had bargained for and I was about to refuse. But then I changed my mind. I really didn't feel like going home to my empty house and I couldn't remember the last time I had been out for lunch.

'Sure, that would be great,' I said.

'Right,' said David. 'We're booked into a place in Surry Hills. Is that okay?'

'Sounds fine,' I answered. 'Do you want me to give you a lift or is it easier if you bring your car too?'

'I'll bring my car. That way I can go straight home after lunch and pack, then head to the airport. Are you parked under the building next door?'

I nodded.

'Okay then, why don't you follow me?'

I was grateful that we had brought separate cars as I followed David into the nearby suburb of Surry Hills. Sarah had obviously lost all patience with being dragged in and out of cars and prams, and soon reached full-throttle screaming levels. Had David been with us I was sure he would have suddenly remembered a pressing business engagement in the opposite direction and escaped at the first red traffic light.

My attempts to soothe Sarah by dangling a brightly coloured toy octopus in her face did nothing but give me stabbing pains in my elbow. However, I'd made the amazing discovery a couple of days earlier that singing nursery rhymes to Sarah made her stop crying immediately. (I obviously had a child with discerning musical taste, though, as the next time I'd sung to her I'd tried Madonna's 'Material Girl', which caused her to cry harder. So, nursery rhymes it was.) In desperation I now tried a rendition of 'Three Blind Mice' but it didn't have the desired effect and Sarah continued crying at the top of her voice.

I groaned as I saw David indicate and pull up beside a swank little restaurant about which I'd read rave reviews. For some strange reason I'd been hoping that we were heading for a basic coffee shop full of shoppers and mothers with children, rather than a power-lunching mecca such as this one. David had obviously never eaten in the company of a baby and didn't realise that they weren't exactly conducive to the perfect dining experience.

Scrambling out as soon as the car stopped, I managed to have Sarah in her pram before David had locked his car and wandered back to join us. The change of position improved her temperament dramatically and she sent David one of her most winning smiles. I had already noticed that Sarah seemed to produce her cutest smiles for men. Perhaps Debbie had been indoctrinating her in feminine wiles during the couple of times I had left them together. If Debbie had her way, Sarah would be putting on eyeliner when other babies were still scrawling with crayons.

Throwing every toy I could find into the pram, I hoped desperately that Sarah's newfound good humour would last.

David stood back and gestured for me to precede him up the three small steps that led to the door of the restaurant. My pram stair-mounting technique was still a bit shaky and I managed to wedge the front wheels against the bottom of the top step. David saw my predicament and squeezed himself between the pram and the terracotta-tiled wall. Together we awkwardly heaved the pram onto the small landing in front of the door, only to discover that the door swung outward and there wasn't enough room for both it and the pram in front of it.

'Ah well,' I said brightly, inwardly cursing the stairs, the restaurant, the pram and the people who had designed each of them. 'I guess we'll have to hold it up over the steps while we swing the door open.'

David hefted the pram and held it awkwardly out to his side as I swung the door open, trying to ignore the queue of men and women in business suits behind us. The pram hit the floor of the restaurant with more force than I had intended and I looked up into the startled eyes of the maitre d.

'I have a booking for Fletcher,' David said,

appearing not at all fazed by our undignified entrance.

The maitre d scanned the appointment book perched on the chrome lectern in front of him. 'Ah yes, please follow me,' he said, leading the way through the bright restaurant with its blond wood, starched white tablecloths and sparkling glassware.

I concentrated on not colliding with any of the tables we passed and tried to ignore the interested glances we were given by the other diners. We stopped at a table for four in the middle and a hovering waiter whipped away one of the chairs to make room for the pram.

As I settled back in my chair, I realised that I couldn't leave feeding Sarah much longer. But should I disappear into the toilets to feed her, which would mean leaving David twiddling his thumbs for twenty minutes or so? Or should I just feed her where I was?

I decided on the honest approach. 'David, I've got to feed Sarah. How would you feel if I did it here?'

'Sure,' he replied easily. 'Do you want me to call a waiter over and ask him to heat the milk?'

'Ah, no, it's actually already warm,' I said. 'You see, I breastfeed Sarah.'

'Oh, right,' said David uncomfortably. 'Sure, go ahead,' he said, with a bit less of his earlier bravado.

I pulled Sarah out of the pram and across my lap as David buried his head in the wine list. My discreet public feeding abilities were improving and I put a little pink cotton sheet over Sarah's head and my chest, unclipped my bra and started feeding. David looked up briefly and seemed surprised to see nothing but Sarah's legs sticking out from under the sheet. A look of relief spread across his face and I could only imagine he had been expecting me to throw off my shirt and bra and sit in the restaurant topless.

'Will you have some wine?' David asked.

'Sure,' I replied, hoping that no members of the Mother Police were within earshot.

A waiter approached to take the wine order and I leant forward to move Sarah into a more comfortable position. As I did, I dislodged a decidedly wet breast pad and it fell with a thwack on the floor at an equal distance between myself, David, the waiter and the two neighbouring tables. Seven sets of eyes looked at the white concave pad and then up at me, obviously not knowing what it was, but in no doubt that its presence on the floor was inappropriate. In a less stressful situation I would have sympathised with them, never having encountered a breast pad myself until Sarah was born.

I froze for what seemed like an eternity but was probably only a couple of seconds as I tried to figure out how to deal with the situation. Picking the breast pad up seemed like a good place to start, so I leant over to grab it, only to realise that with Sarah wedged between my chest and knees I couldn't reach it. I mentally ran through the possible options. I could detach Sarah from my breast and slide off my seat to pick it up – that seemed likely to produce a screaming baby and an exhibition of my newly acquired breasts. Alternatively, I could ask David or the waiter to get it for me – that didn't even bear thinking about. In a sudden fit of inspiration I stuck my foot out, secured the breast pad under my heel and dragged it towards me until it was close enough to pick up.

Grasping it in my hand, I realised that I still had to figure out what to do with it. Stuffing it back in my bra didn't seem like a good idea, nor did depositing it on the table, so I threw it into the basket under Sarah's pram.

Vainly I searched my mind for a witty comment that would relieve the tension and unfreeze this tableau of horrified expressions. The only thing that came to mind was a comparison with dropping condoms or tampons (until now something I'd thought of as the ultimate in embarrassment), which I decided could only make the situation worse. In desperation I smiled faintly and murmured an apology, which seemed to do the job. Conversation resumed at the neighbouring tables and David looked back at the menu to find the wine he'd planned to order.

As the waiter left I sneaked a look to see if David was still sitting there or was halfway to the door. To my surprise he was actually smiling, which gave me the courage to say, 'Well, I think we can safely say that Sarah and I are the last mother and baby team that will be let in here for the next ten years or so.'

David laughed. 'I think you could be right.'

Sarah finished feeding, and I reassembled my clothing and laid her back down in her pram without further incident. But when she closed her eyes, I didn't relax. Nothing had gone to plan so far and I didn't really expect that she would just fall into a blissful sleep now.

Every time someone scraped back a chair loudly or cutlery clattered, I tensed, all the while searching my mind for something vaguely interesting to say.

'How long will you be in Perth?' I asked. Not exactly inspired, but better than nothing.

'Just a few days,' David replied. 'I need to meet with the general manager of our Western Australian stores to figure out what we should be stocking for next season. I always enjoy my trips to Perth – it's such a laid-back city compared to Sydney and I'm lined up to crew on a boat race tomorrow.'

'I noticed the photo of the boat on your desk. Do you sail often?'

'Not as often as I'd like. I love to race but I have to travel a fair bit, which makes it hard to do regularly.'

'From memory it looks like a nice boat.'

He flashed a smile. 'You might regret saying that. I picked up the photos from our last race this morning and I haven't had a chance to open them yet – do you want a quick look?'

His enthusiasm was infectious and I nodded.

He produced a photo wallet from inside his suit jacket and broke the seal. He glanced at each photo before handing it to me with a glowing description.

'The boat's gorgeous,' I said, meaning it. 'The pattern on the spinnaker looks great.'

'Spinnaker? Sounds like you can sail.'

I nodded. 'I haven't raced much but my dad's a

mad keen sailor. We used to spend lots of weekends on the water in our eighteen-foot TrailerTri.'

'Lots of weekends' was definitely overstating my occasional nautical venture, I thought. But as I opened my mouth to set the record straight, David spoke.

'You should come out on *Aslan* sometime, then. In fact, our yacht club's annual fun race is on next weekend. Are you interested?'

Regretfully I shook my head. 'I'd love to, but I don't think Sarah is quite up to it yet. Maybe next time.'

David glanced at Sarah almost as if he'd forgotten she was there. 'I must admit, I've never seen a life jacket quite small enough. Sorry – I guess I do get a bit carried away when it comes to my boat.'

'Don't apologise. I'd love to go out when Sarah is a bit older.' As soon as the words were out of my mouth I regretted them.

A waiter arrived to take our orders. The breast pad incident hadn't given me time to check the menu. Glancing at it quickly I looked for meals that I could eat with one hand – in case I had to hold Sarah with the other. I ordered the risotto, mostly because it was the only dish that I could identify from the description.

'Is it just me or do you think that restaurants deliberately invent new and obscure names for ordinary ingredients?' I asked David as the waiter left. 'I eat out a lot, or did until Sarah arrived, and read the occasional food magazine but every time I open a menu at a place like this I have to guess what half of the things listed are.'

David laughed. 'I know what you mean,' he said. 'The last time I took a gamble and didn't ask a waiter what was in a dish, I ended up with lamb's brains in my pasta. Not something I'm dying to repeat.'

Sipping the very good riesling David had ordered, I felt myself relaxing. Sarah was fast asleep, I was sitting in a great restaurant with a surprisingly pleasant lunch companion, and it was looking as though our baby book venture might just work.

Discovering that we had tastes that were similar in books and opposite in movies, we chatted easily as we ate our meals.

'I must say I was surprised that Debbie stayed at Mr Cheapy as long as she did,' said David. 'It really didn't seem like her kind of thing.'

'That's something of an understatement,' I replied. 'Do you know her very well?' I asked, trying to fish subtly for information.

'Not really,' he replied. 'I've come across her in work situations a number of times and at a few social events, but that's all.'

Not from any lack of effort on Debbie's behalf, I thought to myself.

'From what I've heard, though, she's very good at her job,' David continued.

I nodded, 'I think she'll make a great partner.'

'And what about Sarah's father?' David asked in a sudden change of subject, obviously having noticed that I wasn't wearing a wedding ring. 'Is he involved in the business as well?'

'Sarah's father and I aren't together any more,' I replied. 'It's just Sarah and me.'

There was an awkward silence as both of us tried to think of what to say next. Thankfully the waiter chose that moment to take our dessert orders.

Both David and I just ordered coffee and moved back to safer topics of conversation. The time passed quickly and I was surprised when he said, 'Well, it's two-thirty. If I'm going to make my plane, I really need to get moving.'

'Yes, of course,' I said.

David signalled for the bill. When it arrived I tried to take it but he pushed my hand away firmly. 'Sophie, this is a business lunch and you're my guest; please let me get this.'

For some reason I felt deflated. Of course it was a business lunch. Why else would he be taking me and Sarah out? The man passed up *Debbie*, for heaven's sake – if he wouldn't entertain thoughts of infidelity with her, there was no chance for someone with a baby.

'Sarah's lunch manners are impeccable,' David continued, oblivious to my thoughts.

I decided not to disillusion him.

Stopping next to my car, David opened the door and stood beside me as I lifted Sarah out of the pram. She opened her eyes and I tensed, expecting her to cry. Instead she bestowed another beaming smile on David. Little hussy, I thought.

'Well, I'll talk to you next week.'

'Sounds good,' I replied as I straightened up and held out my hand to shake his. 'Have a good trip.'

Sliding into the front seat, I started the motor and pulled out into the traffic, wishing that our potential buyer wasn't quite so attractive and personable.

SIXTEEN

Debbie and I were seated at my kitchen table making plans for her trip when the phone rang.

'Hi, Sophie, it's Max.'

'Max . . . Hi,' I stuttered.

'I hope I'm not interrupting anything.'

'Ah, no,' I replied inanely.

'Listen, Sophie, I know it's short notice, but I wondered if you and Sarah felt like a picnic dinner.'

'A picnic?' I repeated, wondering vaguely when I was going to get my brain back.

'Yeah – I was thinking maybe Bondi. You don't need to worry about food, I'll deal with that.'

As I recovered from my surprise at hearing Max's voice, my anger that he'd disappeared so suddenly after seeing Sarah for the first time resurfaced. 'Look, Max. I haven't heard from you since you ran out of here three weeks ago. I didn't even know you were in the country, so a phone call asking me to go on a picnic isn't exactly what I was expecting.'

I could hear the strain in his voice as he replied. 'I know. I'm sorry. Why don't you have a think about it and give me a call back? I'm staying at the Park Hyatt – room 310.'

I paused. 'All right. I'll talk to you soon.'

'Bye,' he said softly as he hung up.

Debbie was staring at me as I replaced the receiver. 'I gather that was Max wanting to catch up?'

I nodded. 'Sunset picnic at Bondi. I really don't see the point.'

Debbie had obviously made up her mind about this before I had even got off the phone. 'You need to talk to him, Sophie. It's a beautiful day and it will do you both good.'

'Maybe you're right. I just wasn't expecting to have to deal with it today. Anyway, what about our business meeting?'

'There's not much more that we need to do. Call him back and tell him you can meet him at four. That gives us another few hours to finish what we're doing here.'

The prospect of a couple of hours at the beach did sound nice. I called Max back and was surprised to hear his relief at my decision.

Once our plans and budget were finalised, Debbie put her pen down and sat back. 'I now officially adjourn this meeting. You need to go and meet the father of your child. At least it's too cold to swim so you can't produce that damn swimming costume.'

Like ninety-eight per cent of the population, I used to only go swimwear shopping when my costume was practically falling off me, and even then I would go to extraordinary lengths to avoid looking at myself from behind in a mirror. But after years of being traumatised by swimwear shopping trips, I had come up with a technique which I was so proud of I had even considered patenting it.

It all began about three years before Sarah. I had braved the first day of the post–Christmas sales during my lunch hour and all around me was chaos as women of varying ages snatched up twenty different outfits and then locked themselves in the change rooms for the rest of the day. I was just about to leave when I spied a black two-piece in my size on sale for less than a third of the original price. Feeling reckless (and happy to find an excuse to skip the change rooms) I paid for it and took it home.

It turned out to be the best costume I had ever owned – even Debbie had approved. Debbie not only owns more than one costume, she has a matching wrap and shoes to go with each one. Not for her a beach towel slung over one shoulder. A visit to the beach is just another opportunity to reach the dizzy heights of fashion.

From then on, I bought exactly the same pair from the same shop at the start of every season (although admittedly at full price). I have vowed that I am going to keep doing this until the day I die. Although I live in terror that one day the manufacturers will change their design.

As was usual on a Sunday, the parking at Bondi was appalling and it was well after four by the time we arrived at the spot we'd arranged. Max, whom I spotted when we were still a distance away, seemed agitated, looking at his watch and then gazing towards the road.

'Hi. I'm glad you could make it,' he said when we reached him. He was talking to me, but his eyes slid to Sarah, who looked particularly cute in her pink corduroy overalls.

'It's a perfect evening for a picnic,' I said, trying to pretend that this was just an ordinary get-together and not our first family outing.

'It is,' he agreed as he shouldered the esky and hamper at his feet and we moved towards the grassy slope overlooking the beach. 'I hope you like what we're eating. Are you still obsessive about Manchetti's lime cheesecake? I convinced them to let me have two pieces to take away.'

'Now, come on. Some things might have changed since we were going out but you should know better than to think I wouldn't still kill for lime cheesecake.'

When we reached a clear space amongst the large, noisy families and chased away the seagulls, I spread out the old picnic blanket I had brought. As usual, Sarah was oblivious to the tension in the air, waving her arms in excitement at a sparrow on the ground. Her lack of awareness was just as well, I reflected, otherwise the situations I constantly found myself in would have made my daughter neurotic before she was three months old.

Max moved around setting up the picnic. First he opened a bottle of chilled wine and handed me a glass. Then he produced an antipasto platter heaped with stuffed mushrooms, olives, marinated tomatoes and cold meats.

When, to Debbie's great amusement, I'd drawn up my first-ever budget a couple of months before Sarah was born, I had been horrified to discover the amount I spent at the little delicatessen down the road. Luxuries such as those spread out before me didn't make it into my now home-brand-dominated shopping basket and it was only with great difficulty that I stopped myself from falling on delicacies I hadn't tasted in months. Sarah lay happily playing with her feet as Max and I ate the food, which, with the sea breeze blowing and the sun setting behind us, tasted delicious.

'So what brings you back to Sydney?' I asked.

'There was some follow-up work for the pitch I was here for last time, and the Sydney office wanted me to be involved,' Max replied. 'Look, Sophie, I'm sorry I ran out on you last time,' he blurted. 'The idea that Sarah was my child really freaked me out when I saw her. I've been feeling awful about how I reacted.'

'Having a baby hasn't been easy for me, you know. But running away isn't an option,' I replied tersely, unable to forgive him so easily.

'I know,' he said, looking genuinely upset. 'I realise I've handled this whole thing badly and I wouldn't blame you if you didn't want to see me again. All I can ask is that you'll give me another chance.'

Nothing could change the fact that Max was Sarah's father, and my dad's words about letting Max be involved had stayed with me. 'Okay,' I said slowly. 'I do want you to be able to spend time with Sarah. So let's just take it one step at a time.'

'Thanks,' he replied. 'Do you miss work?' he asked after a moment, in an obvious attempt to change the subject.

I thought about it. 'I certainly don't miss doing the work — all the stresses of coordinating everything and always something not going to plan. But I miss the buzz I used to get when we pulled off a big event.' Somehow the baby book venture still seemed like a pipedream and I decided not to mention it.

'Yeah, I know what you mean,' he said. 'You should see the performance that goes on in the San Francisco office when anyone does something big. There's a huge party at the bar across the road. Just about everyone ends up dancing on the tables and there's almost no work done the next day.'

'Sounds like my kind of office. Don't tell me that you dance on tables now? Two years we were together and I only saw you dance once.'

'I just figured, you know, when in Rome . . . The whole thing gets a bit exhausting after a while, though. In fact I've been thinking about coming home.'

'Wow. That's a big change. Would the company transfer you back?'

'I don't know.' Max hesitated for a moment and then went on. 'Do you remember the old guy who chased us off his farm one weekend? We were after some of his goat's cheese?'

'I do remember. How could I forget?'

'Turns out that someone in our Sydney office is his nephew or something. Don't even ask me how that came up in conversation. Apparently the old guy's planning to move up north to Queensland to retire and he wants to sell the farm.'

'And?' I couldn't quite fit Max into this picture.

'And I've been thinking about buying it.'

'What?'

'I know it sounds crazy, but I really think it could work. There's a full-time manager there already, and he doesn't want to leave. I could still live in Sydney during the week – maybe work four days or something, and then go to the farm on weekends. Just think of the great ad campaigns. Sydneysiders are into good food; I just need to tell them about it. I've seen the figures and it's a pretty stable business.'

My eyes widened in surprise. Even though owning a business in the country was something we'd talked about, I was stunned that Max was thinking about actually doing it. 'That's a huge change from living the high life in San Francisco. Can you afford it?'

'I met with a bank on Friday and I should hear next week whether they'll give me the loan. They seemed pretty positive, though.'

'That's great. I hope it works out for you,' I said, not sure that I really meant it.

Max turned to Sarah and began to talk to her. 'So. Do you think your mummy might like some cheesecake now? It's her favourite in the entire world. What was that? You don't think she would? Well we wouldn't like her to feel obliged, would we? Maybe we should just leave it in the esky?'

Sarah seemed to think the whole thing was pretty funny, but I punched Max in the arm and pulled out the cheesecake myself. True to his word, it was genuine Manchetti cheesecake and it tasted even better outdoors.

I looked over at Max. His face was much closer than I had expected, and almost as if by accident his lips brushed mine. His breath was warm and tasted of wine, and his lips felt exactly as I remembered. The kiss lasted only a second or two, but it made me forget that I was fine all on my own and that Sarah and I didn't need anybody's help. Suddenly I could think of nothing more wonderful than to curl up on Max's chest and let him sort everything out.

But then our lips separated, we moved apart and the spell was broken.

Max's face came towards me once more. I thought he was going to kiss me again, but instead he put his mouth to my ear and whispered, 'I've missed you, Sophie.'

And with that, leaving me dazed and confused, he sat up and started to stack the platters and glasses as if nothing had happened.

Without a word we packed up the picnic and stood up.

'I guess I'll see you later,' I said, desperate to say something to break the uneasy silence that had fallen.

'I'll call you,' Max said.

'Sure,' I replied, not really believing him, and headed to the car with Sarah without looking back.

SEVENTEEN

My growing library of baby manuals conflicted widely about when you should first give a baby solid food. One book said that if Sarah had anything other than milk for her first six months, she would have a much greater likelihood of being obese later.

Talk about a guilt trip. As well as worrying about turning my child into a responsible, non-drug-taking adult, now it seemed her waist size was my problem too.

Flicking to the end of the second book in the pile on the coffee table, I ran my finger down the index. 'Feet, inward turning', 'Follicles, clogging'. I shook my head, convinced that these books could turn a well-balanced and confident mother into a paranoid stress ball.

Locating 'Food, when to' I turned to page 252 as directed but the commentary was vague and I couldn't find any enlightenment about exactly when I should start.

Snapping the book shut, I decided to consult my most reliable reference material – Karen.

'Karen,' I pleaded as soon as she answered the phone, 'I need some adult contact and some advice. Could I drop around?'

'Sure,' she replied. 'As long as you can live with some minor pandemonium. Emily has two friends over and they're charging around the house like demons.'

As I'd spent the morning in the house with Sarah, pandemonium sounded like a welcome change.

Swinging my 'MacGyver Bag' (as Debbie insisted on calling it, given that she was convinced I could pull something out of it to cover any eventuality) onto my shoulder and sticking my sunglasses on my head, I picked up Sarah and headed out.

As Karen opened her front door, three figures darted out from behind her and raced past me.

'Sorry, Sophie,' she apologised as I blinked in surprise. 'Sam took Emily to the movies on the weekend and every time I walk around a corner I come across her pointing a gun at me and yelling, "Freeze!" Anyway, come in.'

Once we were inside, Karen reached over and took Sarah from me. 'Hello, sweetheart,' she said, balancing Sarah in the crook of her arm in a way I still hadn't mastered. Sarah rewarded Karen with a smile as I followed them into the kitchen, which was the nerve centre of the Jackson household.

It took up the entire front corner of the house and the morning sun streamed in the big windows, lighting up the marble benchtops and forming puddles of light on the huge pine table.

Pat, Karen's youngest, was in a highchair at the end of the table and with great concentration was smearing his piece of Vegemite-coated bread across the armrests. Kissing him on the head (about the only part of his body not covered in black paste), I seated myself beside him.

Karen propped Sarah in a corner of the big yellow armchair next to the window and gave her a rattle. 'Emily and co shouldn't be able to stomp on her there,' she said. 'Right, coffee?'

I nodded vigorously and Karen moved across to turn on the chrome coffee machine on the corner of the bench. When she had finally accepted that the pain factor of taking Emily to a coffee shop far outweighed the enjoyment she got from the experience, she had bought a top-of-the-range coffee machine and tried to grab at least ten minutes to herself each day to sit in the yellow armchair, read the newspaper and drink her coffee.

While I still loved the time I spent with my childless friends, I definitely felt more relaxed in Karen's busy house where a crying baby or a leaking nappy weren't even worth mentioning. Karen twisted the knob on the side of the coffee machine and it made a comforting hissing noise as she began steaming the milk.

'So what was the advice you needed?' she asked.

'I'm trying to figure out when I should start giving Sarah solid food,' I said.

'Oh, damn. Is that all?' she replied, obviously disappointed. 'You know that as a happily married woman I need to live through you. I was hoping you had a torrid sexual dilemma for me.'

'Okay, okay,' she continued on seeing my expression. 'You've probably been stressed out by the books telling you that you can cause all kinds of lifelong problems for your children if you start feeding them at the wrong time or feed them the wrong foods.'

'Exactly,' I nodded.

'Well, forget it,' Karen said as she put the coffee cups under the machine and pressed the button to half fill them with coffee. 'As far as I can see from my tireless research at years of playgroups, it doesn't matter a bit. Just do it when you feel like it, although, trust me, the novelty wears off very quickly,' she added, nodding at Pat who was now pulling his bread into pieces and dropping them over the side of his chair. 'But on to more interesting topics. How was your weekend?'

I'd been trying to put Max out of my mind but it was no use. While my situation probably didn't qualify as a 'torrid sexual dilemma', it was certainly something I needed to talk to someone about.

'I saw Max yesterday,' I said, spooning sugar into the coffee she had set in front of me and stirring it absently. 'We had a picnic at Bondi and it was just like old times. He brought loads of great food and a nice bottle of wine and we sat and talked for a couple of hours.'

'And?' Karen pressed, sensing there was more.

'He kissed me.'

Karen breathed out in a soundless whistle and looked intently at me. 'And?' she asked again.

'And I kissed him back,' I said. 'God, Karen, I don't know what to think. I was starting to convince myself that I was getting over him, but now I don't know.'

'How was he with Sarah?'

'He seemed really taken with her. He kept looking at her and talking to her. But nothing has changed. The only reason he's over here is because of work. Kissing me doesn't change the fact that he doesn't want a proper relationship and doesn't want to be a father.'

'Is he enjoying San Francisco?' Karen asked.

'I think so,' I said. 'His work is going well and it sounds like he's living life pretty hard socially.'

Now that I'd started talking about Max, I didn't seem able to stop.

'I've thought about it a lot,' I continued, 'and I figure that even if Max vowed undying love to me now and said he wanted Sarah too, it still wouldn't work. He's lived happily without me for a year and didn't even know what Sarah looked like or what we were doing until he arrived in town for his pitch three weeks ago.'

'Are you going to see him again?'

I shrugged and went to pick up Sarah, who had grown bored with looking around the kitchen.

'Who knows. I don't think even Max knows what he wants. It'll probably be best for all of us when he goes home. Although he's talking about moving back here to buy a farm.'

'That's something the two of you talked about from time to time, isn't it?' Karen recalled.

'Yes,' I answered miserably.

'Back to food,' said the ever-sensitive Karen, changing the subject. 'I'll bet you've been given at least one book of recipes for babies.'

'Yeeess . . .' I answered cautiously, not sure where she was leading.

'Let me save you hours in the kitchen,' she said. 'I guarantee that whatever book you've been given was written by a woman who was a gourmet cook and determined that her child wouldn't eat boring food. So she adapted her recipes to suit her children and serves them things like asparagus and chicken risotto and Mediterranean couscous. But she'll promise you that it takes no time at all and that the recipes will produce enough to feed your child for a week.'

Karen paused and then narrowed her eyes. 'Don't believe a word of it. I got the guilts after months of feeding Emily various combinations of mushed vegetables, and so tried a couple of those recipes. They took me hours and I managed to use every pan in the house, and to add insult to injury, Emily wouldn't have a bar of them. So I went back to the boring basics and now I have trouble keeping Emily away from all the olives, anchovies and capers in the fridge.'

'Potato and pumpkin it is,' I laughed, once again comforted by Karen's practicality.

Later, as I turned back to wave goodbye to Karen, who was standing in the doorway watching me leave, her eyes suddenly widened in surprise. She smiled ruefully as she raised her hands in surrender and turned back into the house, trailed by three little girls with their guns pressed firmly in her back.

EIGHTEEN

Despite the fact that I was thirty and had a baby, I still couldn't quite get past feeling that spending Friday nights at home meant that I had become a social outcast. To make things even sadder, my father had taken to calling me on Friday nights. Although I'd never asked him why, I was pretty sure it was because he figured he would always find me in.

The terrible television programs on Friday nights just added to my paranoia. The only conclusion I could reach was that I must be the sole person in Australia home regularly on Friday nights, otherwise there would be a viewers' uprising at the number of times one of the sixteen *Lethal Weapon* movies was rerun.

Despite the 'entertainment', I had developed a Friday-night ritual that made me feel at least a little as though I was still capable of celebrating the weekend. As soon as I put Sarah to bed, I'd pour myself a glass of wine, open up a bag of cheese and onion potato chips, and lie on the couch to plan my woeful television viewing.

I was just in the middle of deciding whether I could stomach yet another do-it-yourself program, when the phone rang.

'Hello, Sophie. It's David Fletcher.'

'Uh, hi, David. How are you?' I stammered in surprise. He had called a couple of days earlier to ask me if we could get him a finished product and firm prices within two weeks. He was confident that if we could, he would be able to do a deal for four thousand books. I hadn't expected to hear from him again until our deadline, and certainly not on a Friday night.

'Fine, thanks. I'm pleased I caught you in.'

There was no need to enlighten him about my standing date with a packet of chips. Instead I made a noncommittal noise, which I hoped he would interpret as meaning that there was some degree of luck in my being there to answer the phone.

He started speaking again but the background noises were so loud I could hardly hear him. I could only make out a few words, none of which made much sense. 'Late . . . Tomorrow . . . Broken thumb.'

'David,' I interrupted, almost shouting until I remembered Sarah upstairs. 'I can't hear you. Where are you? You sound like you're in the middle of a circus.'

'Hang . . . second,' he said, obviously moving to a quieter spot.

'Sorry, I'm just heading in to see *Bohemia* and it is absolute chaos.'

I had never heard of *Bohemia*, which wasn't surprising given that I didn't exactly have my finger on the entertainment pulse of Sydney. 'Is that the new Julia Roberts movie?' I asked, vaguely recollecting an article I'd skimmed in the newspaper the week before.

There was a brief silence while he obviously chose his words carefully. 'Um . . . no, it's the Australian Ballet's latest production. Tonight is opening night.'

'Right,' I muttered, deciding not to try to explain how I'd totally missed all the publicity that must have accompanied such an event.

I couldn't quite think of anything to say next, but fortunately, David continued. 'Listen, I'm really sorry to call you on a Friday night but I'm desperate and thought you might be able to help. My yacht club's annual fun race is on tomorrow. But I've just had a call from my race partner. He's broken his thumb and can't do it.'

'Right.' Stop saying that, I thought desperately.

'I've tried calling everyone else I can think of but they're either racing themselves or busy. You seemed to know a fair bit about sailing at lunch the other day. I know it's late notice, and you told me it wouldn't work with Sarah, but I wondered if you could possibly sail with me?'

'Um.' Oh yes, I thought to myself, that was a huge conversational improvement.

'I know it's a lot to ask, but I'm really in a jam. Is there someone you could leave her with for a few hours?'

'Well, yes.' Karen had felt so guilty that I'd had to

236

take Sarah to my meeting with David that she'd made me promise to leave Sarah with her for a few hours sometime soon.

'Do you have something planned?'

'Well, no.' At least I'd moved onto two-syllable answers, I thought forlornly.

I couldn't bring myself to tell David that I'd been so desperate to change the subject after the breast pad incident, that I'd somewhat overstated my boating experience. 'David, I'd love to, it's just that I haven't sailed for years. I'd hate to make you lose.'

'Nonsense,' he replied, obviously thinking that I was just being modest. 'Let's meet at the marina an hour before the race and I'll run you through everything. Thanks, Sophie, I really appreciate this.'

As I hung up I realised that at no point had I actually agreed to race. I made a mental note never to try to negotiate with David – he was clearly not a man who heard no very often.

I wondered how David's girlfriend felt about him calling up strange women and asking them to race with him. She was probably racing on another boat and would be delighted for him to be saddled with a liability like me, I decided.

Despite what I had led David to believe, I had only been in one sailing race in my life and that was in the ten-year-old category in Brisbane. The whole experience was a bit of a blur, but I did have a vague memory of an enormous boat almost running over me after I lost control of my tiny dingy at the first marker. Not surprisingly, I hadn't been keen to repeat the experience and had taken up hockey instead. I hadn't exactly made the national team in that either, but I had figured that at least I was unlikely to drown.

I did what I always do when I'm in a tight spot. I called my father. I couldn't imagine Dad not being on the other end of the phone whenever I called. Although he kept insisting that it had been nothing, his heart attack had made me very aware that he was getting older.

'Darling. How are you? How's Sarah?'

One of the great things about talking to Dad was that nothing Sarah did was too minor to be celebrated. The big news this week was that she had rolled over for the first time.

'How's my genius granddaughter? Walking yet?'

Having spent quite some time describing Sarah's latest manifestation of genius, I briefly filled Dad in on my sailing dilemma. I was always grateful that Dad never asked if I'd heard from Max and, true to form, he didn't ask any questions about David either.

He talked me through a typical race and what I would be required to do. It seemed it was most likely to be a class race, which meant we'd be competing with boats of a similar size.

Apparently, as a new crew member I was most likely to be handling the ropes (or 'sheets', as Dad insisted I start calling them).

'Remember, if you want to look like you know what you're doing, follow the skipper's instructions exactly,' were his last words before we said goodbye.

★

So I knew I was in trouble when, during the final leg of the race the following afternoon, I found myself rummaging around in the bowels of the boat unable either to see or hear David.

Up to that point, the race had been surprisingly good fun. David had met me at the marina walkway and given me a rundown on how things would proceed. He assumed that I knew what he was talking about, and my occasional nods seemed to be all that was necessary.

I mentally blessed my father when David asked me if I'd be happy to handle the sheets. I'd figured out without any major calamities what I had to do and, despite the fast pace, actually enjoyed the first half of the race. Completely forgetting I couldn't actually sail, I started having fantasies of buying my own boat and teaching Sarah to sail. David obviously loved being on the water and his excitement was contagious. Apparently, the deal for this race was that all the losing boats were to pool together and buy the winner a case of expensive champagne. As a result, the rivalry was more intense than usual.

These boats had been racing against each other for years, and the catcalls and heckles echoing across the water only added to the atmosphere. So when David suddenly started shouting instructions at me as we approached the mark around which we had to turn for the final leg, I was brought back to reality with a thud.

'Okay, this is the bit that separates the men from the boys,' he yelled. Bearing Dad's instructions in mind, I didn't question him about the political correctness of his expression. 'The wind will be behind us once we've changed course, which means we can use a spinnaker to take us in.'

Unable to add anything, I just nodded and tried to look intelligent.

'We won't have time to change it once it's up so we need to pick the right spinnaker now. I can feel a change coming in the wind. I reckon it's going to freshen and swing around to our port side. What do you think?'

'Ah . . . Yes, I think you're right,' I said with a conviction I didn't feel. There was certainly no way I was going to disagree with him.

'Okay. We'll need the small spinnaker. Go down to the front hatch and grab it. We need to have it up just as we reach the mark.'

He was back in businessman mode and it was less a question than a command. Reluctantly, I headed down below.

Dad had also warned me that because the wind was so unpredictable, things could change suddenly in a race. I knew that a spinnaker was the big, pretty sail that went at the front (bow, I corrected myself mentally), but why we needed a small one was a mystery. There seemed to be canvas bags of varying colours everywhere and I had no idea which was the right one.

'It's the one in the red bag.' I could only just make out David's words through the wind, but I could clearly hear the impatience in his voice. He added something else but I couldn't hear him. I looked around frantically and finally saw an edge of red canvas poking out from behind some other bags.

When I emerged from the cockpit, I saw that the competition had changed dramatically. About half the boats in the race had dropped behind us, but three were well ahead and were just about at the mark.

As I watched, the first boat made the turn and I could see its spinnaker unfurl, creating a beautiful splash of colour. As soon as the big sail filled, the boat leapt even further ahead.

'We need the spinnaker up now!' David was almost shouting, the frustration showing on his face. 'Here, you take the tiller and I'll do it – I'll be quicker.'

As he glanced down at the bag I saw him wince. 'This is the wrong spinnaker,' he shouted through the wind. 'It'll be too big. When the wind picks up, the whole thing will blow out.'

The mark was now only about six boat lengths away and closing fast. There was no time to find the other spinnaker even if I'd known what I was looking for – I'd obviously blown it. All the fun had gone out of the afternoon.

Suddenly David turned, hauled the bag up to the bow and attached the spinnaker.

He turned to me and with a wicked smile shouted, 'Here we go. It'll either kill us or cure us!'

I tried not to think about how much a new spinnaker was worth and managed a tense smile back.

As we reached the mark, David called, 'Ready about – lee-ho!' (At the earlier marks I had once again blessed my father for preparing me for this.)

I pushed the tiller away from me, which brought the nose of the boat around so that the wind was behind us.

The spinnaker filled with wind and it felt as though Moby Dick himself had come up behind us and started pushing. Our spinnaker was at least double the size of those of the other boats and we quickly overtook the one in front. Within about another twenty boat lengths, we overtook the next yacht and suddenly found ourselves in second place.

There was no time for celebration, though, as *Aslan* was travelling at a very precarious angle and felt to me like she could flip over at any second. Suddenly, just when I was sure we were going to be tipped into the water, the wind eased a little and the boat slowed, returning to a healthier angle.

David's triumphant cry made the crew of the boat ahead turn around. The lighter wind meant that their smaller spinnaker wasn't able to keep pace and we edged past them just before the finish line.

David's ear-to-ear grin didn't look like dimming any time soon as he pulled the spinnaker down. 'That was fantastic! I have to confess, though, I really thought we were going to go over.'

I nodded. I'd been prepared for absolute disaster – a ripped spinnaker, capsized boat and a very annoyed business colleague – and I hadn't quite taken in the abrupt turnaround of events.

We motored back to the marina in the midst of the other boats, whose crews shouted their grudging congratulations, some asking whether they could recruit me, figuring I was David's secret weapon. If only they knew, I thought, trying to look as though I'd expected no other result.

As we tied up in the berth, David looked at his watch. 'Our timing couldn't be more perfect. The club bar opened ten minutes ago – fancy cracking open some of our champagne with our opponents?'

I looked at my watch with regret. 'I'd love to, but I can't. I need to be back by five so that Karen can get away – I'm already running late. Have a glass or two for me.'

For an instant I resented having to go home and miss the celebrations, then immediately felt guilty for feeling that way. 'I'll do better than that,' David smiled, then added, 'how about we catch up some-time to share some of the champagne? After all, I certainly couldn't have done it without you.'

'Sounds great.' I felt a small stab of excitement. Surely his interest couldn't just be business, but then how did his girlfriend fit into the picture?

'Excellent,' David replied. 'I'm off to Hong Kong next week for a trade show but I'll give you a call when I get back.'

At his mention of the trade show, my stomach dropped. We should have realised David would be there too. But it would look pretty strange if he ran into Debbie when we were supposed to have our suppliers all sorted out.

'You might see Debbie while you're over there,' I replied as casually as I could. David looked surprised and I hurried on, making it up as I went along. 'Our supplier has to be there, so it seemed the logical place to meet them and finalise the shipment of the covers.'

243

'That makes sense,' David acknowledged. 'Well, anyway,' he flashed that smile at me again, 'thanks for helping out.'

He refused my offer to help clean the boat down and I headed for the car park, relishing the feeling of the salt in my hair and the sun on my back.

NINETEEN

'Debbie, tell me you're kidding,' I exclaimed into the telephone the following morning. 'You can't have chickenpox. You're thirty-one, for God's sake. No one gets chickenpox at thirty-one.'

'Do you think I'd joke about something like this?' Debbie replied. 'I have itchy red spots all over my body, a headache that rivals those of some of my hangovers and I feel like I could sleep for a week. The doctor told me that when adults get chickenpox they have a much worse time than children do. He said I should smear some disgusting white cream all over myself and stay in bed for at least the next five days. He nearly jumped down my throat when I asked if he thought I'd be all right to fly to Hong Kong on Tuesday.'

'This is an absolute disaster,' I said in despair. 'The pages are looking great but if you can't find the covers there's no way we'll be ready for the meeting with David.'

'You're right, Sophie, which is why you have to go,' Debbie said forcefully.

'What?' I said. 'Be serious, Debbie, you know I can't leave Sarah.'

'So take her,' Debbie replied. 'I know it's not ideal, but if we can't line up those covers in the next week we may as well kiss the deal with Handley Smith goodbye.'

'Debbie, it's not just "not ideal", it's a nightmare – just picture me trying to get around Hong Kong and do a deal with a manufacturer with Sarah in tow.'

'I really think it's possible,' Debbie insisted. 'The trade fair is at the big conference centre in the middle of town and I've already booked a room at the Grand Hyatt, which is right next door – using my frequent flyer points, before you ask. You could go straight from the airport to the hotel and just walk to the trade fair. If you don't want to you don't have to go anywhere else. Sarah already has a passport so you can take her to visit your father. Just think of this as a warm-up for the flight to London.'

Much as the thought of a buying trip to Asia with Sarah daunted me, I had to agree with what Debbie had said. We were both excited about the prospects for this deal and it would be hugely disappointing to see it slip by.

'You're right,' I decided suddenly. 'I've always said that I wouldn't let a baby dictate my life. We can't let this all fall apart now because I'm too scared to try.'

Now that I'd made the decision, I felt a touch of excitement. It was years since I'd been overseas and I realised that in less than forty-eight hours I would be in Hong Kong, a city I'd wanted to visit since reading James Clavell's *Noble House*. David would be at the trade fair too, and I couldn't suppress a feeling of anticipation at the thought of seeing him again.

Pushing the prospect of an overnight flight with a small baby to the back of my mind, I focused on what I would have to do before I left.

'All right, Deb,' I said. 'Can you stop scratching for long enough to tell me who I should talk to and what I need to do?'

'Absolutely,' she said. 'Grab a pen.'

For the next thirty minutes Debbie gave me a rundown on what I needed to do at the trade fair. After finishing our final topic – what I should wear – I called the airline to cancel Debbie's ticket and arrange new ones. Knowing that Debbie would never ask for help, I also made a quick call to Andrew, letting him know what was happening and that Debbie would be on her own. He lived near Debbie and promised to check on her while I was away.

Sarah had been watching all of this from her play gym (which wasn't quite as active as the name suggested). 'Well, darling,' I said, picking her up and waltzing her around the room in time to the music on the radio. 'You and I are off to Hong Kong!'

As I struggled down the plane with Sarah in one arm and my overstuffed shoulder bag banging against each seat, I noticed that none of my fellow passengers would meet my eyes. I could almost hear the silent chant, 'Please don't let her sit next to me, please don't let her sit next to me.'

I paused beside one seat to pull my boarding card out of the back pocket of my trousers and check my seat number. As I moved on, a look of pure relief spread over the face of the man I'd stopped next to. Finally I found my seat, which was by the aisle in a row of four. Everyone in sight (other than the three people already sitting in the row) visibly relaxed, while the lucky three next to me immediately craned their heads to see if they could spot a spare seat to escape to.

As I sat down, Sarah decided that it would be an appropriate time not only to dirty her nappy but to do it at a volume loud enough to be heard at the back of the plane. All those heads that were busily looking elsewhere suddenly snapped back towards us. Everyone had obviously concluded that such a loud noise could not possibly come from a being as tiny as Sarah and that, as well as my social ineptness at daring to take a baby on an overseas flight, I also had serious personal hygiene issues.

After briefly toying with the idea of standing up and showing the whole plane the evidence in Sarah's nappy, I decided to pretend that it hadn't happened and deal with getting myself sorted out for the flight. As I did so, a passing flight attendant saw the bag at my feet and picked it up to put it in the overhead locker.

'No!' I yelled in panic.

She paused with the bag in midair. Pulling myself together, I said as calmly as I could manage,

'I'm sorry but I need some of the things in there for the takeoff.'

'Fine,' she said frostily as she replaced the bag on the floor, and I cursed myself for having managed to get her offside before we'd even left the ground.

Balancing Sarah on one knee, I rummaged around in the bag with my spare hand to try to find all the things I might possibly need. Karen had told me that feeding a baby during takeoff and landing was the best way to avoid a screaming session caused by the pressure on their ears, and I'd spent the whole day working towards timing Sarah's feed for takeoff. Thankfully, we left on schedule and Sarah fed happily during the whole process, only finishing as we levelled out and the seatbelt sign was switched off.

I decided that I could no longer ignore Sarah's nappy and, standing up, grabbed my bag from the overhead locker where the flight attendant had put it just before takeoff, after very pointedly asking me if I had finished with it. Sarah, the bag and I just fitted through the narrow toilet door and I pulled down the baby change table that hinged onto the wall over the toilet and laid Sarah across it. After changing her nappy, I tried to figure out exactly how I could go to the toilet myself, given that the change table would have to be folded up, which meant that I would have to hold Sarah at the same time.

IQ tests have never been one of my favourite things, but after a couple of minutes pondering the situation, I managed to figure out a way to execute the manoeuvre, discovering as I did so the evolutionary reason why women's ligaments and joints become looser during pregnancy. It is not to facilitate childbirth, as is commonly believed, but actually to enable a woman to perform the otherwise physically impossible act of going to the toilet in an aeroplane cubicle with a baby in her arms.

By the time I returned to my seat, a flight attendant had hooked a baby bassinette onto the bulkhead in front of my seat. I settled Sarah into it and, to my delight, the hum of the plane and the vibrations seemed to soothe her, as she immediately closed her eyes and went to sleep.

Resisting the urge to high-five the flight attendant walking past, I instead took two of the Hong Kong immigration forms she was distributing. The 'occupation' section on the form gave me some problems. There was no way that I could see to fit 'I used to be a high-powered executive but am now caring for my daughter and investigating business opportunities,' into the space for twelve characters. After chewing the end of my pen for a few minutes, I became aware that the man next to me was peering at my form, obviously trying to figure out what was causing me so much trouble. Reminding myself that the Hong Kong immigration officials weren't going to be making judgments on my lifestyle choice, I quickly wrote 'mother', before signing the form and putting it away in my handbag.

After glancing through the entertainment section in the in-flight magazine, I decided that sleep was more important than having an uninspiring airline meal and watching a movie I didn't want to see. I pushed my chair back, closed my eyes and drifted off, only dimly aware of the noise as the flight attendants served and collected drinks and meals.

When I heard Sarah's rustling several hours later, the plane was dark and silent. I picked her up, fed her and laid her back down in her bassinette. She went to sleep and stayed that way until the rattle of the breakfast trolleys woke both of us an hour out of Hong Kong.

As I settled Sarah on my lap for her morning feed, I felt a lot of eyes on us. I looked up, expecting more of the malevolent stares from the evening before, only to see about ten beaming faces.

'What a wonderful little boy,' gushed the man sitting next to me, who had not uttered one word last night.

'Thanks,' I said uncertainly. 'Although she's actually a girl.'

'Wasn't he good during the night?' added the woman across the aisle. 'I didn't hear a peep out of him.'

'She's a good sleeper,' I said, emphasising the 'she'. 'Although this is her first plane trip, so I didn't really know what to expect.'

'Well, I think he is adorable,' said a woman from the row behind who was peering over the seat at us.

I didn't know what to make of all this. Last night Sarah and I were pariahs, and now, after she had slept all night, we were the best things since sliced bread. Sarah obviously felt the glare of all the attention and stopped feeding. As I sat her up, she vomited a full stomach of milk over herself, down the front of my shirt and into my lap. At least that got rid of the onlookers.

Blessing Karen, who had insisted that I take a change of clothing for myself as well as for Sarah, I squelched into the toilet where, after a few Houdiniesque contortions, I managed to get both Sarah and myself into clean outfits.

As I walked back to my seat the captain announced that we were commencing our descent. I'd been disappointed when I'd heard that the legendary descent into Hong Kong amongst apartment buildings and office blocks no longer existed as the airport had moved away from town, but the view I glimpsed was still magnificent.

My heart sank as I felt warm liquid seeping through the top of my trousers. I looked down to see that Sarah had managed to be sick again, this time only on me. Unfortunately, the contents of my bag did not stretch to two changes of outfits and I resigned myself to staying sodden until we reached the hotel.

It may have been the fact that I had a baby, or that I had borrowed Debbie's matching luggage, but something obviously convinced the airport officials that Sarah and I weren't drug traffickers. I suddenly felt very grown up as they nodded us through without any flicker of suspicion.

The train to the city was waiting as Sarah and I stepped onto the platform behind the arrivals area and it left as soon as I'd sat down. Within twenty-five minutes we were in the steamy heart of the city, and twenty minutes after that we were in our room at the Grand Hyatt.

Sarah fell asleep in the cot the hotel had provided and I decided to take advantage of the quiet and have a quick nap too. I'd arrived the day before the trade fair was to start, and so once Sarah woke we hit the streets.

People had told me that the thing which struck them first about Hong Kong was the smell of money. There were certainly a lot of different smells floating around as we joined the throngs on the footpath, although I wasn't convinced that money was one of them. After spending a couple of minutes trying to figure out which side people walked on, I came to the conclusion there were no rules and just followed on the heels of the person in front of me. I was very thankful that I'd decided to put Sarah in her sling and so didn't have to manoeuvre a pram through the mass of humanity on both sides of the street.

Sarah and I took the Star Ferry from Hong Kong Island across the harbour to the bustling madness that was Kowloon. Wandering through the maze of streets, I passed Chinese medicine shops with barrels of dried objects, the identity of which I could only guess at, and street markets selling haunches of meat, live fish and types of fruit and vegetables I'd never seen before.

When I felt hungry, I stopped for a bowl of noodles at a little shop I was sure I wouldn't be able to find again even if I had a month to do so. My noodles were very tasty but I didn't want to dwell too long on what was in them, having been unable to communicate at all with the man behind the counter and deciding that this was a time when ignorance was indeed bliss.

We went back to the hotel for a siesta and then,

once rested, headed out again, catching a tram which climbed perilously up the side of the mountain just behind the business district to what was unimaginatively known as the Peak. The day was fine and clear and the view was amazing. Sipping a cappuccino on the balcony of a coffee shop at the top, I gazed down at the sprawl of the city at my feet and across the busiest harbour in the world to the rows of buildings on the other side, which were backed by a circle of blue mountains.

By the time I made it back to the hotel, fed and bathed Sarah and had a shower, it was seven p.m. and I was starving. While the thought of room service tempted me momentarily, I decided this was not an acceptable option in a new city and changed into a pair of black trousers and a tailored purple shirt. I pulled a little red velvet dress – a present from Debbie – over Sarah's head, ran a brush through my hair and together we headed out to see what Hong Kong had to offer at night.

The concierge told me that there was a bar on the top floor of the hotel and, on walking in, I saw that it had spectacular views. Sarah and I settled on a sofa right next to the double-storey plate-glass windows and I ordered a Bloody Mary from the hovering barman. This had always been my standard tactic whenever I found myself alone in a bar. Times had changed, though, and I couldn't help but think that I didn't look quite as sophisticated with a baby in a pram beside me.

I took a sip of my drink and settled back to admire the lights on the buildings ranged across the other side of the harbour. The trade fair started at nine in the morning and I decided that I would have a quick meal at one of the Chinese restaurants near the hotel and then go to bed early, so that I was prepared to deal with whatever faced me tomorrow.

My drink was almost finished when I heard a familiar voice behind me. 'I need to see some ID for you ladies. We've had some reports that the blonde in the red dress is underage.'

I'd decided against calling David to tell him I would be coming to Hong Kong, thinking that to do so would look as though I was angling for an invitation to meet up (which, if I was honest with myself, would have been the truth). Since we'd arrived, I'd been half expecting to see him and I felt a leap in my stomach as I turned and saw him smiling down at me.

'What are you doing here, Sophie? I thought Debbie was coming to the trade show.'

'Believe it or not, Debbie broke out with chickenpox three days ago, so Sarah and I are her emergency replacements,' I answered.

David laughed involuntarily and then stopped himself. 'Sorry,' he apologised. 'Chickenpox isn't funny. It's just that it's such an . . . unglamorous illness. I'll bet that's upsetting Debbie as much as the symptoms.'

'You're right,' I smiled. 'She's convinced she caught it from her last store visit before she left Mr Cheapy. She said the place was full of mothers with snivelling babies and that she could just about feel the germs settling all over her.'

'It's a pretty big undertaking bringing Sarah all

this way,' said David. 'Did she handle the flight all right?'

'She slept the whole way. And we've had a great day today exploring the place.'

'Oh, so you flew over last night, did you?' he asked. 'That explains why I didn't see you on the plane. I caught the day flight up and just got here half an hour ago.'

David wouldn't have seen us even if we had been on the same flight, I thought, sure that he would have been sitting at the front of the plane in business class, a respectable distance from the hordes crammed into economy. Figuring that pointing this out to him would only make me sound bitter and twisted, I decided to let it slide.

'Would you like to stay for a drink? I can vouch for the Bloody Marys,' I suggested, my voice sounding a lot more casual than I felt.

'Thanks for the offer, but I'm heading out for dinner with a supplier,' he replied. 'I just dropped in here to check out the view before I left. But do you have any plans for tomorrow night?'

'Oh well . . . Sarah and I thought we'd have a bit of a girls' night,' I joked. 'You know, drink some beer, do a couple of tequila shots, see if we can tag along with a hen's party or two. The usual things.'

David laughed. 'Delightful as that sounds, I do believe I have a better idea. Have you ever heard of Felix?'

I shook my head. 'Only the cat.'

'Felix is a restaurant on the Kowloon side of Hong Kong. You shouldn't die without visiting it. I actually wanted to go there tonight, but decided it would be wasted on the people I'm seeing. Now I've got the perfect excuse. Why don't you come with me?'

His invitation caught me off-guard. 'That sounds great,' I replied impulsively.

As soon as the words were out of my mouth I realised what a bad idea it was. Not only would it not work with Sarah, there was also the small matter of his girlfriend.

'Sorry, David. I forgot for a moment that I'm a mother. From the sound of this place, Sarah's presence would definitely not be cool. Maybe another time?'

'Would you be happy leaving her with a baby-sitter here?' David asked carefully. 'I'd have my mobile phone so they could call us if there was any problem.'

Sarah slept from seven until early morning these days, so it was possible, but I didn't think I could enjoy myself if I'd left her with someone I didn't know when I wasn't close by. My thoughts obviously showed on my face, as David spoke again while I was still choosing my words.

'All right, here's another option. Felix is in the Peninsula Hotel. What about if I speak to them about arranging a babysitter there?'

It sounded like the perfect solution. Pushing the girlfriend to the back of my mind (and the thought of how much a babysitter might cost in a town that charged fifteen dollars for a Bloody Mary), I smiled broadly. 'That sounds great.'

'Excellent,' he said, looking at his watch as he

stood up. 'I'm late so I've got to go, but how about I pick you and Sarah up from your room tomorrow night at, say, seven?'

'Fine,' I replied. 'We're in room 1708.'

'I think you and I have a date for tomorrow night,' I whispered to Sarah as I watched David walk out of the bar towards the lifts.

TWENTY

The Hong Kong Convention Centre, which the hotel information pack told me had been built to celebrate the handover of Hong Kong from the British to the Chinese, protruded out into the harbour, its sail-like roof reminding me very much of the Sydney Opera House.

Just what kind of celebration they'd had in there I didn't know. But as I gazed at the huge windows which stretched up to the ceiling at least ten metres above my head, and the expanse of building stretching out in front of me, I figured that they should have been able to invite most of the Hong Kong population.

My assumption that the gift trade show would be the only thing on at the convention centre was obviously way off and I paused in front of a board listing the huge number of events taking place that day. After figuring out where I had to go, I followed the signs and pushed the pram onto one of the many escalators and along the length of one of the floors. Stopping on the way, I gazed out of the windows across the choppy harbour towards the buildings of Kowloon, which were only just visible through a soupy kind of mist, which I hoped was fog but suspected was actually smog.

A huge plastic banner stretched over a double doorway proclaimed the '10ᵗʰ Gift Trade Show'. Debbie had already paid the registration fee, and after stopping at the registration booth to pick up my 'Debbie Campbell' name tag, I pushed Sarah towards the entrance. As I walked through the doors I stopped dead in my tracks. The flow of people entering the room parted around me and continued on, leaving us in the middle of a moving sea of people.

I hadn't known what to expect, but it certainly wasn't acres of booths crammed with samples of merchandise. From where I stood I could see displays of everything from gift boxes to porcelain figurines, and the rows of plywood stalls continued both to my left and right as far as I could see. The noise echoing through the room wasn't the cacophony that accompanied all the retail markets I'd been to, but was a businesslike hum which rose to the ceiling high above, as vendors and potential purchasers discussed pricing, dimensions and shipping.

What was I doing here, I wondered suddenly. These people were traders who bought and sold products for a living. I was a mother who had pipedreams of making money some other way than by sitting in an office for forty hours a week. The obstacles of sourcing a product and shipping it to

Australia, which had seemed manageable in my lounge room, now looked insurmountable.

Conscious that I was standing in the main thoroughfare, I pushed Sarah towards the edge of the room and stood with my back to the wall, surveying the people striding purposefully past me. All my excitement at being in a new city had vanished and I wished fervently that it was me in Sydney with chickenpox and Debbie standing here. At the thought of Debbie, though, I felt a surge of confidence. She was one of these people and she believed we could make a success of this deal. I'd come halfway around the world to find what we wanted, and standing meekly in a corner wasn't going to achieve anything.

Debbie had marked the trade show map, sent with the registration details, with the location of the vendors who sold the covers we were interested in. Orienting myself, I turned left and then headed down the third row on the right. Sarah and I attracted a lot of curious looks, but I concentrated on looking at the stalls we were passing, determined to look confident even if I didn't feel it.

It quickly became obvious that the vendors were arranged into groups of related products. I passed a series of stalls that held stickers of all sizes and types, which appeared to be designed to cheaply brand products. Following on from them were stalls displaying piles of boxed stationery. Towards the end of the aisle I spotted what I'd been looking for – silk-covered books of all shapes and sizes. Taking a deep breath I headed to the stall closest to me.

An hour later I reached the last stall to hear the same thing the other seven vendors had said to me. Yes, they would love to manufacture four thousand books for the lady with the lovely little boy. But the suggestion that they could be finished and ready for shipping to Australia in six weeks was absolutely hilarious.

Even my desperate suggestion that maybe we could discuss a fee for a rush order proved useless. It seemed that Thai silk books were in huge demand and producing anything this side of Christmas would be impossible. The feeling in the pit of my stomach which had started when the first vendor laughed at my proposed timetable had become progressively heavier. By the time I heard the note of incredulity in the voice of the man in the last stall as he explained my proposal in Thai to his colleague, I felt physically sick.

Sarah had mercifully slept through the whole process but was beginning to stir, and as I looked at my watch I realised she was overdue for a feed.

Focusing on the problem of where to feed Sarah allowed me to concentrate on something other than my sense of failure. Somehow I didn't think that the hall was likely to have any parents' rooms so I headed back to the entrance, figuring that I'd find some-where outside to feed Sarah and call Debbie.

The aisle I'd come down was quite busy and I decided to go back up the next one. Definitely the lacquer aisle, I thought, as I walked along, spotting plates, drink coasters, platters and boxes in varying vivid colours. About to turn the corner and head back out the door, an object on the stall to my left caught my attention. Heading over to it, I saw that it was a book cover, made of two thin lacquer pieces held together by a brass hinge.

The man standing next to the stall smiled at me as I picked the cover up and turned it over in my hands. It was fabulous. The one I held was a vivid green, but judging by the colours of the other objects on display, a cherry red, shimmering blue and silver and gold were also options. Somehow the silk-covered books had never seemed entirely right to me. I'd always been concerned that the corners would rub off and the silk wouldn't stand the test of time. But these would look the same in thirty years as they did now, and the unusual nature of the hard covers and wonderful colours would give our books the distinctive look we'd been after.

Reining in my enthusiasm I told myself that timing was sure to still be a problem and that the price was likely to be way too high to make it worthwhile.

'Hello, my name's Sophie Anderson,' I introduced myself to the young salesman.

'Hello,' he replied in a gentle voice, handing me his business card. 'Please call me Kim. Do you like the book covers?'

'I love them,' I replied frankly. 'My business partner and I –'

He glanced at Sarah and raised his eyebrows.

I smiled before continuing. 'My business partner and I are interested in buying about four thousand covers like this. Could you give me some idea of your pricing?'

At the mention of the price my heart leapt. With shipping and other costs we would be able to land the books in Australia for about four dollars each. That was slightly more than what we had budgeted for, but not significantly so. I'd have to talk to Debbie, but it was definitely an option.

'Would there be any possibility of you producing the order within six weeks?' I asked, holding my breath as I waited for the answer.

Kim didn't reply immediately but frowned and turned to pick up a book that was sitting beside him. Leafing through the book he scribbled some numbers on a piece of paper, stared at them for a few seconds and then looked up.

'Yes, madam, we could do that.'

With great effort I retained my poker face, knowing enough about business negotiations to realise that showing my delight would not help me secure a good deal. Debbie had spoken to me sternly about the things I had to investigate before I placed an order with anyone. Resisting the temptation to throw myself at Kim's feet and ask him to make me four thousand book covers as quickly as he could, I visualised the list Debbie had given me.

'Where is your factory, Kim?'

'In Vietnam, madam.'

I paused to interject, 'Kim, please call me Sophie.'

'Yes, madam,' he replied, smiling as he realised what he'd said. 'My family has a small lacquer factory outside Hanoi,' he continued. 'For years my father has had a shop in the city where he sells our products. However, I believe we should be selling to people outside Vietnam, and after many months I convinced him that I should attend this trade fair and talk to people who wish to sell lacquerware in their countries.'

The serious young man in front of me had as much at stake as I did, I realised. A trip to Hong Kong must represent a fortune for a family with a small business in Vietnam and I couldn't imagine his father letting him attend another such gathering if he wasn't successful at this one.

'Can you tell me about your business and your products, Kim?' I asked.

'Perhaps you would like to sit down and have a cup of coffee, mad – Sophie?'

Suddenly I remembered that Sarah needed feeding. 'That would be lovely, but first I need to feed my baby. I'll come back as soon as I've finished.'

'Please feel free to feed her here,' Kim said. Seeing my obvious reluctance he continued, 'My wife and I have three children.'

Well, I thought, I'd fed Sarah in bars and restaurants all over Sydney, why not add a stall at a trade show in Hong Kong?

Kim pulled out a chair and as I took Sarah out of her pram and positioned her on my lap, he busied himself with something under a shelf behind me. After a couple of minutes I could smell the aroma of strong coffee drifting towards me. Kim looked around and smiled mischievously.

'We aren't supposed to have a stove here, but a friend who had been to Hong Kong years ago told me that the coffee here is terrible,' he said, looking genuinely pained. 'So I brought a small burner and can make my own.'

By the time the coffee was ready, I had finished feeding Sarah and put her back in her pram.

Pouring two cups of coffee from the stovetop percolator, Kim pulled a can of condensed milk off another shelf and held it over the top of each cup for several seconds.

'You have had Vietnamese coffee?' he asked.

'No, I haven't,' I replied as he handed a cup to me.

The idea of an inch of condensed milk sitting at the bottom of my coffee cup sounded very odd. For the sake of politeness, though, I took a sip and was surprised by the lovely bitter coffee taste, which was followed by the separate taste of the buttery, sweet condensed milk.

'This is delicious, Kim,' I exclaimed.

'Thank you,' he smiled happily, handing me a spoon, which he explained I needed in order to be able to eat the condensed milk as well as drink the coffee.

For the next forty-five minutes we discussed Kim's set-up, products and capacity and he showed me photos of the factory and their shop, as well as several of his wife and children. At the end of the time I felt convinced that Kim's family had a small but well-established business, and we had discussed practical issues such as payment and shipping.

With Debbie's instructions ringing in my ears, I left Kim and spoke to the other dealers at the surrounding stalls. Only a few of them had the lacquer book covers and while their pricing was similar to

Kim's, none of them gave me the same feeling of confidence. Figuring that I had done my homework well and that I couldn't go any further before speaking to Debbie, I headed back to the hotel with a bundle of samples under my arm.

Blessing the whim that had made me throw my black cocktail dress into the suitcase, I pulled it over my head, trying not to dislodge the rollers I'd put in twenty minutes before. The phenomenal humidity of the last couple of days had caused my hair to stick flat against my head, but to my great surprise the hotel's housekeeping department had been able to produce some big rollers, which I hoped would give it some semblance of body.

Debbie and I had talked for about half an hour after I'd arrived back at the hotel and she was enthusiastic about the change of product, although she was reserving judgment until she saw the covers. She had never trusted my taste since the time in the early eighties when I had worn a fluorescent 'Wake me up before you go-go' shirt. We'd agreed that I would speak to Kim the next day and tell him that we were very interested and I would contact him once I was back in Australia.

Stuffing my feet into the white hotel slippers, which were about five sizes too big, I walked back to the bed where Sarah was lying.

'Right, young lady, time for you to slip into something fabulous,' I said brightly, feeling happy about the prospect of a night out.

Pulling Sarah's shirt over her head, I froze when I saw that her stomach was covered in pink dots.

Debbie's doctor had said there was a chance Sarah could have picked up chickenpox from her, but I'd thought the symptoms would have shown up by now and so had assumed she was safe.

I felt a sudden stab of panic. Chickenpox in a small baby could be serious and I'd have been worried enough at home, let alone in the middle of Hong Kong. Where on earth would I find a doctor or a hospital here, I wondered frantically.

Taking a grip on myself I tried to think rationally. Suddenly I remembered that I was staying in a five-star hotel. Picking up the phone, I dialled reception. 'My baby is sick, I think she has chickenpox,' I managed in a shaking voice. 'Can you help me find a doctor?'

'Of course,' the receptionist answered smoothly. 'I'll call our doctor and have him come up to your room immediately.'

Replacing the receiver, I felt slightly calmer. At least I didn't have to traipse around the streets of Hong Kong with a feverish baby, trying to find medical attention.

I stripped off Sarah's clothes and examined the rest of her body for spots, but didn't find any. I put my hand on her forehead as I'd seen Karen doing with her children. Was she hot? I suddenly had no idea what her forehead normally felt like.

The doorbell rang and I looked at my watch with a start, realising that it was seven o'clock and David must have arrived to pick us up. I crossed the room, but stopped suddenly with my hand on the doorknob as I remembered I still had my rollers in. Pulling them out with both hands, I threw them over the other side of the bed and opened the door.

David was standing there looking incredibly sophisticated in a black single-breasted suit and dark grey shirt.

'Hi . . .' He trailed off as he registered my very unready state. 'Am I a little early?'

Shaking my head I said, 'No, David. I'm really sorry, please come in.'

He stood awkwardly next to the bed, obviously noticing that Sarah was in a similar state of readiness to her mother.

'Sarah has spots all over her stomach. I think she must have picked up Debbie's chickenpox.' My voice wobbled as I finished speaking and I bit my lip fiercely, determined not to cry.

David seemed to realise that too much sympathy would bring floods of tears and, no doubt thinking of the damage I could wreak on the front of his suit, he became suddenly businesslike. 'Have you called a doctor?' he asked.

I nodded. 'They're sending someone up straightaway.'

As I finished speaking, the doorbell rang and I opened it to see a slight Chinese man carrying a doctor's bag.

'Good evening, Ms Anderson, I'm Dr Chen. Your baby is sick?'

'Yes, I think she has chickenpox. A friend of mine in Australia has it and Sarah must have caught it from her.' I stood back and gestured towards Sarah on the bed.

'Okay, let's have a look.' Placing his bag on the bed beside Sarah, he looked down at her. As he did, Sarah suddenly started crying.

Without even touching Sarah, the doctor turned back to me. 'That's not chickenpox, Ms Anderson. Your daughter just has a heat rash.'

I looked at him blankly.

'I'll check her anyway,' he said. 'But I think she's fine.'

After listening to her chest and looking in her ears and mouth, the doctor pronounced her perfectly healthy and left, leaving me with a still-crying Sarah and feeling incredibly stupid.

'Sorry, David, you must think I'm totally neurotic,' I muttered, looking over at him.

'Not at all,' he answered with a smile. 'Chickenpox sounded like a perfectly reasonable diagnosis to me.'

Relief that there was nothing wrong with Sarah hit me, and as her crying subsided I felt my tension levels drop.

'I guess we need to get moving then,' I said.

I fished around in my suitcase for clothes for Sarah. The case was overflowing and I discreetly buried some dirty underwear that had been hanging over the side. Despite the fact that each item of Sarah's clothing took up about a tenth of the space of mine, her wardrobe and assorted bits and pieces took up three-quarters of the suitcase. I had no idea how I had managed to fill a case before I had her.

Laying Sarah on the bed, I pulled a singlet over

her head. It seemed to me that singlet manufacturers deliberately made the head hole about three sizes too small. I had distinct memories of having my nose and ears squashed against my head when my father put my singlets on and had thought it was his technique that was lacking until I found myself doing the same thing to Sarah.

The singlet safely on, I pushed Sarah's arms and legs into the outfit and did up the zip which ran down the front.

David looked on with great interest. 'Aren't you worried that you're going to snap off a couple of fingers or toes when you do that?'

'Somehow it doesn't seem to happen,' I answered. 'Trust me, that was a gentle exercise. Sarah lets me know if it becomes too brutal.'

'You seem to be very good at all this baby stuff,' David said.

'It's amazing how quickly it all becomes normal,' I replied. 'Before Sarah was born I struggled out of bed at seven-thirty each morning and needed two coffees before I could even start to think about the day ahead. I'd hardly ever held a baby, let alone changed a nappy or dressed one. Now nine in the morning seems like lunchtime and it feels as though I've been feeding and looking after a baby for years.'

'Would you mind if I held her?'

'Of course not.' I handed Sarah across to him.

'Hang on, not so fast,' he stuttered. 'I need some instructions about how I should do it first.'

'Her neck's strong so you don't need to worry about holding that,' I replied, smothering a smile.

'Here, sit down, put your arms together and just rest her in the crook of your arm.' I pulled his arms into place and laid Sarah on top of them.

David sat bolt upright, looking down at her as though she might explode any second.

'Relax, she won't bite you,' I laughed.

Gingerly David moved around so that he was in a more comfortable position and moved Sarah so that she was facing his chest. Lucky girl, I thought.

Sarah started squirming and began crying again. Suddenly I thought about the process of getting her to the other hotel and settling her with the baby-sitter. The prospect of things going smoothly, and getting to dinner without David wishing he'd never suggested it, seemed very remote. There was no other option, though, and I moved around the room, quickly throwing things into a bag.

David seemed to have sensed my thoughts. 'Look, Sophie, is this all a bit hard?'

My heart sank. We hadn't even got out of the hotel room and already he was sick to death of my dramas. 'No, no, it'll be fine,' I said with an optimism I didn't feel.

'Maybe it would be easier if we took a raincheck on dinner and did it when we were home in Sydney,' he suggested.

'That's probably a good idea,' I answered, trying not to show my disappointment.

'Or what about having dinner in the room?' he continued. 'You could put Sarah to bed and we can have a drink and order in some room service.'

'That sounds great,' I replied with relief. The

prospect of having David's company without having to deal with the whole Sarah factor sounded like the perfect scenario.

'All right, can I use your phone for a second?'

I nodded and heard him cancelling our dinner reservations and the babysitter.

As if Sarah felt me relax, she stopped crying and yawned. I took her into the walk-in dressing room where I'd had the hotel staff set up the cot, and laid her down. After kissing her goodnight, I pulled the door shut behind me and walked back into the bedroom. To my surprise there was silence – she'd gone straight to sleep.

David was sitting at the desk poring over the room service menu. He looked up and smiled.

Suddenly I realised I was still wearing the hotel slippers. Looking down at myself, I grimaced. 'I'm not sure what the room service dress code is. Do you think I'm appropriately attired?' I stuck one hip out in a model's pose.

'Hmmm,' he considered, narrowing his eyes as he looked at me. 'I'd say that's just about spot on. I particularly like the two rollers on top of your head. I've heard that's what everyone is wearing in Paris this season.'

My hands flew to my head and I realised in horror that I'd missed two of the rollers when I'd pulled them out earlier. About to apologise, I started laughing and threw the rollers onto the desk. 'Anything else I should know about?' I asked.

'Nope, everything else is perfect,' David replied seriously, looking at me intently.

Unsure of how to respond, I broke his gaze and moved behind him to look at the menu. 'Wow, the food sounds great,' I said. 'After a steady diet of noodles the last two days, that rack of lamb looks very appealing.'

'Rack of lamb, it is.' David picked up the phone and ordered the food and a bottle of wine.

'Would you like something to drink while we're waiting?' I asked as he put the phone down.

'A beer would be terrific,' he replied.

I pulled two beers out of the bar fridge and poured them into glasses. We moved the chairs up to the window and sipped our drinks, looking down over the bright lights on the other side of the harbour and chatting easily. The time passed quickly and I was surprised when I heard the doorbell ring.

Obviously I'd never stayed at the right hotels before. Until now my room service experiences had always meant a lukewarm meal delivered on a tray, but as I watched, the waiter wheeled in a narrow table covered in a crisp white cloth with a rose in a crystal vase on top.

Briskly the waiter flipped up and secured the edges of the table and produced two fabulous-looking meals from what must have been a hot box underneath. After showing the wine to David, he pulled the top off, poured some for him to taste and then filled two glasses.

David whisked the bill in its black leather cover off the trolley, wrote in his own room number and signed it, despite my protests.

With a small bow the waiter was gone and we were alone.

'To Hong Kong,' David said, holding out his glass. Smiling, I touched my glass to his and then took a sip before tucking into my dinner, which tasted as good as it looked.

'How's Debbie's chickenpox?' David asked, unable to keep the smirk off his face.

'She's spotty, itchy and miserable,' I smiled. 'I'm actually quite glad I'm on the other side of the world. Debbie's one of the world's worst patients.'

David's reference to Debbie gave me the opportunity I'd been looking for since I'd allowed myself to believe that maybe his interest in me was not just a business one. 'David, Debbie mentioned to me that you had been living with someone for a few years,' I began awkwardly.

'When I met Debbie I was,' David replied easily. 'But Angela and I decided that we were together more out of habit than anything else and that our relationship wasn't making either of us happy. So we broke up a couple of months ago. Unfortunately, though, we work together, which means we still see each other every day. I wish we could just move on and be friends but it's not that easy when you've been together for five years.'

'Relationships certainly aren't simple, are they?' I mused, regretting the trite words as soon as they were out of my mouth. God, I thought, next thing I knew I'd be telling him life wasn't meant to be easy.

'What about Sarah's father?' David asked.

'Kind of similar, I guess. Max was transferred to

the States and it brought things to a head. It had got to the point where I wanted some kind of commitment from him which he didn't want to give.

'Not marriage or anything,' I continued hurriedly, concerned that David would think I was sizing him up for a walk down the aisle. 'Just some kind of feeling that we could plan past the next dinner party.'

Deciding that was enough sharing of past relationship sagas, I tried to think of a way to change the topic. Determined not to talk about Sarah, I searched my memory for some item of current affairs. As I did, I realised that I hadn't read a newspaper for at least a fortnight and that for all I knew world war three could have broken out.

'So do you play any sport?' I asked, cursing myself as I heard how awkward I sounded.

'Yes, and my hobbies are stamp collecting and horse riding,' David replied.

We both burst out laughing and, ice broken, talked comfortably for the rest of the meal. Once we'd finished, I picked up the phone to order some coffee, which arrived quickly. After the waiter had left, taking our dinner table with him, we settled back into the lounge chairs.

'Before the airport was moved, you used to be able to watch the planes landing and taking off over there every few seconds,' David said, pointing across the harbour.

'You seem to know Hong Kong well,' I said.

'Pretty well,' he replied. 'I come here a few times a year.'

He looked out across the harbour again.

'Look,' he said, standing up. 'You can actually see Felix at the top of the Peninsula.'

I stood up to see where he was pointing. 'Yes, I can see it,' I lied, too aware of David's proximity to concentrate on picking one brightly lit building out from the hundreds lining the opposite shore.

Feeling David's eyes on me, I turned my head to look at him. He reached out a hand and threaded it into my hair then pulled me towards him, touching his lips gently against mine. But as much as my body wanted to be carried away on a wave of passion, my mind wouldn't let it. Debbie's taunts about my not wanting even to think about sex for months after Sarah was born echoed in my ears. Competing for attention was my worry about whether, three months post birth, my body was in a satisfactory state for viewing by anyone else.

Pulling back, I looked at David. 'I really . . .' I began.

'Sophie,' he interrupted, 'I think you're beautiful and it doesn't bother me in the slightest that you have a baby. Just relax, would you?'

Flattery has always been one of my weaknesses. While I was under no illusions that I really was beautiful, if David wanted to tell me I was, then he was a friend for life. At the sound of the compliment my sensible mind threw in the towel and surrendered to my lustful body and I let David lead me towards the bed, with only a vague wish that I'd bothered to read the 'Sex after Baby' chapter in my book, which I'd dismissed with a snort at the time.

When Sarah's cry woke me hours later I automatically went to sit up. Usually I could make it into her room without opening my eyes. However, this time there was a weight across my chest, which my forever-damaged abdominal muscles were unable to shift. Lying back down I opened my eyes and looked sideways at the arm flung across my chest and the unfamiliar body lying beside me.

The events of several hours ago flooded back; but, oblivious to the fact that I was engaging in a pleasant reverie, Sarah continued yelling. Realising that being woken to the sound of a screaming baby might be slightly more than David was prepared for at this stage, I carefully lifted his arm off my chest and eased my feet onto the floor before slipping into the dressing room to feed Sarah.

Sitting in the dark, I ran the evening over in my mind, unable to believe that it had happened and that I'd actually slept with David only the third time I'd met him. To my surprise, I realised I didn't have any regrets. It had been a long time since Max and I had split up and, despite the horror stories I'd heard, the sex had been great, regardless of whether or not anything came of it. After feeding Sarah I slipped back between the sheets, enjoying the feeling of having someone else in bed with me.

It was David's voice, not Sarah's crying, that woke me for the second time. He was standing over the bed fully dressed, looking down at me. Damn, I thought. I knew I should have turned off the bedside lamp while we were having sex.

'Sophie, it's seven o'clock. I've got a flight to

Beijing in two hours. I'm really sorry but I've got to leave.'

I sat up with the sheet clutched to my chest feeling ridiculously self-conscious. My clothes were scattered on the other side of the room and I had no intention of collecting them while David was watching. I had learnt from bitter experience that, while it always looks effortless in the movies, wrapping a bed sheet around you is best left to the experts. On my one and only attempt, I'd spent a couple of minutes dragging the sheet out from under the mattress and then found myself suddenly naked when the corner caught on the foot of the bed.

Seeing my predicament, David passed me one of the white hotel robes hanging in the cupboard. I quickly slipped it on and stood up.

We spoke at the same moment.

'David, I . . .'

'I had a good . . .'

I smiled and gestured for him to go on.

'I really do have to go, but I'd like to see you again . . . Can I call you?'

'That would be great,' I said, trying not to look as pleased by his words as I felt. David hesitated and then stepped over and deposited a stiff kiss on my cheek. Turning quickly, he walked to the door and I tried desperately to think what Debbie would say in this situation. However, before I could come up with anything, he was gone.

TWENTY-ONE

Accusing me of being too soft in my negotiations, Debbie, still spotty but no longer contagious, had taken over ordering the books while I finalised the designs. So a few days after we'd arrived home from Hong Kong, I left Sarah with her while I went to meet the designer. My house looked and sounded amazingly calm as I put the key in the lock on my return.

As soon as I walked inside I spotted what must have been two dozen red roses crammed haphazardly into a vase which was perched precariously on top of the television.

Debbie was sitting in the lounge room, *Vogue* in one hand, glass of champagne on the table, and Sarah kicking happily on a rug at her feet. When she saw me come in, she stood up. The look of glee on her face made my heart sink. Maybe she'd stolen the flowers from a neighbour or, my breath caught in my throat at the thought, maybe she'd found my credit card and decided she should celebrate her emergence from the social oblivion of chickenpox quarantine.

'What have you done? Debbie, if you've bought all these with my money, I swear I'll kill you.'

Her smile increased, which only made me more nervous. 'Darling, how little you think of me. I understand perfectly that your days of fun are over. At least I had thought so until that nice deliveryman showed up. Who've you been sleeping with and, more importantly, why didn't you tell me?'

I still didn't believe her – she looked way too innocent. 'Debbie, it's not funny any more. Tell me what you've done.'

'Sophie, read my lips. I haven't done anything apart from accept your delivery. For once I'm perfectly innocent. You might find a clue in the flowers, though – they came with a card.'

Still not entirely sure what to believe, I pulled out the envelope stuffed in amongst the flowers.

As soon as I saw my name on the front of the envelope I knew Debbie had been telling the truth. I'd never seen David's handwriting, but my name was written with the kind of flourish I would have expected from him. I tore open the envelope and scanned the white card inside.

Sophie. Thanks for a great night in Hong Kong. David.

Debbie was standing with Sarah on her hip and looking at me with raised eyebrows. Something, probably the fact that I suspected nothing would come of it, had stopped me telling Debbie about David. Figuring there was no point in trying to hide the truth now, I flicked the card across to her. Catching it deftly with her free hand she looked at it in puzzlement.

'David . . .' she mused. 'Do you know a David?' Her eyes widened suddenly as she made the connection. 'Not David Fletcher!' she exclaimed.

Seeing my guilty look she continued, 'It *is* David Fletcher! No wonder he's giving us a good deal if you've been bestowing your charms on him!'

Smiling bashfully I said, 'We had dinner together in Hong Kong and I figured that I was in grave danger of being expelled from the King Street Cafe mornings if I let this celibacy thing continue any longer.'

Debbie's jaw dropped. 'You slept with him?' she exclaimed. 'But Sarah's only three months old, what about . . .?'

She interrupted herself and held up a hand. 'Nope, forget that, I don't want to know. I can't believe you didn't tell me, you dark horse. Have you seen him since you've been back?'

I shook my head, pleased by the look of grudging admiration on Debbie's face. It wasn't often that I managed to impress her where men were involved.

'Well, he's certainly making up for that now,' Debbie crowed, examining the card again as if looking for further clues.

'But what about the girlfriend? Don't tell me he's cheating on her.'

'They broke up two months ago, apparently.'

'Well, I have to hand it to you, Sophie,' Debbie said. 'You've only had a few months without a pregnant belly and you're already dating one of the most eligible men in Sydney. Whatever will Max think?' she continued mischievously.

Despite myself, I couldn't help feel a flicker of guilt at the mention of Max. 'This has got nothing to do with him, Debbie,' I said fiercely.

She threw her free hand up in mock surrender. 'Okay, okay, just joking. Are you really interested in David?' she asked, suddenly serious.

'I think maybe I am,' I said. 'He's good fun and easy to be with.'

'Not to mention drop-dead gorgeous,' Debbie interrupted.

'And he seems totally relaxed about Sarah,' I continued. 'It's all taken me by surprise, though. A relationship was something I really hadn't counted on, and it's strange enough thinking about being with anybody, let alone someone who isn't Max.'

'Well, I think it's great,' Debbie said. 'Don't think too hard about it and just see what happens. If it's not something that's meant to last, then at least you'll have had a good time.' She looked at her watch. 'Speaking of men, I've got to go.' She handed Sarah to me, kissed my cheek and headed out the door.

Things were looking up, I thought, as I punched David's number into the phone. I'd just received fabulous flowers from a man I was definitely interested in, and we now had a supplier as well as a buyer for our baby books.

Suddenly I changed my mind and put the phone down before it connected. 'Come on, Sarah,' I said. 'Let's go and thank David in person.'

Even though I knew that buying fake designer

clothes was theft of copyright, I hadn't been able to resist picking up some fabulous pieces for Sarah in Hong Kong which had cost me about a tenth of the amount of the real thing. Deciding that a trip into the city justified a change of outfit for her, I pulled off her white cotton grow suit and slipped on a bright pink pinafore of a brand I was sure would have impressed even Debbie.

My wardrobe was still in its pre-pregnancy time warp. The few maternity clothes I had reluctantly bought certainly didn't count, and since Sarah's birth, the mind games involved in choosing which of my existing clothes I'd try for size had given me enough traumas without venturing into the world of shops, pushy salespeople and full-length fluorescent-lit mirrors.

The only piece of clothing I'd bought since Sarah's birth was an orange and white striped sleeveless top. I'd found it in a store that boasted of selling no item for more than ten dollars and had felt proud of my budgetary inspiration the first time I wore it with a pair of trousers I'd paid about twenty times as much for. However, the next time I'd gone to wear it, I'd discovered that the intervening wash had caused it to shrink so that it only reached halfway down my stomach and that the arm and neck holes now sagged towards the bottom of my bra. As a result I'd abandoned my trawling of bargain bins and decided to give up clothes shopping altogether until my finances improved.

The sun was beating down out of a cloudless sky, leaving no doubt that the heat of summer wasn't far away, and so I changed my jeans and T-shirt for a pair of black three-quarter length trousers (which admittedly had always been rather loose) and a sleeveless lime green top that hadn't seen the light of day for at least a year.

I pushed away the vague recollection that the 'Hot and Cold' section in last month's *Cosmopolitan* had identified both Capri pants and lime green as definitely 'cold'. Sliding my feet into a pair of black mules, I picked up Sarah and my bag and headed for the door. Catching a glimpse in a mirror on the wall, I paused for a moment. We looked pretty good, I acknowledged with a burst of optimism.

My attention to what I wore when out and about with Sarah had been sharpened by a recent episode in the nearby park.

Needing a change of scenery one afternoon, I had put Sarah in the pram and wandered down. Given that Sarah couldn't move, she wasn't exactly old enough to make the most of the play equipment the park had to offer, but I figured that she should see more of nature than our little back garden could provide.

The park was fringed by gum trees and on the street side was an area of play equipment which had brightly coloured swings, tunnels and climbing platforms. Without making a conscious decision, I drifted around the edge of the park and ended up at the play area, where I propped Sarah up in her pram so she could see what was going on.

Looking around, I noticed three other mothers. They had their backs to me and were playing with their children on the plastic play equipment. Except they couldn't be real mothers, I thought, they all looked too good.

The woman closest to me had on a light pink linen top and a pair of straight black trousers, which tapered beautifully over her high-heeled black boots. Even in my most ambitious moments since Sarah's birth, I hadn't considered wearing any of my linen clothes, having no doubt that I would look as though I'd slept in them for three days before I even left the house.

The second woman was wearing a brightly patterned skirt, black lycra top and patent leather sandals with a small heel. The third woman had on tailored cream trousers, tan boots and a top that simply had to be dry-clean only.

I swivelled my head to see if I could spot a TV crew, thinking that maybe I had stumbled across the filming of an American sitcom. Unable to see anything, I resumed my inspection of the women and moved closer on the pretext of showing Sarah a nonexistent butterfly. As I did so, two of them turned slightly towards me so that I could see what I'd suspected, but had been hoping wasn't the case – they were wearing full faces of makeup, including foundation and glistening lipstick.

The articles featuring movie stars and models looking fabulous with their angelic babies hadn't prepared me for seeing glamorous mothers in Erskineville. In LA maybe, or Central Park, but not the Lion's memorial park at the back of the local supermarket. These women had definitely never arrived home after several hours in public to discover a trail of vomit over their shoulder and down their back, as I had the week before.

I'd felt underdressed at restaurants, bars and parties, but feeling underdressed in the playground was a new one for me. Oh well, I comforted myself. They were obviously all friends who felt they had to compete with one another for the position of best groomed mother on the block. However, this last illusion was shattered as I caught some of their conversation and realised that the three of them had only just met and were making small talk.

The woman in the skirt caught sight of me and smiled welcomingly. 'Hi, how old's your little girl?' she asked (I had figured out recently that 'How old is your boy/girl?' was the baby group conversational equivalent of 'So what do you do?').

'She's three months,' I answered, pleased to see that dressing Sarah from head to toe in pink was finally making her recognisable as a female.

'Duncan is eight months,' she said, gesturing towards the baby crawling around the ground picking up cigarette butts and attempting to swallow them.

Despite their friendliness and willingness to tell me exactly what Sarah would be doing shortly (I was hoping she might miss the cigarette butt obsession), I felt somewhat out of place in my washed-out jeans, old T-shirt and deck shoes, and shortly after made my excuses and headed off. However, the incident had stayed in my mind and I had been trying at least to iron my clothes since then.

Sarah gurgled happily the whole way into town. In an inspired move the previous week I had hung one of her toys from the top of her capsule and it still hadn't lost its fascination. Debbie was convinced that the 'goldfish theory', which maintains that goldfish have such short memories that every trip around the bowl is a completely new experience, applied equally to Sarah. While hoping that my daughter's brain power was significantly larger than that of a small fish, I had to admit there seemed at least some truth to what she said.

There was always a fair degree of luck involved in just where I ended up when I drove into the centre of Sydney. Even after five years, the maze of one-way streets still confounded me. Today I not only ended up exactly where I wanted, but a free parking space (the existence of which in Sydney was significant enough to be a topic of conversation at dinner parties) appeared in front of me. As I reversed into the spot on my first attempt, I made a mental note to buy a lottery ticket and make the most of this purple patch.

Sarah and I set off down the street to do the shopping I was trying to convince myself was my main reason for coming to town. After drifting through a few shops and making a couple of totally unnecessary purchases, I headed for Handley Smith.

The receptionist looked at me without any sign of recognition.

'Sophie Anderson here to see David Fletcher,' I said in response to her raised eyebrows and questioning look. 'I don't have an appointment,' I continued as she looked at the diary in front of her. 'But if you could just tell him I'm here, I think he'll see me.'

'He has someone with him at the moment, Ms Anderson,' she replied. 'I'll let him know you're here just as soon as he's free.'

With a sudden flash I remembered that people in the nonbaby universe actually worked and for the first time I wondered whether it was a good idea to drop in unannounced. As I paused, considering whether I should manufacture an excuse and leave, the door to David's office snapped open and a tall, thin girl with long fire-red curls marched out and down the corridor.

Framed in his office doorway, watching her go, was David. Obviously feeling eyes on him, he turned towards the receptionist and gave a visible start as he registered my presence.

'Sophie . . . Hello,' he said lamely, managing a watery smile. 'How lovely to see you; come on in.'

It didn't take a genius to figure out that the girl must have been Angela, and as I pushed Sarah's pram into David's office, I cursed the whim that had propelled me into the city to thank him in person. Once inside I paused awkwardly, uncertain how I should greet him. Shaking hands was clearly inappropriate given the events of Hong Kong, but bridging the acres of beige carpet which separated us and attempting a kiss didn't seem right either.

Taking the cowardly option, I bent over Sarah's pram to totally unnecessarily rearrange her toys. When I looked up, David, who was no doubt as grateful for the reprieve as I, had settled himself behind his desk. Following his lead, I perched awkwardly on the edge of the chair opposite him.

We both started speaking at once, stopped, then started again.

'You go,' David smiled.

'I was just in town doing some shopping,' I said with crossed fingers, 'and thought I'd drop in to say thank you for the flowers.'

'I'm glad you liked them,' he said, sounding anything but glad and looking at the desk in front of him rather than meet my eyes.

He's changed his mind, I thought glumly, concluding that the reality of having a relationship with someone with a baby had sunk in and that he was trying to work out how to get out of the situation he now found himself in.

Right on cue Sarah started crying. Not now, I thought fiercely. Our telepathic thought channels obviously weren't working, though, and she increased her volume sharply.

Picking Sarah up, I held her over my shoulder, rocking her from side to side. 'Look, I should go. I just dropped in to say thanks but I don't want to hold you up.'

'No, it's fine, Sophie. Actually I need,' David paused to let a particularly loud cry of Sarah's subside, 'to talk to you.'

'Okay,' I said, jiggling Sarah vigorously. She seemed to be quietening so I sat down, which caused an immediate resumption of her full-throttle crying.

Bouncing up again I said with forced cheerfulness, 'I don't think this is going to get much better. Why don't you just go ahead?'

'Sorry?' he asked with his hand behind his ear.

'Go ahead,' I repeated louder.

'Well . . .' he yelled. 'There's a problem with the order for your books.'

I froze midrock. 'Pardon?' I asked, hoping that I'd misheard.

'We've got a problem with the order for your books,' David repeated. 'I've just had notice that Handley Smith is under huge pressure to drive the share price back up and so the top management have put a total freeze on all hiring.' He paused and took a breath. 'And all new purchases have been stopped too. That means I can't add any new suppliers until the freeze comes off, Sophie, and I have no idea how long that could take.'

The enormity of what he had said hit me. 'But we were so close to a deal,' I stammered.

'I know,' David replied, looking as though he'd rather be anywhere but here. 'But we hadn't formalised it, and now this directive has come down, I can't put the purchase through. I still think the books are a great product and they'll sell, but there's no way around it. I'm really sorry, Sophie.'

I slumped into the chair. Sarah was mercifully silent. My visions of a business empire slowly collapsed as I realised what had happened.

'So that's it?' I asked David. 'There's nothing you can do to convince your management that they should make an exception?''

David shook his head. 'There are no exceptions, Sophie. I've only seen this once before, about three years ago. It's an across-the-board freeze that applies to everyone. We were about a day away from hiring another buyer, but the freeze has put an end to that too.'

Sarah had lost interest in the situation and started to cry again. I was about to speak but paused as I saw her take a deep breath in preparation for another yell. Both David and I watched her, wincing involuntarily as the silence stretched and was then abruptly shattered as she let her breath out in an ear-splitting wail.

'Look, David, I can't even think straight with this noise,' I said. 'I've got to go. I'll call you later.'

David watched silently as I dumped Sarah unceremoniously in her pram and pushed her to the door. Head down, I muttered my goodbyes and went straight to the lifts. After what seemed to be an agonisingly long time, one arrived. Once we were safely inside and the doors had shut, I breathed easier and smoothed Sarah's cheek, which was red from crying.

The crowds in the mall, which had parted smoothly for us earlier, now forced us to move at a snail's pace. When I was about fifty metres from the car I realised that the reason there had been no one parked there was because it was a no-standing zone. With a sigh, I spotted a parking inspector standing beside my car. As I watched, he completed the ticket, tore it off and carefully lifted the windscreen wiper to slip it underneath.

Having been through this a number of times, I knew that rule one of the parking inspector guidebook forbade them cancelling a ticket once they'd started writing it out. Several humiliating experiences had taught me that there was no point in throwing myself on their mercy. I briefly considered using Sarah to assist my case, but quickly concluded that wouldn't help, given my firm belief that parking inspectors are grown-up versions of boys who play golf with cane toads.

Hanging back until the inspector was gone, I pulled the ticket free of the wipers and glared at it before stuffing it into my handbag.

Hardly conscious of where I was driving, I found myself heading to Debbie's flat. Pulling up outside, I took Sarah out of her capsule and puffed up the four flights of stairs to Debbie's door (another reason a move before Sarah's arrival had been unavoidable).

Debbie had wanted me to keep my key when I moved out but I had insisted on giving it back – somehow, coming across Debbie with a male friend was one thing when we were flatmates but quite another when we weren't (and I was likely to be bearing my innocent young daughter).

Hearing male laughter through the door I was doubly glad I had made that decision. But when Debbie opened up, it was Andrew and not one of her bevy of men I saw on the sofa behind her.

'Hello, Andrew,' I said in surprise. 'What are you . . ?' I began, before I noticed that Debbie was wearing running gear.

'Unbelievable!' I exclaimed. 'Don't tell me you've managed to get Debbie to do some exercise?'

'I've decided to get fit,' Debbie announced.

'You're kidding,' I said incredulously. 'The only time I've even seen you walk fast is in the Boxing Day sales.'

'Yes, well, things are different now,' she said. 'Now that I'm not devoting all of my energy to scouring the earth for self-cleaning soap dishes, it's amazing what I've got time for.'

Upon reflection, I realised that it had been a while since Andrew had collected my weekly exercise summary sheets, which he had given me when Sarah was born. His finding another person to focus his energies on could only be a good thing for me.

Remembering why I was there, I suddenly stopped smiling. 'Deb, we've got a big problem with the Handley Smith order.'

'I'll leave you both to it.' Andrew leapt off the sofa. 'I've got a client in half an hour.'

Debbie had heard the serious tone in my voice and didn't take her eyes from my face as Andrew left. 'What's the problem, Sophie?' she asked quietly.

'There's no order from Handley Smith,' I stated flatly. 'Apparently there's a company-wide freeze on all expenditures, including new purchases. Something to do with pushing the share price up.'

'Shit!' Debbie exclaimed with great force. 'And we were so close.

'I've come across this before,' she continued as she paced across the room. 'Some big companies' top management get bonuses based on share price increases and profits. If they can't increase revenue, the only other way they can increase profits is to reduce expenses. It's incredibly short-sighted, but it keeps happening.'

I sat down on the couch Andrew had just vacated. Debbie sat down beside me and reached over to take Sarah, who smiled up at her endearingly. Sarah had recently taken to dribbling in large quantities. A middle-aged lady, a harassed-looking woman trailing two kids and, bizarrely, a thirtyish man with dreadlocks and a ring through his lip, had each stopped me on the street to tell me that the dribbling meant Sarah was teething. As a breastfeeding mother, the thought sent shivers up my spine, but I had explained clearly to Sarah that one bite and she was on the bottle, and I hoped we had an understanding.

Another dribble was threatening to drip off Sarah's chin and I watched as Debbie absently wiped it on her purple Nike running singlet. However, even the sight of the change Sarah had wrought on Debbie couldn't take my mind off the depressing development in our business venture.

'The good news is that we haven't placed the order yet,' I said in an effort to be positive. 'At least we don't have a container-load of baby books arriving tomorrow.'

'Sophie . . .' Debbie began awkwardly, staring at the top of Sarah's head.

'What?' I asked, my voice rising with worry. 'What don't I know?'

'Well . . .' Debbie continued, lifting her head to look at me. 'I spoke to Kim the day you arrived home. He said that they were backed up with orders and that if they didn't put ours through straightaway then it would be five weeks before they could start, which would have been too late.'

She paused and took a deep breath before saying what I'd already guessed. 'So I told them to go ahead.'

Closing my eyes, I leant forward and put my head on my knees.

'Sophie, I'm so sorry,' Debbie continued. 'I know I should have told you but I was so sure it was a done deal and I knew you'd just worry about it.'

I only vaguely heard Debbie's words through the roar of blood in my ears. My share of the amount we owed for the books was more than the savings I had left. We needed to pay for the books before they left Vietnam and there was no way a bank would lend money to a single mother with no assets who wasn't currently working. So I'd decided the only option was to cover my share using my credit card. Although the concept of paying horrendous interest on a large amount of money terrified me, I'd decided that as it would only be for the couple of weeks until we delivered the books to Handley Smith and received payment, it would be all right.

But this changed everything.

'What on earth are we going to do?' I asked, my voice trembling.

'Sophie, please look at me,' Debbie implored. 'I know how much that money means to you. It was my decision to place the order, I'll pay for it all. Committing ourselves without having Handley Smith tied up was a bad business decision, but the other option was losing the order and I really thought we weren't taking too much of a risk. I guess I was wrong,' she finished glumly.

After a few more seconds I looked up. 'No, that's not fair. If I'm honest, I would have made the same decision you did and I understand why you didn't tell me. You've worked as hard for your money as I have and this is going to wipe you out too. I'll cover my share, I've just got to figure out how.

'Maybe we can reduce the order if they haven't started producing all of them yet,' I said with sudden inspiration.

Debbie shook her head. 'Kim explained that they'd be producing all the books at the same time. Each one has heaps of different layers of lacquer and it's putting all those layers on that takes the time.'

'So we're stuck with four thousand baby books and no one to sell them to. God, what a mess,' I said morosely.

'Look, let's not give up yet,' Debbie said briskly. 'You know, this all happened so quickly and easily that we haven't looked at the business economics as closely as we should have. The shipment is due to leave Vietnam in ten days, so we've got until then to come up with the cash for the books themselves and then another two weeks before they arrive here. As I see it we have two options. We either try to offload the covers to someone in Australia and hope to cover our costs, or we spend the money to get the pages printed and the books packaged and try to sell them ourselves.'

The thought of spending more money I didn't have on printing and packaging sounded like madness and my feelings must have shown on my face, as Debbie went on quickly, 'But we don't have to decide yet. Let's at least investigate other buyers before we go making any drastic decisions.'

'All right,' I said slowly, figuring we had nothing more to lose.

'I'm sure that one of the other big stores will jump at the chance to take the books,' Debbie said positively, and it was only because I knew her so well that I could hear the unfamiliar ring of uncertainty in her voice.

I tried not to think about my savings being turned into a pile of useless books, and forced myself to concentrate as Debbie outlined what we should each do over the next couple of days.

TWENTY-TWO

That evening I was doing some sums to figure out just how long I could carry the interest cost on my credit card, when I heard a knock and opened the front door to see David standing there. I cursed whatever god it was who ensured that when I wore decent clothes at home absolutely no one dropped in, but turned my house into a veritable Melrose Place as soon as I donned leggings that had lost their elastic in all the critical places.

David had his suit jacket over his arm, had undone the top couple of buttons on his shirt and loosened the knot on his tie, which was pulled to one side. He'd obviously been running his hand through his hair and it stood up in little peaks on one side. Seeing him standing there made me realise that I'd hardly thought about my feelings for him since he had given me his news. Well, not fretting about my love life was one benefit of suddenly being up to my eyes in debt, I decided.

'Hi,' he said. 'That was really awful in my office today. Do you mind if I come in to talk?'

'Of course not,' I said, standing aside to let him through.

David stood in the middle of the room looking around. 'This place is great,' he said. 'It looks like a real home.'

'I'm guessing that baby rugs and toys don't really feature in the décor at your place,' I joked, trying to ease the tense atmosphere.

'Sophie, this is really difficult,' David began nervously. 'I enjoyed your company when we were in Hong Kong, which is why I sent you the flowers. I'm so embarrassed about what's happened. We were really close to tying things up and I feel incredibly bad about pulling the rug out from under your feet.'

'Don't worry about it, David,' I said. 'It's not your fault.'

'At least you haven't placed your order yet,' David said.

I wondered whether or not I should tell him the truth, but decided I didn't have much choice. 'Actually, our order is already being manufactured. We're just going to have to find another buyer.'

David looked aghast and started to speak again.

'David, stop,' I interrupted, cutting him off. 'Would you feel this bad if we hadn't slept together?'

He considered that briefly, and then shook his head.

'Exactly,' I continued. 'I've felt uncomfortable about this not being a totally businesslike relationship.

The order being cancelled is a nightmare, but it isn't your fault and Debbie and I will deal with it.'

I had gone this far, I figured I might as well keep going. 'I enjoyed your company when we were away too – let's just pretend that we met some other way and see what happens.'

'That sounds great,' David said, smiling for the first time since he'd arrived.

'I'm cooking some pasta for dinner. Would you like to stay for something to eat?' I figured some company might help take my mind off my dire financial position.

'I'd love to,' David replied. 'But I've got a work dinner I can't get out of. Actually, I should be there now.'

I tried to suppress my concern that it was the leggings that had put him off and pasted a bright smile on my face. 'Okay. Thanks for coming around to talk – we can take a raincheck on the pasta.'

'It'll have to be a week or so,' David answered. 'I'm heading back to the Perth office first thing in the morning and I'm not sure when I'll be back.' I was mentally cursing the leggings when he added, 'But I'll call the moment I'm home.'

'If you're back by Friday week, keep it free. A group of us are going out to dinner for my birthday.'

'Sounds good.' Looking much happier than when he arrived, David pecked me awkwardly on the cheek and moved towards the door. A thought obviously hit him and he turned back to me. 'You know, if you do find another buyer, there's a chance I could help out with some publicity. Do you have anything prepared yet?'

'I've done a couple of drafts. I could email you something once we've sorted things out,' I answered without a lot of enthusiasm, knowing how hard it was to get press coverage for products.

'Okay, just let me know.'

With a small smile, he was gone.

I sighed, wondering how I was supposed to deal with these abrupt departures of his. Celibacy was beginning to look as though it had some advantages after all.

The phone began ringing as soon as I'd closed the door. Just before the answering machine kicked in, I found the phone wedged down the back of the sofa and hit the button.

'What the hell does "blanch de-zested lime rind" mean?' Debbie's voice had a hint of hysteria.

'Sorry?' I asked, trying to figure out what on earth she was talking about.

'I've been buying these damn food magazines for years and the first time I actually go to cook something from one I discover it's written in some language other than English which I cannot for the life of me decipher!' Debbie yelled.

'You're cooking?' I asked incredulously.

'Yes, well, that's what people do on weeknights if they don't go out, isn't it?'

'I guess so,' I answered, still stunned by the picture of Debbie doing something in the kitchen other than brew coffee. 'I didn't really think you'd be in the mood after today's news, though.'

'There's no point in sitting at home alone moping,' she answered strongly, making me feel pathetic, given that was exactly what I planned to do.

'Okay, so take me through this slowly,' I said. 'What's going on?'

There was a pause and I heard the clatter of saucepans before Debbie spoke again. 'I'm having someone around for dinner in . . . forty-five minutes and at the rate I'm going I'll have to throw the lot in the bin and order in a pizza.'

'Who is this person you're cooking for?' I asked curiously.

'Oh, a guy I met, you wouldn't know him,' she replied vaguely.

'Debbie, aren't you the person who always says that if you need to try to win a guy through his stomach, you're doing something seriously wrong with the rest of him?' I was suddenly worried that Debbie had taken some nasty drugs which were making her delusional.

'Oh, he's already well keen,' she replied and I was comforted to hear the usual Debbie arrogance in her voice. 'It's just, you know, I thought maybe a quiet dinner at home might be a nice way to spend a Wednesday night.

'But I can't talk about this now,' she said suddenly, the note of hysteria back in her voice. 'I have a total crisis on my hands.'

'All right, what's the situation?' I asked. I figured it must indeed be serious if she was resorting to calling me for cooking advice and bit back the questions about her sudden domesticity and why she hadn't mentioned this dinner earlier today.

'Right,' she replied in an efficient voice. 'This guy is a vegetarian, so I thought zucchini soup to start, spinach and ricotta tortellini in a tomato sauce, and then pineapple with lime caramel sauce for dessert.'

'You designed this menu, did you?' I asked disbelievingly.

'Of course not. Do you think I spent the day trawling through cookbooks? The recipes are all in this month's *Food, Food, Food*,' she said, referring to a popular magazine she never read but always bought, figuring it looked good on her coffee table.

'I've made the zucchini soup, which actually looks edible, but I've just realised that I put chicken stock in it. What do you think, will I go to hell if I lie and say it's made with vegetable stock?'

'Hmmm, tough one,' I mused. 'But I really think that feeding chicken bits to a vegetarian has got to have some pretty bad karma associated with it. Don't think you can do it.'

'All right,' she said. 'I figured you'd say that and have already given up on the soup. Main course is easy, even I can fry some onions, garlic and canned tomatoes, and I bought the pasta from the deli.'

Thank God for small mercies, I thought.

'But dessert is a disaster. It looked really easy in the magazine. The recipe said to boil the sugar and water until it turned a caramel colour. But I've been boiling it for thirty minutes now and it's still pure white and starting to look very solid. So I decided to ignore that for a bit and do the rest, but I didn't read this far down the recipe before and I have absolutely no idea what "blanching" or "de-zest" mean.'

'Debbie, where does the magazine say the recipe came from?' I asked.

'Oh, I don't know,' she replied impatiently. 'Hang on . . . Okay, it says that a chef from Angie's Restaurant contributed it. Their food's great, so what's the damn problem?'

'Ah, Debbie, you have fallen into the food magazine trap,' I intoned darkly.

'Sophie, my dinner date is now coming in thirty-five minutes, what the hell are you talking about?'

'Do you think the chef from Angie's wants you to be able to cook sensational lime caramel pineapple for your guests?' I asked. 'Of course not. If you could, why would you ever go to his restaurant? A lot of these supposedly simple recipes turn into the world's greatest disasters. I'm sure that the chefs leave out a vital ingredient or step to ensure that your take on their signature dish is a debacle.'

'So you think my sugar's not going to turn into caramel?' she moaned.

'Not a chance,' I replied. 'Ditch it, smother your pineapple bits in Cointreau and stick it in the fridge until you want to eat it,' I instructed, describing my standard dessert when I couldn't avoid cooking. 'Please tell me that the pineapple's not from a can?' I pleaded as an afterthought.

'Of course not,' Debbie replied haughtily, as if her entire home cooking career to date hadn't been performed with a can opener in one hand.

'Good. Do you have any oranges in the fridge that are younger than Sarah?' I asked hopefully.

'Hmmm, I'm not sure,' Debbie said doubtfully.

'I think you actually bought the ones that are in the crisper.'

'Okay, forget the oranges, just feed him the pineapple and Cointreau, and if you have any, stick some ice-cream or sorbet on top.'

'You're a genius, Sophie, thanks,' she gushed before hanging up the phone.

'You're welcome,' I told the dial tone, distractedly wedging the phone back between the sofa cushions as I tried to figure out exactly what was going on with Debbie.

Ten minutes later the doorbell rang. Opening the door I saw Max standing there. What on earth was it about these leggings?

'Sophie. Hi,' he said. 'Sorry to drop in unannounced but I was nearby and I thought I'd stop and say hello.'

I hadn't seen or heard from Max since the picnic at Bondi two weeks before and my feelings on seeing him were just as confused as they had been then. Irrationally I had a rush of guilt as I thought of David and was glad that he and Max hadn't crossed paths – that was one complication I didn't need at the moment.

'For someone who lives in San Francisco, you seem to be spending a lot of time in Sydney,' I commented.

'Yeah, well, I don't actually think I'll be living in San Francisco much longer,' Max replied.

'Really!' I stopped still, wondering how that would affect Sarah and me. 'Come in, anyway,' I said, realising we were still standing on the doorstep.

Max followed me into the kitchen.

'Do you want a glass of wine?' I asked. I knew I should be angry at him, but didn't have the energy.

He nodded. 'That'd be great.'

'So what's the story?' I asked as I pulled a bottle of white wine out of the fridge.

'I've had a few discussions with the old guy who owns that farm and I flew back yesterday so I could have a look around. I spent the day there,' Max said. 'The place is fantastic and the potential to turn it into a real money-earner seems huge.

'So,' he took a deep breath. 'I made an offer to buy it.'

I paused with the wine bottle suspended over a glass. 'Are you serious?' I asked, seeing immediately that he was.

'You certainly don't waste any time,' I continued, unsure what to say in response to this unsettling news.

'I know I should probably think it all through a bit more, but it feels so right,' Max replied, taking the bottle of wine from my hand and filling two glasses. 'My boss in the States has said he'll arrange for a transfer back to Sydney if I really want it – although I did have to threaten to resign if he didn't.'

Max had always been impulsive. It was one of the things I'd loved about him.

'I really hope it works out,' I said and if Max noticed anything wrong with my tone of voice, he didn't comment on it. Although it had never been more than a pipedream, the idea of owning a place in the country was something we'd talked about together, and if I was honest with myself, the fact that Max was making it a reality without me kind of hurt.

'Do you mind if I have a quick look at Sarah?' he asked suddenly.

I shook my head and he tiptoed up the steps.

When he returned, he swirled the wine around his nearly empty glass before looking up at me. 'Actually, Sophie, I wasn't just in the neighbourhood, I was on the other side of town, but I really wanted to see you and had a suspicion that you might put me off if I called first.'

'I'm trying to be fair. It's just . . . hard.'

He nodded. 'I know.'

An uncomfortable silence fell and we both took a mouthful of wine.

'Would you like to stay for dinner?' The words were out of my mouth before I had thought them through and I instantly regretted them.

Max replied before I had a chance to say anything else. 'Sure, dinner would be good. Did you have any plans or would you like me to get some takeaway?'

'I wasn't planning anything too fancy. Just some rocket and tomato pasta. We can get takeaway if you prefer.'

'Nope, pasta sounds good. Can I help?'

Accepting his offer, I smiled as he instantly took control in the kitchen, chopping and cooking the components of the sauce and putting the water on to boil. Falling into the old familiar pattern we'd developed over the years, I wandered into the lounge room, chose a CD and then sat up on the bench to watch him work.

After many fierce arguments, we'd come to the conclusion that this was the only way we could cook together – one of us actually cooking, the other one keeping the wineglasses full and the music going. Despite everything that had happened, the scene suddenly seemed very familiar and comfortable. I quickly reminded myself things had changed dramatically.

My mind wandered and I began to worry again about what I would do if we couldn't find anyone else to buy the baby books. I was strongly tempted to tell Max everything that had happened. But I knew that would mean a discussion about money and Sarah, and I decided that was something I could do without for the time being. One thing I was sure about was that I wasn't going to borrow any money from Max, even if he had some spare at the moment, which I seriously doubted.

Max dished up the pasta and we carried the plates to the table. When we had finished our meals, Max glanced at his watch and did a theatrical double take.

'Do you realise what time it is?' he demanded.

I shook my head and looked at my watch. He'd stayed for almost two hours but I didn't think it was that late.

'What's happened to you, woman? *ER* is on in exactly four minutes. What were you thinking?'

A passion for *ER*, which had survived George Clooney's departure, was another thing we had shared, although since Sarah's arrival, I had got out of the habit of watching it. When Max and I had been together, Wednesday nights had been a ritual. We always planned to be home at either flat and made sure there was a tub of Sara Lee Pralines and Cream ice-cream in the freezer.

We moved into the lounge and turned on the television.

'Why don't you sit there?' I suggested, gesturing towards the armchair.

Apprehensively I eyed the designer Italian sofa. I'd paid a ridiculously large amount for it when I'd first moved to Sydney, but it had recently begun disintegrating and I was never quite sure which part of it would give way next. My friends had all been sucked into its spring-studded depths often enough to learn to avoid sitting on it at all costs, and I was becoming quite adept at steering visitors towards the other chair, so my current plan was just to ignore the problem.

'How about a neck massage?' Max asked slyly.

I knew he was throwing down a challenge. A neck massage had been another of our rituals but, as we were both only too aware, a ritual that had more often than not ended up with us in bed.

At least it solved my dilemma of where to sit and, determined not to show my feelings, I sat down in front of him, trying to relax as his hands ran up and down my neck and shoulders.

As the opening credits rolled I asked him to fill me in on the most recent developments. Max couldn't believe that I didn't know what had been happening. 'What planet have you been living on?' he exclaimed.

'In case you hadn't noticed, I've been looking after a baby. That kind of mixed up my priorities!' The words came out more sharply than I had intended and his hands were suddenly still on my neck.

'Sorry,' he said quietly. 'I was only joking.'

We watched the television in silence. Max resumed his rhythmic massage and I tried to concentrate on what was going on. When his lips pressed into the back of my neck, it wasn't entirely unexpected but it still sent jolts of alarm through me. He traced a path of kisses towards my shoulder and then down the top of my spine.

Slowly I turned and our lips met. *ER* was forgotten. Even Sarah was forgotten as the kiss deepened into something that neither of us wanted to stop. All I could think about was that this felt so good. All the reasons Max and I had separated seemed to disappear.

He slid down so that he was beside me on the floor, his hands still stroking my arms, my throat.

Suddenly an image of David flashed into my mind, how he'd touched me in the same way less than a week earlier. Guilt flooded through me and I stiffened and pulled away.

'Max . . . I can't. Please stop.'

Reluctantly, Max pulled away and I managed to sit up straight.

Neither of us knew what to say and we turned back to the television wordlessly, avoiding each other's eyes.

As soon as *ER* had finished, Max stood up and stretched. 'Well, I guess it's time for me to head off,' he said half-heartedly, no doubt hoping for an invitation to stay.

Half an hour of thinking while I was staring sightlessly at the television had given me time to get my feelings straight again. Things were different now and a night with Max wasn't worth the consequences. I had Sarah to think about and I wasn't going to throw away my chances of something good with David.

Max kissed me briefly on the lips as he left and then was gone.

Ten minutes later, when I was changing into my pyjamas, I heard another knock on the door. My heart sank. Whoever it was, I didn't want to talk to them. All I wanted was my bed, and the oblivion of sleep where I didn't have to think about money or men.

Reluctantly, I headed back downstairs and pulled open the door. On the doorstep was a tub of Sara Lee Pralines and Cream ice-cream.

TWENTY-THREE

With the twin motivations of Debbie's determination and my desperation, the two of us contacted all the big department and home furnishing stores in the country over the next couple of days.

Given Handley Smith's interest, I had been holding out hope that one of the other big chains would snap up our books, but none of them seemed remotely interested. Almost every response was the same. 'We think it has potential in theory, but our buyers have already completed this season's range. We'd be interested in looking at any other products you develop.'

'That is the business equivalent of "I'll respect you in the morning",' Debbie fumed. 'I'd like them more if they just said, "Hate it — can't use it." Why can't anyone see the potential here?'

'I don't know, Deb, maybe we just got it wrong. Maybe people do want their baby books traditional,' I said miserably.

Next we moved on to smaller retail outlets. However, after contacting every store in New South Wales that could conceivably have been interested in our product, we had interest for a grand total of eighty books.

Things were looking so bleak that Debbie started talking about the need to find another job. As for me, I'd even thought about asking Dad and Elizabeth for help. Dad always insisted that he was 'as fit as a fiddle' but I could hear the tension in Elizabeth's voice whenever we spoke about his health. The last thing I wanted to do was to give him something to worry about, so I decided to keep my money problems to myself.

Andrew's week wasn't going any better. One of his biggest corporate clients had been taken over by an American company, and word had it that all 'nonessential' expenditure was to be reduced, or eliminated completely.

As a result, Saturday's cafe session was a subdued affair. With the exception of the employment section, which both Andrew and Debbie had trawled through, the thick piles of newspapers remained unopened and the conversational tone veered from miserable to pathetic.

Only Karen, fuelled by a white chocolate muffin with double cream, and Anna, nursing a coffee, attempted to remain positive.

'You can't just give up!' Anna insisted. 'There must be something else you can look into – what about trying the baby wear shops?'

'Good idea,' Karen agreed. 'At least you'd know

for sure that you're reaching the right market. I can't imagine who would be in a baby wear shop other than people with babies.'

'Friday,' was all Debbie managed in response.

'Friday?' asked Anna, obviously sensing that she and Karen were fighting an uphill battle.

'On Friday, I visited or rang every babywear store in Sydney. They'll only take the books on consignment and even then I would have shifted a grand total of fifty. Not really enough to solve our problem,' she added miserably.

Andrew looked up from his latte thoughtfully. 'You know, I read an article a couple of weeks ago in *BRW* about a guy who had been backpacking around Asia and bought a whole heap of stuff home, thinking he could sell it for a quick profit to a retail chain. Similar sort of story, really. He couldn't get anyone to stock it for him so he took over an empty shop and sold it himself. I think the article said he now has something like twenty outlets around the country and is making megabucks. His big thing is that he starts work at five in the morning and finishes by one, so that he can concentrate on the other stuff he's doing. At the moment he's raising money for some charity by running the London Marathon. Maybe he's the kind of person you could talk to.'

'So what's the name of this guy's business?' I asked, thinking maybe we'd missed an opportunity.

'Um . . . I can't remember.'

'It wasn't House Arrest, was it?' I said. 'They sell all kinds of homewares and have a baby range. But if it was, we can forget about it. They have the scariest receptionist in Sydney, who wouldn't even tell me the managing director's name, much less put me through to him.'

'I really can't remember, but I should still have the magazine somewhere. I'll check it out when I get home. It's not like I'll have anything else to do,' he added gloomily.

'Come on,' I said, trying to remain positive even though it was the last thing I felt. 'You don't even know yet if your business will be affected. I thought Americans were all into proactive workplace programs. Max tells me his company has a permanent tab going at the bar across the road. They maintain it keeps up morale. Maybe the new company will think the same way.'

Andrew didn't seem convinced, but Ben arrived with more coffees as I finished speaking. Max was a topic I always avoided around Ben, not wanting him to feel he had to take sides, and I was sorry now that I'd mentioned his name.

'So what do you think of Max's news?' Ben asked.

The others looked at me inquiringly so I filled them in.

'Max is going to live on a goat farm in the country?' Andrew asked incredulously.

I smiled. 'Not exactly. He's done a deal with his company to work four days a week and he'll spend the other day and most weekends out there. He's really fired up about it all. He's taken a couple of weeks holiday to sort everything out before he heads back to the States to pack.'

'What do you think about it?' Anna asked quietly.

I couldn't be bothered being anything but honest. 'I don't know, really. He seems keen to see Sarah, which I guess is a good thing.'

'C'mon, Sophie, don't be modest. It's not just Sarah he's been showing an interest in,' Debbie piped up. 'I don't think he bought Manchetti cheesecake for her benefit.'

Sometimes I wondered why I ever told Debbie anything. It would be more efficient to just cut out the middleman and take out an ad in the newspaper.

Anna looked at me intently. 'Do you think Max wants to get back together?'

'It's not like that,' I hedged. 'He is Sarah's father, after all, and it's perfectly natural that he'd want to be around.'

My feelings about Max were still all over the place and I was reluctant to expose them, but these people were my good friends and they were obviously concerned. 'We had some great times together but it was all over a long time ago and I've come to terms with that. I don't know . . . I mean, he didn't even call until Sarah was over two months old. I can't suddenly flip a switch and pretend he didn't let me down.'

Ben hesitated for a moment and then said, 'I guess you never know what's going on in someone else's head, do you? At least you're not seeing anyone else, so that's one less complication.'

At this, Debbie looked gleeful and I glared at her, hoping for once she'd use a little tact and not tell everyone about David.

'Enough about my relationships,' I said briskly before temptation overpowered Debbie's very limited discretion. 'We haven't had a man paraded past us for ages. Don't tell me the amazing Debbie has hit a flat spot?'

Now it was Debbie's turn to shift uncomfortably. 'It's not a flat spot,' she said. 'I'm just taking it easy.'

Having known Debbie since primary school, I knew that where men were concerned 'taking it easy' wasn't a concept she understood.

'And another thing,' I continued, warming to my 'attack is the best form of defence' tactic. 'I could swear that I've seen you wearing that shirt before. Would I be right in thinking that was part of last year's Donna Karan summer collection?'

Debbie squirmed again. 'Well, yes . . .' she admitted. 'But it's really comfortable and it seemed silly to give it away when it still looks as good as new.'

Everyone's eyes widened at this statement. At the end of each season, Debbie ritually bundled up the clothes she'd worn for the previous few months and dropped them into the St Vincent de Paul shop around the corner from her flat, which I was convinced existed solely on her donations. Six months ago she would have regarded any suggestion that she wear a shirt for two seasons in a row as akin to heresy.

There was definitely something different about Debbie these days. Quitting her job and focusing her energies on something she wanted to do had changed her, and maybe she didn't feel she needed constant male company and up-to-the-minute clothes any more.

But not even the topic of Debbie's love life and fashion choices, and a fresh injection of caffeine, could raise the spirits of the gathering. After desultorily staring into our coffees for another ten minutes, we paid the bill and headed our separate ways, Karen looking as though she was more than happy to be leaving our suicidal ranks for the infectious happiness of her children.

The following Monday night, Debbie called an emergency business meeting at my place. Fortified by takeaway Turkish pizza and a bottle of red wine we tried to look at the situation dispassionately.

'So basically we're in deep shit,' Debbie summarised. 'We have four thousand books which we're going to have to pay for before they're shipped on Saturday, designer bills for the pages that aren't even printed yet, and nowhere to sell them.'

'And I've got nowhere to leave Sarah when I go back to work,' I added flatly.

At about three that morning I'd finally faced the fact that as no one seemed willing to leap in to fill Handley Smith's shoes, I was going to have to go back to work very soon. My boss was delighted when I called him with the news, which had at least given my ego a much-needed boost.

However, my next call was to the local childcare centre, whose administrator calmly informed me that their waiting list was currently twelve months long. A series of panicked calls to other centres in an increasing radius from my house hadn't found anywhere with a waiting list of less than four months.

Unless I could somehow do a deal with my boss to work from home, I was going to have to try to find a private child minder until a place in a child-care centre came up. Between those costs and the interest on my credit card, I figured I'd be lucky to have enough money for Saturday coffees.

I tried to find something positive to say about the situation, but failed. 'If we could just move some of the books, at least we'd be able to cover our costs and be back to where we started before we came up with this ridiculous idea.'

'By the way,' Debbie said, 'Andrew gave me that article he was talking about in *BRW*. The chain of stores he was talking about is House Arrest. The guy's name's Peter Davies apparently.'

'Oh,' I said, disappointed. 'I called them again today, just on the off-chance I'd get someone other than the nasty receptionist. No such luck. She is obviously under strict instructions not to put anyone selling things through. She just told me to put it in writing and they'd get back to us within six to eight weeks. We'll have starved to death by then.'

'Talk about forgetting his roots,' Debbie scowled. 'You'd think that if he really did open his own shop because he couldn't get any retailers to talk to him, he'd have a bit more sympathy for other people start-ing out.'

The way Debbie was slugging back the wine showed how disheartened she was. At this point I wished I could join her and get outrageously drunk. The way things were going, I probably wouldn't even be able to afford to do it once I'd weaned Sarah. Now that was a cheering thought.

Debbie spoke again. 'Maybe he doesn't know

that the receptionist is such a Rottweiler. What about if we try to contact him directly? We must be able to find out where he lives.

'Hold on,' she said suddenly. 'Remember Victor? He'd be able to give us this guy's home address – even if he isn't listed.'

Victor was an undercover detective Debbie had seen for about three weeks last summer. I had always had my doubts about him, but when he got horribly drunk one day in a Bondi hotel beer garden and started boasting to anyone in earshot that the police rules didn't apply to him, even Debbie knew it was time to move on.

'Well, Deb,' I said, 'there are a couple of things wrong with that plan. One is that Victor is a psychopath and it was a miracle he didn't plant some evidence in our flat so that his team could raid us in the middle of the night for kicks.' I looked at her meaningfully until she nodded reluctantly. 'And the second thing is that it's illegal.'

'All right, all right. It was just a thought.'

We sat in silence for a while.

'This might seem like a bad idea . . .' I began. 'But if this guy really does start work at five a.m., maybe that's when we should call him. Surely the Rottweiler couldn't be there then?'

'Well anything's worth a try,' Debbie said. 'Better still, maybe we should actually go to his office and show him the mock-ups? The article said that this guy refuses to pay city rents and so their head office is in some little building in Kingsgrove. It's not like we'll have to get through security.'

'You think so? Wouldn't that have the opposite effect and irritate him?'

'Maybe. But at least he'd remember us.'

'I guess . . .' I said doubtfully.

'Look,' Debbie interrupted, 'we've both got our life's savings riding on this. I'm not going to let it all go just because we don't want to be rude. What have we got to lose except some dignity?'

'All right,' I surrendered, knowing better than to try to oppose Debbie when she'd made up her mind about something. 'When do you want to do it?'

Suddenly Debbie was very efficient, and at least moderately sober. 'Okay, here's the plan. Five o'clock tomorrow morning. We'll meet here. You bring all the samples, I'll bring all the paperwork.'

'What about Sarah?'

I couldn't help but notice my friends had a tendency to assume Sarah would be fine left in her cot with a TV remote control and a packet of chips.

'Um . . . Well, let's bring her. She proves we've really done our market research. Plus she's very cute. No one could be mean to her.'

TWENTY-FOUR

When the alarm went off the next morning, I couldn't believe I'd actually let Debbie talk me into this.

Swearing, I dragged myself out of my warm bed. I'd fed Sarah an hour and a half ago, and thoughts of leaving her with a stranger so I could go back to work to pay off a huge credit-card debt had kept me awake ever since.

Feeling rather like a criminal, I had a sudden desire to don a black catsuit and balaclava. Instead, I pulled on the black trousers, boots and grey knitted polo-neck I'd left out the night before having spent fifteen minutes pondering the dress code for an early morning gatecrashing of a successful businessman.

After all these months, I had come to the conclusion that there was only one unbreakable rule of motherhood. Never, ever wake a sleeping baby. As I looked at Sarah peacefully asleep in her cot I almost decided to call Debbie and cancel this ridiculous escapade.

The situation was desperate, I reminded myself, and once I was ready, I reluctantly picked Sarah up and carried her out to the car. She stirred and let out a cry as I gently lowered her into the capsule. I froze and thankfully she settled back to sleep.

What on earth was I doing? Much as Debbie protested that we were just being assertive, what we were about to do was pretty close to stalking. By the time Debbie pulled up, looking even less thrilled about the situation than I did, I had decided to call the whole thing off. One look at her set face, however, and I knew there was no getting out of it now.

'This had better bloody work,' she grumbled as she bundled herself into my car.

There were some faint fingerprints of light creeping across the sky as we pulled up outside a building sporting the House Arrest logo. I didn't know whether to be relieved or disappointed when I saw the top floor was lit.

'Well, at least it looks like someone is here,' I commented.

Debbie didn't even respond and I looked at her. Her gaze was fixed firmly on a bakery three shops down. Lights were on in there as well and I could detect the unmistakable smell of coffee and hot bread drifting through the cold air.

'Wait here,' she ordered and disappeared into the darkness.

Less than five minutes later she returned bearing half a dozen coffees and a bag full of warm bagels and croissants. It smelt wonderful, but I wasn't in the mood for a picnic.

'Deb, we hardly have time to stop for breakfast. Let's just go inside, get humiliated and leave. We can eat after that.'

'Sophie, have a little faith. I have a plan. There are very few human beings in the world who can resist the smell of coffee and fresh bread, particularly at this indecent hour. At least if we come bearing gifts, he might hesitate before he throws us down the stairs.'

In the absence of any better plan, I agreed with her.

Thankfully the door at the bottom of the building wasn't locked, so, laden down with our provisions, samples and Sarah, who by some miracle had stayed blissfully asleep during her transfer to the baby sling, we trudged up two flights of stairs. I couldn't help but think that Peter Davies might not be so cavalier about his security after this morning.

Putting the bakery supplies on the reception counter, Debbie hesitated and then rang a buzzer attached to a sign saying 'Please ring if desk unattended'.

There was a rustle from behind a partition and then a face appeared around the corner. 'Hello?'

Feeling particularly silly, I stood frozen to the spot, but Debbie stepped forward. 'Peter Davies?'

The face nodded suspiciously – clearly he was not used to unannounced visits at this hour.

'Mr Davies, my name is Debbie Campbell and this is my colleague Sophie Anderson. We have a product we believe would work really well in your stores and we'd like to show it to you.'

Obviously deciding that we weren't axe murderers, the man stepped forward. He was about fifty, with the lean, wiry body of a long-distance runner. He didn't look pleased by the interruption.

'And you decided that,' he checked his watch, 'five-thirty in the morning was the best time to catch me in a good mood?'

I almost turned and ran out the door, but Debbie stood her ground. 'No, Mr Davies, I don't believe five-thirty is a good time for anybody. We came this morning because we really believe our product should be in your stores, but we can't get past your receptionist during conventional hours.'

His expression changed slightly. 'Susan does have a tendency to be overly protective,' he admitted. 'But,' his face became stern again, 'that doesn't give you the right to just waltz in here whenever you like. How did you know I would be here, anyway?'

I thought it was probably time I gave Debbie a hand. 'We saw the article in *BRW*. It said you started work early. And,' I added, as he didn't respond, 'we brought you some coffee and bagels.'

He hesitated. For a moment I was certain he was going to tell us to leave, but then his gaze rested on Sarah. 'All right, you'd better come in. And call me Peter. Mr Davies is too formal for this time of the morning.'

It wasn't exactly a warm invitation, but at least he hadn't kicked us out. We followed him to his office, which was surprisingly small, and covered with posters promoting the London Marathon. Debbie and I exchanged glances. This guy made Andrew look unmotivated.

'I didn't know what kind of coffee you drink, so I bought every kind I could think of,' Debbie began, pushing the tray towards him. 'Take your pick.'

As he selected a flat white, I pulled our samples out of my bag. I figured we had less time than it took to drink a coffee in order to convince him. To add to the pressure, I could see Sarah starting to stir.

'Our product is baby books,' I began and saw him grimace. 'Baby books that are designed for real people,' I hurried on. 'Not books that have storks and cherubs all over them.'

I passed him a vibrant pink book and followed it with a green one. 'The concept is that people buy a cover and the pages and they then mix and match whatever pages they want. Christenings might be relevant for some people, naming ceremonies for others.'

'Makes sense,' he said, nodding as he flipped through the mocked-up pages. 'Do you have costings?'

Debbie handed him her file. While he looked through it, Debbie and I chose our own coffees and sipped nervously. None of us touched the bagels.

'And how soon could you have them delivered?' he asked, still reading.

'The covers are arriving in three weeks.' I couldn't see much point in hiding the truth. 'The pages could be printed by then too.'

That got his attention.

'You've ordered the products and are still looking for distribution? That was brave.'

Neither Debbie nor I responded. Brave wasn't the word I would have chosen.

Peter put the file down and looked at us. 'Look, ladies. This isn't how I do things. I have twenty outlets and people to source products for me. I don't get involved with decisions about small product lines any more.'

My hopes, which had started to build as he read through the file, vapourised. Another knockback, I thought.

'But . . .' Peter interrupted my vision of Sarah and me queuing for soup and bread at the Salvation Army, 'I actually think these look great and I admire your energy. The coffee and bagel bribe didn't go astray either. So if you'll reduce your price to give me fifty-five per cent of the retail value, I'll buy five hundred of them. If they sell I'll take more.'

He scribbled a name and number on a piece of paper and pushed it across the table. 'Call this person later today to sort out the details.'

'Sorry, Peter, we can't do that,' Debbie said calmly, ignoring the piece of paper in front of her.

I looked at her incredulously. This man was offering us money and as far as I was concerned we should just take whatever he was prepared to give us and get out of there before he changed his mind.

'We can absorb the price drop, but only if you take one thousand copies,' she continued.

Peter pursed his lips and scribbled some numbers on the pad in front of him. 'All right, I'll take nine hundred,' he said, a faint smile playing across his face. 'Deal?'

'Deal,' Debbie replied, scooping up the piece of paper and then standing and holding out her hand.

I smiled in what I hoped was a businesslike manner as we left, resisting my urge to hug him for saving my daughter and me from poverty.

'Yes!' I punched the air as we reached the stairwell. Nine hundred books at the lower price meant we wouldn't quite cover the costs of importing the covers, but if I could swing a longer credit period for the printing and artwork fee, I would only have to borrow money for a couple of weeks. And if we could sell some more books to House Arrest or someone else, then maybe we could actually make some money too. The feeling of relief that rolled over me made me light-headed.

Debbie grinned at me. 'Know anywhere that will serve us champagne at this hour?'

TWENTY-FIVE

'Debbie, what are you doing in there?'

Banging on the door to the spare bedroom where Debbie had closeted herself, I had a sudden feeling of déjà vu, as though we were back in high school and my dad was waiting downstairs to take us to a school social.

Instead, I was about to belatedly celebrate my thirtieth birthday, my daughter was in the next room, my daughter's father was about to arrive, and my date was waiting impatiently downstairs.

I looked at my watch – seven fifty-five.

'Debbie, you said yourself it was a miracle we got a table at Eat Drink for eight-thirty on a Friday night. I reckon they'll wait for about thirty seconds before they give it away.'

Debbie opened the door to the bedroom. Despite the fact that she had been in there for almost an hour, she was still wearing nothing more than her underwear.

'I can't decide what to wear.'

This was amazing coming from Debbie. While I often went through five different outfits before settling on the first one I'd tried, Debbie always seemed to know exactly what she was going to wear days before any event. She even managed to coordinate her toenail polish with her outfits. However, I noticed that tonight even her toes were bare.

'Deb, what's going on? I'm the one who is supposed to be stressed. It's my party.'

'Sophie, I can't explain now. I just need your opinion. Should I wear the black dress or the black trousers and paisley top?' Before I could answer she added, 'Or the gold top?'

'Well, considering I've never even seen any of this stuff before, I don't really know. When did you buy all this?' Seeing the look on her face I realised now was not the time to lecture her about clothes expenditure. 'Okay, forget it. Let me see what the dress looks like on.'

As she pulled the dress over her head, I pondered this very un-Debbie-like behaviour. She hadn't even invited anyone along, insisting that she'd get ready at my place to keep me company.

The dress looked great and I convinced her to leave it on without showing me all the others. I left her to finish off her makeup and headed downstairs.

My birthday had been months earlier, but having had visions of nursing one glass of champagne while all my friends became riotously drunk in my honour, I'd refused to have a celebration while I was pregnant.

When we'd finally set a date for the festivities, I'd been in favour of going to a bar in Newtown, followed by a meal at Sahib's, the Indian restaurant around the corner. But Debbie had insisted that Eat Drink was the place to be seen, and that she and everyone else wanted to take me out for something slightly more glamorous than a dodgy curry.

However, as I tottered downstairs again in my ridiculously high Prada heels (courtesy of Debbie) I had my doubts. There was something very appealing about celebrating moving into my thirties in jeans and a T-shirt, propped up at a low-key bar with my friends. After all, I reasoned, who was I trying to impress anyway?

When we were together, Max and I had spent a small fortune on trying out new restaurants and we had developed a theory that the most successful of them operate on a policy of fear and intimidation, which their highly trained staff carry out with great skill. We had concluded that the purpose of this is to ensure that by the time you actually have your meal you are so confused and cowed that there is no chance you could ever complain, no matter how bad the food is.

But it was far too late to change my mind now. As I looked at my watch again, I realised that if we didn't get a move on, we were going to be very late.

'How's she going?' David seemed more amused than stressed about the lateness of the hour.

'She's pretty close to ready. Are you sure I can't get you a drink while you wait?'

'No thanks, I'm fine.'

Despite his last visit, and the fact that Debbie and I had managed to place the order with House Arrest, things were still strained between us and we were both trying a bit too hard. As if that wasn't enough pressure, I had also let Max talk me into letting him babysit Sarah for the evening.

'Sophie, I'm going to have to learn how to do it some time – I might as well start while she's asleep. She won't even know you're not there,' he had argued. 'I'll line my mum up so she's at the other end of the phone if I need some advice. You can take your mobile and if things really get serious I'll call you and you can be home in fifteen minutes.'

I didn't want to tell him that I was less worried about Sarah's wellbeing than my own, that I didn't know how I'd feel about getting all dressed up and going out with David and leaving Max at home. The whole thing was just too weird to contemplate.

'And besides,' Max had continued, 'who else are you going to get to babysit? Won't everyone be out at the party?'

He had a point. Karen had been looking forward to the dinner since we had first started planning it and had already arranged for her usual babysitter to look after her kids. I hadn't been out enough to develop my own network of babysitters and I hated the idea of leaving Sarah with a stranger.

Debbie had looked at me strangely when I'd told her my dilemma. 'Just take him up on his offer, Sophie. I thought you two had decided to be grown-ups?'

I didn't feel very grown up, though, when Max

arrived on the dot of eight with a video and plastic bag full of containers of takeaway Thai.

'David, this is Max. Max, David,' I said, trying to act casual.

If I hadn't felt so stressed, I would have had to laugh. Each looked seriously unimpressed by the other's presence, although I had already warned both of them separately. Max had promised to be on his best behaviour, but I could feel the chill in the air as the two of them shook hands.

Despite having told myself many times that I didn't have to fill every conversational void, I couldn't help myself from babbling as I prayed desperately for Debbie to hurry up. 'Sarah's already asleep,' I told Max.

'She shouldn't wake up until three or four,' I continued. 'And I'll be home by then. But just in case, there are some bottles of milk in the fridge. She likes them warmed up, so if you just put the bottle in the microwave for about thirty seconds, that'll take the edge off it . . . Make sure you test it before you give it to her, though.'

'Got it,' Max answered. 'Relax, Sophie, we'll be fine.'

'I know you will. But if you do need me, here are some contact details – my mobile and the restaurant and also some emergency numbers just in case.' I waved a page covered with numbers in front of him.

Max took it and put it down on the table beside him without a glance. 'Got it.'

I hoped I only imagined the look that passed between the two men.

'We'd really better get going,' David spoke up. 'Do you want me to have a go at yelling at Debbie for a while?'

After a couple more shouts up the stairs, Debbie finally emerged, having changed outfits again. She was now wearing a pair of fitted black trousers and a stunning halter-neck.

Max looked very relieved to see us leave. 'Have a great time,' he said and I couldn't help but feel a pang as he closed the door behind us.

When we arrived at Eat Drink, I was greeted with yet more evidence of just how far out of the social loop I had fallen. The burly, not-too-bright doormen I was used to seeing at restaurants that had a happening bar attached had been replaced by a new breed of security guard, which Debbie informed me quietly were known as door bitches. Tall, razor thin and with dead straight black hair, the woman outside Eat Drink looked more like a model than a bouncer. However, she was definitely making the decisions about who was getting into the bar and who wasn't.

According to Debbie, the theory was that women were better than men at negotiating their way out of tricky situations and were therefore less likely to have to resort to unseemly violence. Apparently this new trend had begun after a series of unpleasant and highly publicised incidents in which patrons had been badly injured by overzealous security staff.

This particular woman didn't appear to have a great deal of confidence in her negotiating ability, as she was flanked by what looked like the entire Manpower troupe. Tight black T-shirts emphasised huge biceps and thick necks, and I was seized with a desire to give them some simple maths problems, to check if they were really as dumb as they looked.

Our reservations worked like a secret password and we moved inside without incident. Karen, Sam, Ben and Anna were already there. They all eyed David with undisguised interest.

'We need champagne,' Debbie declared after I had finished the introductions. 'And lots of it.'

Standing in the cool, if decidedly pretentious, restaurant surrounded by good friends I was glad that Debbie had insisted on us coming here. By some kind of miracle the champagne Debbie had ordered arrived straightaway and everyone raised their glasses as she said, 'To Sophie, our wonderful friend and now Sarah's devoted mother. Happy birthday!'

Andrew arrived as we drank, attracting approving glances from a number of women as he pushed his way through the other people at the bar to join us. I noticed with surprise that he was wearing a very fashionable three-quarter length black jacket over a light blue shirt, neither of which I'd ever seen before. The only clothes Andrew ever showed interest in buying were made of special sweat-absorbing material and I could only remember him buying a handful of going-out clothes in the whole time I'd known him.

He and David shook hands in what I could see was the usual male 'I have stronger grip than you' tussle. Debbie handed Andrew a glass of champagne and he took a deep sip and said something to her that I didn't catch.

David turned to me and said quietly, 'I couldn't say it before when Max was around, but you look great.'

'Thanks,' I smiled.

I felt great. Figuring I had a double reason for celebrating now that we'd done the deal with House Arrest, I'd splurged on a red dress from a shop on King Street. I'd been looking at it through the window for months and it had miraculously been on sale. I hadn't bought anything other than fat clothes, as Debbie called them, for a year and it felt fantastic to be wearing something new.

'I have some good news,' David said as Debbie and Andrew turned back towards us.

'The *Sydney Morning Herald* is running your baby book story tomorrow morning – including those glam photos of the pair of you.'

Debbie and I looked at him incredulously. The kind of exposure the article would give us was something we could never have contemplated paying for, even if there had been room in our business plan for an advertising budget. With all the people who would read the article over breakfast and morning coffees, our business had just gone from being a candidate for a chapter in a 'How not to run a small business' textbook to something that could take off.

'How did you manage that?' Debbie asked, always the cynic.

'I went to school with the features editor and he owed me a favour,' David answered, ignoring Debbie's sceptical tone. 'Besides, it's a good story.'

'That's unbelievable news, David. Thank you.'

'It was the least I could do after what happened,' David said happily. 'I'm really glad I could help.'

'This definitely calls for more champagne,' Debbie declared, catching the eye of a passing waiter. We polished off the champagne as the waiter arrived to show us to our table.

David was sitting across from me. He seemed to be very comfortable with everyone and was chatting animatedly to Anna beside him. It was only after the waiter asked us for the third time if we were ready to order that we all made an effort to stop talking and look at the menu.

The meals, which were presented on huge moss-green plates, looked like works of art and tasted great too. They were also decently sized, something to be thankful for in Sydney where you could easily pay fifty dollars for a beautifully presented but minuscule piece of meat in the middle of a plate half the size of the table.

A silence suddenly fell over the group and I realised that looking down at David was Angela; tall, thin, gorgeous Angela, whom I had last seen leaving David's office in a fit of pique. She looked stunning in a pale blue suit – at least she would have looked stunning if her eyes weren't bloodshot and she wasn't swaying slightly.

'Hello, David,' she said and I could hear the effort she was making not to slur her words.

'Hello, Angela,' he answered, with a decided lack of enthusiasm.

A strained silence descended.

'How are you?' she tried again.

'I'm well, thanks,' he replied. Obviously deciding that it would be rude to go any longer without introducing her, he turned reluctantly to the table.

During the introductions Angela's eyes didn't move on past me. After several excruciatingly long seconds she obviously realised that she was staring and wrenched her gaze away.

'I'm here with the usual crowd,' she explained, gesturing towards the other side of the restaurant. 'Well,' she continued, 'enjoy your dinner,' and with that she walked back towards her table, negotiating the gaps between the tables with some difficulty.

'Sorry about that,' David apologised. 'We used to go out together and it's still pretty awkward,' he added unnecessarily.

Ben changed the subject expertly and before long the conversation was back in full swing. The whole scene had unsettled me, though, and I excused myself, heading to the bathroom to gather my thoughts.

I was standing at the basin washing my hands when Angela walked in. She was obviously as surprised to see me as I was to see her.

She smiled awkwardly at me and went to walk into one of the cubicles but then stopped suddenly. 'Sophie, I'm really sorry. I didn't mean to cause you so much trouble,' she said to my back, taking me totally by surprise. If anything, I'd expected her to be unpleasant. 'I wasn't really thinking straight after David and I broke up.'

'Why would you be sorry?' I asked, turning around.

It was her turn to look confused. Even three sheets to the wind, she obviously realised she had made a mistake. 'Um, nothing,' she muttered and turned towards the cubicle.

There was something about her manner (and maybe the champagne and wine I'd already consumed) that made me reluctant to let the matter drop. What did Angela have to apologise for?

I made a big show of reapplying my makeup, even though I'd just done it, and was still standing at the mirror when she re-emerged.

She looked anything but delighted to see me still there.

'Angela, maybe I'm missing something, but I don't know what you were talking about just then.'

She put her handbag on the counter and started rummaging around inside. Her mascara had started to smudge but she seemed oblivious to this and started haphazardly applying more.

'Forget it, Sophie. Can't you see that I'm drunk? What do I know?'

It must have been obvious to her that I wasn't going to be easily dissuaded and eventually she spoke again. 'All right. I was jealous that David had bounced back so quickly from our break-up while I felt like I was dying inside.'

Tears welled up in her eyes and I realised just how fragile she was.

'Five years,' she said bitterly. 'And he moves straight on to someone else. I still can't think about anything but him.'

I had a sudden flash of having a similar teary

conversation with Debbie after Max and I broke up. 'I'm really sorry, Angela. I know how it feels.'

'Yeah, well, I just wanted to hurt him, so I threatened to tell the managing director that he was compromising his position by ordering your products while he was sleeping with you.'

A sick feeling formed in my stomach as it dawned on me what she was saying. 'So, let me get this straight,' I said slowly. 'There was no spending freeze?'

'No what?' Angela asked, not understanding.

'Never mind.' I shook my head.

It was logical that she'd think David had told me the real reason why he'd had to cancel the order. As much as I would have preferred to dislike Angela, I actually had the feeling she was probably a nice person.

Obviously feeling she'd said enough, Angela smiled uncomfortably and backed out the door, leaving me alone with my thoughts.

The least I could do was talk to David before I jumped to any conclusions. Trying to reassure myself, I thought that maybe there was something Angela didn't know about.

When I got back to the table everyone was poring over the dessert menus. Determined not to create a scene, I did the same, but my appetite had vanished. David had either seen Angela disappear at the same time as me, or had just sensed something was wrong, as he kept trying to catch my eye.

I tried not to show my mental turmoil as I sipped my coffee. Once the others had paid the predictably horrendous bill, Debbie announced that the next stop was The Scene, one of the many new bars I'd never even heard of. One of the waiters deigned to call cabs for us and I found myself alone with David in one.

Dropping my pretence that nothing was wrong, I turned towards him. 'David, I spoke to Angela in the bathroom. She told me that the reason you cancelled our order was that she threatened to tell your boss you were compromising your position by doing a deal with me. Is that right?'

His hesitation gave me my answer.

'Yes, it is, Sophie,' he said finally. 'Graham believes everything Angela tells him and I knew I'd be causing huge problems for myself by putting your order through. Angela had just dropped her ultimatum on me when you walked into my office that day, and somehow I couldn't bring myself to tell you the truth. I said the first thing that came into my head. I didn't realise you'd actually ordered the books and I truly believed you'd find it easy to get a deal with one of the other big stores. I'm really sorry, Sophie, I've almost told you about ten times.'

I could no longer pretend that there might be another explanation. David had lied to me. I had a sudden surge of anger as I thought about the dire financial position he'd put Debbie and me in because he had refused to stand his ground and explain to his boss that our product stood on its merits.

As well as being angry, I felt humiliated. I'd slept with David and had even been starting to think there could be a real place for him in my life, while all the time he'd been keeping something like this from me.

'You know, there were so many other things you could have done,' I said coldly. 'You could have talked it through with Angela – she strikes me as a pretty nice person who was really hurt by what had happened. You could have explained things to your boss. Or, you know, you could have just told me the truth. Were you really intending to pretend it had never happened? Or did you think it wouldn't matter anyway as there wasn't anything serious between us?'

'It definitely wasn't that,' David said earnestly. 'I really enjoy being with you and with Sarah – this hasn't just been a fling for me.'

Strangely enough I believed him, but it didn't change anything. 'Well, you should have thought about that a bit more before you started telling me a pack of lies.'

I leant forward and tapped the driver, who had been doing his best to pretend he wasn't listening, on the shoulder. 'Could you pull over here, please?'

The cab stopped on the side of the road and I turned to David. 'I don't feel like going out any more. I'm going home.'

As I opened the door David grabbed my arm. 'Sophie, I really am sorry. It was a selfish and stupid thing to do, but I care about you. Don't let this ruin everything.'

'How can you say that, David?' I asked. 'What kind of relationship do you think we could have if you dealt with the first difficult situation you found yourself in by lying to me?'

I stepped out onto the footpath and started walking. For a few seconds I thought David was going to follow me, but after a long pause the taxi pulled out into the traffic again and drove past me. I didn't look up as it did.

I marched furiously along the side of the road, not going anywhere in particular. After a few minutes, however, my insteps, wedged in Debbie's ridiculous shoes, hurt so much I had to slow my pace and then stop. I leant against a shop front, rubbing the side of my foot and reflecting on the disaster area that was my love life.

As my anger faded, it dawned on me that I wasn't devastated by it not having worked out with David. Being around an attractive man who obviously enjoyed my company had caused me to ignore the fact that we were quite different people. David was used to a well-ordered and sophisticated life, which bore no resemblance to Sarah's and my chaotic existence, and if I was honest with myself I couldn't picture him being part of that. I felt slightly depressed at the thought of losing that exciting feeling being involved with someone new brings, but I couldn't be bothered being with someone just for the sake of it. Hopefully, I wouldn't spend the rest of my life alone, but for now it probably wasn't such a bad thing.

Giving my foot a last rub, I hobbled in the direction of home and Sarah, hoping that the gods would bless me with an empty taxi.

TWENTY-SIX

Sarah seemed to have some kind of sixth sense which alerted her that I'd had a late night and the next morning she woke at three and then again not long after dawn.

The confrontation with David had sent me home earlier than I had anticipated, but it had still been after midnight when I'd made it in the door to find Max fast asleep on the sofa. There'd been no discussion about him staying the night. But after hovering uncertainly beside him for a couple of minutes, I'd decided there was no way I could wake him up and shove him out the door.

I fed Sarah now, and then put her back in her cot in the vain hope that she'd take pity on her sleep-deprived mother and go back to sleep. It quickly became obvious that wasn't going to happen, so I picked her up again before she could wake Max. A stimulating play session was just not going to happen this morning. Pulling her into bed, I put my head next to hers so she could play with my face, deciding that the pain of little fingers grabbing my hair and my nose was a small price to pay for the benefit of being able to close my eyes.

The novelty of that game lasted for a blessed half hour, after which I forced my eyes open and managed to entertain her with various toys while still lying in bed, trying not to think about the fact that Max was downstairs. Eventually I acknowledged that there was not the remotest chance of any more sleep, so I dragged myself off into the bathroom, where I propped Sarah on a towel on the floor so she could watch me showering.

I have always felt that a hot shower is one of modern man's best inventions, by far surpassing advancements as trivial as the wheel. As usual the warm water did wonders, and by the time I'd dried myself and dressed both of us, I felt almost human.

Just then I heard the noise I'd been waiting for – the sound of the newspaper delivery van pulling up outside, followed by the soft thunk of the newspaper landing on the path. Not even Max's presence could keep me from seeing the article about our business in print and I headed down the stairs.

Sarah let out a cry as I stepped into the living room and Max sat up with a start, blinking sleep away and obviously trying to figure out where he was.

'Hi,' I said awkwardly.

'Hi,' he replied, looking warily behind me. Obviously concluding that David hadn't stayed the night, he smiled with more warmth. 'Good night?'

'Great night,' I answered. 'Although I could have lived without my little blue-eyed alarm clock at a quarter to six.'

'Everything was fine here too,' Max said. 'I didn't hear a peep out of her. Sorry for crashing on the sofa,' he added, slightly sheepishly. 'After the movie finished I just closed my eyes for a moment and the next thing I knew it was morning.'

'I think you deserve some kind of award for actually managing to sleep on that collection of springs,' I said admiringly. 'Most of my friends won't even sit on it for more than five minutes.'

'Yeah, well, getting to sleep has never been one of my problems,' Max grinned.

'No . . .' I replied, thinking of the many nights I'd lain awake beside him after he had fallen asleep within seconds of his head hitting the pillow.

Max was obviously having similar thoughts and the silence stretched uncomfortably.

'I guess I should get going,' he said half-heartedly.

'There's something you have to see first.' I opened the front door and picked up the hefty Saturday edition of the paper from the front path. After depositing Sarah in the armchair, I pulled out the features section. Staring at me was a quarter-page photo of Debbie, Sarah and me.

'Oh my God,' I exclaimed in shock, having expected our article to be tucked away at the back of the paper. 'Take a look at this.' I turned the paper around to Max.

He blinked in surprise. 'What? "Sacking the Stork – Babies in the new millennium",' he read the headline out loud. 'The article's about your business?' he asked incredulously. 'How on earth did you manage that?'

'David did, actually,' I replied, turning the paper back around.

Ignoring Max's silence, I scanned the article. They had printed what I'd written almost word for word, but seeing it in the paper was very different to looking at it on my computer screen. Karen's husband Sam was a keen photographer and he'd taken some black and white shots. The one they'd included had us sitting on some metal steps in front of an old warehouse. Debbie looked predictably glamorous with her hair flowing over her shoulder in the breeze. But Sarah and I looked pretty good too, I thought with pleasure.

'This is unbelievable, Max,' I exclaimed, thrusting the newspaper at him. 'Can you imagine what this could do for us?' I grabbed the phone. 'I've got to talk to Debbie.'

'Damn,' I muttered when I heard the engaged tone. Debbie often took the phone off the hook after a late night. Without much hope, I dialled her mobile number, exclaiming in frustration when her voice mail clicked on straightaway.

Surely she couldn't have forgotten that the article was coming out this morning. I stood up and grabbed my car keys. 'Max, I've got to show this to Debbie. I'm going around to her place.'

Max finished scanning the article and looked up. 'Do you want to leave Sarah with me?'

I looked at him in surprise. Sarah always went

everywhere with me, so I hadn't thought about whether or not it would be convenient to bring her now. But it would be much easier to leave her here rather than drag her in and out of the car. She wouldn't need feeding for a while yet and I could easily be back in time.

Still, I hesitated. Looking after Sarah during the day was a different story to doing so at night when she was fast asleep. While I admired Max's willingness to help, I wasn't sure he was up to dealing with Sarah if she decided to be difficult.

'Sophie,' Max said before I could voice my concerns. 'I'll be fine. Give me a rundown on what to expect and I'm sure I'll be able to manage for an hour or so.'

He was right. Sarah was due for a sleep soon anyway, and I couldn't think of any mortal danger that might befall her within the four walls of the house. So I changed her nappy and explained to Max when and how he should put her down to sleep, then I headed towards the door.

I hesitated and turned back. 'Max, you're not thinking of taking her out while I'm gone, are you?' I asked, trying not to sound obsessive.

'Oh, I thought we might head down to the pub,' Max said offhandedly. Seeing my expression he laughed. 'Sophie, I'm kidding. Talk about a sense of humour loss. Go!'

'All right, all right,' I laughed, dropping a kiss on the top of Sarah's head and walking out the door with the newspaper under my arm.

The traffic was mercifully light and I was at

Debbie's flat within fifteen minutes. Feeling happy with the world, I bounded up the steps. Well, actually I bounded up the first two flights and trudged up the remainder, my exercise regime having lapsed significantly in recent weeks.

Trying to still my panting, I rang the doorbell. Unsurprised at the fact that no one answered, I tried again, knowing that the noise would eventually break through Debbie's sleep. Sure enough, after my fourth bout of ringing, I could hear footsteps trudging across the lounge.

'Whoever you are, I'm coming,' Debbie yelled. 'Just please stop that terrible noise.'

Grinning I stood back and waited as she opened the door.

Debbie threw the door open and stood there, her robe held together with one hand and her hair uncharacteristically tousled. As she registered that it was me, the thunderous look on her face changed to confusion and I could see her swallowing the curses she'd been about to bestow on the person waking her so early on a Saturday morning.

'Sophie?' she said. 'What are you doing here? Is everything all right?'

'Everything's fine, Debbie,' I answered. 'In fact, it's great. Have a look at this.' I held the article out in front of me.

Debbie squinted at the page, trying to focus her bleary eyes. Comprehension struck suddenly. 'The article! My God, how could I forget?' She grabbed the paper with her free hand and stared at it.

'This is unbelievable,' she exclaimed after a quick

scan. 'David is now officially forgiven for everything after this little effort.'

I suddenly remembered she didn't know the latest instalment in the David saga and my mood dipped. I'd tell her later, I decided, not wanting to spoil one of the rare moments of celebration in our fraught business enterprise.

Debbie turned and walked into the flat, reading the article as she went, and I followed behind her. I was about to sit down on the sofa but I stopped suddenly. Thrown across the back of the armchair was a man's black jacket.

'I didn't realise you had company,' I said with raised eyebrows.

'Ah, yes,' Debbie muttered, uncharacteristically reticent about her latest conquest.

Looking closer at the jacket, I realised what had been staring me in the face for a long time.

Turning around, I saw Debbie looking at me apprehensively. 'You and Andrew?' I asked, still not quite believing it.

Debbie nodded with a rueful smile.

I dropped onto the sofa and tried to readjust my thinking to accept something I previously would have considered impossible.

'I've been wanting to tell you for a while now,' Debbie said. 'When it first started, we both thought that, given our respective track records, it wouldn't last a week and so we decided not to announce it to the world.'

She noticed the hurt expression on my face and hurried on. 'I know you're not the world, but I felt so strange about it all, I couldn't face having anyone else watching us as we tried to figure out what was going on. Not even you.'

I nodded slowly, understanding what she was saying. 'When did it start?' I cast my mind back in time and tried to think of a likely opportunity.

'Remember how a couple of days after I resigned, we were going to the movies with Ben and Anna but they cancelled at the last minute? Nothing happened, but I think both of us were surprised by what a good time we had. Then when you were in Hong Kong and I had chickenpox I ran out of calamine lotion and asked Andrew to buy me some and drop it around. He said he'd had chickenpox and so couldn't catch it and, well, one thing led to another . . .'

'You had sex with Andrew for the first time, dotted in pink cream?' I asked incredulously, amazed she'd even let him in the front door.

'Well, yes,' Debbie said in embarrassment. 'It did occur to me at the time to wonder if he had some kind of fetish for sick women,' she added dryly.

I was still trying to fit all this together. 'So, if you were going to tell me, does that mean it's something you think might last?'

Debbie hesitated and looked over her shoulder before saying in a low voice, 'Sophie, I've never felt this way before . . . I think this might be it.'

At this point, nothing could surprise me. The possibility of seeing Debbie in love had always seemed remote, but the concept of her being in love with a man who was happiest in a tracksuit, running up and down hills, simply defied imagination.

I stood up and walked over to the hallway that led to Debbie's bedroom. 'Andrew Hardy, come out here,' I demanded imperiously.

Andrew walked out, sheepishly, a towel wrapped around his waist. He had obviously been listening to what he could of the conversation.

'I should refuse to speak to either of you ever again,' I said in a serious voice. Involuntarily I smiled. 'But bizarre as the concept is, I actually think this is fabulous news.'

I meant what I said. As my initial surprise faded, I realised that they could actually be very good for each other. Although on the surface they seemed complete opposites, they were actually pretty similar. Both of them were generous and ferociously loyal and there was no way I could have survived the last year without either of them. They were also both outgoing and loved a good time – although admittedly they had very different definitions of fun. No matter how happy they were together, I still couldn't imagine Debbie getting a kick out of jogging on her toes – my guess was that Andrew hadn't shared that wild and crazy activity with her yet.

'Excellent. Well I'm glad we sorted that out,' Debbie said, the look of relief on her face belying her businesslike tone.

'This calls for a celebratory coffee,' Andrew declared, turning towards the kitchen, clearly very much at home in Debbie's flat.

'Sorry, Andrew, I can't. I have to keep going,' I said, looking at my watch. 'Sarah is with Max and I need to be home pretty soon to rescue him.

'It's a long story,' I said in response to Debbie's quizzical look. 'I'll fill you in some other time.'

'You're the only one who knows about this so far, Sophie. We're going to break the news to everyone else, but can you not mention it to anyone until then?' Debbie asked.

'My lips are sealed,' I replied. 'Just promise me that you make sure I'm there when you break the news at the cafe.'

As I headed out the door, Andrew put his arm around Debbie's shoulders.

This was definitely going to take some time to adjust to, I thought to myself as I waved goodbye and headed back down the stairs.

TWENTY-SEVEN

As I was pulling up at home, my phone rang.
'You are not going to believe this,' Debbie
crowed as soon as I answered.

'Don't tell me you have another surprise for me,'
I replied. 'Let me guess . . . You're giving away all
your clothes to the poor.'

Debbie ignored me. 'I've just had a call from the
buyer for Johnson Brothers and she's very interested
in putting the books in all their stores. She wants to
meet with us on Monday.'

Johnson Brothers were Handley Smith's main
competitors and had over one hundred stores across
the country. I pulled a pen and an old shopping
receipt out of the glove box and scribbled some figures, staring at them in surprise.

'Debbie,' I whispered. 'We could make some
serious money.'

'I know!' she yelled. 'Bloody fabulous, isn't it?'

'But I thought Johnson Brothers weren't interested.'

'I couldn't talk to anyone there with more clout than the postboy when the Handley Smith order fell through, but all of a sudden their head buyer thinks our books have "marvellous potential",' Debbie answered. 'Goes to show the wonderful effect of a bit of publicity, doesn't it?

'You'll be glad to hear that I managed a civil reply when she asked me why we hadn't approached them before,' she added.

After talking for a few minutes longer, I rang off.

Despite Debbie and I having assured each other we weren't going to count on this order until we had something in black and white, I sat in the car staring at the figures on the paper in front of me. If this really did happen it would totally change things. Our original thoughts of building up a range of similar products suddenly didn't seem as ridiculous as they had yesterday, and, best of all, I wouldn't have to go back to work.

Things were definitely looking up, I thought, hurrying up the front path to tell Max the good news. I stopped short as I walked into the lounge room, which looked like a bomb had hit it. Sarah's crying reached me from upstairs. Heart racing, I took the stairs two at a time, following the noise to her bedroom.

She was lying on the change table, crying at the top of her lungs. Max was shirtless and standing in front of the open closet vainly rifling through the stacks of clothes. It took me only a second to realise that Sarah was perfectly fine, if a tad out of sorts, and then another one to recognise what was happening. I burst out laughing.

Max spun around at the sound. 'Sophie. Thank God you're here,' he exclaimed and began rambling like a condemned man. 'Sarah was crying and wouldn't go to sleep and the book said it might be because she had a dirty nappy.' He gestured towards the floor where a baby book lay open. 'I checked and it was dirty, so I decided to change it. But then I discovered that it had gone all the way up her back and soaked through her clothes.

'How can she do that?' he asked in mystification. 'Does it bounce off the bottom of her nappy or what?' Without pausing for breath, he continued. 'So I took off her clothes to change them. Then she did it again and it squirted all down the front of my shirt.'

'It's okay, Max, relax,' I said, putting my hand on his arm and trying not to laugh. 'Here, this will do.' I pulled an outfit out of a drawer and led him back to the change table.

Max stood to one side, obviously having no intention of giving Sarah a second shot at him. Gently I coaxed him through the process of putting a new nappy on her and dressing her. When that was finished Max picked Sarah up, and as he did, she stopped crying and closed her eyes, obviously exhausted by the whole ordeal.

'Put her into bed,' I whispered.

Sarah stirred as Max laid her down and he froze, not moving again until she had settled back into sleep.

We left the room in silence and Max closed the door. 'Phew,' he breathed, running his forearm across his forehead. 'That was harder than making a pitch to a new client.'

As we walked downstairs I told him about the approach we'd had from Johnson Brothers, trying hard not to let myself get too excited about the prospect.

'What would you say to breakfast at the King Street Cafe?' I suggested impulsively, enjoying having someone around in the morning who actually talked back to me. 'It's still only nine and I'm not meeting the others there until eleven.'

'Sounds great,' he replied. 'But, hold on, we can't go anywhere until Sarah wakes up.'

I couldn't help but smile at the abrupt role reversal. 'If we give her another ten minutes or so she'll be sound asleep and we can move her into the pram without waking her. You're going to want a shower anyway, aren't you?' I looked pointedly at his chest.

'Ah yes,' he replied with a grimace.

Twenty minutes later Max had showered and dressed in one of my rugby tops, which had once belonged to him anyway, and we were ready to go. After manoeuvring Sarah's pram over the doorstep and onto the footpath, I noticed Max looking uncomfortably at me.

'Would you mind if I, uh, pushed it?' he asked nervously.

'Of course not,' I replied, happily relinquishing the pram.

Max put one hand on the handle and pushed it tentatively. Gaining confidence he picked up speed and soon we were strolling along the footpath. I was very conscious of the family scene we portrayed and I assumed Max was too. My attempt to make small talk failed, and we walked in silence for most of the way.

The clouds that had been hanging threateningly finally began dropping rain as we reached King Street, and we ran the last few metres to the cafe just as the heavens opened. When we burst through the door we were greeted by a scene which looked more like Debbie's kitchen than the usually spotless cafe.

Although there were no customers, empty cups and saucers littered most of the available tables. The usually pristine counters were stacked with plates and glasses and Ben was standing behind the coffee machine looking unusually stressed. Spotting Max and me together, he brightened momentarily.

'You two are up and about very early,' he said, obviously fishing for information.

'Max went to sleep on the sofa while he was looking after Sarah,' I said quickly.

'Oh, right,' he replied with a smile, obviously not convinced. Turning back to the mess in the cafe, Ben's mood darkened again. 'Last night two of my staff members decided they were soul mates and ran off to Melbourne together. They didn't feel that cleaning up from the afternoon session would be in keeping with this romantic revelation, and to make matters worse, they were both rostered on this morning. As a result, I have an absolute pigsty on my hands and no staff.'

'Two of your staff members . . .' I repeated. 'That'll teach you to break Anna's rule and hire someone female.'

'I didn't,' Ben replied flatly.

'Ah . . .' I said, trying not to smile. 'Would it help if we started to clear tables?' I hadn't worked in a cafe since my uni days but I was sure I could manage to wash a few plates and cups.

Ben looked ridiculously grateful. 'That'd be great. What about Sarah?'

'If I can find somewhere to put the pram, she should sleep for an hour or so. Can I leave her in the kitchen?'

'Sure. Look, if you could just get the crockery clean and ready for the morning rush, that'd really help. I've called in more staff, but they're probably still an hour away.'

Quickly I pushed the pram through the double doors and squeezed it into the tiny space between the wall and the paper-laden desk in an alcove off the kitchen. For the next three-quarters of an hour Max and I stacked and scrubbed cups and plates, and by the time Sarah woke, the place was starting to look more like its usual pristine self.

Finishing one last load, I dried my hands and took off my borrowed apron. I'd forgotten how hard cafe work was and I was pleased to have an excuse to stop and sit down. Max left the kitchen ahead of me and as I followed him with the pram, the handle dislodged a teetering pile of papers which spilt all over the floor.

Cursing, I bent down to collect them. As I stacked them back on the desk, I noticed a sheet of paper bearing the logo of the real estate agent I used. That made sense. It was a big agency and they probably rented Ben the cafe premises. What didn't make sense was the fact that my address was on there.

I stared at the page dumbly for a moment. The document was an invoice made out to Max, care of the cafe. In the details column was $320, being for four weeks rent at my address.

What was going on?

Just then, Ben walked into the kitchen. Something in my face must have alerted him that all was not well because he suddenly looked concerned.

I thrust the offending page into his hands. 'What's this?' I demanded.

When he saw what I was holding, he blushed a deep red. 'Sophie, I'm sorry. I wanted to tell you.'

'Tell me what?'

'Max has been paying some of the rent since you moved into your place. He said you wouldn't accept any money from him but he didn't want you struggling on your own with Sarah.'

'What are you talking about? How did Max even know where I was living, let alone how much I was paying?'

Ben went an even deeper shade of red. 'Well, that bit of it is my fault. You came in the day you first saw your place. You seemed really excited about it, but didn't think you'd have a chance as they were asking for too much rent.'

'What, so you thought you'd call Max in San Francisco and ask him to kick in for it?' I was starting to feel like the victim of a conspiracy and couldn't stop the sharp edge that had crept into my voice.

'No. It wasn't like that.' Ben touched my arm. 'Max called me a couple of days later. As usual the first thing he asked about was you. I told him about the house and that you weren't hopeful about getting it at the price you'd offered. He asked me if I could find out who was renting it. It turned out that the estate agency was the same one that I've been renting through for years and I called them and pulled in a favour.'

I couldn't believe what I was hearing. So much for my strong words about managing without financial help from Max. He had been paying nearly a quarter of my rent the whole time. Wordlessly I turned around and began manoeuvring Sarah's pram out of the tiny kitchen. In the process, I managed to dislodge yet another pile of papers, which I ignored.

Max had settled into a comfortable corner seat and was looking at the menu.

The pram caught a table leg and I swore under my breath. Wielding a pram made it hard to do anything with dignity.

'I can't believe that you have been paying part of my rent all this time,' I stormed when I finally reached the table where Max was sitting. 'You knew how I felt about you paying for a child you didn't want. You knew I wanted to manage by myself.'

Ben had followed me out of the kitchen and Max looked from one of us to the other, obviously guessing what had happened.

'What, were you planning on sneaking around paying for things until Sarah turned eighteen? God, you must think I'm so thick!'

'Sophie . . . I'm sorry. I just wanted to help and you seemed so determined to do it all the hard way.'

'Great. So you just went behind my back and lied to me. I'd rather be living in a shoebox on the edge of town than take guilt-inspired handouts from you. At least I'd know that it was mine. Just forget about it. I'm leaving. I'll call you once I've sorted out what I'm going to do.'

As I jerked the pram through the doorway and out into the rain, I wished that I was one of those witty people who could think of good one-liners to exit on. No doubt the perfect thing would come to me in about a week.

I couldn't believe how angry I was. Managing to support Sarah by myself had given me a lot of pride. Discovering that I hadn't been, made me feel as though I'd been punched in the stomach. How could I have accepted the drop in rent so naively?

As soon as Sarah and I were out of sight, I stopped under an awning. Ignoring the fact that she was already more than damp, I slipped on the pram's waterproof cover. Far from being upset, she seemed to think the whole thing was pretty funny.

'Yeah, you just sit there laughing. You're not the one who has to worry about finding somewhere else for us to live.'

About to brave the deluge once more, I felt a hand on my shoulder. I turned to find Max standing beside me, gratifyingly looking as sodden as I felt.

'Sophie. I'm really sorry. I didn't think you'd take it like this. I had just handled everything so badly and I wanted to make up for it somehow.'

The awning wasn't having much effect against the near-horizontal rain and Max looked up at the sky. 'Look, we don't have to have this conversation here. Won't you come back into the cafe with me?'

I shook my head. 'We don't have to have this conversation at all. I've moved on, and Sarah and I are fine. You don't need to feel guilty or that you have to look after us. The fact that you've been paying some of my rent doesn't change anything, except that maybe now I'll have to get a cheaper place. Or a flatmate.'

Impatiently Max pushed his wet hair out of his eyes. 'All right, I'll say it here. Sophie, I love you and I love Sarah and I want the three of us to be together.'

I shook my head again, more violently this time. 'Max, we can't become a family just like that. Being a parent is not about lazy breakfasts and cute toys. The longest you've ever spent with an awake baby is an hour this morning. I'm really pleased that you love Sarah and want to spend time with her, but I've been through so much stuff that you weren't there for.'

'Sophie, just hear me out, okay?' Max interrupted. 'San Francisco was never as great as I thought it would be. I couldn't figure it out. The work was good, I met some fantastic people, the restaurants and parties were amazing, but I wasn't having a good time. I'm a pretty slow learner and it took me a few months to figure out that what was missing was you.

'I seem to have always been waiting for the perfect woman to come along. So I never wanted to get too serious with anyone just in case it meant I missed out when she finally appeared. What dawned on me once you were no longer around was that even if she existed, I didn't want her.'

Max's words definitely sounded as though they were going in a positive direction, but I couldn't stop myself pulling a disbelieving face.

He smiled briefly. 'Well, all right, maybe if her dad had made his money in pubs . . .' His smile disappeared again and he stuck his hands in his pockets, scuffing his shoe against the cement footpath. 'Seriously, I've finally realised that my obsession with a ridiculous fairy tale stopped me from seeing that I had already met the girl who's perfect for me – you.'

My hand paused mid wipe across my face as I realised that not only was Max saying the words I'd only ever fantasised about hearing, but that he really did mean them.

Catching sight of a black smear on my hand, I quickly wiped my face again with my sleeve – I was sure Juliet hadn't had to contend with running mascara when Romeo was comparing her to a summer's day. If he ever had, that was – my Shakespeare was very shaky. I mentally shook myself. Max was standing in front of me spilling out his heart and I was thinking about a long-dead Englishman.

Thankfully Max was staring at his feet, not having noticed either my ruined makeup or my lack of reaction.

'But, not only am I a slow learner, I'm also a coward,' he continued. 'It still took me another couple of months to decide that I wanted you on any terms, baby or no baby. By the time I got to that point, you were just about to have Sarah, and even with my lack of sensitivity I figured that wasn't a great time to descend and vow my undying love to you.'

I was about to inform him that as far as I was concerned, that would have been the perfect time, but decided to keep quiet.

Max drew a breath and continued. 'So I waited. The opportunity with the rent came up and it seemed like the perfect way to help. Once Sarah was a couple of months old, I couldn't wait any longer and flew back. There was never any pitch, I've just been taking holidays each time I was here.'

I opened my mouth to speak but Max held his hand up. 'No, let me get this off my chest. I'm trying to remember all the things I should have told you before. As I said, before I came back I had already decided I wanted you even though that meant a baby too. But now I've spent time with Sarah, she's not just something I feel I have to live with. I think she's amazing and the fact that she's my daughter is still sinking in. I want to be around and see her grow up, every day, not just on alternate weekends.'

Max's words stunned me. I'd always thought that if he hadn't been back for work we wouldn't have seen him at all. Now he was telling me that he'd made a decision about what he wanted months ago and had been working towards getting it ever since.

I took a deep breath. 'Look, Max, this is a lot to take in. A year ago you couldn't even cope with the idea of having a serious girlfriend and now all of a sudden you're in the running for father of the year? Sarah and I have got things pretty well sorted now and I don't think I can live worrying when the reality of having a baby will become too much for you. One look at me in my dodgy slippers after a bad night with Sarah and you'll run screaming back to San Francisco.'

'I know it sounds pretty weak,' he acknowledged. 'I've never believed that people can change, but they can grow up and I think I have finally moved out of adolescence.'

The already torrential rain became cyclonic and the sound of the water hitting the concrete was deafening.

'Sophie, I don't know how else to say it,' Max yelled over the noise. 'For God's sake, I bought a bloody goat farm for you. Can't you just give me a chance?'

Maybe it was his question, or maybe it was the cold water trickling inside the collar of my jacket, but I suddenly realised what a ridiculous situation this was and made a decision.

'Look,' I said. 'Where are you living these days?'

'I'm still in a hotel in the city. Why?'

'This is just an idea, but seeing as how you've been paying rent already, what about moving into my spare room until you find somewhere permanent?'

Seeing the look on his face I added quickly, 'As a flatmate only. Don't go getting any ideas.'

Max smiled at me.

'I wouldn't dream of it.'

Dianne Blacklock
Wife for Hire

*Sam knew she was a model wife, a prize wife, the
kind of wife men secretly wished they had. But
now Jeff wanted to leave her for someone else.*

All Samantha Driscoll once wanted out of life was
to be somebody's wife. She would marry a man
called Tod or Brad and she would have two blond
children, one boy, one girl.

But instead she married a Jeff, had three children,
and he's just confessed to having an affair.

Sam's life purpose crumbles before her eyes, with
the words of her mother playing in a continuous
loop in her head, 'You've got no one to blame but
yourself, Samantha.'

Spurred on by an eclectic bunch of girlfriends and
her nutty sister Max, she finds the job she was
born for: *Wife for Hire*. Sam handles the domestic
affairs and acts as personal shopper and social
coordinator for many satisfied customers.

But when attractive American businessman, Hal
Buchanan is added to her client list, Sam soon
realises she can organise many things in life, but
not her emotions.

Ilsa Evans
Drip Dry

*Because sometimes coffee isn't nearly enough
and you have to take a deep breath, maintain
control, and assess the situation . . . or just reach
for the scotch.*

The twice-divorced mother of three is back. New,
improved and stronger than ever – but still struggling
to keep her head above water, even in the bath.

And what a week it is in the Riley/Brown/McNeill
household. There's one wedding, two babies, three
engagements and four birthdays. Then ex-ex-
husband Alex's long-awaited return from overseas
heralds unexpected results, which in turn heralds
the arrival of a most unwanted guest.

Meanwhile, Sam wants to join the armed forces, Ben
is setting up embarrassing money-making schemes
and CJ's wreaking havoc with sharp fairy wands.

Along the way there's an infectious disease
outbreak, a mysterious death in the family, a
broken nose, a bruised rump and several bruised
egos. Can life get more frenetic than this?

Praise for Ilsa Evans' first novel, *Spin Cycle*:

'Wildly entertaining'
WOMAN'S DAY

'A hilarious novel'
THAT'S LIFE

Liane Moriarty
Three Wishes

*It happens sometimes that you accidentally star in
a little public performance of your very own
comedy, tragedy or melodrama.*

The three Kettle sisters have been accidentally
starring in public performances all their lives,
affecting their audiences in more ways than they'll
ever know. This time, however, they give a
particularly spectacular show when a raucous,
champagne-soaked birthday dinner ends in a violent
argument and an emergency dash to the hospital.

So who started it this time? Was it Cat: full of
angry, hurt passion dating back to the 'Night of the
Spaghetti'? Was it Lyn: serenely successful, at
least on the outside? Or was it Gemma: quirky,
dreamy and unable to keep a secret, except for
the most important one of all?

Whoever the culprit, their lives will have all
changed dramatically before the next inevitable
clash of shared genes and shared childhoods.

Louise Limerick
Dying for Cake

Life has suddenly taken an unexpected turn for the
women in a Brisbane mothers' coffee group. Baby
Amy disappears, and her mother, Evelyn, broken and
distant in a psychiatric hospital, won't utter a word.

Desperate to find Amy, desperate to understand, the
women cope with the loss in their own ways. But
Evelyn's withdrawal has altered them irreverisbly,
and each begins to look for something to satiate the
cravings they had not allowed to surface before . . .

Joanne is dying for cake. Clare is longing to paint
again. Susan wants to claw back all the time she's
lost. Wendy is trying to forget the past. Then
there's Evelyn. Nobody knows what Evelyn wants.
But how can she not want her baby back?

'. . . a great read . . . a thoroughly diverting book that
plunges us wholeheartedly into the lives of its five
characters: all mothers of young children, but all different
from one another . . . her depictions of the minutiae of
raising children are lovingly realistic but not overly
sentimental . . . this novel is essentially about the validity
of different ways of mothering, and the importance of
self-fulfilment for women, however that is gained.'
THE AGE

'It is an intriguing plot . . . Where Limerick's writing shines is
in her buoyant evocation of the sticky, constant, exasperating
and loving realm of small children and their carers. There are
many such delicious scenes in this novel . . .'
Andrea Stretton, THE WEEKEND AUSTRALIAN

'Dying for Cake is honest, original, thoughtful, emotional,
mature and suspenseful.'
SYDNEY MORNING HERALD

Jessica Adams
I'm A Believer

Mark Buckle is one of life's natural sceptics. He's a
science teacher who'd rather read Stephen Hawking
than his stars and he's highly suspicious of Uri
Geller. And don't even mention feng shui or crystals.
Most importantly though, Mark Buckle absolutely,
positively, doesn't believe in life after death.

But then his girlfriend, Catherine, dies in a car
crash. And everything changes.

Within days of her death, Mark sees Catherine sitting
by his bedside wearing the dressing gown that he
packed away in the bag bound for Oxfam. Next, he
discovers that he can hear her and she him. Mark
has some questions he wants answered . . .

By the end of the year, Mark Buckle, super-sceptic,
will be a believer. But not before his dead girlfriend
finally sorts out his love life for him.

Praise for *I'm A Believer*:

'Even complete cynics will fall for the many charms of
I'm A Believer'
NICK EARLS

'Adams puts a refreshing spin on the boy meets girl
scenario, guiding her flawed but likeable hero to the
heights of love from the depths of despair'
VOGUE

'Funny, sad, quirky – and very real. Adams has done it
again'
MAGGIE ALDERSON